THURSDAY'S CHILD
THE MONEYLENDERS OF SHAHPUR

Helen Forrester

THURSDAY'S CHILD

THE MONEYLENDERS OF SHAHPUR

WHSMITH
EXCLUSIVE
· BOOKS ·

Thursday's Child first published in Great Britain in 1959 as
Alien There Is None by Hodder and Stoughton Ltd
First published as *Thursday's Child* in 1985
by Fontana Paperbacks

The Moneylenders of Shahpur first published in Great Britain in
1987 by William Collins Sons & Co. Ltd

This edition first produced exclusively
for WH Smith in 1990 by Harper Collins Publishers Limited

ISBN 0 00 223715 6

Printed and bound in Great Britain by
The Bath Press, Avon

CONTENTS

Thursday's Child 1
The Moneylenders of Shahpur 203

THURSDAY'S CHILD

When one knows thee, then alien there is none,
then no door is shut.

Gitanjali-Rabindranath Tagore

Chapter One

'Dawn't be a fool,' shouted James as he slapped me hard across the face.

I stopped shrieking and began to weep, rocking myself backwards and forwards, my hands clutching at my nightgown as if to tear it.

James, with tears running down his face, was saying: 'Now, dawn't take on so, luv.'

His Lancashire accent, usually carefully suppressed, was homely and comforting, and gradually my weeping lessened and I lay back on the pillow. The medicine bottles on the mantelpiece changed from red blobs to definite shapes, and James's face, so like Barney's, ceased to be a blurred mirage and I saw how exhausted he looked.

That last winter of the war had seemed particularly long and cold. Although in Wetherport bombing raids had ceased some time before, most of its inhabitants were worn down by overwork and poor food, and Mother was not surprised, therefore, when at the end of March I caught influenza. On the morning that James called, I was feeling better, and, with the promise that on the following day I should get up, Mother had tucked me up in bed with two hot-water bottles, and had gone out to shop. She had been gone only five minutes when the doorbell rang.

I let it ring twice, in the hope that whoever was at the door would go away, but the third ring was such a prolonged one that in desperation I got out of bed, hastily wrapped myself in a blanket and pattered along the icy upper hall and down the equally icy Victorian staircase to answer it.

On the doorstep stood James, looking as white as if he had just seen the sticky result of a direct hit on an air-raid shelter. Mist had formed little globules of moisture on his red hair and on his muffler; his face was blue with cold.

'What's the matter?' I asked apprehensively, and shivered in the draught from the open door.

'Get back into bed and ah'll tell thee,' said James.

In spite of ten days of illness, I ran up the stairs and scrambled into bed, my heart pounding with foreboding.

'It's Barney,' I muttered, my teeth chattering. 'Something has happened to Barney.'

James limped slowly up the stairs, drawing off his gloves as he came, entered my bedroom and sat down heavily on the bedside chair.

One of my hands lay on the coverlet and he took it in his.

'Peggie, dear, Barney was killed the day before yesterday. Mother got the news this morning.' The words came in the precise, clear tones he used when clarifying a point of law for one of his clients.

Although the news was something I had feared daily for months, I was stupefied by it and could not for a moment grasp the implication of his words. It was said that lightning did not strike twice in the same place, and it seemed impossible to me that in one war a woman could really lose two fiancés.

Jackie had gone down in the *Swallow* in 1939, a month before our wedding, and it broke my heart, but I was young then – and young hearts mend – so that when Barney proposed to me four years later life once more became worth living.

I had known Barney all my life. He was big, red-headed and impetuous, and I fell in love all over again. His only sorrow seemed to be that his twin brother, James, was lame and could not, therefore, join the Army with him. This had separated them for the first time in their lives – and now they were separated for ever.

'Kill me, Lord, kill me too,' I had shouted in my agony, as James's words bit into my heart and mind.

I must have had hysterics; otherwise James would never have struck me, but I remember only an enveloping, physical pain. Barney was dead, and the knowledge of it killed part of me.

I clung to James's hand: 'Why did he have to die?' I sobbed. 'Why not take a useless fool like me, not a good man like him? Why couldn't I die instead?'

James loosed his hand and put his arm around me. He smoothed the hair away from my eyes: 'The good God must have other work for you to do,' he said.

James was not the kind of man to talk about God, and his words stuck in my mind, but at that time I just lay in his arms with his face close to mine, and thought only of my own misery and not of his. He and Barney were identical twins, and he must have felt as if one of his limbs had been amputated without anaesthetic – yet he never mentioned his mother's or his own suffering.

James was still nursing me against his damp overcoat when Mother returned from shopping. She could never tell the brothers apart unless she saw James limp, and she thought it was Barney sitting beside me.

'Barney, how nice to see you. Leave at last!'

James said, 'I'm James,' and Mother understood.

'My poor darlings,' she said. 'Your poor mother.'

In her time, Mother had faced many crises, and she was wonderfully patient with James and me that day. It was she who remembered to telephone James's office – James was a solicitor, as was Barney – to ask his clerk to cancel his morning appointments, and it was she who later bundled him off to work, after letting him talk to her about Barney while she prepared lunch for him.

'Is someone with your mother?' she asked.

'My aunt is with her.'

'Then when you have eaten this, go away and work. Work is a good opiate.'

When he had gone, she came and sat on my bed and talked to me. She did not talk about Barney, but about James, of his brilliant brain, his sensitiveness and the sorrow he must be feeling. She said firmly that Angela, who is my younger sister, and I must help to comfort him and his widowed mother.

I listened dully. At that moment I did not care about anybody except Barney, and every time I thought of his lying, blown to pieces, in a German field, sobs shook me and I writhed in my bed, so that the pillows grew damp and the sheets became hopelessly twisted.

When Mother realised that it was too soon to divert my thoughts to other people, she sat quietly by me until Father and Angela returned from work. Perhaps she knew what I had not realised, that James loved me more than Barney did; and maybe she hoped that when the pain had worn off, I would transfer my love of one brother to the other.

Father came in and stared down at me with pitying eyes.

'I am sorry, child,' he said.

He bent and kissed me: 'Have courage, little girl.'

He went away to eat his dinner, and I heard the quiet murmur of his and Mother's voices in the room below.

I heard also Angela's key in the lock of the front door, and the patter of Mother's slippers as she went to meet her in the hall. I heard Angela give a little cry of anguish; Mother must have told her the news immediately, so that she did not blunder when she came up to see me.

There was a pause and then Angela's dragging footsteps up the stairs. Enwrapped in my own misery as I was, even I thought how tired she must be to come so slowly.

Angela came into the room. She had taken off her hat and coat, but still wore the slacks and the overall she used in her work as a 'back-room girl'. She had studied electronics, but none of the family really knew exactly what she did in the closely guarded Government laboratory where much of her life was spent.

She shut the door behind her and leaned against it. Her face was an unearthly white and, despite the heat of the sickroom, she was shivering.

'Pegs.' Her voice was only a whisper.

She looked so stricken that I motioned her to come to me. I had not imagined that my elegant, sophisticated sister had so much feeling in her, and I was jolted out of my self-pity.

She came and sat down on the bed, her shoulders hunched and her hands dangling hopelessly between her trousered knees. This ugly posture was enough to tell me how deeply she had been affected by the news of Barney's death; usually she sat very gracefully, with straight back and ordered hands.

Suddenly she flung herself across me and wept, her breath coming in harsh gasps. I said nothing, feeling too full of grief myself to speak.

'Dinner's ready, Angela,' called Mother.

'Give me a handkerchief,' said Angela, looking up quickly, her sobs hastily stifled.

I gave her a very wet handkerchief and she wiped her eyes and blew her nose. She tried to smile at me, as she said: 'Woman must eat as well as weep.'

She went across to the dressing-table and powdered her nose with my puff, then came back to the bed, and in almost motherly fashion, straightened my top sheet and kissed me on the forehead. I could feel her lips trembling as they touched my skin, although she looked fairly composed as she walked to the door.

As she went out, she said: 'I'll come up after dinner and keep you company while you eat your supper.'

'I can't eat,' I said.

'My dear, you must. In times like this, one must keep strong – and you have a long way to go yet.'

'I wish I was dead,' I said.

After Angela had gone downstairs, I lay for a long time, thinking of Barney. I had always had a great affection for him, hot-tempered and ruthless as he often was; when we were younger, I had imagined that he preferred Angela to me as he had taken her out frequently, but it was to me that he proposed during the last Christmas he had spent at home. I had been so happy; it seemed as if the war could not possibly last much longer, and we planned to be married as soon as Barney was demobbed. He had survived the invasion of France safely and had enjoyed one more leave when his badly mauled regiment was brought home to be reformed. He had been tired and morose during that last leave, as if he had a premonition of what was to come, but after he was rested he became more cheerful and we spent two or three happy days together before he went back to his barracks.

I had begun to collect linen and china for the small flat we hoped to find. I wanted Barney to enjoy all the comforts I could scrounge for him in a tightly rationed country. I had bought sheets on the black-market, made pillowcases out of bleached flour bags, begged old curtains from Mother, and had bought from auction sales pieces of painted china and prewar silverware. Even now, on the bedside table, lay a half-finished tablecloth, which I was contriving by faggoting together tiny pieces of linen left over from the manufacture of aeroplane wings.

In a paroxysm of rage, I sat up and flung the tablecloth and the coloured embroidery silks across the room. Unfortunately, I flung the water glass as well; but the explosion it made when it crashed released the tension in me, and when Mother came running into the room, I was crying with steady, hopeless sobs.

Mother picked up the cloth and folded it carefully. It was to be a long time before I would spread it on a table, and if some, self-appointed prophet had told me where the table would be, he would not have been believed.

Chapter Two

When I was seven, my father, Thomas Delaney, came to Wetherport to work in the Income Tax Offices. In order to be near his work, he bought a Victorian house not far from the middle of the city. It had a walled back garden, in which my father managed to grow the daffodils for which he was famous locally. In spite of the heavy fall of soot and the fact that the surrounding houses had long since deteriorated into apartments or boarding houses, the family was very fond of its home and we refused to be dislodged from it, even during the heaviest bombing; and when we surveyed it on Victory Day, five weeks after Barney's death, we were happy to find that it was in as good condition as when we first entered it.

From this house, I had gone out to school and later to the University; and now when my long day's work was done, it was the place to which I thankfully returned each night.

About half a mile from home there was a very old part of the city, which bordered upon the docks, and it was in this area that, after taking a degree, I took up social work amongst unwanted and neglected children. A scar on my lung kept me out of the Forces during the war, and I was left undisturbed by the Ministry of Labour and National Service to continue my work. Most of the prostitutes of Wetherport lived in my district, and the place swarmed with troops and sailors of every nationality. Many of the residents were coloured – part West African Negro, part Arab and part Chinese, with a few Indians scattered amongst them. Their poverty was great and was intensified by the bombing which they bravely endured. They knew me as 'the lady from the Welfare' and I was classed with 'the man from the parish', that is, the Relieving Officer, as someone to whom the front door could be opened without hesitation. The war brought work to those who were dock labourers and seamen, and the young men were called into the Army, so that their fighting cocks tended to languish in their backyards, but games of fan-tan and crown and anchor flourished, and betting and drinking carried away much that was earned; the poverty and filth of their homes remained.

As the war progressed, illegitimate children seemed to be born faster than I could cope with them and my work was always far behind. I therefore returned to the office a week after James's visit, still feeling shaky from the effects of the influenza.

The elderly voluntary workers, who were my staff, were horribly kind. They had seen Barney's name in the 'Killed in Action' column of the *Wetherport Telegram*, and they handled me as if I was a delicate ornament, liable to breakage. They tiptoed in and out of my room, brought me specially made cups of tea, and murmured that I was looking better or looking worse. I felt like screaming at them to stop, to be normal, to make some vulgar joke, so that the automaton that was me could try and laugh.

One day James rang me up and asked me to join his walking club – it was surprising how far his lame leg could carry him over rough country. By the end of the summer, I had become, at his instigation, an unprotesting member of a music club and an opera society. He kept me in circulation firmly; every time I showed signs of slinking back to the family fireplace to weep he hauled me out again.

Very few of our friends came home from the war, and, in the topsy-turvy world in which we found ourselves, Angela also seemed glad of James's company, and she frequently came with us on our outings. She was witty and she often made James laugh; he had the same throaty chuckle as Barney – and it hurt me to hear him. I love to hear merriment, but a dead man's laugh is saddening, especially when you still love him.

Occasionally it was very like torture to have James striding along beside me, looking just as Barney always did, and then to catch his eye and see a different soul, a strange mind, peering out at me; but he was an old friend and I did not have to make a special effort to be pleasant in his company, so I clung to him, and for nearly three years saw him from time to time, either at the various clubs to which he had introduced me or at his mother's home, which I visited occasionally. His mother welcomed my visits and, presumably, hoped that I would marry him. This solution had not occurred to me and James gave no hint that it had occurred to him; he continued to behave in his usual silently courteous manner and asked nothing except my company. He had other women friends, with some of whom I was also acquainted, but he never showed any particular preference for one of them.

I gradually picked up the fragments of my life and stuck them together again as best I could. The sickening reaction from the effort entailed by the war had, however, set in, and like many others I felt low and dispirited. I had been the only young woman left in our organisation at a time when our work was increasing; the war itself had brought many problems which were not the concern of any particular authority and I often found myself doing work far removed from the care of children. Many were the days when there was no time to eat and many the nights I spent on an old sofa in the office rather than waste time by going home. Once the Japanese war had been brought to a horrifying finish by the atom bomb, however, new social workers were recruited and my hours of work became normal. I should have been grateful for a life once more returned to a peaceful routine, but I found myself intolerably bored and very tired of solving other people's problems.

In the autumn of 1948, however, James's love of chocolate caused a sharp change in my life. We were attending a first night at the Royal Theatre, and I had elected to wait in the foyer, while James carried on a delicate negotiation with the girl in the sweet shop next door, for the purchase of a box of rare, handmade chocolates, for which he had not enough ration coupons. I stood idly watching the people arriving for the show. Every tram that stopped outside unloaded a fresh mass of shabby humanity; a few small private cars added their quota of patrons. Dressed in old sweaters, tweeds and raincoats, the women hatless like myself, they poured into the theatre. They certainly did not care much about outward appearances, but I knew they would form an attentive and critical audience.

I had just seen a Duchess slip quietly into the auditorium, chivvied from behind by two students who were afraid of being late, when a voice behind me gushed: 'My deah, where have you been all these years?'

The voice was familiar, and I turned round quickly, to face a middle-aged woman who was extending a black-gloved hand to me.

'Bessie,' I cried, overjoyed at meeting someone I had known before the war. The last time I had seen Bessie she had been in khaki uniform – a sort of female brass hat – but there was nothing of that about her now. Her black suit and frilly, red hat made her completely feminine.

'My deah, you are just the woman for whom I've been looking. Can you dance?'

'Yes,' I said blankly.

James came up to us, triumphantly bearing his box of chocolates, and was introduced. The foyer bell rang, and Bessie said hastily: 'Come and see me, my deah, tomorrow evening at 42 Belfrey Street – the McShane Club. Come at seven.' She looked about anxiously. 'Please excuse me – I must find my party.'

She waved one plump hand vaguely in the direction of the front door and tripped across the hall, her high heels clicking merrily on the marble floor, and to my amazement, joined a party of Negroes. She greeted them gaily and vanished with them into the auditorium.

James's eyebrows lifted, as he asked: 'Who are they?'

'No idea,' I said.

'Have a chocolate,' said James, tearing off wrappings.

James had invited a young married couple to join us, and as soon as they arrived we went in to see the play. It was a good play about the escape of a prisoner of war from a German stalag – but my mind was on Bessie.

Bessie Forbes used to live in a flat near to us. Her husband had been a lieutenant in the Regular Army and had been at Wetherport Barracks for nearly a year before the war broke out. He had been sent to Norway and had been posted as Missing. Bessie waited for further news but none came, and, as she had no children, she enlisted in the Army Territorial Service. I knew she had done very well in the Service, but presumably she had now taken her discharge. I wondered if she had married again. And what was she doing in the company of Negroes? Negroes were an everyday part of my working life – but that was unusual. It was not reasonable to suppose that a woman of Bessie's station in society would be well acquainted with any – the colour bar still functioned in England quite effectively in respect of Negroes.

At the end of the second interval, as the audience was surging back to its seats, I was tossed against Bessie, and she smiled at me.

'Who are you with?' I whispered, nearly dead with curiosity.

'Nigerian chieftains,' she said. 'See you tomorrow,' and she was swept away from me.

The mystery was beyond me, so I ate James's chocolates and tried to concentrate on the play.

James and I walked leisurely home together. The night was clear and there was a sweet smell of rotting leaves in the park. We did not talk much on the way, knowing each other well enough not to have to make conversation. He lingered at our gate and I asked him in.

'No, I – I won't come in tonight,' he said.

He made no move to depart, however, and leaned awkwardly against the gate pillar, his fingers drumming on its dirty, granite sides.

He said abruptly: 'Peggie, will you marry me?'

My mind was on Nigerian chieftains, but the answer came without hesitation, and I surprised myself with the certainty of it.

'No, Jamie,' I said gently, 'I can't.'

James stopped drumming on the gate pillar and gripped it hard.

'Why not, Peggie? Ah love thee.'

'I know, dear, and I'm sorry.' I paused, and looked at him in the light of the street lamp. 'You are so like Barney, Jamie, that I would love you because of the likeness and not because you are you. It would not be fair to you.'

He stood there, silently biting his lower lip, just as Barney used to when puzzled.

'Ah might've guessed it,' he said at length. 'Are you sure, Pegs?' The light-blue eyes gleamed suddenly in the poor light and there was pain in them.

My resolve faltered; James would make a good husband, I knew. He had a depth of character which Barney had lacked. I looked up at him again. The light was playing tricks with him and it seemed as if Barney was standing there, instead of James; like a tormenting dream, I thought bitterly.

'I can't, Jamie. You're the finest man I know – but I can't marry you – I just can't.'

'Dawn't fret yourself, luv. Ah do understand.' He lifted my chin with one hand, so that the lamplight fell upon my face. His lips were curved with pity. 'Just remember, that ah'm always around if you want me,' he said softly. His arm dropped to his side and he turned to go. 'Good night, Peggie, luv.'

'Good night, Jamie – I'm truly sorry.'

He looked back at me as I stood by the gate: 'Ah told thee – dawn't fret,' he called as he limped into the darkness.

I knew I had hurt badly someone who loved me very much, and as I climbed the front steps I reproached myself mercilessly for being so foolish as to see so much of him when I had no intention of marrying him.

I let myself in. Everybody was in bed, and only the tick of the grandfather clock broke the quietness. On the bottom step of the staircase lay Tomkins, our cat, and I sat down by him and scratched his ears. He stood up, stretched, and leaped up on to my shoulder, to rub himself against my neck. The house seemed so peaceful, so normal, just as it had been since I was a little girl. Only the little girl had grown and changed into a disheartened woman.

I burst into tears, and Tomkins fled up the stairs.

A door opened and Angela leaned over the banisters.

'What's the matter, Peg?'

'Nothing much,' I whispered, 'I am all right,' and I picked up my handbag and went slowly up the stairs.

Angela was standing in a shaft of light from her bedroom, fairylike in a nylon nightgown, her fair hair tumbling about her shoulders. She looked tired, however, as if she had not slept well for a long time.

I smiled wanly at her and she followed me into my bedroom.

'You look tired,' I said.

'Me? Oh, I am blooming. I never did sleep much.'

'Go to bed now – there's nothing the matter with me – I'm just grizzling – it was nice of you to come, though.' I caught her by the shoulders and kissed her impulsively. 'You're a darling, Angela,' I said.

'Am I?' Her lips were tight across her teeth in a wry smile.

'Of course you are. Now go to bed and don't worry about me.'

A look of weariness crossed her face. She seemed suddenly much older.

'Sure you're all right? No more tears?'

'No.'

'I'll go then. Nighty-night.' And she trailed across the passage to her own room and quietly shut the door.

I switched on the electric fire, undressed in front of it and then went to the dressing-table to take the pins from my hair. Although I was shivering a little from the clammy coldness of the big room, I paused to look at the shadowy reflection in the mirror.

My hair fell thick and brown to my waist. I lacked the courage to bleach it golden as Angela did. Large hazel eyes peered anxiously between the tousled locks.

'You are abominably average,' I addressed myself. 'Stock size figure and long legs included.' I peered closer. 'What on earth can a man see in that?'

Tomkins meowed at my feet and I bent to stroke him.

'Tomkins,' I said, 'if I was half as beautiful as Angela, I would have married a king – and he would not have had to be killed,' I added sharply.

Why, I wondered idly, as I got into bed, had Angela not married? She must meet many scientists in the course of her work – but science is not a lucrative profession, I reminded myself, and Angela is distinctly expensive-looking.

Tomkins heaved himself on to the bed and settled down in the curve of my knees.

'Tomkins,' I said, 'you'd better have some kittens to keep Angela and me company when we grow old – because it doesn't look as if either of us is destined for matrimony.'

I turned over and Tomkins meowed protestingly, as if to say that he would if he could.

'Well, find yourself a pretty lady pussy,' I said drowsily, and fell asleep.

Chapter Three

I was still puzzling about Bessie and the Negroes as I walked swiftly through the badly-lit streets, to keep my appointment at 42 Belfrey Street. I felt a subdued excitement at the thought of seeing her again – after all, Bessie belonged to that part of my life which had been sunlit and full of hope, when the war was still a long way off in places like Poland and Norway.

I had been unable to remember what kind of a club the McShane was, but the moment I walked through its swing doors and a gust of conversation swept round me, I wondered how I could have forgotten.

Angus McShane, a native of Wetherport and a great believer in the excellence of British culture, had at his death asked that his considerable fortune be used to build a club for the purpose of propagating British ideas amongst foreign visitors to Britain.

The City Council, faced with all the difficulties inherent in ruling a port full of foreigners of every nationality, had supported the idea, and the result was a suite of pleasantly furnished rooms in the middle of the city, where foreign visitors and students could entertain their friends and also make friends with English people. Dances were held; English was taught; a canteen dispensed English food – and confirmed the opinion of its customers, that the British were the world's worst cooks; a library held an assortment of donated books ranging from classics to the latest Ernest Hemingway and the newest magazines; and the lounge into which I walked that autumn evening seemed to contain a representative from every country in the world – and they were nearly all men.

Shyness swept over me and I hesitated, while the doors behind me made a steady plopping sound as they swung back and forth. Four men in American-cut suits stood near me. They were coffee-skinned, and I could feel their eyes looking me over. Their gaze was not insolent and they seemed to approve of me, for they sighed softly as I passed. Two Negroes sitting near bowed their heads self-consciously over a magazine as my skirt brushed the small table in front of them. They made me feel thoroughly womanly, and I enjoyed the change from being Miss Margaret Delaney, the lady from the Welfare.

A white-haired lady was sitting by one of the two fires that blazed in the room, and she was playing chess with a young Chinese. As I looked round, she cried, 'Checkmate,' triumphantly, and her opponent's eyes vanished into slits as he laughed.

'Excellent play, most excellent,' he said.

The lady looked up and saw me and I went to her, and asked where Mrs Forbes could be found.

'She is probably in her office on the floor above.' The voice was quiet and cultured.

The Chinese bowed slightly: 'Permit me to take the lady up,' he said.

His opponent smiled graciously and said that Dr Wu would be pleased to direct me.

Dr Wu rose and bowed to me: 'Come this way,' he said.

He led me out of the lounge and up a flight of stairs to a series of offices.

'This is your first visit here?' he inquired, his eyes twinkling behind rimless spectacles and his hands making neat, small gestures to guide me along the passage.

'Yes, it is.'

'I trust that we may have the pleasure of seeing you here again,' he said, as he knocked at the door. He bowed again and left me, as Bessie called, 'Come in.'

'My deah,' said Bessie, 'I'm delighted to see you. Sit down and have a cigarette.'

Bessie, out of uniform, had more charm than most women. That evening she was wearing a pink cardigan that gave colour to her naturally pale complexion. Her dark hair was brushed up in a Pompadour style. As she lit my cigarette I tried to imagine her drilling on a parade ground, but failed hopelessly. The determination and discipline which had lain under her uniform were still with her, however, as I was soon to find out.

'Bessie, what are you doing here?'

'I'm the Entertainment Secretary – it's my job to see that visitors here enjoy themselves.'

I nodded. That explained the Nigerian chieftains at the theatre.

'Do you like it?'

'Rather. I meet anybody who is anybody – and no two days are alike.'

'What have you in mind for me to do?'

'I'm starting a dancing class – very good teacher, but not enough partners. If you are free, I wondered if you would volunteer to come along on Thursday evenings and act as a partner. I can assure you that there are less amusing ways of spending an evening.'

'But women are two a penny in this town, Bessie. Why pick on a rather dull person like me?'

'Two-a-penny women are not required in this establishment,' said Bessie. 'Every woman crossing the threshold of this club has to be vouched for personally by a member of the staff or by some other responsible person. Each member has a pass which she must show to the commissionaire at the door.'

'No commissionaire was there when I came in.'

'Oh,' said Bessie, and seized the telephone. Her conversation was brief and frigid. The commissionaire never again left his post without being relieved by his colleague. After Bessie had dealt with him, I think he would have stuck there like the guard at the gate of Pompeii, even to being engulfed by boiling lava.

Bessie turned back to me.

'You always struck me as someone whose head was well screwed on, and I badly need helpers like that. I noticed at the theatre that you are still single. Any ideas of matrimony?'

'No,' I said, my throat tight.

Bessie looked at my plainly combed, long hair, my tailored suit and my far too sensible, flat-heeled shoes: 'No, I suppose not,' she said in a specially kind tone of voice.

I felt angry. I am not beautiful and my work demanded that I should dress very plainly, but Barney, James and Jackie had loved me, so I could not be entirely lacking in charm. Still, the dancing class promised to be a new experience, so I asked her to explain exactly what was entailed by acting as a partner.

Bessie explained about times and lessons, and I agreed to come the following evening. Then a little silence came between us.

Hesitatingly, I asked if she had ever heard what happened to Lieutenant Forbes.

She gave a fluttering sigh: 'No,' she said. 'He was presumed killed.'

'I'm sorry, Bessie.'

She sighed again and fiddled with the fountain pen on her desk: 'It's quite all right, deah,' she said, 'I was lucky to have him for as long as I did.'

I saw that it was time to go and I rose. She got up and walked with me downstairs and as far as the swing doors, which the commissionaire opened. She told him that I would be coming on the following day and that I was to be brought straight up to her. Then she shook my hand.

'You will enjoy it here – meet some new people – have some fun,' she said.

I murmured that the nicest thing was seeing her again – and I meant it.

When I got home, Father was sitting by the fire reading Gibbon's *Decline and Fall*. He rose and kissed me. Our house always smells of polish and flowers, and the outside door is invariably open and welcoming; his warm greeting and the habit he has of pushing forward the most comfortable chair for you, make the shyest visitor feel that his arrival is a pleasure. He has long since lived down the fact that he is 'in the Income Tax', and everybody knows him as Mr Delaney who has such a lovely show of daffodils.

'Where's Mother?' I asked, taking off my dark jacket and eyeing it disgustedly.

'She's in the kitchen, making chili con carne for your supper.'

'How good she is,' I said. I love hot dishes, but as no one else in the family liked them, I did not eat them often, so I kissed Father on his bald patch and wandered hopefully kitchenwards.

The house may be Victorian, but the kitchen is not. Father had the old kitchen ripped out, just before the war began, and Mother worked in an atmosphere reminiscent of the advertisements in American magazines.

Mother was really cooking chili con carne.

'The butcher gave me some extra meat,' she explained, 'and I've had the beans for years.'

I sniffed appreciatively and sat on the primrose-coloured table, while I told her about the McShane Club. I also told her ruefully about Bessie's tone of voice when marriage was mentioned.

Mother looked at me shrewdly from the corners of her eyes. She said: 'The war lasted too long. Now it is finished, it is time to wear pretty clothes again. You should buy a "new look" dress.'

'Good heavens, Mother, they are too ultra-fashionable. I've never seen anyone in Wetherport wearing one yet.'

'Don't be silly,' said Mother, 'they are in the shops – I've seen them – and you have just the figure for one. You've plenty of money – you saved all through the war for – ' she stopped.

'For my marriage,' I finished off.

'Yes, dear,' said Mother sadly.

It was true. I had three hundred pounds in the bank. I sighed; but when on the following day I had finished a round of visits to foster-parents, I slipped into a dress shop and spent an hour buying a dress and coat, followed by another hour in hat and shoe shops. I wondered if I would ever have the courage to wear my purchases, but it did not take much bullying from Mother to make me put them all on, and, when I arrived at the club, Bessie was full of admiration for my appearance. She ushered me into the room in which the dancing class was being held, with the advice that many of the pupils were Muslims, who had not mixed much with women before, and that I should be careful.

Fifteen male pairs of eyes took in every detail of me. Seven female pairs of eyes smiled with relief.

'Welcome to the battleground,' said one young lady.

'How do you do,' said the teacher. 'Will you kindly partner Mr Popolopogas. We shall just go over the basic steps of the waltz again.'

We went over them – Mr Popolopogas went over my feet as well. He was a willow of a man, topped with outsize horn-rimmed spectacles, and upon inquiry he informed me in slow, correct English that he was a Greek and was studying medicine.

I graduated from Mr Popolopogas to Mr Ramid Ali, Egyptian cotton merchant's son, sent to Lancashire to see our methods of spinning. Then I did a quickstep with an officer in the French Air Force, who was about a foot shorter than me. Finally, the dancing teacher picked out one or two advanced pupils to teach them another step of the tango. I was asked to partner a Negro. Although many Negroes lived in the district in which I worked and I knew some of them quite well, I had never been touched by a Negro, and I was nervous – not nervous because he was as black as I was white, but because I knew the shy reserve of black people and I wanted him to feel that I liked dancing with him.

We did the exercise while he held me very stiffly and at a distance, but to dance a good tango the partners must be close and the woman must be held snugly against the man. I, therefore, stopped dancing and explained the proper stance. He immediately held me correctly and it was obvious that he knew the proper hold, but had been too afraid of me to use it. I could feel him trembling slightly against me as we moved off again to the throbbing notes of 'Jealousy'. We were to dance the whole record through, and after a minute I realised that the man guiding me was far more expert than I was.

I concentrated on the steps and followed carefully. He did not dance with the polite diffidence of an Englishman, but with the full ardour that the South American rhythm demanded. My heart beat faster and I began to enjoy myself. Soon there was nothing in the world except the piercing wail of violins backed by the steady beat of drums, and a compelling body which gently but insistently persuaded me into figures I had never danced before. I did not even notice the slight gap between two records. A wild, sensuous happiness enveloped me. The dark cheek above me rested very close to mine. A separate me appreciated the beauty of the line from chin to ear, finely chiselled out of ebony. Sweat was pouring from him but he smelled clean and sweet, and he danced as nature intended us to dance, to the complete relaxation of mind and body.

Suddenly a burst of applause hit me. My partner let go of me and pulled out a pocket handkerchief to mop the perspiration off his face. He was laughing joyously. I was embarrassed to find that we were the only couple on the floor and had indeed danced alone through the last record, while the rest of the pupils formed an interested audience. I blushed hotly as everyone began to laugh, but it was all so good-natured that I had to laugh too.

The dancing teacher came to us and explained to my partner that he should now lead me back to my seat and say 'thank you very much', which he did, still laughing exuberantly.

The class then broke up, and I went with the other girls, who were all younger than me, to powder my nose. They were ordinary, middle-class girls, some of them students, with pleasant, accentless speech. They were full of little jokes about the dancing class and teased me about the tango I had danced. They told me I had danced beautifully and said they hoped to see me the following week. I felt very cheerful and I was glad that Bessie had found such nice young women for our foreign visitors to meet. From my work, I knew very well how difficult it was for strangers to know English families, more especially so if the stranger's skin was not white.

On the bus going home, I realised guiltily that for a whole day I had not thought of Barney, and I wondered if he would mind. Then I thought of how he would have laughed at my discomfiture after the tango and I giggled behind my gloved hand. Looking out through the rain-lashed window I seemed to see him laughing with me, and I thought that perhaps he would be happy that I was feeling happier.

Chapter Four

I soon became acquainted with all the staff and most of the members of the McShane. Bessie introduced me to the Director, Dr Gantry, a short, wiry man of uncertain temper and many accomplishments. He spoke seven languages well and managed to make himself understood in several more. He was almost womanly in his insistence that the club must have a homely atmosphere; it must look like a well-cared-for house, not too fashionable or too shabby; there must be flowers and it must be warm and airy. He went through the premises daily, inspecting every corner like the Chief Steward of a liner; he met diplomats when their ships docked at Wetherport, and found digs for vegetarian students; he kept up a lively correspondence with ex-members of the club, who had returned to their own countries; he encouraged every kind of Anglo-Other Country society to meet at the club, provided they steered clear of political pitfalls; he led panting young men up and down mountains in the Lake District and in and out of the best country pubs – he would say: 'You haven't seen England if you haven't been in a pub'; he took great care of the women who helped him with their voluntary work in the club, and any man about whom they complained was summoned to his office and if he did not mend his ways his pass was taken from him. This last was a delicate problem, but Dr Gantry had a fair idea of when a man had made a genuine mistake or when a woman's behaviour might be at fault. He used to say, however, that he sometimes thought he was running a marriage bureau, not a club. So many visitors were men, still young and single. They outnumbered their sisters by four to one, and as a result of the Committee's care in the choice of ladies allowed inside the club, these men met very marriageable young women. Almost every week Dr Gantry gave his blessing to a new couple about to marry, and he always said that Britain's best export was wives.

At the end of two months of helping with the dancing class and sometimes helping Bessie with a particularly large influx of visitors, Dr Gantry offered me a position on the staff of the club.

'The Government has made so much use of our services that we have been able to obtain a grant from them to extend our work,' Dr Gantry said one day, as he chatted to me in the lounge, where I was waiting for the dancing class to begin, 'and it has long been my opinion that lady visitors to this country have many problems peculiar to women. I put this point to the Committee the other day and it was agreed that we should ask you to join our staff and look after our lady members.'

His offer was very unexpected but I was most interested and murmured that I was flattered by it.

'Mrs Forbes tells me that much of your present work is in connection with women and children. She said also that you have a degree in Economics – is that so? and that you can speak French and German?'

'Yes, it is so.' My face must have shown my interest, because he went on to tell me about the salary and the working hours. The staff worked in shifts, and sometimes I would have to be on duty during week-ends and in the evening; this did not trouble me as I had often worked irregular hours; and as he went on to describe the work to be done, I felt a great desire to leave my present employment, in which I saw only the more sordid and degraded side of women, and do work of a pleasant nature.

'I can be free in two months' time,' I said, my mind made up. 'Will that be all right?'

'Just in time for the rush of summer visitors,' said Dr Gantry, wringing my hand, and then, before I could take breath, he shot across the room to talk to an Indian in a pink turban.

So I became part of the life of the McShane. It was for me a new and exciting life after the many years I had spent amongst the less fortunate inhabitants of the city. I helped Indian ladies with their shopping, shepherded American ladies round castles and museums, introduced wan German girls, imported as nurses, to the delights of having enough to eat, arranged tours for Gold Coast ladies whose knowledge of Shakespeare was frightening and who always wanted to see Anne Hathaway's cottage. I led hikes into the Welsh mountains, into the Lake District and into the Peak District, arranged tours round biscuit factories, cotton mills, docks, power stations and new housing estates; and I enjoyed every minute of it.

I encouraged my often-shy bunches of ladies to talk to everyone they met, with the result that many a factory hand heard of Somaliland for the first time, and many a farmer saw India as a cluster of multicoloured saris fluttering round his cow-shed.

I rediscovered England myself, and the beauty of it was intensified for me by the many years spent working in an industrial town. When nowadays I sometimes feel a little homesick, I think of Tarn Hows in a rainstorm or the green pools of Snowdonia glittering in the sun, and my mind is diverted and the mood passes.

So the summer and autumn passed in a holocaust of work. Father was amused at what he called my Wogs, but he was pleased to see my enthusiasm, and Mother was delighted about my improved health – plenty of fresh air was putting pink into my cheeks and improving my appetite. I no longer wept. The pain that was Barney was with me still, although I tried not to disturb the wrappings with which time was insulating it.

James sometimes invited Angela and me to the theatre or to a concert, but he was careful not to be alone with me, and marriage was not mentioned by either of us again.

I never forgot the tango which I danced with the Negro, Paul Stacey, and neither did he. Whenever I attended one of the dances given at the McShane, he always danced a tango with me, and I always felt slightly drunk after it. He had a girl friend, a Polish refugee, and they clung to each other through many social difficulties. She could not tango, however, and she used to stand and watch us dance and clap her hands to the rhythm of the music. She had been in a concentration camp and her eyes were full of the horrors she had seen, and yet when she was with Paul she was completely at peace. He knew exactly how to chase the ghosts from her mind and bring quiet to her restless body, and he never deserted her except to dance the tango.

The tango undid the good which many months of quiet discipline had done. When I knew that Barney would never come back to me, physical desire had raged within me. I knew, however, that to live I must find peace of body as well as of mind, and I therefore worked long hours and concentrated painstakingly on the problems of my clients. Gradually some respite came until, consciously or unconsciously, in the space of five minutes Paul made naught of all my efforts. At first I felt humiliated and ashamed that, without encouragement, I could feel such desires – but comon sense told me that I was still young and must expect such feelings, so again I did my best to channel my energies into my work.

One day Bessie came and told me that a party of Egyptians was expected that evening. They were a rich and influential group of young men, who were touring Britain. It was Sunday and they were stranded in Wetherport until morning. Their guide, a harassed Government official, had telephoned to ask if we could entertain them for the evening, and, since a dance was held every Sunday evening, Dr Gantry had said that we could.

'They're Muslims,' said Bessie in disgust. She was normally extremely tolerant, but for some reason she had taken a dislike to all followers of the Prophet, and it took her all her self-control to be pleasant to them. Like everything else about the staff, this was well known in the club. Probably she did not like them because, on their arrival in Britain, she was often the first Englishwoman – sometimes the first woman outside their family – to whom they had ever addressed themselves; and she suffered from their lack of knowledge of Western conventions.

Anyway, Bessie galvanised the canteen into baking in their honour, rounded up by telephone some girls with whom they could dance and begged me to help in the ballroom as well, although I protested laughingly that I was tired, after tramping round the cathedral with a party of American ladies.

When the Egyptians arrived, I was having a cheerful argument with Dr Wu, who believed ardently in the Chinese Communists' cause and wished to convert me to his views, so I did not see them enter the room.

A silence stole over the lounge and I turned to see about a dozen exquisitely tailored young men surveying the room languidly, while a very indifferently tailored Englishman with a decidedly hunted look was dithering in front of them.

'Excuse me,' I said to Dr Wu, and went to the rescue.

The Englishman clutched my hand, said he was delighted to meet me and introduced me to his charges as Mrs Forbes. All the Egyptians immediately voiced their delight too, so it seemed pointless to explain that I was not Mrs Forbes.

I took their coats from them, found them easy chairs near the fire and asked the steward to find out what they would like to drink. The party was split evenly between whiskies and sodas and cups of tea. Since Bessie had not appeared, I asked Dr Wu, in a whisper, if he would kindly find her for me. Then I sat down amongst the new arrivals and chatted to them about their tour. Their English was a pleasure to hear, every word being clearly enunciated.

Dr Gantry arrived, followed by Bessie, so I moved away from the circle and went to speak to the group of American ladies, who had congregated in one corner. They were curious to know who the new visitors were, and when I told them that they had come to dance, the ladies promptly announced that they wanted to dance too and charged off to the cloakroom to 'pretty up', as they called it.

It looked as if the evening would be lively, so I sat down in a corner to rest for a few minutes. I had hardly seated myself when Dr Wu came up and silently handed me a cup of coffee – he must have seen my fatigue and gone specially to the buffet to get it. I was touched.

'Please don't mention it,' he said when I thanked him, 'it is a pleasure to me.'

I looked at Wu with new interest. Up to then he had just been another Chinese with Communist ideals, but when he expressed his pleasure he became suddenly a real person to me for the first time.

'You are very kind, Dr Wu,' I said, as I sipped the coffee appreciatively.

Wu smiled. 'You are very kind to us,' he said. 'Madame Li has told me of your many kindnesses to her and to the other ladies in your charge.'

'It is nothing,' I said, the old shyness creeping over me. 'I just do my work.'

'You do much more than your work,' said Wu. 'We all know that,' and he waved one hand as if to associate with his remarks the many faces in the background.

This was the first indication I had had that anyone other than the ladies I escorted appreciated the amount of work which I put into the club, and I was pleased. Through Wu's polite remarks I glimpsed also how much foreigners like himself depended on the club for its friendly atmosphere.

'I must desert you and go to the dance,' I said, hastily finishing my coffee. 'I have promised to help Mrs Forbes.'

Wu rose, bowed and smiled so that his eyes nearly vanished.

'Alas,' he said, 'dancing is beyond me. My stupid feet fail to understand what the music tells them to do.' His hands fluttered hopelessly.

I laughed.

'Soon my friend will arrive and we will both come to the ballroom to watch you dance. Mr Stacey says that you dance most excellently.'

'Mr Stacey is too kind. Do I know your friend?'

'I think not. May I have the pleasure of introducing him to you later in the evening?'

'I should be delighted to meet him,' I said, and went away to dance with the Egyptians.

Chapter Five

The usual mixed crowd was gyrating slowly round the ballroom floor to the strains of a waltz. The room was already overhot and the Englishman in charge of the radiogram was perspiring. The lights had been lowered for the waltz and the whole room looked dreamy and unreal. I felt very tired.

Bessie ushered in most of the Egyptians – one or two older ones had stayed with their English guide and Dr Gantry in the lounge, preferring the cosy fire and Dr Gantry's lively conversation to dancing.

I went to Bessie. She was wearing a pink dress and her best hostess manner; and I noted that she had already enchanted a rather portly, but extremely aristocratic looking, member of the party. She promptly pushed him on to me and we finished the waltz together.

The club had long since found that to encourage new members to dance, it was advisable in the first instance for one of the staff to ask them to dance, after which they usually had enough courage to ask someone else to dance. I therefore went to each Egyptian in turn and took him on to the floor, after which I let him loose amongst the other women present. Most of them danced very well and their conversation was polite.

The lights had again been lowered for a waltz, and I swam out with my fifth Egyptian. This one hugged me tightly to him, and we had hardly circulated once round the room before he asked me to accompany him to Manchester the following day and spend the evening with him.

I regretted that I was not free as I worked at the club. He said calmly that he would arrange it with Dr Gantry, who was a friend of his father's. He wanted, he said soulfully, to take me to a ball and dance the whole evening with me. Retreating, I said that it was impossible and that I had no suitable clothes.

He said he would buy me all the clothes I could desire.

I was in real difficulty. Dr Gantry had expressly asked that we be careful in handling these young men, whose fathers were either high-ranking Government officials or well-to-do aristocrats. All his life this young man had probably had everything he wanted, and it would not be easy to gainsay him.

The record player seemed to be playing for an interminable time, and the Egyptian's lips were brushing my ear as he murmured: 'We are agreed that there are many more beautiful women in England, but you – you are the most seductive woman we have seen.'

I wanted to giggle. Miss Delaney, until lately helper of girls in distress, to be called seductive and to be so tempted! I had to get out of my predicament somehow – and get out of it gracefully. I looked round for a staff member or some English helper to whom I might have introduced my partner and thus created a diversion and made my escape; but almost everyone was dancing and the record-playing Englishman seemed to have vanished.

My partner was saying: 'You should wear pearls in your ears – you must let me buy you some.'

I resisted a temptation to slap his face. Then over his shoulder I saw

Dr Wu enter with a brown-skinned man – presumably the friend he had mentioned earlier. Dr Wu would do very nicely – but by the time we had danced round to the door where he had been standing, he had gone and there was only his friend, leaning against the doorpost and puffing at a pipe. I did not know this man and so continued to dance. The Egyptian had taken my silence for acquiescence and was breathing sweet nothings down my neck. Once more we came near to the door. I looked up and straight into the eyes of the brown-faced stranger. They were the most honest eyes imaginable, and when I looked they had such an unexpectedly gentle expression that I felt I had inadvertently peeped into his private life, and I dropped my own eyes. The music stopped and I guided the Egyptian firmly towards his friends. He was saying: 'Please say where I shall meet you tomorrow.'

'I am sorry I cannot come,' I said, and turned round and fled.

Just at the door I looked back. The Egyptian was fighting his way through the swarm of dancers. Whatever should I do? 'Come with me,' said a voice.

I looked up. The stranger was laughing down at me. A thousand times better than twenty Egyptians, I thought. He opened the door opposite the ballroom door. The library, of course. So simple a means of escape – across the floor and down the tiny back staircase to the canteen on the floor below.

'Thank you very much,' I said, as we descended the staircase. 'How did you guess?'

The stranger looked embarrassed and said shyly: 'I was looking at your face.' He stood uncertainly before me, pipe in one hand, the other making nervous gestures. I smiled, and he gained enough courage to say: 'I come here every Saturday and Sunday to see you.'

I was surprised. 'But I have never seen you before,' I exclaimed.

'You have to take care of all the ladies. How is it that you will see me?'

'But – but . . .' Words would not come. The evening was getting to the stage of fantasy, and I was so tired.

'Is your work ended?' asked the stranger, seeing my embarrassment and trying to change the subject. He drew out of his pocket an old-fashioned gold watch. 'The time is ten o'clock.'

'Oh, yes, Mrs Forbes asked me to stay only until 9.30.'

'May I obtain for you a cup of tea before you go? We could – we could sit and drink tea safely in this corner, where you cannot be seen from the door by the Muslim.'

My legs were feeling unaccountably wobbly, my head ached and the canteen was quiet, except for two German girls talking with their English escorts. I sat down where he had indicated.

Mrs Barnes, the Canteen Manageress, evidently knew the stranger who liked to look at me every Saturday and Sunday, because she drew from under the counter and gave to him some cheese straws and some chocolate biscuits, which were in short supply at the time. Armed with these and some tea he came and sat down by me. My head was clearing and when I thanked him I took a good look at him. He was dressed in an old tweed jacket and baggy, grey trousers; his white shirt made his skin look very dark but his features were clear cut and delicate; both in expression and outline his face reminded me of a Saint in an old Italian painting; his hands also, as they invited me to eat and drink, used the gestures portrayed in the same paintings.

'From which country do you come?' I asked, 'and may I ask your name?'

'I am from India and I am called Ajit Singh. You are Miss Margaret Delaney and you live in this city, yes?'

'Yes,' I said, and inquired if he was at the University.

'I am writing my thesis – I spend much time, however, at the Berkeley Street power station – for experience.'

'Oh,' I said blankly, wondering what kind of experience a power station offered.

'Instruments,' said Ajit, as if divining my thoughts.

The tea was reviving me. My eyes twinkled with the mischief I felt, as I asked suddenly: 'Why do you come to see me on Saturdays and Sundays?'

'I have to work very much from Monday to Friday,' was the calm rejoinder.

I laughed outright: 'But I have never met you.'

'There was no one to introduce us.'

'That does not seem to deter the others.'

'My father has said that in England an introduction is necessary before a gentleman speaks to a lady. Tonight I see the Egyptian frighten you – and I know Father is right.'

'The Egyptian was introduced to me – he was not, however, acquainted with our customs. It must have been difficult for him to understand the subtle relationship between men and women in the West.'

'It was difficult for me – but I have not frightened you, have I?'

'No,' I smiled.

He looked as if he was about to say something that was important to him, but changed his mind and said merely: 'This evening my friend, Dr Wu, had promised to introduce us, but we have managed very well by ourselves, have we not?' He flashed a little grin at me, as he took out his tobacco pouch and filled his pipe: 'May I smoke?' he asked.

This then was Dr Wu's friend. Presumably they had met at the University.

'Please do smoke,' I said. 'I must go – otherwise I shall miss the last bus home.'

He rose as I did, and opened the door for me.

'Thank you again for rescuing me,' I said, pausing by the door.

'It is nothing,' he said, his face inexplicably sad.

'I hope to see you next Saturday,' I said, desiring to clear the melancholy shadow away.

The sun shone immediately. 'I wish that I will see you,' he said, and I went to fetch my coat and hat.

As I hurried through the swing doors on my way out, I met Dr Wu looking harassed.

'Are you looking for Mr Singh?' I asked.

'Yes, Miss Delaney, I am.'

'You will find him in the canteen,' I said, and ran down the stairs. As I went through the glass outer door, I turned. Wu was standing at the top of the stairs grinning down at me, as if I were the subject of some private joke.

Chapter Six

My term of duty on the following day did not start until two o'clock, so I missed the fun when Bessie received a telephone call. As a result of the Egyptian invasion, poor Bessie had worked until late on Sunday evening but had returned to work at her usual hour on the Monday morning, in order to act as Chairman at a meeting of an Anglo-Polish organisation. She was at the meeting when the club telephonist called her out of the room and said that someone who would not give his name wished to speak to her urgently.

She lifted the receiver and a reproachful voice immediately upbraided her. Could she not recognise love when she saw it – his heart was broken – one day was all he asked.

'Who are you and what do you think you are talking about?' asked an outraged Bessie.

When he gave his name she became more polite – the stony politeness reserved for Muslims.

'I think a mistake has been made,' she said guardedly.

'You are the Mrs Forbes, the beautiful Mrs Forbes with whom I danced last night?'

'Well, I am Mrs Forbes, but I did not dance with anyone last night – I was too busy.'

'Yes, I remember – I remember – there were two Mrs Forbes – you are the lady of the blue dress?'

'No,' said Bessie. 'I'm the lady of the pink dress.' Then she thought of my blue dress. All Bessie's latent motherly instincts came to the fore. Deliver me to this lunatic? No. She dealt summarily with the Egyptian and returned, full of apologies, to her Committee.

'Bessie, dear, what did you say to him?' I asked, after I explained the confusion over the initial introductions the previous evening.

Bessie looked at me sideways. 'I told him that your reluctance to accompany him was natural, because you had an Italian husband six feet tall and expert with a knife.'

'Bessie,' I gasped, 'you're a dreadful scallywag.'

'It was effective,' said Bessie dryly.

During the afternoon I took two Americans round the docks, after which they were to take dinner with an English family. I left them at their hotel and walked through the crowded streets towards the club, meaning to do a couple of hours of work at my desk before taking dinner in the canteen. One way of avoiding the more crowded pavements was to take a short cut through a store which had its front and back entrances on adjoining streets, and this I did, only to collide with Mother.

'Hello, dear,' said Mother, clutching her parcels to her.

'Hello, Mum. What are you doing here?'

'Christmas shopping.'

Mother was looking worn, so I asked her to come and have some tea. We turned back into the store, and were fighting our way through the Cosmetics Department, towards the lift which would carry us up to the restaurant, when I suddenly saw a familiar face bent over an array of perfume bottles, while a bored shop assistant stood behind the counter and dealt with other customers between addressing the perfume buyer. I heard her say: 'Passion of Paris is considered most alluring.'

'Mr Singh,' I said.

'Who?' asked Mother, peering through her eye veil.

'Mr Singh. Come and meet him – he is quite amusing.'

Mother loves meeting new people, so we walked across to the perfume counter and I asked if I could help him, and then introduced him to Mother.

'Please do help me,' implored Mr Singh. 'My friends at my digs say that dragons like scent for Christmas – they do not tell me which perfume to buy – it is most confusing.'

'Dragons?' I queried.

'Landladies,' said Mr Singh unsmilingly.

I heard Mother stifle a laugh behind her parcels, and I hastily straightened my own face and looked gravely through the collection of bottles. I was very conscious of Mr Singh standing by me. He did not look at my face, but he watched my hands as I sought for the best bargain for him. He took out a finely tooled leather pocket book and paid for the present, and then looked hesitatingly at Mother and me.

'Will you join me to drink tea in the restaurant before continuing your shoppings?' he asked.

Before I could open my mouth, Mother said that we would be delighted. She had never met an Indian before and was evidently excited at the prospect of examining further the specimen before her. Her neat, grey curls danced as she talked vivaciously to Mr Singh, and it was obvious that she enjoyed the tea party that followed. Mr Singh held open the doors for her and helped her with her parcels, pulled out chairs, and insisted on ordering masses of buttered toast, since the restaurant had sold out of cake. Mother was conquered by him before the meal was ended.

At the end of an hour I remembered guiltily my piled-up desk and said that I must return to work. We collected the parcels and Mr Singh paid the bill.

As we were waiting for the lift to take us down again, Mr Singh asked: 'We are – that is – the Indian community is giving a Christmas party – I wonder – Mrs Delaney – Miss Delaney – would you like to come?'

This was a rare honour. The small Indian community tended to mix amongst themselves and rarely asked outsiders to their entertainments. In any case, no opportunity to refuse was given me. Mother accepted with alacrity for both of us.

'We are mostly students,' said Mr Singh. 'It will be held in the club canteen.'

The canteen was decorated for the occasion with the Indian national flag and a picture of Gandhiji framed with flowers. It was a good party, although everything went wrong. The lights fused, the hot food, cooked by the students themselves, arrived cold, and the ice cream melted, but nobody was upset. Leisurely our hosts lit matches while the Canteen Manageress mended the fuse, somehow the Indian food tasted good, though strange to Western taste – and Mother felt like an empress.

As the eldest lady there she was specially looked after, and she was enchanted by the respect shown to her. She was soon surrounded by an assortment of men in Indian costumes; and three girls were almost tearing off their saris in an effort to show her how they were put on. As soon as their first shyness had worn off, they all talked at once, and I could hear her clear English voice rising above theirs, as she asked questions about their studies, their costumes and their homes.

Mr Singh looked after me and brought his special friends to meet me. He was very nervous and seemed fearful that I would criticise the arrangements for the party.

'This food is not typical of India. The ladies who cooked it are not used to cooking – in India each family employs a cook.'

I assured him that the food was excellent.

'We should have put up more decorations – the room looks bare.'

I reassured him on that point too.

Gradually he relaxed and soon he was laughing and joking with the little circle who had gathered round us. I sat quietly and listened, occasionally adding some small remark to the conversation. He was very popular amongst his own people, of that there was no doubt. Occasionally he broke into his own language and after these interludes there was always a roar of laughter.

'Singh knows more jokes and riddles than anyone here,' confided a small, handsome woman in an orange sari.

'He should tell me some in English,' I said, 'I'm sure they must be good.'

Singh looked at me, full of contrition. 'I forgot,' he said.

'Afterwards you shall tell them all over again in English,' I teased.

He salaamed. 'It will be my pleasure,' he said.

I could see some of the girls present giving each other knowing looks at this promise of a private conversation; it meant nothing to me at the time, but it meant everything to them, and speculation as to Singh's intentions ran high.

Mother asked Ajit – for Ajit he had become by the end of the party – to Christmas dinner at our house, and although I was pleased at her offering hospitality to a visitor, I wondered with some trepidation what Father would say about an Indian coming into the house.

Father did not make any special comment. He just looked very shrewdly at the man before him, the same careful look with which I am sure he scrutinises income tax returns, and then made him sit down and drink sherry, while Angela, Mother and I arranged the dinner table.

Although I had lived the whole of my life with my parents, I learned something new about Father that evening. It was apparent that he did not feel at all awkward about his foreign guest; there was none of that strained manner which is often apparent when even the most courteous man of one colour meets a man of another colour. It was as if Father had never heard of a colour bar – and I was proud of him. Strangely, too, I felt proud of Ajit. Father yarned happily about how he had fought with the Japanese in Russia and how well they had endured the cold winter, and Ajit told him how the Madrasi soldiers had successfully fought in a Kashmiri winter. Then they went on to the adaptability of mankind in general, from there to religions, and, by the time the port was served, they were old friends.

Angela sat down at the piano and played carols as we sat round the fire; and I watched the face of this stranger, who had tumbled into the middle of our family. The flickering firelight sometimes silhouetted the almost Greek profile and sometimes lit up the full face, so that its calm gentleness was fully revealed.

Father must have been looking too, as he smoked his after-dinner pipe and plied his guest with tobacco. He asked to which caste he belonged.

'I am kshatriya – warrior caste,' answered Ajit. 'That is the second caste.'

'A very gentle warrior,' I thought.

When our guest took his leave and Father was bolting the front door for the night, he said to me as I started to mount the staircase: 'The first young man I have met for a long time who has both brains and manners. Got any more like him at your club?' And he grinned a little wickedly.

'Plenty,' I said, blowing him a kiss, 'of all shades.'

Upstairs Angela was hanging up her frock in the big wardrobe in my room. She said, without preamble: 'He's rather a pet, isn't he?'

'Who?'

'Ajit Singh.'

I started to pull the hairpins out of my bun. 'Yes,' I said almost reluctantly, 'I suppose he is.'

On the evening of Boxing Day I was on duty at the club to make sure that the few ladies who had no private invitations had something or someone to entertain them. As I went from one easy chair to another in the lounge, I found myself looking for Ajit Singh. The room was lit with coloured lights half hidden in evergreens. A German architect had amused himself by decorating the room and the result was a soft glow with an occasional sparkle of tinsel or silver balls. It would be easy to miss someone in such dim light, and I had just decided that he had not come, when a voice from a particularly dark corner said: 'Hello.'

I jumped, the cushion I had been shaking up still held in one hand.

'It is Singh.'

He was sitting cross-legged in a deep settee and was smoking his pipe.

I said: 'Good evening. How are you?'

'Very well. Can you sit with me – today everybody is out, and I think your work is not great.'

'I haven't much to do.' I sat down beside him. He continued to smoke, saying nothing and looking reflectively at me.

'Will you come to the University Ball with me on New Year's Eve?' he asked.

Before I could stop myself I had answered in the affirmative, and when I saw his face soften, I was glad I had said yes. I foresaw all kinds of complications arising from that simple 'yes', but his pleasure was unbounded and I did not regret it. He thanked me effusively and also added thanks for the previous day's invitation.

I said we were glad to have him and then asked him about Indian Festivals, which subject kept up the conversation until Dr Wu came in with Madame Li and the conversation became general.

Ajit Singh did not dance well, but the University Ball was fun. I knew several people present and was amused to see their eyebrows shoot up as they noted my Indian escort.

I did not care. I was enjoying being made a fuss of by a man who liked to come and look at me on Saturdays and Sundays.

We were eating ice cream when a very tall Indian, with a very short redhead on his arm, came up to us and roared: 'Ajit, old chap, introduce me.'

'Miss Delaney, may I introduce to you Mr Chundabhai Patel – my friend.'

My hand was enveloped in an enormous brown one. Chundabhai was the biggest ugliest Indian I had ever seen, but I could not help liking him. Six feet six inches was topped by a bullet head, blessed with small, twinkling eyes. His hair was cut to within an inch of his head, like a dog's coat. His suit was of a quality rarely available in England at that time, and his shirt was silk.

He pulled forward his lady friend. Her name was Sheila Ferguson and she was doing chemistry under the same Professor as Chundabhai. Her freckled nose wrinkled and she tossed her red hair, as she described the Professor's despair over the work of both of them.

When they went away to dance, I asked Ajit who Chundabhai was.

'He is a Banya, the son of a rich chemical manufacturer. Soon he will go home to Shahpur to work with his father.'

So I heard the name of Shahpur for the first time; but it was just the name of an Indian town, a name more easily pronounceable than many. I asked where it was and whether it was a big city.

'It is one of the richest of Indian cities. It has many industries – cotton, metalware, chemicals – but it has little water as it lies at the juncture of three deserts.'

'Is the Government trying to improve the water supply?'

'Certainly it is. Further north there is a river which is being dammed. From it they will obtain power for Shahpur and with the power water will be pumped from new deep wells. One day perhaps there will be a better way of bringing water to Shahpur, but Government has much work to do – it cannot do it all at once.' He grinned at me, and added: 'The British did not expect to harvest much tax from the district round Shahpur, so they did not care about providing water for it.'

It was the first time I had heard him criticise the British régime in India. His usual attitude was to ignore the past and speak only of the future of his country. Other Indians sometimes said that the Germans or the French would have been worse taskmasters and would have made their struggle for freedom both longer and bloodier.

'Don't be too hard on my fellow countrymen,' I said.

He thought he had hurt me and to comfort me he said immediately that India had much that was good to learn from England, and that India was indebted to many fine English administrators.

Chundabhai came back to the table. Sheila followed with two English friends of Ajit and Chundabhai, and the party became hilarious.

This was the first of many occasions that Ajit and I enjoyed together, sometimes with a group from the club, sometimes just the two of us. It was a peculiar relationship. Ajit never asked anything of me – he seemed just content to be with me; and I was grateful for his peaceful presence. Part of me cried out to be loved, but I could not imagine being loved by anyone but Barney – and Barney was dead.

Very occasionally Ajit came to our house for an hour or so on Sunday evening, when I was not on duty. Mother always made him stay to supper and he basked in the comfortable, domestic atmosphere. After one of these visits, as we walked down the path to the gate, he said to me rather wistfully: 'You have a splendid home.'

'I think you must have a nice one too,' I said.

'I have,' he said absently, 'but I cannot hope to provide for my wife what Father provided for Mother. Middle-class people in India do not have so much money in our days.'

'It is the same in England,' I said. 'If Angela or I got married, we would probably start in a two-roomed flat.'

'Would you?' he asked eagerly.

'Of course.'

He shook my hand and went through the gate. I leaned over it and watched him out of sight. I was troubled because I saw myself hurting yet another man by refusing his proposal.

But I flattered myself. No proposal came.

Chapter Seven

A year went by, a year full of contented work for me. I began to have friends all over the world. After our visitors had gone, they often wrote to members of the staff, inviting them to spend holidays in cities as far apart as Delhi and Santiago. The feeling that I could go to almost any large town in the world and find a friend there to make me welcome, gave me a confidence that I had not enjoyed before.

I met also many English people, who took an interest in the club's activities, and I learned how hospitable they could be, rationed and servantless as they were. I sometimes accepted an invitation to tea myself, and Mother helped me to entertain in return. By this means the number of her acquaintances was enlarged, and she found new interests to replace the slackening demands made on her by her daughters.

It was after one of these tea parties, when we were washing up, that Mother said: 'Are we going to have a marriage in the family, darling?'

My hands froze amongst the soapsuds of the washing-up water. Had she misunderstood Ajit's and my relationship, and if she had, how could I explain its special quality?

'I don't know, Mummy,' I said guardedly.

'I think so, dear – Angela and Jamie.'

I sighed with relief. Mother knew nothing of James's proposal to me; all she knew was that he used to pay equal attention to both her daughters, but recently he had taken Angela out alone on one or two occasions.

'I hope you are right, Mother,' I said, as I shook more soap flakes into the water.

Mother looked troubled.

'I sometimes worry about Angela,' she said. 'I can never get close to her as I can to you – even when she was a small child she seemed remote and independent.'

'Don't worry, Mother. Angela is a very capable young woman and well able to take care of herself.'

Mother sighed.

'I expect you are right, darling – it would be so nice if she married James – he's so dependable.'

So Mother felt the same as I did about Angela. As far as her personal affairs were concerned, she was bafflingly unapproachable – and yet we both loved her. Whenever I thought of Angela I thought of kindness. We had shared our toys, lent each other clothes for special occasions, rarely quarrelled. When we were at Grammar School we had confided in each other about our boy friends and small triumphs and disappointments; but when I preceded her to University that closeness seemed to vanish, probably just because we saw less of each other.

What did I know of Angela, the grown-up, sophisticated Angela, who, now that the war was over, was beginning to publish modest papers on her work?

She was a shadowy figure who had rejoiced with me over my engagement to Jackie; held me tightly while I got over his death and had been glad when I became engaged to Barney – or had she been glad? She had seemed surprised, almost shocked at first.

As I carefully laid the plates on the draining-board for Mother to dry, I thought again of that terrible last year of the war and of the events that led up to my engagement to Barney.

The twins had lived down the road from us since they were small boys and we had often played together. Barney, James, Angela and me, and as we grew older we had occasionally paired off – my heart missed a beat – not Barney and Peggie, and James and Angela, but Barney and Angela, with James and me left to our own devices.

I dropped a cup and smashed it.

'My love, I hope you are not upset about James and Angela,' said Mother, helping me to pick up the bits.

'Oh, no, Mummy,' I said truthfully, 'I am very pleased.'

I put the bits of broken china into the sink basket and apologised for my clumsiness.

Barney's actual wooing of me, apart from odd kisses at children's parties, had been short and sweet. It had been compressed into fourteen days' leave during which we had become engaged, and one subsequent leave. In between there had been letters every two or three days – love letters.

I had been very flattered by the sudden special attention from a man who had stood high in my affection from childhood. His hot, almost desperate passion had awakened an equal passion in me, and the idea of spending the rest of my life with him made me glow with happiness.

Mechanically I emptied the teapot as I thought back to the days before Barney had volunteered for military service – and I was afraid. A fine sweat trickled down my back and I clutched the teapot firmly in case its fate should be the same as the broken teacup. I began to remember odd times when the four of us had gone out together, when we were all students – and I saw sudden little pictures of Barney hauling Angela up Scafell, Barney and Angela picking gooseberries in our garden and quarrelling at the same time, only to fall silent when I approached, Angela kissing someone good night under the laburnum – I had thought it was James she kissed, but it could have been Barney – Angela making a point of meeting the postman on her way out to work during the war and taking her letters from him.

I tried, as I scrubbed the kitchen sink, to remember Angela's other men friends. There were one or two vague figures escorting her during her teens, but I realised with a growing feeling of nausea that, if I excepted a fellow scientist who had written a paper with her, I knew of no man with whom she had gone out alone either during or since the war, except Gaylord, an American officer, towards the end of the war.

I tried to crush down my fears. I did not really know who were her admirers – she could have been in love with the entire British Army – and we should not have known at home.

I was afraid to pursue the subject further and yet a morbid fascination led me on from one damning consideration to another. Try and be sensible, I told myself. He is dead anyway. Maybe he did admire Angela, loving her like a sister and you like a wife-to-be. But the kiss under the laburnum tree was not a sisterly kiss, said my memory.

I dried my hands. 'Mother, I think I will lie down for a while before going to work.'

I felt like lying down to die, like the laddie in the Scottish song.

The winter twilight had already closed in, as I lay down on my bed. Why had I never thought of this before? Probably because I had never thought of being in competition with Angela. I was nearer the age of the twin brothers, being three years older than she was – and I had always imagined that her sweethearts would be younger men. Three years' difference in age is nothing between adults – but it is between children, and I was still carrying on the same childish attitude that I had when she was four and I was seven. She had always been my little sister – too young to really feel what I was feeling. Too young to suffer what I was suffering.

Too young to suffer what I was suffering? My heart leaped with pity for Angela. If she and Barney had been sweethearts, what must she have suffered when he was killed? I remembered her tears on the day the news came and I mentally kicked myself for being so stupid. What must she have felt when he became engaged to me? How did it come about that he proposed to me instead of her? I buried my head in the pillow as if to shut out further thought.

The light was switched on – Angela walked to the clothes cupboard, singing under her breath. She hesitated when she unexpectedly discovered that I was resting on the bed.

'Sorry to disturb you, Pegs,' she said. 'I wanted a dress from the wardrobe.'

'It is all right,' I said, 'I have to go to work soon.'

She took out the dress and came and sat on the bed by me. She was in her petticoat, and I looked at her coldly. She was beautiful, I thought regretfully, in comparison with my English prettiness.

'At this minute you look just like Father,' she said, and then broke off. She must have seen my eyes glistening with unshed tears.

'Don't cry, Pegs,' she said, her voice full of sympathy.

My eyes examined her face critically. It was lined quite heavily under her powder, and there was a maturity about it that spoke of acquaintance with pain. Something had taken away her springy youthfulness.

I tried to behave like my normal self, and smiled at her.

'That's better,' she said.

'Angela, is it true about you and James?'

'James and me?'

'Yes, Mother was saying she thought you might be getting married.'

'Well – er, no – he's never asked me. We went to the Law Society Ball together – and to a popular lecture on nuclear physics, that's all.' She laughed. 'Mother is romancing.'

'Would you marry him if he asked you?'

She opened and closed the zip fastener on the back of the dress she was holding, before she answered thoughtfully: 'I suppose I would – I'd be stupid not to – he's a good catch.' She looked at me mischievously. 'Would you mind if I did?'

'No, no, I'd be delighted.' I did not say anything about his proposal to me. I looked at her through my lashes and imagined Barney kissing her shoulder. It hurt.

'Angela – ' I faltered, and yet I felt if I did not know I should die. 'Angela, will you tell me something – I won't be angry, whatever you reply.'

She looked mystified and although she answered 'certainly' her voice had a defensive note.

I raised myself on my elbow until I was looking closely into her eyes.

'Angela, were you in love with Barney?'

A flush crept over her face and neck and perspiration started on her forehead, but she answered me steadily: 'Yes.'

I took a long breath.

'Was he in love with you?'

'Yes.' She half rose, to leave me, but I restrained her by catching her wrist, and looking at her imploringly.

'Angela, why in the name of Mercy did he become engaged to me?'

'It was the best revenge he could think of.'

'Revenge? On whom?'

'On me.' She stood up, and there was anger in her voice as she spoke: 'Our heroic Barney was nothing but a handsome jealous cat.'

'Tell me,' I said, a chill creeping over me, 'were you his mistress?'

'We were always lovers – ever since my seventeenth birthday party.'

I shivered. That party was in 1939. I remembered it well – everybody had got a little drunk and Mother had been upset about it – but the first months of the war had upset all of us.

'Why did you not get married?'

'At first he was studying and had no money. When he and James took over his father's practice, he said that before either of them married they must re-establish the firm. Then he volunteered.' Her voice trembled. 'When he came home on leave he expected to make love, though he never mentioned getting married. Once I asked him – but he laughed it off – said the end of the war would be time enough. A man never wants to marry his mistress,' she finished up bitterly.

'Well, what did you do?'

'Gaylord came along. He was really sweet to me, so I thought I would marry a man who loved me rather than one whom I loved. After about twelve months, he told me he was going home to his wife – it was the first indication he had given me that he was married.' She shrugged her shoulders, and continued: 'I suppose he was no different from most men away from their homes.'

There seemed to be more to come – Angela's lips were quivering, so I said: 'Go on.'

'Barney came home on leave unexpectedly and caught us one night at the gate. He glared at the pair of us as if we were scum, and marched on into the house. He never spoke to me again, except when I was amongst the family. He wanted everything without responsibility, and, when he saw that he was going to lose me to someone else, he tried to punish me – perhaps he though when he became engaged to you I would crawl at his feet rather than see you marry him.'

'And how soon after that did he become engaged to me?'

'During his next leave.'

I felt sick, horribly sick. Barney making love to me to revenge himself on my sister, whose only fault it seemed to me was that she had trusted a lifelong friend too well.

Angela crouched on the bed and hid her face in her hands. I felt a great anger against Barney – such disregard of the damage he had been doing was unforgivable. I sat up and put my arms around Angela.

'Angela,' I said softly, 'he's dead. One day you will marry a more worthwhile man – perhaps James – he is a good man.'

'Pegs,' she wailed, clinging to me, 'it was awful.'

Now it was my turn to comfort her. I stroked her head and thought how many times she had comforted me.

'My love,' I said, 'why didn't you tell me? I would have boxed his ears and told him to stop acting like a child. I would have sent him back to you.'

'I have some pride – and you were so happy.'

'Of course.'

Dazed with misery, I sat for a while, automatically stroking the blonde head. In those minutes I realised how little I knew about men. Most of my knowledge of them had come at second-hand through the cases I had handled and through books. Jackie, my first fiancé, had been the brother of a girl friend of mine and had been at sea for months at a time. The club had been my first opportunity to meet many strangers – previously I had gone to balls and dances as one of a party. How blind I had been, not to realise what Barney was doing. How blind and how full of false pride. Hatred surged through me – hatred of a man who had humiliated me in my own sight.

The alarm clock whirred and brought my sanity back sharply. Time to go to work.

Angela and I got up together and dressed silently, Angela to keep some mysterious appointment, and I to make out a list of cultural centres in which South African schoolteachers visiting the north might be interested.

Before we went downstairs, I kissed Angela and the kiss was warmly returned. I felt humbly grateful for the comfort of the forgiveness it conveyed.

Chapter Eight

I worked until midnight, when the club closed. The thought of going home to bed made me feel sleepless, and, as the last bus had just left, I decided that, rather than take a taxi, I would walk home. I walked slowly through the night mist and, when at last I reached our gate, I thought irritably that I would never sleep if I went in, so I walked round the block. The policeman on the beat knew me, and said: 'Good night, Miss.'

I returned the salutation. I came again to our gate but continued past it, walking the same route. The constable met me again and asked if I had lost anything.

Wearily, I said: 'No, thank you. I am just taking a stroll before going to bed.'

'It's not too safe round here late at night, Miss.'

I agreed, and walked back to our gate with him. It appeared that I would have to go to bed, but my nerves were jangled and I felt that to scream would be a great relief.

At home I made myself some cocoa and at three o'clock I got into bed. Every time I closed my eyes I saw Barney laughing at me, until I could have shrieked at him to go away and never haunt me again.

I switched on the bedside lamp and took from the side table the studio portrait which he had given me just before leaving on his last journey back to barracks. I sat up in bed and for a long time examined the face portrayed. The lips smiled at me, but when I covered them up and looked at the eyes alone, they were cold and staring.

At five o'clock I got up. It was Sunday morning, and the church bells soon began to ring for the first service of the day. Mother heard me washing in the bathroom and called to ask if I was poorly. I said I was quite all right and was preparing to go to church. I heard her bed creak as, satisfied, she turned over to sleep again.

I had no intention of going to church, but it was the simplest explanation to save Mother getting up to see what she could do to help me. Garbed in slacks and woollen sweaters, I went out into the garden. Lighted only by the shaft of light from the front door, it was as bleak and shrivelled as my heart. I went inside, boiled some water and washed up the supper dishes for Mother, after which I laid the table for breakfast.

I had just refilled the sugar basin when, to my astonishment, the telephone bell rang. I answered it quickly, to avoid its waking the entire household.

'I wish to speak to Miss Delaney,' said Ajit.

'Speaking,' I said. 'Hello.'

Ajit's cool tone melted into a warm hello.

'I am reminding you that you must be ready at ten o'clock,' he said.

'Oh, Lord!' I ejaculated.

'Is there trouble?'

'No, no,' I said. I had forgotten that I had promised to walk along the coast with him to a village inn which specialised in bacon and egg teas. He had taken great trouble to pick a Sunday when I would be free and when the tide would be high and at its wintry best. The thought of being bright and entertaining throughout the day was too much for me. I opened my mouth to make an excuse.

'I hope I do not telephone too early. We Indians rise rather early.'

'No, I was already up.'

'Then we will meet at ten o'clock.'

It seemed unkind to disappoint him, so I said that I would be ready and would bring some sandwiches for lunch.

The happiness of his response when I said this could hardly be construed as enthusiasm for sandwiches, so I was glad I had not refused to go.

Ajit had not been at the club the night before. He was working very hard, trying to cram in as much experience and study as he could before going home. He had just finished an arduous round of visits to the factories of electrical instrument makers, and had determined to make this Sunday a holiday.

He met me at the corner of the road in which my home stood. I was early and shivering in the north wind which whined through the leafless trees. The sun peeped only intermittently through the clouds, and the deserted streets looked dismal. I turned up the collar of my leather windjammer.

Ajit was apologetic about my having to wait for him. He glanced at my face, which I knew looked drawn in spite of careful make-up.

'Are you well?' he asked. 'We need not go if you do not wish it.'

I assured him, with a brisk smile, that I was quite well. He looked doubting, but the bus came and we boarded it.

The sea was a heaving mass of grey, except where far out the waves were hitting a sandbank and breaking into white spray. As we started along the top of the sea wall, only the slapping of the water against the base of it and the cries of gulls broke the silence. We walked steadily, the wind behind us, and gradually my body warmed with the exercise and the fresh air cleared my head.

In the coarse grass covering the sand at the back of the wall, I saw a rabbit peeping up at us and, laughingly, I pointed it out to Ajit.

He had been looking at me from time to time rather anxiously, but he was apparently satisfied when I laughed, because he laughed too. He told me about the squirrels that lived in the neem trees in the garden of his home in Delhi, and of the lizards that always made a home in the window curtains, no matter how frequently they were shaken out. I shivered at the idea of lizards in the house, but he said they were harmless creatures with yellow bodies and sparkling eyes, and they kept the room free from insects. He told me also about the mongoose that lived in the inner courtyard to guard it from snakes.

'Snakes are sacred, are they not?'

'Village people sometimes worship cobras as a manifestation of God – but it is the cow which is really sacred – she gives us milk, clarified butter and curd, and in return she must be fed and protected and on no account slaughtered.

'It would be merciful to kill some of the cows which are sick and old,' he added ruefully.

'I read once that one of the Hindu Gods is a destroyer. Is that true?'

'Yes, Shiva destroys – without thought or mercy,' he said, bitterness in his voice.

I thought of the famines, the floods, the earthquakes, the riots of India. It was not surprising that they believed in a God who destroyed.

'Well, who creates?'

'Brahma creates. From the holocaust which Shiva makes, he recreates. So life is born anew and nothing is wasted.'

Nothing is wasted. From the devastation which emotions leave, does Brahma spin again the threads of life? I wondered. It was a new idea to me – a harsh idea – that destruction was a necessary preliminary to the creation of fresh life.

'Do you believe in such Gods?'

'No, these Gods are for simple people. I must seek the truths behind them.' He glanced at me and saw that I was not bored, so he continued: 'There is a part of an Indian's life which is given to the study of religion. When his sons are grown up and he can rest from his work, he spends many hours of his day in contemplation and in the study of Sacred Books, such as the Gita and the Upanishads, and he prays for enlightenment. A few renounce their wealth and their families and become beggars, asking only for food from the householders and cotton cloth to cover their bodies.'

'By ridding himself of worldly ties, he expects to give all his thoughts to God?'

'The same idea exists in the Christian religion,' he said, nodding his head in assent to my question. 'It is, however, in one particular different. In Christianity blind faith is required. In Hinduism faith is not asked. A man must by earnest contemplation discover what he feels to be true, and in that only he must believe.'

'It is a hard religion.'

'On the contrary. It provides for every man. It asks only belief to the best of a man's ability – no more.'

Mother and Father had brought up their daughters to go to church on Sundays and babble the Lord's Prayer every night. They had also taught us the accepted rules of conduct in society. Good children, they said, did not lie or cheat. Good young women lay only with their husbands; they were not too vain; they did not gossip unkindly, and so on. I had often questioned these teachings, but it was clear that they contributed to the peace of the community, so I accepted them. But when the war came to our city with all its savagery of persistent air raids, when most of the boys with whom I had grown up were dead in an apparently futile war, my mind sought for a reason for all the suffering I saw – and found none. And subsequently had not found any.

I had dug amid rubble with nothing but a coal shovel and bare hands to free a mother and children from the cellar of their ruined home, and had prayed at the same time that God would not let the tottering walls around me fall and crush me too. They had not fallen – but I had not then believed in God. With a crushed child in one's arms it is hard to believe in any kind of Divine Mercy. My confused mind seemed symbolic of a whole world which faced the same issues.

Rather than continue a discussion which threatened to resurrect old worries, I suggested that we have lunch, and we sought shelter from the wind in a deep hollow ringed with rough grasses. It was a pleasant place, and the sun which had strengthened as we walked warmed us as we munched the sandwiches that I had brought. Afterwards we sat and smoked in silence.

Ajit took my hand and opened it. Very lightly he traced the lines upon it with his finger.

'Your hand is full of good,' he said finally.

'I suppose I am really a fortunate woman,' I said, 'but I do not feel so.'

He puffed at his pipe, and looked again at the hand.

'The early life is broken, full of small illnesses and disappointments – later on it greatly improves.'

'Does it?' I asked hopefully, leaning closer to him to have a better look.

He caught his breath as I moved nearer, but went on: 'Yes, there is a husband – and three children.' He broke off and then asked: 'Have you been married? Forgive me for asking.'

It was my turn to catch my breath. 'Not quite,' I said, 'I have been engaged twice and both my fiancés were killed.'

'Forgive me,' he repeated. 'I should not have asked, although it is written in your hand.' He closed the hand but kept it in his own firm grasp. His head was bent as he stared at our clasped hands; his hair was glossy, like the back of a cat.

He looked up, straight into my eyes: 'Why are you so unhappy today?' he asked.

Although I was totally unprepared for such a question, I tried to evade it lightly, as I said with forced gaiety: 'Do I look unhappy? It must be old age creeping up on me.'

'Age – you?' he exclaimed. 'No, some shock has come to you – and I wondered if I could be of comfort.' He stroked my hand absentmindedly.

At his words, my mind was flooded with the pain and humiliation of yesterday. The quivering of my lips became a general trembling, which he felt in the hand he stroked.

'Say to me,' he said very gently.

'I – er – it is rather a personal matter.'

'Naturally it is personal – that much I realise. It is good when in trouble to speak to another of one's personal matters – it makes better.'

His voice was full of sympathy and, after a hesitating start, the whole story poured from me in short, bitter sentences, and, just as he had said, it made me feel better.

Finally I said: 'Unknowingly I hurt Angela, who loved me enough not to let me see the jealousy she must have felt.'

During the recital he had continued to hold my hand as he sat stiffly cross-legged, but as I finished he let go of it and lay down on his back and relit his pipe. The smoke rose in cloudlets, as he thought. Then he looked at me and grinned mischievously. Feeling very self-conscious at having confided in a stranger and a man, I smiled rather tremulously back at him.

'You are lovely when you smile,' he said, as if he had not heard the story at all.

The incongruity of the remark struck me and I laughed a little harshly.

'That is not a good laugh,' he said, raising himself on his elbow, so that he was quite close to me, and taking my hand again. 'I have some advice to give you.'

'Yes?'

'Let me marry you. Let me show you what life and love can really be.'

I started up as if to run away, but he would not let go of my hand.

'Don't go away. Hear me to the end.'

I looked down at him and was astonished at the beauty which flooded his face; it was transfigured. There was love in it such as I had previously seen only upon the face of a new mother – no lust – just a glow of affection. I knew I was seeing something rare, and I sat down again, hardly knowing what I did but fascinated by a loveliness I did not know a man's face could show.

'I have loved you from the first day I saw you – you must know it.'

I did know it although I had not acknowledged it to myself. I nodded.

'We would have to fight many difficulties together, as we are of different races – yet those difficulties could also make us cling together and know each other.' His eyes were imploring. 'I would love you so that sadness and weariness left your face, and contentment filled your life.'

'You do not ask me if I love you.'

'I do not ask your love now – only the chance to win it – and the privilege of giving you happiness.'

I felt curiously humble before him, very uncertain of myself, but the desire to run away had gone. It was as if unimagined treasures had been laid before me; and it seemed to me that I had done nothing to merit such a gift.

I tried to think clearly, to imagine what living with a man who was brown would be like. My mind refused to grasp anything, however, except that a delicate, brown finger was stroking my wrist and that a man of known integrity and ability was looking at me with adoration, and had just offered me all that he had and an entirely new life.

'Ajit – I am not worth all the sacrifice it would mean.'

'My Rani – my Queen, you are worth everything to me.' He slipped his arm round me and drew me closer. Suddenly I turned my face to his shoulder and wept wearily. I wept the last tears I had for Barney, who had been such a scallywag in life and was so pitiful in death. And for the first time for years I desired to make someone else happy instead of hugging my own miseries to myself.

The Chinese say that the time to court the widow is immediately after the funeral, and there had certainly been a funeral the day before, a funeral during which love had been replaced by hate and then by pity – pity for Barney, pity for Angela, pity for myself.

He let me cry until the sobs became less. Then a brown hand turned my face to his. Very carefully he pushed back the loose hairs from my face which must have been ugly from crying. He bent his head and softly caressed my cheek with his nose. A butterfly kiss went across my lips, and I lay still, too tired to protest.

Infinitely patient, he courted me as if I was a girl bride who had never seen him before and was afraid of being alone with him. He did not attempt to kiss me as Barney had kissed me. Just light kisses, softly across my mouth, until I began to desire more. His breath was sweet in my nostrils, and my arms almost of their own accord went up and round his neck.

When he felt my whole body stir uneasily, he said: 'Marry me?'

'Yes,' I said, and he released me slowly. He was beaming.

'You will be the Lakshmi of my house,' he said, 'the Goddess and Giver of all Good Things.'

The winter sun grew sharply stronger, as the clouds rolled away. I smiled at him very shyly although my pulses were pounding. I had just accepted a very difficult set of ties and yet I felt released from bondage. I sat back on my heels and surveyed my future husband.

Because I was for the first time imagining him as a partner, it was as if I had never seen him before. He lay and puffed his pipe contentedly and hummed under his breath, as if nothing had happened, his eyes shadowed by their dark lids and enormous lashes. A patient man, I thought. Anyone else would have followed up the advantage which my acceptance had given him. Some inner perception must have warned him to go slowly – or was it an infinitely subtle skill in the making of love?

At the thought of his really making love to me, a hot flush rose to my face and I scrambled to my feet. He got up too. He was shivering, whether with cold or desire I did not know, but I arranged his scarf for him and made him button his raincoat to the top.

'Hot tea and bacon and eggs,' I said as I pulled on my woollen gloves.

'These English women,' he said. 'So practical – and also so impractical,' and he swung me towards him and kissed me hard until my body slackened against his. I pulled myself away hastily.

'Bacon and eggs,' I said firmly, and ran up the sea wall to the top. The wind hit me as it blew straight off the sea.

'It's really cold,' I said as he joined me.

'Let us then run.'

So, laughing, we ran along the sea wall to get warm. As I raced Ajit, the wind tearing at my hair and the waves roaring at my feet, some youth came back to me, and I was filled with young hope for the future.

Chapter Nine

There was a log fire in the parlour of the pub where we had our tea, and as we were the only customers, we afterwards sat hand in hand on an old wooden settle and watched the sparks fly up the chimney.

The landlady who served us looked upon us with disdain, but when she heard our voices, she confided audibly to her daughter behind the bar that: 'She isn't a common sort,' and she unbent enough to ask Ajit if he was a student from India. She also asked me if I was a student. I said vaguely that I was a social worker, not wishing to invite further questioning. The landlady was nonplussed by my answer and said to her daughter, as she took our dirty dishes to the sink behind the counter, that: 'It was a right rum combination – an Indian and a social aid worker.'

Both Ajit and I giggled when we heard this remark; but it reminded Ajit of another problem.

'What will your father say about your marriage to me?'

I was secretly worried about my parents' reaction to the marriage, although I did not want to communicate this worry to Ajit.

'Father likes you very much,' I said cautiously, 'although he will be very upset at my going to live so far away as in India.'

'We shall see – I do not wish that he should grieve.' He let go of my hand, picked up the poker and poked at the fire, while his fine eyebrows knitted and a frown broke the smoothness of his forehead.

'Peggie, in one month's time I have to return to India.'

'So soon?' I asked in astonishment.

'Yes, my Queen, I have obtained a post at the new power station at Pandipura, near Shahpur – where Chundabhai lives – and I must start work in two months' time.'

'But, darling . . .' I expostulated. I got no further, the rest of what I was about to say being smothered in a kiss. It was the first time I had used an endearment when speaking to him, and he was delighted. I had to laugh. He had picked just the right second in which to kiss me – the barmaid had bent down beneath her counter to put away a glass.

'Darling,' I protested, fighting my way free, 'not in public.' I relieved him of the poker which he had been brandishing in the air.

He immediately let go of me. 'I am sorry,' he said, looking very crestfallen.

I slipped my hand into his and said: 'You are sweet – and don't be sorry – the kiss meant a great deal to me – ' I stammered and could feel the colour mounting to my cheeks.

'I understand,' he said. 'It was naughty of me – in Bombay I would have been liable to a fine for such behaviour.'

'It was a little naughty – but very nice,' I said. 'Now, tell me about your return home.'

He did not immediately reply to my prompting about his journey home. After a moment or two, he said slowly: 'I have not yet told my father about my marriage to you.'

'How could you? You have only today asked me.'

'I have had the intention for twelve months,' he said calmly.

I grinned. I could imagine it. Although his ideas erupted suddenly into words, it was obvious that much preparatory thought had been given to them. I was glad that he, at least, had given thought to our marriage; I was still bewildered at the change he had brought into my life and at my temerity in accepting his proposal.

'Are you going to write to your father now?'

He did not answer the question directly, but said:

'My father will not wish us to marry. He will wish me to have a bride of his own choice from our own caste. It is possible that he will be most angry.'

I knew that the old customs were dying out in India and I queried his remarks.

'They are dying,' he said, 'but still they linger in families. I love my parents and I do not wish their anger – but I love you more and am determined to marry you.' His face darkened as he said this and he put his arm round my waist. 'Peggie,' he went on, his voice full of urgency, 'marry me now, quickly. What has been done cannot be undone.'

I had heard of the power of Indian parents, and I asked him what his father was likely to do if he defied him, as he suggested.

'I am fortunate,' said Ajit. 'I have a post and do not have to depend on my family. I do not think Father will use his influence to have me dismissed – he will not wish to ruin me. We shall, therefore, be assured of our income.' He stirred uneasily and went on, 'It must be hard for you to understand the tight bonds of an Indian family – here you leave your parents as a matter of course, but in India it is not so. It is the unity of our families which makes life bearable in a country where there is no other protection against catastrophe except the family.'

I thought this over. Then I asked: 'Why don't you get a job in this country, where life is easier and a quarrel with your father would not affect you so much?'

'Peggie, you have often told me of the difficulty of getting employment for coloured people in this city. You know the difficulties.'

I did know the difficulties. Although before the law all citizens had the same rights, when a man came before a prospective employer he had to balance his brown skin by being twice as good as the white man applying with him, even if they had been born and bred in the same district. It would be even more difficult for a foreigner. He might be lucky and obtain a post, but I writhed at the thought of the petty insults he might well have to endure from the men who served under him.

'I do know,' I said, my mind made up. 'We shall go to India, and we shall hope to win your parents' goodwill. You shall teach me carefully the customs of your caste, so that after a while people will half forget that I am English, and then perhaps your father will not be so angry and you can make peace with him.'

'You are good,' he said. 'You would not have to alter completely your way of life – you need only conform in public – perhaps wear a sari.'

His face cleared, and I said: 'You are right about being married soon. We will put up the banns immediately and we can then be married a week before you go.'

'What are banns?' he asked.

I explained about a registry office marriage. He was full of excitement. 'I will go to the Registrar tomorrow,' he said. He squeezed me hard against him, and then got up abruptly, fumbling in his pocket for money to pay our bill.

We decided to go back to town by bus, and as we waited in the darkness at the bus stop near the inn, he came close to me and held me to him, and talked quietly about our future life together.

Our children could be Christians, he said, if I wished it, but he would prefer to bring them up as Hindus as they would have to live in India. This question had already occurred to me, and I said that they should be Hindus. I knew from previous conversations with Ajit that the rules of conduct laid down for Hindus were wise, and all I asked of Ajit was that what we taught our children should be free from corruption or bigotry.

He chuckled. 'Don't be afraid,' he said, 'and put out of your mind most missionary writings about us. You will find purity of thought in India as well as here.'

'I shall be happy if our children are like you,' I said.

He trembled. 'I am not good,' he said. 'I . . . I want that we do not wait three weeks for our marriage.'

'The time will go quickly,' I said, unclasping myself from him, as the lights of the bus swept us.

As the bus jogged back to town, I puzzled over the best way to break the news of my engagement at home. My head was heavy from lack of sleep and I could not think very well, so I decided to leave the question until the following day.

Knowing that Ajit's dragon did not provide supper, I insisted that he should come home for a meal.

As our shoes were dirty, we went in through the back door. My heart was pattering and I think Ajit's must have been too, but Mother was too busy to notice any difference in us. She was just taking a pie out of the oven.

'Come in, children,' she said. 'I hoped you would come soon. I have made a pie for supper. Peggie, pass me that cloth. Ajit, I am glad you have come. Perhaps you would like a wash. Hang the rucksack on the door.' She flew round the kitchen like a plump robin.

Ajit smiled at her, his slow, sweet smile, and my heart leaped. I gave her the oven cloth and took the rucksack from Ajit and hung it on the hook which she had indicated.

Father came out of the living-room, the Sunday paper in his hand, his old leather slippers on his feet.

'Hello,' he said. 'Have a good day?'

Ajit assented. I looked at Father with new eyes while I said: 'Yes, thank you, Daddy.' Father was getting on. Why, his hair was quite white; I had never noticed it before. It is going to hurt me to leave him, I thought, and a little pain nagged inside me when I realised that if I went to India it was possible that I would not see him again.

Mother did not give me much time to brood. 'Wash your hands, Peggie,' she said, as she filled the kettle at the tap, 'and lay the table for me.' To her, I was still a small girl, and I found myself thinking that I had been too long at home. It would be good for me to go away.

Ajit wiped his feet carefully on the mat by the kitchen door and went up the heavily carpeted staircase to the bathroom to wash, and then came down again to the living-room, where he sat down to chat with Father.

Father knew from experience that he would have to tell him to smoke before he would do so in front of an older man, so Father unscrewed his tobacco jar and passed it to Ajit. Ajit took out his old pipe and lovingly packed it with tobacco, while I laid the table and Father talked about the news in the paper.

'I see Nehru has had another try at getting the Hindu Code Bill through parliament,' he said. 'There is an article on how it would improve the status of women. What is the real status of a woman in India today?' he asked.

Ajit lit his pipe before answering.

'It depends,' he said, 'on the community to which they belong. They have equal rights with men before the law, they can vote and they can hold public office.' He leaned back in his easy chair and looked at the moulding on the ceiling. 'The Code Bill would give them rights of divorce and inheritance – it will clarify their position generally.'

He went on slowly: 'In our community, we are proud that our womenfolk are said to be the best taken care of in India. We do our best to see that they are nicely dressed and properly fed. We listen to them with respect, and in the home, of course, their rule is absolute.'

Father chuckled.

'I am in the same boat,' he said, 'ruled with a rod of iron by three women – they eat me out of house and home – and take all my clothing coupons into the bargain.'

I leaned over the back of his chair and pulled his hair, then fled to the kitchen as he rose in mock anger, brandishing his newspaper at me.

Ajit laughed, as I scuttled down the passage. I relieved Mother of our best silver teapot and carried it back into the living-room; Angela came in from church, looking wan and bored, and we all sat down to supper.

Afterwards, as we sat by the fire, I looked round the shabby comfortable room. Much of my life had been spent in it. I had done my homework on the oak table, cut out my first evening frock on the Axminster carpet, written up case histories as I sat by the fire while the guns outside roared and the shutters rattled, sewn two trousseaux under the light of the reading lamp; and now, in the same room, sat the man who was to take me away from it. What would he give me in its place? Would I, through days of heat, long for the steady warmth of our living-room fire, for the welcoming easy chair, for Father reading his endless history books and Mother doing her equally endless knitting? I must be mad, I thought, to want to leave such peace. But I did want to leave it – I felt stifled, penned in. I wanted to go out and know adventure, suffer hardship, be myself – not Mr and Mrs Delaney's elder daughter.

Angela had been talking about a conference she was to attend in Manchester, and then we fell silent. I was feeling sleepy.

Suddenly I was roused to paralysed attention, when Ajit said: 'Mr Delaney, Sir – Mrs Delaney, I want to ask you something of special importance.'

Mother looked up from her knitting pattern. 'What is it, Ajit?' she asked.

Ajit took a long breath. 'Today I asked Peggie to marry me and she accepted. I ask your blessing.'

'Good heavens,' said Father, dropping his newspaper and clutching the arms of his chair. 'Good heavens, boy.'

Mother and Angela turned to me and said in chorus: 'Darling, how lovely.' Angela's face was lighted up with pleasure, and Mother took my hand and patted it: 'I am so pleased.'

She beamed pointedly at Father, fearing that he would make a fuss.

Father looked at Mother furiously. There was a great fear in his expression. I am sure all the missionaries' appeals for funds, the whole text of 'Mother India' and the contents of half a dozen books by British Army Colonels must have rushed into his mind at once, and he saw me facing all sorts of horrors, ranging from cholera epidemics to a sutti on Ajit's funeral pyre.

'Singh, do you realise what you are saying? Peggie, is this true?'

'It is true, Father,' I said, 'and I am very happy about it.'

I went over to him, sat on the arm of his chair and put my arm round his neck. He looked up at me. His eyes were moist and he was shaking. He was not angry, I realised, but only shocked.

'I want you to be happy about it, too,' I said.

Ajit saw that he had wounded my father deeply, and his voice was concerned as he said: 'Sir, do not fear for Peggie's life with me. It will not be the same as in your beautiful home here, but it will be a fairly comfortable life.' He continued, his voice very gentle, as Father held my hand tightly: 'I cannot promise to send her home for a holiday during the first year, but probably during the second year she could come, and, as my earning increases, she shall come as often as possible.'

Mother's featherweight brain had not taken in the full implications of Ajit's announcement: she was just pleased that I was to marry a nice man after all, even if he was brown. She saw, however, that Father was upset and she said comfortingly: 'Now don't get upset, Tom. Ajit's a nice boy – he will make Peggie happy,' and she beamed on Ajit and me. Turning again to Father, she patted his knee: 'There, there, my dear, Peggie will be all right, I am sure.'

Father was recovering his composure, but he held on to my hand, as he said: 'Singh, I cannot hide from you that this is a great shock to me – a very great shock – although I should, of course, have foreseen it.' He looked anxiously at me. 'Peggie is old enough to know what she wants, but I had hoped – hoped that she would marry someone in our own circle. She has had a lot of sorrow and I don't want her to have any more.'

'I understand, Sir – perfectly,' said Ajit in a polite, small voice.

Father turned to Mother. 'I would like to talk to these young people alone, Margaret, if you would not mind.'

It looked as if Mother minded very much, but she got up and said: 'Come, Angela,' and they both left the room.

There was silence for a moment. I had not imagined that Ajit would take the responsibility of telling my parents of our plans. I had been prepared to face alone the denouncements, upbraidings and tears, and had dreaded them.

Father said in a controlled kind of voice: 'Singh, I appreciate your coming to tell me yourself about this matter, especially as both Peggie and you are of an age to make decisions without advice from your parents.' He hesitated while he thoughtfully smoothed my fingers between his. 'You know that mixed marriages can cause a lot of sorrow, and they bring problems that do not arise in ordinary marriages.'

'Yes, Sir. I have given thought to this for two years – two years is a long time, Sir, to think about marriage – and I have asked Peggie to marry me because I believe that the problems of which you are thinking can be overcome.' He leaned forward, his voice earnest. 'India is changing rapidly, and I feel that Peggie would be able to adapt herself to the life of my people.'

'Have you got a job? What will you do about your children?'

Ajit told him about the Shahpur post and about the prospects of better posts later on, and then said: 'I have to speak further with Peggie about our children. I can say to you, however, that they will be considered to be of my caste and we shall save to educate them for professions. It would be easier for them if they were brought up as Hindus – if Peggie objects to this, I should not, of course, forbid a Christian upbringing.'

'You feel that their mixed blood would not stand against them in India?'

'No, Sir, as long as they are trained from the beginning to think of themselves as Indians, and not as people superior to or apart from Indians, there is no reason why they should not be happy. There is not much prejudice about whom one marries – as long as one's family has given its approval.'

'Does your father approve?'

'I have not yet told him – he will be distressed. Naturally he will wish that I marry into our own caste – but he has much wisdom and he is also benevolent – he knows that India is changing and the caste system is breaking down.'

Father told me afterwards that when Ajit said this, he immediately pictured a father in flowing robes and a turban, reading a holy book and counselling his son in a sing-song voice, using his hands in strange oriental gestures to emphasise his words. Somewhat different, he remarked ruefully, from a dry as dust civil servant like himself who lived in a Victorian house and had a garden full of daffodil bulbs.

'What is your father like?' asked my father, his voice becoming more natural, as fear gave way to curiosity. 'Have you a picture of your home?'

'Why, yes, pictures of home and of Father and Mother are here in my pocket.'

He rummaged in his wallet and handed a bunch of photographs to Father. I had not seen them, so I leaned over his shoulder to look. I had not said one word during the discussion, feeling it was better for the two men to talk without interruption.

After scrutinising them carefully, Father handed me two studio portraits, one of a plump lady whose grave expression was belied by laughter lines at the corners of the eyes. Her head was draped with a veil, and in the middle of her forehead was painted a round dot. Her carefully posed hands were small and the fingers were covered with numerous rings. On either wrist hung several bracelets. She wore also an elaborate necklace and ear-rings.

'Your mother looks very pretty,' I said, 'and her jewellery is exquisite.'

'Do you like the jewellery?' asked Ajit, anxious to make a point. 'You will have the same as soon as I am able to buy the gold and stones. Some also my parents will give you, and at Father's death he will give you gold and silver for ornaments.'

I must have looked a little incredulous and Father looked most surprised, for Ajit added: 'Truly it will be so.' He turned to Father. 'All jewellery given to a wife is her property – and can be her standby in time of need.'

'Hmm,' said Father non-committally. 'What is the dot in the middle of Mrs Singh's forehead?'

'It shows that she is a Hindu. She paints it each day with vermilion – now it is worn mostly for fashion – I have even seen Muslim ladies wear it.'

The second portrait was that of a man of great dignity, heavily moustached and black browed. He did not wear a turban. He had on instead a round, black cap, and he was buttoned into a high-necked black jacket.

I covered the lower half of the face with my hand and looked at the eyes alone. Without the moustache to distract attention, the eyes and forehead were surprisingly benign.

There were several snaps of relations and friends, all looking untidy in an assortment of draperies, and finally there was a photograph of a large, white building, reminiscent of a tiered wedding cake.

'What is this building?' asked Father.

'It is my father's house.'

'Really?' said Father. I echoed his surprise. The building had two floors and at each corner there was a tower like a minaret. There was a pillared entrance, and carved veranda rails ran the width of the house at both ground and first-floor levels. A fine sweep of steps led from a well-laid-out garden up to the front door. In a corner of the picture I could see the outline of a gardener at work.

'What is your father, Ajit?'

'He is a retired District Magistrate.'

Father asked many more questions, to which Ajit replied patiently. Both of them were doing well, considering their differing backgrounds.

In his youth Father had been taught, as indeed I had been at school, that Indians were natives who existed to serve the long-suffering British in return for our 'protection'. Englishmen went to India to rule or to make money and, in either case, they returned to England, to retire in comfort to a house in Harrogate or Bath. Probably the only history of India Father had learned at school was of Clive, the relief of Cawnpore, the Black Hole of Calcutta and, possibly, of the indictment of Hastings. Fortunately he had compensated for his public school education by much reading on every conceivable subject. During the First World War, he had fought in Russia in a polyglot army sent to fight the Bolsheviks. He always said he learned more about people during that period of his life than at any other time. I knew that he had learned Japanese and Russian from his fellow soldiers. It was upon these experiences that I think he drew in trying to understand Ajit, and because he had worked, fought, lived and eaten with men from the East that he regarded them as real people, who desired, loved, quarrelled and struggled through life just as he did – only their struggle was harder. He had always taken an interest in my work amongst coloured people in the city, and he was, therefore, prepared for the possible advent of coloured friends – but it had never occurred to him that I might take a brown husband.

Gradually the conversation petered out and he was left with an uneasy feeling that although he could find no concrete arguments against it, such an unconventional marriage should not take place. He said, with a sigh: 'Well, think this conversation over, Singh – and you too, Peggie – before you do anything rash.'

We assented and Ajit rose, shook Father's rather limp hand, and I saw him to the door. His face had the tightly shut-off look that I had seen before when he was thinking deeply. He knew he had not really convinced Father, and I was suddenly afraid that Father might have implanted in him doubts that would make him retreat. As this fear rose in me, I knew with certainty that I did not want to lose him at any cost – not at any cost.

He kissed me gently on the lips, said he would see me the following day at the club, and walked with the flat-footed gait of a man used to loose sandals down the path, out of the gate and along the road. I stood on the steps as long as I could hear his footfalls on the pavement, and then, feeling intensely lonely, I went slowly up to bed.

I lay sleepless for a long time, remembering how each time I had imagined I was to be happily married, the man concerned had been taken from me. Would Ajit, not wishing to harm me, voluntarily leave me?

When I slept I saw in my dreams Shiva dancing his dance of death; and he was laughing at my puny efforts to escape him.

Chapter Ten

On Monday, my hours of duty at the club were from ten in the morning until six in the evening, and when they had dragged to an end, I sat by the fire in the lounge, which was empty, and waited for Ajit. I had told Mother that I would take my dinner at the club, but the thought of food nauseated me; apprehension about the future filled me. Supposing Ajit backed out of his proposal, feeling that Father was right and I should marry amongst my own people. Supposing we did marry and it was not a success. What should I do?

A hand came over the back of my chair and lifted my chin. Ajit leaned over and kissed me. My fears left me; just by the assured touch of his fingers, I knew we would be married, and the rest would be what we made of it.

We announced our engagement, and Mother had a fine time preparing for a wedding. Father was sadly silent; he barely spoke to me, although he expressed his pleasure at my joy over the first presents which Ajit gave me – a red silk sari embroidered in gold, and a thick, gold bracelet. With the exception of the two engagement rings which lay in cotton wool in my dressing-table drawer, they were the most beautiful gifts I had ever received, and it was with some pride that I exhibited them to my friends.

The engagement announcement caused a fuss amongst Ajit's Indian fellow students, and arguments for and against the union raged in many cheap digs, but Ajit went steadily on with his arrangements, despite the dismal prophecies of his friends. All he hoped was that no one would write and tell his father, before he could get home and tell him himself. It was not possible for me to fly with him to India as passages were hard to obtain and, furthermore, I wished to give the McShane Club a month's notice of my intention to leave. It was, therefore, arranged that I should travel by sea, arriving in India about the middle of May.

'It will be very hot at that time,' said Ajit.

'Never mind, the sea voyage will give me plenty of rest, so that I shall be better able to cope with the heat,' I said cheerfully. 'Besides, to come by plane with you would be so expensive.'

'Miser,' he said, but he was pleased. Long afterwards he told me that he would not have dared to marry me, if it had not been apparent that I was careful with money. In India, he would not earn so much that he could risk having an extravagant wife.

The question of guests at our wedding was a difficult one. Grandma – my mother's mother – who was a product of a strict Victorian upbringing, thought it was a tremendous lark, she said she only wished she was young enough to kick over the traces too, and promptly spent hours putting fine stitches into petticoats for me. Her single daughters, Mother's elder sisters, were horrified, and refused to associate themselves with the marriage at all, regarding Grandma as someone who had suddenly lost her senses. Father had one younger brother, living in London with his numerous family, and in reply to the invitation sent him, he wrote that he was sorry he could not come but he could not approve of such a union, to which his wife, Louise, had added a postscript that I should not take any notice of him – he just could not afford to come – but if things went wrong in India their home would always be open to me, and she and the children sent their good wishes with the enclosed. The enclosed proved to be two Benares brass vases made in Sheffield.

My friends' attitude generally was that sorrow had turned my brain, but that it was not their responsibility to interfere; and those I asked to the wedding accepted and were cordial to Ajit. A few, bless them, saw the calibre of the man I was to marry and congratulated me with enthusiasm.

Ajit asked a peculiar assortment of people, all sharply different from each other, but all with one interest in common – Ajit.

There was his Professor, who afterwards became a close friend of Father's; there was the riproaring Chundabhai and his Sheila Ferguson; there was a precise, quietly spoken English physicist with a plump, untidy wife, and an Indian physician with his English wife who impressed my parents greatly by her serene manner. There was also a large, important-looking business man with an equally large, important-looking wife, and although petrol was rationed, they arrived in a car which matched them – big and sleek. This man was the Production Director of a firm with whom Ajit had at various times done some practical work on instruments. Both he and his wife did much to make the reception a success – they moved amongst the other guests, talking politely all the time and being most helpful to my hard-pressed parents. They met Dr Gantry and Bessie and eventually became Committee members of the McShane.

Lastly, there was Dr Wu, who, encased in a new, dark suit for the occasion, was the best man. Although his hair had been carefully combed, it hung down over his forehead like a shaggy dog's, nearly touching the narrow eyes which crinkled up in laughter every few minutes. That same laughter softened his thin face, giving a kindly curve to the wide mouth and exposing unusually small, perfect teeth.

He greeted Angela as if she were an old friend although he had not met her before. He was acquainted with her work through the papers which she had published since the war, and she in turn knew about his work, so they had plenty to talk about in between discharging their respective duties at the wedding.

We were married before the law with a garble of words intoned over us by a disapproving Registrar; and with a flow of tender understanding between us we were married before the Creator.

The reception, which I had expected to be cold and stiff, was, on the contrary, a merry affair. Mother had opened up our big dining-room and lounge, and had asked a firm of caterers to supply the wedding breakfast. With prewar opulence, fires roared in both rooms, and the last of Grandfather's wine cellar flowed in our honour. Angela worked like a honey bee to make the party a success.

Father was much relieved when Ajit's Professor, warmed by several glasses of port, confided to him that his sister had married a Bengali Brahmin some twenty years before, that it had caused a near scandal but it had proved a great success – she was most happy – had come home on a visit only the previous year bringing two shy, adolescent sons – the elder boy was going to attend his lectures next year. He went on: 'Fine young man – this Singh – will make a name for himself one day.'

Father expanded, and when it was time for us to go, he came over to Ajit and wrung his hand.

'Take care of her,' he said.

'I will, Sir.'

A taxi was waiting and Ajit was calling. I was kissed by everybody. James whispered: 'Good luck, old girl,' and then I was really alone with my husband for the first time since he had proposed to me – the taxi driver being kind enough not to turn round during the whole eight miles of the drive to the small inn where we were to spend three precious days together.

During the war, Angela and I had sometimes come out to this inn in order to get a night's sleep free of air raids, so I knew its clean, cold bedrooms well, and they did not inspire romance. I was astounded, therefore, when the Polish maid opened the door of our bedroom.

The brass bedstead had been pushed back, and a wood fire blazed in the hearth. In front of it was a table laid for a meal. A bottle of wine glowed warmly on a side table, which held also a basket of fruit and a bowl of flowers which looked as if it had been arranged by an artist. A box of chocolates, its lid alluringly half off, sat on the dressing-table. Some parcels tied with coloured ribbon lay on the bed.

'Ajit,' I cried, 'what have you been doing?'

Ajit grinned shyly.

'Chinese gentleman – he come this morning and see all is right – he make flowers in bowl,' the Polish girl said.

'I asked Wu to arrange for me, as Mother is not here to make ready for you,' said Ajit.

I looked with gratitude at the room and went and lovingly touched the flower arrangement. Two men had done all this! How could they have guessed at the shyness, the innermost fears of a not very young woman, and know how to divert her?

'You like dinner now?' asked the girl.

'In about three-quarters of an hour,' said Ajit, taking off his overcoat.

He helped me to remove my outdoor clothes and I kissed him. I had never done so before – he had always kissed me. He led me to an easy chair by the fire and sat down with me on his knee. I laid my head on his shoulder. I could feel his heart pattering furiously. He stroked my cheek with one finger. 'Rani,' he said.

There was a knock on the door. I sprang up. Mrs Samson, the innkeeper's wife, had come herself to serve our dinner. She pottered about the room, congratulating Ajit and at the same time serving us with roast chicken. She was fat and full of jokes, pressing us to eat more and telling anecdotes of her own youthful days in service. Finally, she added some logs to the fire and, taking the dishes with her, she left us to our port and ourselves.

Ajit took his port and climbed on to the bed and seated himself cross-legged as if he was on a divan. I curled up by him. While I sipped my port, he made me open the parcels. There was a pearl necklace, some nylon stockings, some embroidered handkerchiefs and some perfume. He watched me intently while I exclaimed over the various gifts, but gradually silence fell between us. He put down his glass on the side table and took mine and placed it beside his own. He lay down close to me and the slender fingers caressed my throat.

As we sipped our early morning tea and gossiped lazily, Ajit asked me if I did not find his brown skin ugly in comparison with my exquisite whiteness.

I stopped drinking tea. In the three days that we had been together it had never occurred to me that he was a different colour. All I could remember was a feeling of admiration that a man could look so handsome. I told him this, and his teeth sparkled in a grin and the eyes with their incredibly long lashes crinkled up wickedly.

Chapter Eleven

As I saw the London plane take off and circle round the airport, I could feel my legs giving way under me. No matter how many times I told myself that Ajit was going on an ordinary journey done every day by hundreds of people, I could not eradicate the feeling that this was a final farewell and I would never see him again; it was a feeling left over from the sad goodbyes of wartime, tied to the fact that his family might exert unbearable pressure upon him to desert me. It happened often enough, and, knowing that everybody had a breaking point, I did not think I would blame him if he failed to send for me. He loved me – but distance does not always make the heart grow fonder, said a cynical voice within me. I tried to think dispassionately of being left alone again, but I could not. I loved him. I ached with love.

Angela was waiting at the entrance to the airport. She had insisted on waiting outside for me, so that I could have a last few words with Ajit. We went home together, but I did no more than have a word with Mother and then took the bus down to the club. My honeymoon was over.

People came forward to shake my hand. Dr Wu had told all the club members about the wedding and they were very courteous about it. The attitude of the Indians towards me changed markedly. Whereas they normally tucked themselves away in corners, forming a tight clique, today they came and asked politely after my health and that of Ajit. They did not shake hands with me but raised their hands, palms together, in their own form of salute. I was one of them now and they were showing that they accepted me. They were charmed when I returned their salute in the same fashion and said: 'Namaste,' as Ajit had taught me. They would have kept me with them to talk, but I had work to do and had to leave them.

'Come soon and visit me,' said one of the girl students, pulling her sari round her.

'I will.'

I went to see Bessie. She told me I looked wonderful and, indeed, I knew I was glowing like a lamp newly lit.

'I didn't see Dr Wu in the lounge,' I said idly, as I pulled off my gloves and took off my coat. I saw that there was a pile of correspondence waiting for me on my desk.

'Haven't you heard?' asked Bessie in surprise. 'He had news yesterday that his father had been executed – his brothers have fled to Hongkong.'

'My God!' I said. 'How terrible!'

I sat down at my desk and stared unseeingly at the letters on it. 'I thought he was a member of the Communist Party – he fought with them – he's got a bullet wound in one leg, I'm told. I always imagined that his family were very happy under the Communist régime – that it was the fulfilment of all their hopes.'

'He's not a party member, according to his application form,' said Bessie. 'I took the trouble of having a look, because it seemed queer to me too – he believed wholeheartedly in their cause – he was always talking about it.'

'Poor Wu,' I said. 'He is bereaved in more ways than one then – and he is such a kind soul. I wonder what he will do now.'

'Can't imagine,' said Bessie, picking up the telephone.

I started to go through the accumulation of letters. I wrote a letter to Wu expressing Ajit's and my sympathy and assuring him of our lasting friendship. Then I sent for a stenographer. Among the pile of letters I dictated was one to a London bookseller asking for a Gujerati grammar, dictionary and reader. Ajit and I had agreed that I should learn first the language of Shahpur district, and later on learn Hindi, which was his mother tongue.

The books arrived three days later. They were dilapidated second-hand copies – the only ones the dealer could obtain – but they answered the purpose. They became my constant companions. I read them on the bus going to and from work, and propped them in front of me while washing dishes or doing my hair. At the end of the week I had mastered the alphabet and the rest came more easily. The Indian girl who had invited me to visit her had a friend who was a Gujerati. The Gujerati girl, on the promise of reciprocal English lessons, was persuaded to come to the club four times a week to hear me read and, after a while, converse. At one time I had congratulated myself on acquiring a working knowledge of German in six months; now I wanted to learn an oriental language in six weeks at an age when languages do not come easily to the tongue. Spurred by necessity, however, I learned at least to understand simple conversation.

On the same day that the books arrived, Mother telephoned to say that a cable had come from Bombay telling of Ajit's safe arrival. A load slid off my back and I could admit how afraid I had been for his safety. As I put the telephone back on to the rest, I saw again the room at the inn, lit only by the falling logs in the fireplace, and I sighed wistfully.

'What did you say?' asked Bessie.

'Nothing,' I said hastily.

Ajit wrote to me every day and I to him. At his request, I sent my letters direct to Shahpur, in care of the Company for whom he was to work. He wanted to choose his own time for breaking his news to his parents, and frequent letters from England would have shown that he had some attachment there. A part of me which was cold and cynical wondered sometimes if he would tell his parents and if I would ever get to India. I went on with my preparations for the voyage, however, and booked a passage in a slow, Indian ship, as P. & O. liners were booked up for months to come.

One evening on the way to the club, I had paused to look at a window full of spring suits when a voice behind me said: 'Good evening, Mrs Singh.'

It was a second before it penetrated that I was Mrs Singh. The only time I had seen my married name used was on letters addressed to me – in the club I was still Miss Delaney, and my friends used my Christian name.

I whirled about.

Dr Wu bowed to me and asked how I was. I said I was very well. He looked heavy-eyed, but his teeth gleamed in a cheerful smile.

He thanked me for my letter. I said I was truly sorry to hear of his bad news.

He dismissed it with a little wave of one hand. 'It is life,' he said, the sadness of his voice belying the airy gesture of his hand. 'If you are going to the club, may I accompany you?'

I nodded agreement and we walked slowly along the busy pavement. I told him that I was off duty and had decided to spend an hour in the lounge and have some coffee.

'Have you had dinner yet, Mrs Singh?'

'No, I haven't.'

'Let us dine together. I know a good restaurant.'

I accepted. I longed for sympathetic companionship to ease the worries which consumed me about Ajit.

He took me to a small, clean, Chinese restaurant. I asked him to order, and, after speaking in Chinese to the proprietor, he gave the order. It was early for dining and the bare room was quiet, the lighting subdued. Two Chinese in a far corner were the only customers.

We chatted desultorily and then became silent. I was wondering what Wu was going to do, in view of the persecution of his family in Communist China and the probability that he would not be looked upon with favour if he returned home. I decided to ask him.

'Dr Wu,' I said. 'As an old friend and as the wife of an old friend, may I ask what plans you have, in view of the sorrows – difficulties . . .' I ran out of words.

His smile was wry. 'I expect to stay here. Today I spoke with my Professor, and it is likely that when I have my doctorate from Wetherport University – I have already, of course, a Chinese degree – I shall take a post in industry.'

Sympathy must have been apparent in my expression, because he went on in a burst of confidence: 'I hoped that the revolution at home would be followed by less bloodshed than was the Russian revolution; I still believe that there will be fewer excesses – the new régime must make itself secure, however, and it is my misfortune that my family must suffer. I do not have as yet any details of what brought the Government's wrath down upon my family, but we owned land and have in the past produced many Government officials – and our interests may well have clashed, although we fought in the army of the Communists against the Japanese.' He fiddled nervously with the spoons which the waiter had laid upon the table in front of him. 'It is likely that I could go home to China and work for the new China – I have not offended personally – but if my family is scattered, for what reason shall I work? How shall I ever feel confident or safe in such a situation?' His voice died to a whisper.

'China's loss will be our gain,' I said. 'You are one of the foremost young men in your field, I am told, and you will be welcome here.' I could not think of anything else to say. Here was a man whose family was scattered, whose beliefs had suffered a fearful blow. He had been so proud of his country's resurgence and it had struck at him through his parents. As he sat and plucked at the tablecloth, he seemed to be the quintessence of the suffering of our generation. Looking at him, I saw the hosts of the homeless, brotherless, dispossessed and disillusioned, and I was wrung with pity.

'Is your wife safely in Hongkong, Dr Wu?'

'I am a widower. My wife was killed in an air raid a few months after our marriage.'

'My God,' I said involuntarily.

My ejaculation brought him back to the realisation that he was supposed to be entertaining me.

'I am a bad host,' he said, 'boring you with my story. So bad of me. Are Mr and Mrs Delaney well?'

I tried to help him by launching into other subjects. Food came – Won Ton soup and chicken with almonds. Both of us felt better after eating; we leaned back and smoked and drank China tea out of handleless cups.

'I will take a few days' holiday,' said Wu. 'I am tired of my good landlady's cooking. I will go into your beautiful countryside and walk – and think about my thesis.'

His courageous acceptance of his loss of beliefs, country and family was at first shocking to me. I looked for rebellion against the forces that had stripped him, and resented the fact that I found none. He bowed his head like an aspen in the wind, and said: 'It is life.'

Then, as he talked quietly of the lovely places in England which we both knew, I realised that to rebel against the inevitable is to waste strength; and Wu, by his acceptance, was saving his strength for the long, tiring battles that lay ahead of him in this England which he loved so much. He needed a little time, however, in which to get his breath, and I encouraged the idea of a spring holiday.

'My sister has gone for ten days to Pentecost Bay,' I said. 'A break is always a good idea after a long winter's work.'

He poured himself another cup of tea, tasted it and found it cold; so he signalled to the waiter to bring another pot.

'I have visited Pentecost Bay,' he said. 'The country there is hilly, is it not?'

'It is,' I said. 'Angela is staying at a farmhouse which takes summer visitors, about a mile out of the town. I hope she is giving herself a good rest – she works far too hard, and she was marvellous about helping with my wedding when she had so much else on her plate at the time.'

The conversation moved to Ajit. More tea arrived and Wu refilled my cup.

'It is so kind of you,' he said, 'to be patient with my long discourses.'

'It has been a most pleasant evening,' I assured him, when I said finally that I must go home.

At the door of the restaurant I paused to examine a showcase full of

Chinese porcelain, and, as we walked down the narrow, dirty staircase, I asked him to tell me about the dragons depicted on the vases. He beamed, and told me about Imperial dragons, fairytale dragons and ordinary dragons, as we strolled leisurely to the bus stop, where he insisted upon waiting for the bus with me.

Tomkins was the only member of the family at home when I arrived there, so I scooped him up into my lap, as I sat down by the embers of the living-room fire. He purred softly as I stroked him while I leaned back in Father's easy chair and thought about Wu's patient acceptance of his sorrows.

'Tomkins,' I said severely, 'I am worrying about Ajit before there is any need to worry and I am ashamed of myself. Tonight a very brave man showed me how to face real troubles courageously.'

Tomkins grunted sleepily and submitted to being carried up to my bedroom to keep me company. Propped up on my dressing-table was a letter from Ajit which must have been delivered during the afternoon. I tore open the envelope eagerly.

Chapter Twelve

In his letters Ajit told me in great detail all that passed after his return home. Later on I learned much more and gradually pieced together the whole story – not only Ajit's story, but also the story of Bhim, Nulini and Khan, whose tragedy was played within the compound walls of my father-in-law's house; and helped me indirectly.

The antiquated aeroplane, in which Ajit had flown from London, chose to land at Bombay instead of going on to Delhi. Repairs might take as long as forty-eight hours, he was told, and as no alternative plane reservation was available, he decided to travel the remainder of his journey by train.

As the train strained its way northwards, it felt strange to him to hear his own tongue spoken with increasing frequency. He found that Hindi no longer came naturally to him and he spoke it stiffly, like a foreigner. He felt foreign in his hot tweed jacket and worsted trousers amongst white cotton shirts and dhotis; and the food that he bought along the route seemed overspiced after years of English cooking.

Still, it was good to be home; to see the Western Ghats in the moonlight, and the barren hills of Rajastan glowering hotly over small villages; to be packed closely in a carriage with a multitude of well-behaved children and stacks of homely-looking luggage. It was comforting to see whole families travelling together, strong in their unity. No need to feel lonely here – these were his own people, whom he understood and who understood him and did not regard him as a curiosity. He took his shoes off and sat cross-legged on the carriage seat. A holy man, who was travelling without a ticket, had climbed through the window when the train paused to take water. He settled himself on an unencumbered part of the floor and arranged his orange robes round him; then he mopped his bald head, noticed Ajit's shoes lying on the floor and asked if he had been abroad. Ajit said he had just returned. Glad to speak in his own language, Ajit talked with him for most of the journey. The man was going on a pilgrimage, and so that the pilgrimage should not be interrupted by irate ticket collectors, he made his namaste and departed through the window again just before the train entered Delhi.

Ajit put on his shoes, collected his unread detective novels and tightened the straps of his bedding roll. There was a general upheaval in the carriage, and the flash of a porter's turban as he leaped on to the step and clung to the outside of the door. The train tore past his brother, Bhim, towering out of the crush of people on the platform, and his father standing close to the train.

'Bhim,' yelled Ajit.

The coolie opened the door as the train came to a sudden halt. Ajit noted the coolie's number on the brass plate on his arm, pointed out his luggage and told him to put it on to the platform. The luggage attended to and one or two children hastily lifted down, Ajit jumped from the train and pushed his way towards the spot where he had seen Bhim.

Bhim saw him and came to him, smiles of greeting obliterating his usual absent-minded expression. His little sister, Shushila, nearly bursting with excitement, ran to him and slipped a garland of flowers round his neck, as he bent down to hug her. Her short plaits waggled as she burrowed her face into his neck. Her frock and white shoes and socks made her look uncannily like the little girls he knew in England; but he was amused to see that she wore a diamond in her pierced nose, and golden ear-rings.

He went to his father and bent to take dust from his feet, but the elder man caught his hands and raised him up.

'My son,' he said huskily, as he ran his eyes over Ajit.

'Father, it's good to be home,' he said.

He had forgotten how absurdly small, but how dignified, the old District Magistrate was. Although his handlebar moustache was flecked with white, he still had the same erect bearing and imperious manner that Ajit remembered.

Bhim attended to the luggage, and then the father, escorted by both his sons, trotted out of the station, receiving with the condescension of a ruling Raja the polite 'Namaste' of the station-master, who happened to be passing.

And so home through the moonlit evening, everyone talking at the top of his voice, and even the new chauffeur venturing an occasional remark.

Bhim had been married during Ajit's absence and accepted with a shy grin Ajit's jokes about it. Shushila, who might have been expected to talk about her new sister, was silent on the subject except to say that she was very pretty. Ajit knew, from Bhim's letters to him, that his father had chosen the bride, just as he had decided that Bhim should be a lawyer, and like a dutiful son, Bhim had accepted her. Bhim had just begun his law practice when he married, and whether it had been the crushing amount of study and new work which he had undertaken at the same time, or whether he did not like his wife, Ajit could not judge, but there had been a singular lack of enthusiasm in his letters mentioning his marriage. He had just said that his father had found a suitable, educated wife for him and that her dowry was reasonable, though not large.

Ajit knew Bhim's ability to shut himself up with his books and some obscure problem of inheritance or of evidence, and he wondered if a young wife had been able to tempt him away from his work. Bhim was an immensely kind person, provided his attention was drawn to a specific need of being kind, but otherwise flood and famine could come and go without his noticing it.

Ajit was sure that his own marriage would come as a dreadful blow to the family, and as the car bumped along the rutted road outside the city, he prayed that they would not be too angry and upset. Would Bhim understand, he wondered? How would Shushila accept a white sister?

While they were passing through the sweetsellers' bazaar, he was full of defiance; a man should be free to choose his own wife. But by the time they had hooted their way through collections of refugees' huts, he was sure he must have been mad to take such a step; even his elders, with a lifetime of experience behind them, arranged a marriage only after every factor affecting the whole family had been considered.

It was with a feeling of helplessness that he descended at last from the car when it drew up in his father's compound. Still, it was marvellous to be home, to see the same neem trees rustling in the corner, with a mongoose playing beneath them, and his mother standing at the top of the veranda steps, waiting to perform the Welcoming Ceremony. Behind her stood Ayah, holding the tray; the oil lamp on it flickered in the wind, casting unearthly shadows on to the two women and the small crowd of servants and nephews and nieces behind them. As he approached, the lamp flared up and showed the scarlet of his mother's sari and a glitter of bracelets. Then it died down to a flicker, making her look like a ghost from an India long dead.

Ajit paused at the foot of the steps; he wanted suddenly to run away, but his father was standing beside him expectantly, his white dhoti gleaming in the moonlight, and Shushila was pushing him impatiently from behind. Bhim seemed to sense what he was feeling, because he touched his elbow lightly, to propel him forward.

He saw his mother's sweet, plump face peeping out of her sari, and he wondered what I would find in common with her. He prayed as he ascended the steps: 'Ramji, Ramji, help me.'

He put his hands together in salutation, bowed low and took dust from her feet. Smiling through her tears, she took vermilion from the tray and imprinted upon his forehead the mark of a Hindu. When he felt her gentle fingers, he knew that the shackles of the family were again upon him. He, Ajit Singh, descendant of a thousand warriors, wearer of the sacred thread, electrical instrument engineer, was back in his father's house, a younger son who must submit to his father, his uncles and his elder brother.

The sweetmeat which his mother then put into his mouth was hard to swallow, but he loved her, and when he raised his face to her he smiled.

Thakkur, the bearer, and Pratap, the gardener, ran forward to help with the luggage and to greet the man they had loved as a child. Thakkur's face, which was normally doleful, was today full of joy. Ajit remembered how he used to spend hours reciting the Gita for the benefit of a sleepy little boy.

'Have you any more grandchildren, Thakkur? And do you recite the Gita to them as you did to me?'

'Ji, hun, ji, hun, no less than three. They recite the Gita to me instead.'

'Pratap, have you grown any lady's fingers for me to eat? I hunger for your lady's fingers; I have not eaten them for so long.'

'Ji, hun, Sahib, plenty of lady's fingers are.'

After washing himself, Ajit went into the big stone kitchen, to take food. He sat on a straw mat and his mother insisted on serving him herself. Her slow, graceful movements seemed restful after the jerkiness of English women. In the background fluttered Ayah, her thin face wreathed in smiles of welcome for the man she had suckled as a baby. In the shadows, away from him, sat his new sister-in-law, Nulini. She was not introduced, nor did they address each other. It was just as if she had been there always, and Ajit had merely returned from a visit to the bazaar instead of from a three-year sojourn abroad. He noticed that her black sari was silk and richly embroidered in gold; he was embarrassed that she stared at him almost insolently. He thought irritably that she should veil her face and sit more modestly.

When the last pakaurhi was eaten and the last drop of tea drained, he sent Thakkur for one of his suitcases, and took from it three silk saris, purchased in Bombay as a wedding gift, and handed these to Nulini. Coyly, she smiled for the first time, and took them from him, taking care that in the movement she showed her hands and rounded arms to the best advantage.

He had an English china doll which he presented to an enchanted Shushila, a gold pendant and a handbag for his mother, a leather wallet from Port Said for Bhim and a leather-cased travelling clock for his father. Ayah had not been forgotten; there was a soft, white woollen shawl for her, and muslin dhotis for Cook Maharaj, Thakkur and Pratap. The kitchen resounded with cries of appreciation – what a good young master, what a good son.

Ajit felt like a traitor.

After chatting for a while with his mother, he picked up the clock and he and Bhim walked slowly across the inner courtyard to the room which his father used as a study. Walking in the half light of the moon the brothers tried to re-establish their old comradeship, but they were shy with each other and spoke only of Bhim's law practice.

Ajit heard his father talking to his clerk and, therefore, he knocked tentatively, but Ram Singh immediately bade him enter, and the clerk salaamed and withdrew.

Their father was sitting cross-legged on a wooden divan; beside him on the divan was a small desk littered with papers. Although Ram Singh had retired, his knowledge of Hindu law, particularly that of land tenure, was so great that he was frequently consulted both by Government officials and lawyer friends; and some hours of every day were still spent at his desk.

He motioned Ajit to a chair which stood by an old, English rolltop desk. The elder brother hovered in the background until his father told him to come and sit down too.

They waited respectfully for the elder man to speak, and he began asking Ajit about his air trip and about the University. They discussed these safe topics and news of his uncles' families for an hour.

Diffidently Ajit proffered the clock as a humble gift.

The old man was touched. He took the clock, opened it, wound it, listened to its subdued tick, and finally closed it, rubbing the leather case lovingly with his thin, knotted fingers. He was pleased that Ajit had not forgotten him in these years. I think he realised that Ajit must have saved carefully to bring back such a good present, and that he imagined the many small sacrifices that Ajit must have made in order to buy it.

'It is a very fine clock,' he said at last in a very husky voice.

Ram Singh's personal servant brought in his dinner to him, and the brothers rose and left him to eat in peace.

Hand in hand, they recrossed the courtyard and went to the dining-room, where the rest of the family was gathered for dinner.

There was general merriment in the big, cool room next to the kitchen. The family sat in a circle on low, carved stools, their brass eating trays before them, while Thakkur rushed back and forth to the kitchen, serving them with the bread that Cook Maharaj made as they ate.

As the light of the brass paraffin lamp glowed over the contented family with its contented servants, Ajit was torn by apprehension that his marriage might well disrupt all its peacefulness.

To marry without his father's permission, without even informing his family, was like spitting into their faces. Above all, to marry an English girl, who knew nothing of their way of life, was inflicting something upon them which was possibly more than they could bear.

In that instant he wished passionately that he had never been sent to England, had never met me, had never stirred from the age-old path of an Indian's life, mapped out by sages long ago and followed by his people ever since.

But then he thought of me, he said, as his lamp in darkness, his Lakshmi. He knew I trusted him, and he felt weak with love.

'Do you feel quite well?' asked his mother anxiously, having observed a spasm cross his face.

He looked at her, and she saw to her concern that something was indeed wrong, but he answered gently: 'I am quite well.'

'It is my imagination,' she said. 'I thought you were troubled.'

Chapter Thirteen

When writing to his father from England, Ajit had, of course, told him that he had obtained the post of instrument engineer at the new power house being built at Pandipura, near Shahpur. The old man, in reply, had said frankly that he had expected to have to pull a number of political strings before getting his younger son settled in life; even in a country short of technicians, competition for the better-paid posts was formidable, and Ajit's qualifications must, therefore, have been considered exceptionally good. Ram Singh had spent thousands of rupees to send Ajit to England to continue his studies, and he now felt that his appointment to Shahpur had more than justified this expenditure.

Ram Singh was, therefore, in an extremely good temper on the morning following his son's return home. Before calling the boy to him, he bathed and dressed and went through his usual routine. He sat cross-legged on a stool in the small, pillared prayer room in a tower at the corner of his house, and said his morning prayers; when the light of the dawn became stronger, he took up his Gita and read some of the Lord Krishna's injunctions to Arjuna, and then meditated on them, after which he went for a short walk.

Ram Singh's life had been a difficult one, a life of constant compromise between the British rulers of India, whom he served, and his revolutionary countrymen, with whom his sympathies lay. As a District Magistrate, his livelihood depended upon the goodwill of the British, and when Gandhiji started to lead India towards independence, he had been faced with the choice of throwing up his career, as did many of his friends, and joining the passive resistance movement, with its inevitable prison sentences and, sometimes, death; or staying where he was and tempering the wind to the shorn lambs of revolution, as they came before him in the courts. Lacking the courage of his convictions he had done the latter, and many a Congressman had been relieved to receive from him the minimum of sentences.

When the day came for the British to leave India and the Congress Party came to power, they had remembered his clemency and his secret contributions to their funds, and he had served them until his recent retirement.

Now, as instructed by the scriptures, he was trying to turn his mind towards God, and to that end he had retired to his house outside Delhi and built himself a prayer room, in which he could pray, meditate and study holy books.

Knowing that he was getting old and that before he died it was his duty to find a wife for his son, he had recently consulted various friends of his own caste, who had families of the same age, and had found one with a daughter a few years younger than Ajit – a girl whose horoscope, cast at her birth, proclaimed her to be a suitable match.

Ram Singh knew the girl well. She was a friend of Nulini, his elder son's wife, and often visited his house, and presumably she would fit in happily if she became a member of the family. She was noted for her hot temper, but she was fair-skinned and healthy, and he had no doubt that marriage would tame her. Being a Punjabi, she was bigger built than many, and that would suit Ajit, who, by Indian standards, was not a small man. He found upon inquiry that she was a talented embroideress and could play the vina well. Furthermore, her father was offering a good dowry; this dowry could in turn be used to dower Ajit's younger sister, and so save her father parting with the dowry he had obtained for Bhim. This latter dowry he would keep in reserve, for use if he should be faced with the dowering of a niece or other relation left unexpectedly fatherless.

There is no doubt that Ram Singh felt very satisfied that his son's future was neatly taken care of; and as soon as he had eaten his morning meal and spent a few minutes gossiping with his wife, he sent for Ajit to acquaint him with his plans.

Although tired out by his long journey, Ajit had not been able to sleep during the night. He had lain and tossed on his hard wooden bed, wondering how to explain his unfilial behaviour to his father. For months he had pushed this gnawing worry into the background. Now it could no longer be pushed away; it had to be brought out, be examined, be tossed about from tongue to tongue through the family, until it would sound as if he had committed a major crime.

He sweated when he thought of how his uncles, who lived in the house next door, would counsel his father to coerce him into breaking the marriage, even to the point of making him marry someone else. They would suggest that his father obtain his dismissal from his new post, that he be confined to his room until his ardour cooled, that he be cast out from his caste and family. He knew them – they would enjoy his disgrace, since it would show to good advantage the virtues of their own sons.

Ajit loved his proud parent, and he desired to love and serve him in his old age as a good son should. He knew that his marriage would come as a great shock, and he winced as he thought of the family humiliation it might well involve, the loss of caste and the domestic calamity.

His father was noted for his toleration of the unorthodox behaviour of others, and, in fact, his own household was by no means orthodox. Many Western innovations had crept in. He had, however, insisted upon the observance of certain customs. No meat or eggs ever entered his house, although he had been discreetly deaf when busybodies told him that his sons ate both of these in restaurants. Prayers were said, fasts and festivals were kept, food was prepared in accordance with caste rules, and his charity was unfailing. He accepted his sons' Western mode of dress, since it had long been adopted by civil servants and he himself wore it on official occasions; but when he was at home he wore the village-woven shirts and dhotis of his own people. When his father, Ajit's grandfather, died, Ram Singh abolished purdah throughout the family, much to his mother's disgust. He expected, however, that his womenfolk would not go out alone and would behave with modesty.

A few modifications to the old ways of life had sufficed up to now to keep his family happy. He still received the veneration of his younger brothers and their families, as well as that of his own family; his word was law in the old family mansion next door, which they shared – and which Ram Singh had deserted, when on the neighbouring plot he built his present house, which was more suited to his position as a senior civil servant.

Ram Singh ruled with justice what was still really a communal family, banded together for safety in troubled times and for the protection of their weak and helpless ones. He considered every action and every question raised from the viewpoint of what was best for the family as a whole, and this frequently meant the sublimation of the desires of one member for the good of the many. For generations this sublimation had been taken for granted; it often stifled the initiative and ability of one individual, causing him much suffering, but it ensured the survival of the family. The family's coffers filled as many toiled together, and their widows, orphans and cripples were fed. The amount of gold worn by their women increased generation after generation; there was gold for necessary bribes and there were plenty of young men to defend the walls of the old house when need arose.

As the family were not Brahmins, there was no taboo about their crossing the sea, and the family had early sent some of their men to study in the West and thus fit themselves for Government posts under the British. One of those chosen had been Ajit, and by their standards Ajit had played the traitor – and Ajit knew it.

So he tossed and turned all night, longing for me to be there, he said, to soothe and advise, and yet cursing his selfishness that put his own pleasure before the family's well-being. The independence of outlook which he had acquired in England slipped from him and he was again a younger son, to be pushed hither and thither at the behest of his elders.

And yet, in his heart, he was sure, he said, that I could be fitted into his family without undue upset, if he could only persuade his father that it could be done. He believed in my discretion and adaptability; I had seen so much in my life that was strange. His family was a normal, kindly one, so that I ought not to find it too difficult to bow a little to their customs and they to mine.

When Thakkur came to ask him to go to his father, he rose reluctantly and his feet dragged as he traversed the verandas. He had put on a dhoti and homespun shirt, and they flapped against his body, reminding him that he was an Indian at home, not a student enjoying the social whirl of the West, dividing his time between study, long technical arguments and dates with girl friends.

In the lounge, off which his father's study led, he hesitated. The chairs and tables, specially carved to his father's order, the green upholstered settees and the brocade curtains all spoke of Western influence, but Ajit knew the room was rarely used by the family, and had been intended for the many European visitors who came to Ram Singh's house before the British left India.

Ram Singh had heard his son's slippers flip-flapping across the drawing-room, and called: 'Come in, my son.'

His clerk, laden with papers, came out of the study, salaamed as best he could under his burden and scuttled away. Ram Singh's personal servant and chauffeur was squatting outside the office door and he quickly got to his feet and salaamed as Ajit approached. He was a new servant engaged during Ajit's absence, and Ajit stopped to ask his name and from where he came.

'I am called Khan. My home is near Dava – near the river Sutlej.' His Hindi was faltering.

'A hill man,' thought Ajit, his interest for the moment obliterating his own troubles, 'from Tibet, presumably.'

He looked at the man with some admiration. He was small but perfectly made, and the muscles rippled under his thin shirt. There was, however, no time to ask more. His father called again: 'Come in, my son.'

There was no escape, so Ajit went in, bowed and touched his father's feet. He stood and waited for Ram Singh to speak.

Ram Singh greeted Ajit jovially, pushed to one side the mahogany desk on which he had been working, and bade him sit down beside him. Ajit removed a pile of files, put them on a dusty side table, and climbed up beside his father. They sat cross-legged, nearly facing each other; and Ajit seemed to be again a little boy about to learn from his father a few more lines from the Ramayana.

'Ah, a dhoti,' said his father with approval and leaned forward to pat his son's muslin-covered knee.

He was in a high good humour. He often said that there was nothing he liked better than a good wedding, with the house swarming with relations, a kitchen stuffed with cooks and storerooms stuffed with food; and probably something of this was in his mind as he sat with his son.

Certainly Kasher Chand Rana would spare no expense over his daughter's wedding – his wife would see to that.

'I am sad,' he said to Ajit, 'that you can stay only a short time with us. I had hoped that you would be able to live at home on your return from England – and that I might soon have a grandson to play with, eh?' His eyes twinkled.

Ajit stirred and hoped that his discomfiture was not apparent. Ram Singh might easily have a grandson quicker than he expected. The thought of my having a son made him feel better, he said, and strengthened him.

'Sir?' he queried, feeling that Ram Singh had something special to say to him.

Ram Singh smoothed his whiskers and knitted the heavy brows that had frightened many a malefactor in the courts. It signalled that he was about to deliver a pronouncement of importance. Then he sniffed and seemed to think better of what he was about to say.

'Describe to me, my son,' he said, obviously changing his tactics, 'the work which you will do in Shahpur.'

Thankful for a subject on which he could talk freely, Ajit explained the irrigation scheme, of which the power house was a small part, and how landless refugees from Pakistan would be settled in the district as soon as deep wells could be bored and electricity was available to pump up the water. In his enthusiasm he foretold an era of prosperity for the whole province. He loved India and longed to see the peasants freed from famine. His work would be to him a crusade against hunger.

Ram Singh had, of course, heard of the scheme, but he was interested to hear details of it.

'The future of India,' he said, 'lies not in the hands of those who rule but in the hands of our village people. Their content or discontent will be the factor which will decide who shall rule. Full stomachs will do more to keep the Congress Party in power than any other reform. I rejoice that you will be concerned, if only indirectly, in the alleviation of hunger.'

He smiled at Ajit, and continued: 'Bhim will one day be a magistrate, perhaps a judge. I have trained him to be incorrupt and to be careful to weight the scales of justice as far as possible in favour of the poorer man. I am happy to think that I have two sons who will be of some use to our patient villagers.' He wagged his finger at his son. 'Never despise a man because he is of lower caste or lives in a mud hut. He feels as we do. Remember!'

Ajit said: 'I do not despise any honourable man.'

This was getting away from the subject of Ajit, however, and the old man asked where Ajit would live and what he would earn.

Ajit explained that he would start on Rs.700. His friend, Chundabhai Patel, had warned him, however, that Shahpur was an expensive town in which to live, as middle-class people were few and the bazaars catered either for the many rich industrialists or for the thousands of poverty-stricken mill workers. There were few districts in which a man of modest means might live comfortably. The Government had, however, found accommodation for the senior staff of the power house, and had allotted to him a small flat in the same building which housed most of the staff of a nearby college. Although the flat was six miles out of town, it was not very far from the power-house site.

'And who will look after you?'

'I thought Mother might have a servant here, who would come with me,' said Ajit guardedly. 'Servants are hard to get in Shahpur – the mills take many men and the building of the power house has attracted most of the surplus labour from the villages round about.'

'Hum,' said Ram Singh, taking out a handkerchief and mopping his face. The weather was already getting hot.

'Doubtless Mother could spare you somebody, but – er – um – would it not be pleasant to – er – have someone else to share a flat with you?'

Ajit said nothing. He saw with horrid clarity the proposal which was about to be made, and he was appalled. Although it was inevitable that his father should have in mind the question of a wife for him, he had hoped that it would have been left unmentioned until he had been home for some time. What in the name of Ram was he to reply to his father?

He stiffened himself. Humility before his father was all very well, but he had some pride. Why should he fear to do what he knew was right just because it was not the custom? He held up his head and again mentally rehearsed the first words of his confession. His father, however, was burrowing in his desk, and from underneath the lid his muffled voice announced: 'I have been thinking of you during your absence – I – er – have not mentioned marriage to you before because I wished you to complete your studies without distraction, but now you are thirty, and – er – your mother and I feel – er – that it is more than time you were married.'

He emerged from his desk looking flustered and clutching a number of papers. Putting down the desk lid, he carefully spread out the papers and smoothed their corners with uncertain fingers.

'Now,' he went on more firmly, 'our good friend and caste brother, Kasher Chand Rana Sahib, has, as you will remember, a daughter a trifle younger than yourself, and it would give us both pleasure to see you united.'

'Father – ' broke in Ajit; but Ram Singh lifted his hand for silence.

'Here is a photograph of her,' he said, as he put into Ajit's reluctant hand a formal studio portrait of a magnificent woman who had the bearing of an Amazon.

'Her father has not pressed her to marry, since she has shown no preference for anyone. He tells me, however, that you would not be unwelcome.' He omitted to say that Bimla Chand Rana's temper was so famous that a number of men had persuaded their fathers to excuse them from marrying her. Ajit knew of it, because ever since he was a small boy he had been teased by his friends about a promise that his mother had made to Mrs Chand Rana, that Ajit should marry Bimla when he grew up.

Ajit looked at the imposing photograph.

'Father,' he said, panic-stricken, 'Father, I can't – I'm – '

'Don't you like the look of her now she is grown up?' asked Ram Singh, taking up a copy of her horoscope. 'If you really don't like her, I could advertise for someone else. I know we should get some good replies – you are an excellent catch, you know.'

He smiled lovingly upon his son. He wanted him to enjoy his wife – and Bimla Chand Rana was a beauty.

Ajit dropped the photograph on to the divan.

'Father, I can't marry anybody.'

Ram Singh looked annoyed.

'Rubbish,' he said. 'It is necessary to marry. Why can't you marry?'

Ajit bowed his head until it nearly touched his father's knees.

'Forgive me,' he said, 'but I am already married.'

'Married already!' exclaimed Ram Singh. 'When? To whom?' And added without much hope, 'To an Indian fellow student?'

'Last month to an English lady named Margaret Delaney,' whispered Ajit, while a second Ajit inside was praying: 'Ramji, don't let the shock make him ill.'

Ram Singh gasped.

'Not in my family,' he muttered. 'It could not happen in my family. Ajit, you have lain with a foreign woman – you, whom I love above everyone – you have married an English woman.' His voice rose to a wail: 'Ajit, you are joking.'

'It is true, Father.' Ajit could feel the pain of his father, and it was a great pain.

'What will your uncles say? This is impossible.'

Ajit said afterwards that while he sorrowed for his father, he could hear my voice at the time of our parting saying: 'Ajit, darling, don't desert me, will you?' Ajit had not resented my entreaty. He knew of the work I had done amongst bitter, disillusioned women, and he knew, too, that I had learned to love him truly and dreaded that somehow he would be taken away from me, as the other men I had loved were taken.

He had promised passionately that I should join him, and that promise he remembered as he faced the disgust in his father's eyes. The old man's face was flushed and his moustache was trembling. He sat in silence, as he collected his thoughts, and regarded steadily the son who had betrayed his family and his caste.

Ajit awaited judgement, his head still bowed. Far away, he could hear the clatter of Cook Maharaj's tava and tongs as he made bread for the house servants' meal. It was a homely, familiar sound and seemed to string together all the quiet pursuits and gentle relationships of the family. Tears stung in his eyes as he listened.

While he sat, Ram Singh's agile mind had evidently already been at work on the question of extricating his son from what must have appeared to him as a dreadful predicament; for he leaned forward, his face passive, and lifting his son's chin with his thin fingers, he said: 'Weep not, my son. We will untangle this unfortunate knot which you have tied.' He dropped his hand to the desk and fidgeted with Bimla's horoscope. 'We can probably come to some arrangement with this woman, whereby for a reasonable allowance, she would relinquish her claims upon you, and if she desired she could later divorce you. For our part, we will invoke the old Hindu law and simply obtain a second wife for you – a good Indian wife, like Bimla.' The dark flush eased away from Ram Singh's cheeks, as he went on: 'I presume that no one here knows of your English marriage, and for all purposes of inheritance the second wife here in India would be considered the first wife. An English woman would probably have no knowledge of our laws and is not, therefore, likely to make troublesome demands upon the family at my death.'

Ram Singh folded his hands in his lap and looked very satisfied about his solution to the problem. He had propounded the popular thesis that an English woman would do anything for money or jewellery. He waited.

Ajit was flabbergasted at the proposal. Such an idea had never occurred to him. It was so cold-blooded and showed such a disregard for the feelings of the persons concerned, such an inability to grasp what a marriage of love meant, that he was speechless for a moment. Then words poured out of him.

'Father,' he said, outrage in his voice, 'I would never agree to such a settlement. I have promised her that she shall come to me here, and she shall come.' He looked round wildly, trying to think of a way in which to appease the wrath immediately apparent in his father's eyes. 'I love her,' he shouted defiantly. 'I love her.' And the walls of the big, bare house echoed back mockingly: 'Love her, love her.'

'Ajit!' roared Ram Singh, infuriated at such a show of passion – but Ajit was past caring.

He thrust his face close to his father's.

'I will not marry anyone else,' he said, his voice cold with rage.

Ram Singh stiffened. Such insubordination was insufferable. He picked up the horoscope and slapped it down again on to the desk. The sharp thwack on the desk brought Ajit to his senses, and before his father could say anything he had pulled himself together and was speaking in a carefully controlled voice.

'Forgive me,' he said, 'for marrying without your permission. I know in that respect I have done you a deep wrong. I had intended to come home and ask you first – but Margaret is so beautiful that I was afraid another would make her an offer before I could. I would have been far away, here in India – and she might in despair have accepted someone else for a husband.'

Afterwards he wrote to me: 'When I was arguing with my father, I kept seeing you in my mind's eye as you were on our wedding night. Never had I seen anyone so fair. I ached to touch you – to be with you – to be part of you – away from people who thought of women merely as useful additions to the family.'

Ram Singh apparently did not take in Ajit's last remarks, and his thoughts were concerned only with avoiding the entry into his house of a casteless English woman. Condemnation burst from him.

'I know English women,' he shouted. 'I have seen them – painted, loud-mouthed, immodest. They bare their shoulders and legs so that any sweeper can goggle at their charms. They take all from their husbands and give nothing.' His moustache bristled, and he shuddered. 'They humiliate their husbands with public discourtesy. They have affairs with other men. Do you know what they say about them in the bazaars? In the zenanas, hey?'

'Margaret is not like that,' broke in Ajit indignantly. 'She is a refined, educated – '

'Educated, you say? All the English women I ever met were supposed to be educated. But to what end? Allow such a woman in my family? No, a thousand times no.' And the little man banged his inoffensive mahogany desk to emphasise his words.

'Margaret is as good and kind as Mother,' said Ajit, his voice again rising in anger.

'How dare you compare her with your respected mother? You know what they call them here. Landlady's daughters – a synonym for a leech, sucking away the wealth of good families and bringing them to shame. Shame on you, my son, shame on you.'

Determinedly Ajit held down his anger and managed to say between gritted teeth: 'Father, I have given my word to an honourable woman. She has married me in good faith, and I will bring her to India. I cannot marry anyone else.'

Ram Singh took a deep breath. 'You dare to say what you will do, indeed.' His voice was full of the fury he felt. 'For the sake of our family, I will not have a casteless woman in this house – an English woman, moreover.'

With a gesture that would have done justice to a prosecuting counsel, he pointed his finger at his son. 'Go to your room. Think carefully of the suggestions I have made. Although you have behaved foolishly I am ready to help you.' His voice rose to a near shriek: 'Go.'

Ajit got up and bowed to his trembling parent, who sat very straight and stared at the opposite wall, on which hung a picture of Gandhi. He did not acknowledge his son's bow, and Ajit marched out of the room, speechless with anger.

Chapter Fourteen

Ajit marched across the drawing-room and into the hall.

Khan was seated cross-legged by the hall door. He had evidently moved from the office door at the sound of altercation.

'What are you doing here?' hissed Ajit, provoked to further rage at the thought that a servant had overheard his father upbraiding him.

Khan lowered the lids of his mild, slanting eyes. 'Burra Sahib said that I must stay within call,' he said.

Ajit grunted, realising that it was not the man's fault if he had overheard.

At that moment there was a roar from the inner room. 'Pani.'

The servant jumped to his feet. 'You see,' he said.

'I understand,' said Ajit with a sigh. 'Get the water for him.'

Ajit walked swiftly along the verandas towards his room. Before he could reach it, however, he was engulfed by a horde of male cousins who had come over from his uncles' house to greet him. He had to stop and sit with them for a while, make jokes and drink tea, which Nulini and Shushila brought as his mother had gone to the cloth bazaar.

He behaved as cheerfully as he could, but Nulini looked at him curiously as she handed round the teacups. She made pan for each man to chew and then withdrew. Shortly afterwards, Ajit was able to escape too, on the promise that he would come soon to his uncles' house to make his obeisances to them.

Thakkur had put chattyas over the windows of his room, to cool it. The water dripped down them in a slow, melancholy fashion. The interlude with his cousins had calmed him, but he felt weak as if he had lost a lot of blood from a wound.

He turned on the table fan, kicked off his slippers, and, to comfort himself, sat down on the divan and wrote to me. In page after page he poured out his troubles and his love. He wrote with the blissful trust that I would surely understand him. And I did understand.

He wrote that the reputation of English women in India was unfortunate. Everybody could quote at least one scandal that had been created in times past by marriages contracted by young Indians sent to study in England. Many students had never mixed with women before going to England, nor had they ever had to think for themselves, since autocratic parents had always arranged their lives for them in detail. The sudden freedom from parental control was often too much for them; they experimented with everything that came to their notice; they smoked, they drank, they had affairs with women.

The fairness of the women was intoxicating and they often fell in love and married a white skin, regardless of the type of woman to whom it belonged, and some proud Indian families had been faced with prostitutes, or little better, as daughters-in-law.

'I am not alone in my fight to choose my own wife,' he wrote. 'There are men here, who, estranged from their families, are facing near-ruination as their parents try to prevent or break up their marriage. But do not fear, my Rani, we shall not go hungry – and I hope that my father will see sense soon.'

There was a break in the letter here as if he had left it unfinished and then come back later to complete it. It continued: 'He has, of course, brought up the question of caste, as you are in our society casteless, and he thinks it is wrong of me to marry outside our caste. I cannot tolerate this point of view. Caste is obsolete and must go. People like us should make the first moves towards its abolition; in fact, many already have. I cannot think of a single acquaintance of mine, who is under fifty, who would hold aloof from you because you had no caste, and you need not fear insult because of it. New ideas are clamouring at our gates and we must let them in.

'Our strength – yours and mine – lies in that we are financially independent of Father. I have saved and so have you and this can be our capital. Never fear, dearest one, that we shall come to real harm – only I would be infinitely happier if Father acquiesced to our marriage.'

And so on, assuring me of his eternal love. I wondered, and I feared. Was he telling me the truth? Could his father ruin us in the same way that other fathers had their sons?

I remembered the dark velvet of his skin and the matching deep timbre of his voice, and I ached for my husband.

Ajit put down his pen. Again and again, he had got up from his chair, to pace up and down the room, and then gone back to write more. How could he explain to me the formal, yet deep, relationship between parents and children in India, the invisible ties which made families and caste more important than the State or the country.

Thakkur came to say that tea was ready, but Ajit said he did not want any. Later, Thakkur brought his dinner on a brass thali and again he refused to eat. Thakkur removed the tray and went away grumbling that Maharaj had made all the dishes his young master liked and now they would be wasted.

Ajit laid his head on his desk. Thakkur made him feel like the unrepentant boy, who had on many occasions been banished to this room to do his homework. Depression flooded through him.

He moved to his divan and lay down on it, and watched listlessly as a few flies danced in the failing light. They would soon die in the summer heat, he thought. How would I endure the heat of summer? Shahpur was hotter than Delhi; he would have to take care that I observed caste rules of cleanliness, so as to lessen the chance of my falling sick. As he thought of me, desire throbbed in him, desire to see, touch and hear me. What was the use of writing? What was the use? He turned over on to his stomach and beat his pillow with one fist.

When there was a sharp swish-swish of skirts brushing along the veranda outside the room, he imagined for a second that the intensity of his longing had brought me to him. But when he looked up, it was his mother who stood uncertainly on the threshold.

He sprang up and went to her, as she surveyed him anxiously.

'Ajit, Thakkur is right – you have a fever – your eyes are too bright – I thought you were studying – otherwise I would have come to see you earlier.'

She entered, and with a graceful movement, sat down on the divan.

'Is it malaria? You have not eaten all day.'

Ajit sat down beside her, and she turned the table fan so that it did not blow directly on him.

'No, Mother,' he said, with a wry smile, 'I have no temperature.'

She took his hand and felt his pulse. 'No,' she said doubtfully, after counting carefully, 'there is no fever.'

She made herself comfortable by tucking her feet up under her and arranging her sari. It was clear to Ajit that she knew something was wrong and wanted to hear more about it. He imagined that his father must have told her at least in part of the quarrel of the morning, and his heart sank. That meant the news would go through the family like a cholera germ. To his surprise, however, she did not mention the matter. She said instead: 'Tomorrow is Holi. We are having a tea party for you and I have asked all your old friends. Your uncles are coming and Dr Chand Rana is bringing Mrs Chand Rana and Bimla. Bimla has grown into a great beauty since you last saw her – I think you will like her.'

'Ji, hun,' assented Ajit without enthusiasm. He shivered slightly. Beautiful, certainly – beautiful as a volcano – liable to eruption.

'Shushila has been buying powder for days, so that she can play colour with you,' went on his mother, all the time watching his face through her veil. He could feel her eyes taking in every slight alteration in his expression. She must have noticed him shiver at the mention of Bimla.

The tension in Ajit eased as he heard of Shushila's preparations for the Spring Festival. Of course, he would play with her. They would have tremendous battles with the small boys nearby, each one of them armed with a pail of coloured water. Honour would not be satisfied until every shirt in the neighbourhood had been drenched with rainbow colours. Her day should not be spoiled by his perplexities, he vowed to himself.

'Of course – both Bhim and I will play with her, Mother.'

Mrs Singh chatted on, her lively hands from time to time flashing out from her lap to emphasise a point. She took Ajit's silence for granted – he was being courteous in allowing his elder to speak uninterrupted, and he let her run on until finally she had exhausted her news. Then she tried to persuade him to take some food, but he declined gently.

Then she said: 'Tell me about England. How do ladies live there? How many servants do they have?'

He did his best to describe to her a servantless country, where even high-caste, rich ladies often did their own cooking, swept their own floors and made their own clothes, and even went to the bazaar by themselves.

All this Mrs Singh could visualise better than many ladies of her caste and class. She herself had been brought up in a village, the daughter of a small landlord, and had been married to Ajit's father when she was thirteen, long before his grandfather had made the money which had laid the foundations for the remarkable prosperity of his sons. She could herself cook, and had as a very young girl worn the blouse and skirt of a village woman and played in the fields, at harvest time. She had known more freedom in her native village than she knew now, in spite of her husband's lifting of her purdah.

She sat and contemplated her sandal which hung precariously from one of her straight, soft-skinned toes.

'Do they wear bracelets?' she asked, fingering the golden collection on her wrists.

Ajit thought of the gold bracelet he had bought for me, at the time of our engagement, and my pleasure at the gift.

'They do wear them,' he said. 'A gold bracelet is much valued.'

His mother must have noticed a sadness in his voice, because she said fearfully: 'My son, you are ill,' and she flung her sari back from her face and looked at him closely.

He lifted his eyes to hers, and all the pain and worry must have been shown to her.

'Ajit, what is this? What is the matter?'

His eyes flickered and then moistened.

'Mother,' his voice faltered. 'Mother – oh, Mother,' he cried and flung himself full length beside her. The misery in him welled up and regardless of ceremony he wept.

She was shaken by the outburst, but she lifted his head on to the lap made by her crossed legs, and stroked the smooth, black hair. For a time she just crooned softly to him, rocking herself as if she were nursing a baby, and wiped away the tears with the end of her sari.

'Say, Ajit, say what is the matter. It is my privilege to love and counsel you.'

'Has Father not told you?'

'Told me what?'

'About Peggie.'

'About Paickie. No. What is Paickie?'

He realised too late that his father had said nothing to his mother, but he could not withdraw and, in any case, she would have to know sooner or later.

Thakkur came to arrange the mosquito net over the divan for the night, but Mrs Singh gestured him silently to go away.

'What is Paickie?' she repeated.

Hiding his face in the folds of her sari and holding her hand in such a tight grip that it must have hurt her, he told her the whole story. He admitted his wrong conduct and asked her forgiveness.

'She is beautiful and good, and she would serve you well, Mother,' he finished up.

As she later told Bimla Chand Rana, she was shocked beyond imagination, and her first instinct was to say that he must accept his father's advice, get rid of the foreign woman and marry Bimla his caste sister.

Then she remembered suddenly, she said, a similar occurrence in Jaipur, where her sister lived. A young man, Mohan, had come home from America and had asked his parents' permission to marry an American. The parents had refused permission, and, as they held the purse strings, they had been able to insist that he must marry a woman of their choosing. Mohan had shut himself up in his room and had fasted for days. One night, he had emerged when the family was asleep, and the next morning he was found dead among the trees at the far end of the compound, dead from a cobra bite, although none knew that a cobra was in the vicinity. It was said that God Shiva had taken pity on him, killed him and taken his spirit to himself, so that he might be spared rebirth.

During his mother's silence Ajit lay with his head in her lap. He could hear the kitchen boy scrubbing the brass vessels used at dinner; he was slamming them on to the stone floor as he turned them round and round, in order to scour every corner with sand and coconut fibre.

The first words his mother said were: 'The new thalis will be dented – I must tell Gopal to be more careful.' Then she said cryptically: 'Shiva shall not have you – no, not even if you have three English wives.'

Ajit looked up somewhat astonished at the remark, and she smiled down at him and stroked his head.

She began to ask him questions, surprisingly shrewd questions, considering that she had seen little of the world and could not even read very well.

'What is the custom of marriage in England?' she asked. 'Do the parents arrange it? How is a girl brought up? How do they deport themselves?'

Ajit fumbled for his handkerchief. No pockets in a dhoti, he thought irritably. His mother picked the errant piece of linen out of his shirt pocket; he took it and blew his nose. Then he sat up, cross-legged, took his mother's hand in his again, and carefully and in detail he answered her questions, just as he had about a month before answered my father's questions.

'What is Paickie like?'

He slipped off the divan, went to his desk and picked up a battered envelope. From it he drew a photograph of me, which he had taken himself. He had draped a silk scarf over my head and had demanded that I should not smile. The resultant portrait was oddly un-English.

Mrs Singh took the photograph, examined it closely and said that I did not look like the English women that she had seen before.

Ajit affirmed promptly that I was fair like an English woman, but had the disposition of an Indian girl, quiet, modest and loving.

On finding that she was not trying to dissuade him from continuing the marriage, he went on to extol my virtues, until I would have found difficulty in recognising myself from the description. His mother heard him out patiently, her forehead creased deeply as she concentrated on what he was saying.

When he had finished she continued to sit in silence, twiddling her gold bracelets. Ajit quietly put the photograph, which she had returned to him, back into the envelope and replaced it on the desk.

Eventually his mother raised her head and said: 'It is a pity that your respected father should feel so strongly about Paickie, because he must know – ' her voice trailed off, then gained clarity again as if she had made up her mind to speak out: 'Father must know that Bhim and Nulini are not content. I had expected that he would be more careful over your marriage. Perhaps he fears his brothers' condemnation.' She sighed and added: 'No grandchild yet.'

Ajit's curiosity was awakened by her remark about his brother.

'What's the trouble with Bhim? He looked all right to me.'

'He may be all right – but Nulini is not. She is not happy. Dear Bhim has been so engrossed in being a good partner in his law practice, that he forgets his little partner at home.' Mrs Singh readjusted her sari over her head, and then continued: 'She is a good daughter-in-law – although she does wear such immodest blouses – and I cannot understand why he does not give time to her. A woman needs her husband near her quite a lot – and – and I am fearful of what may happen if he continues to neglect her.'

'What could happen?' asked Ajit impatiently. 'Bhim is a good husband – only last night I saw him give her money for embroidered sandals to match the saris I gave her.'

'Money for embroidered sandals is very well in its place, and Bhim works extremely hard – far into the night – so that she may have luxuries. Yet – I think she would go barefoot, if she could feel that she was necessary to him and not just a pretty doll to be well dressed and politely tolerated.'

Mrs Singh hitched her sari more closely round her, and pursed her lips thoughtfully.

'She is a doll,' she added. 'Not intelligent enough to know how to entice him from his work. Sometimes I long to advise them both – they could be so happy – but I am mother-in-law and must not come between them – I may do more damage.'

'Your wisdom is great, respected Mother. A chance to help them may come when Bhim feels more safely established.'

'Perhaps. I do not wish you also to be indifferent to your wife. It is time there were grandchildren in this house.'

'Peggie will bear children – and they will be fair. I could never be indifferent to her.'

'I was thinking if Bimla was your wife.'

'I will marry no one else but Peggie.'

Mrs Singh suffered the rebuke in silence, while Ajit paced up and down the room. The house was still, except for the occasional cry of the watchman, as he circled round the compound, and the squeak of the gate as he went through to the uncles' compound. Fainter and fainter grew his cry, as he moved up to the far end of the family's property, thumping his staff as he went, to warn all thieves to beware of his coming.

Mrs Singh began to speak – not of Peggie, but of the generations of women of her caste who had gone before her and how they had kept the honour of the family and of the caste, obeying the scriptures and daily making puja, keeping the feasts and fasts, and sharing life's burdens equally with their husbands, as was laid down in the marriage ceremony.

Ajit's heart sank. There was to be no understanding by his mother either, it seemed.

The old lady sighed. These customs were going. Was she not out of purdah herself? Indeed, yes. Did Nulini keep the fasts? She did not. She could not say that she approved of the modern girl – but then her mother-in-law had not approved of her either. Caste barriers also were going. Did not Ram Singh himself sit down to eat with men of other castes? Why should he fear a casteless daughter-in-law? She would automatically become of their caste by her marriage. What mattered was a kind heart, a forbearing temperament, a suitable humility before the dictates of elders. She sighed again and looked at Ajit when she spoke of the latter requirement.

Ajit laughed quietly in his throat. He wanted to shout aloud. His mother was convincing herself that she could cope with Peggie.

'Did you say something, my son?'

'No, no, Mother.'

She passed her hand wearily over her face, and then said: 'Come here and sit with me. We must decide what to do about Paickie.'

Ajit came and sat beside her, while she opened her pan box, took out a cardamum, peeled it carefully and popped it into her mouth. Then she leaned forward and, speaking in a whisper lest anybody left awake should hear, she counselled Ajit as to how he should deal with his father.

At the end he rose and, bending humbly, he kissed the tiny foot with its swinging sandal. She laughed, withdrew her foot quickly and descended gracefully from the divan. She shook up the pillows, straightened the sheets, and told Ajit to put up the mosquito net and to sleep in peace.

Overwhelmed with gratitude for her advice and understanding, Ajit was dumb, but he went to the doorway with her and held back the curtain for her to pass through. She smiled at him and walked slowly along the veranda towards the kitchen. He felt calmer and leaned against the door jamb. The night breeze caressed him.

A light sprang up in the kitchen and through the big window he saw his mother move towards the small shelf on which the elephant-headed Ganesh sat staring accusingly at her. She struck a match, lit a bunch of incense-tipped sticks and put them into a wire stand before him. Then she stood before the god with hands held out in appeal to heaven.

Ajit had a nasty feeling that she was praying for forgiveness for being an undutiful wife. Her advice to him could hardly be said to coincide with that which his father had given.

Chapter Fifteen

'I have a headache – I could not sleep last night,' said Ram Singh the next morning to Mrs Singh and Khan, when they arrived with his breakfast.

Ram Singh always had a headache when faced with domestic issues, and the whole house always knew about it. Maharaj always received orders to make special tea, Ayah had to get out the rubbing oil, and the unfortunate clerk, who had followed his master into retirement, was sent hither and thither to bring his work to Ram Singh's bedside.

'What has upset him this time?' asked Thakkur of the clerk.

'I don't know,' said the harassed clerk. 'He gets worse as he grows older.'

Khan might have been able to tell him – but Khan was a very discreet man. He stood by Mrs Singh at Ram Singh's bedside, and silently held out his hand to Mrs Singh for the key to the box in which she kept the aspirins. She took the key off the bunch at her waist, and gave it to him, and he went to fetch the bottle from her room.

'My life is eternally filled with new problems,' Ram Singh sighed, as Mrs Singh massaged the back of his neck to ease the ache.

Mrs Singh made suitable comforting noises, although, as she told Ajit, she was a little amused, since she knew the cause of the headache.

'I could not sleep,' he said again.

Mrs Singh neglected to tell him that she had not even been to bed.

'Here are the aspirins. Khan, a glass of water. Now, just take two and lie back on your pillow for half an hour, and then I'll rub you.'

He lay back comforted. His wife had been comforting him ever since he was fifteen and she thirteen, and there is no doubt that he held her in great affection.

Khan went back to his post outside the door.

About an hour later, Ajit came to his father's room, having heard from Ayah that the headache had eased.

Khan was seated on the floor by the door, surrounded with pink knitting wool which he was winding into balls. As Ajit wished to establish friendly relations with the new servant, he inquired of Khan what he was going to make – he knew that many hill men were skilled weavers and knitters, though normally their wives did this work, while the men themselves went on trading journeys between Tibet and India.

'I am winding the wool,' Khan said softly, 'for Miss Nulini. Last time she bought wool, it shrank after washing, so she asked me to buy for her this time – because my fingers know good quality wools.'

Ajit looked at the small, strong hands as they deftly wound a skein into a ball. The man did not look up from his work – he had not risen at Ajit's appearance, because he had the skein stretched over his two feet to keep it from tangling. Ajit, therefore, gave a little cough to indicate to his father that he was there.

Ram Singh was washing his mouth out, after having managed to eat his breakfast; so Ajit stood just inside the door until the elder man gave a final gurgle and spat into the wash bowl. Then he raised his hands in salute and said: 'Namaste.'

Ram Singh dabbed his lips with the towel.

'Namaste. You may come in. Khan, take away this thali.'

Encouraged by the courteous 'good morning', Ajit moved further into the room, while Khan took away the breakfast tray.

Ram Singh climbed on to his divan, crossed his legs neatly, straightened his round, black cap, and took up a paper from his desk.

When Ajit had heard about the headache, he had recognised the sign immediately. It invariably meant that his father was upset and torn by indecision over something, usually in connection with the family; so Ajit hoped that his father was feeling less sure that he was right about his son's marriage, less certain that an Indian daughter-in-law was essential to the family. It might also have occurred to his father, who was a very honourable man, that even English marriage vows were meant to be kept, and that it was not right to expect him to break them.

To go straight to the reason for Ajit's visit would have hardly been proper, so Ram Singh asked him if he had seen any of his friends yet. Ajit mentioned the visit of his cousins, and that there was to be a tea party that afternoon. He had already played colour with Shushila and the neighbours' children, as his blue-stained hands testified.

At the mention of a party, Ram Singh unbent a little. Ajit knew that, despite his efforts at prayer and contemplation, Ram Singh still enjoyed a party, especially a tea party, with lots of hot, spiced samosas and sweet hulwa to nibble.

'The courtyard must be swept,' Ram Singh said promptly. 'Tell Pratap to make sure there are no snakes or scorpions there – it will be full of children this afternoon.' He thought for a moment, and then said: 'No. I will instruct Khan.'

Khan was still winding wool outside the door, and came immediately his master called. He was given the message for Pratap and instructions to help Mrs Singh and Thakkur to put out extra divans for the many matrons who would invade the drawing-room.

'They will enjoy talking scandal – scandal – ' he trailed off. Ajit felt sorry if he was thinking what a scandal his son's marriage could prove to be. At best at such a party there would be lots of jokes about the return of a marriageable son – and Bimla's presence would make all the guests surmise. The samosas would taste flat and greasy to his father during this party.

Ram Singh absent-mindedly picked up a glass pot of wheat seeds which had been lying on his desk, and turned it slowly round in his hands, gazing unseeingly at the contents as they slithered round the pot.

Wishing to divert him, Ajit asked if he was considering planting wheat on some of their land.

'Yes, I am,' said the elder man. 'If this strain does well, I will import some more and distribute it to the cultivators round about. They might get a heavier yield.'

Ajit was interested, and an amicable conversation ensued.

When at last the discussion languished, Ram Singh asked guardedly if his son had considered their conversation of the day before. He asked in the soft, melodious voice that had deceived many a lawyer in the courtroom into thinking that his client had the sympathy of the magistrate.

'Yes, Father,' Ajit replied. 'I have given deep thought to it, and I appreciate the kindness of your offer to help me out of the alliance which I have made.' He paused.

Ram Singh relaxed. So the boy would agree to his suggestions.

'Then?' inquired Ram Singh.

Ajit plunged in: 'Father – I should like to make some other suggestions, if you have no objection.'

The father looked exasperated, but nodded to his son to go on.

'In a week's time I must go to Pandipura to start work – and there also I have a flat. There also live but few of our caste brothers to speak to our family of what I do. I suggest that I send for Peggie and take her there.'

He stopped to take a quick look at his father's face. The expression was wooden and the moustaches stuck out belligerently as if the mouth beneath was compressed with disapproval. Ajit felt his cause was hopeless, but fortified by his mother's advice he continued doggedly.

'Let us stay there for a couple of years. In that time Peggie can easily learn enough of our customs never to offend your good taste and to enable her to fit into this house quite well. Unfortunately, it is not likely that at any time during my working life I shall be able to stay long at home here. When the power house is finished and I have worked there for a few years, there will be better posts in other parts of India.'

Ram Singh was contemplating with great attention the activities of a fly walking on his desk.

'I cannot believe that your objection to my marriage is based entirely on Peggie's lack of caste. You have on many occasions denounced its evils. Rather you must fear the scandal if Peggie should misbehave or should leave me.'

The fly was cleaning its wings.

'If she came straight to Pandipura, you would not have to associate yourself with the marriage.

'If it was not a success and Peggie left me,' Ajit swallowed hard, 'would you – in your goodness of heart – forgive me for my rashness? I would humbly admit myself in the wrong; and our family would feel that you had judged rightly, that I had been headstrong and you had wisely let me learn my lesson in this hard way, rather than cast me off.'

At the words 'cast me off' Ram Singh looked indignant – as if any good Indian father would dream of casting off any of his family, no matter what they had done.

'Nothing was further from my mind than casting you off,' he said defensively.

'If our marriage was a happy one – and I believe it will be – then – ' Ajit hesitated, 'perhaps you and Mother would receive Peggie into the family, forgiving us for our hasty marriage and taking pleasure in your grandchildren.'

He added: 'Thus all would be well. Our respected uncles could not condemn you as lacking in wisdom. They cannot, at the worst, say more than that I have been a very foolish young man and have a very benevolent and long-suffering father. The ladies of our household will not be troubled by someone who does not know their ways; and any scandal would not reflect much on our family as a whole, as it will take place six hundred miles away, in a distant province, and people would hear only vague rumours.'

Ajit stopped, having nothing more to say. He wondered agonisedly if his mother was right in her belief that a compromise could be reached.

Ram Singh brushed the fly off his desk and leaned his elbows on the hard surface. The room was very still. Ajit would have given his meagre bank balance to know exactly what his father's thoughts were, as he stood before him, and he was quite unprepared for the question which his parent suddenly asked.

'Is a child expected?' he asked, his eyes narrowing shrewdly.

Ajit smarted under the insinuation.

'It is unlikely,' he said sharply. 'There has hardly been time.'

'It would be as well,' said Ram Singh reflectively, chewing the end of his moustache, 'if no child arrived for eleven months from the date of the marriage.'

Ajit sighed with relief. His father might be willing to agree. Of course, if there was no child during this period, one subject of gossip would be eliminated. No one could say that Peggie had trapped him into marriage or that he had fathered the child of another man.

'There is also the question of the gold and silver which my daughters-in-law will expect at my death,' said Ram Singh from between bits of moustache. 'Your wife shall have her share, but in practice her sister-in-law may make it difficult for her to claim it.'

Ajit interjected: 'Father, do not think of death – you will be with us many years yet.'

'My son, it is my duty to consider the well-being of all of you at all times. I will specifically mention in my will what she is to have.'

'Father, you are indeed kind. You will not regret my marriage to Peggie.'

'We shall see, we shall see,' said Ram Singh testily. 'In the meantime I have to tell Rana Sahib that I withdraw my offer for Bimla – and a good dowry will be lost, too.

'Shall I never know peace in my life?' he added savagely. 'My sons never consider my feelings – never realise what their foolish actions mean to me.'

Ajit hung his head, and muttered: 'Perhaps one of uncles' sons would do in my place.'

'Possibly – and there is another problem. No mention must be made to your uncles of this woman you have married.'

'No, Father.'

While they had been talking, Ajit had been standing up, since his father had forgotten to tell him that he might sit. His father now said: 'Sit down, sit down, boy. Why do you stand gawking at me? Here I am, trying to mitigate the result of your hotheadedness, and what do you do – you stand and say "No, Father".'

Ajit sat down hastily on the edge of his father's divan.

'Khan,' shouted Ram Singh.

The rapidity of Khan's entrance indicated that he had been very close to the door, and Ajit hoped the servant was as discreet as his looks implied.

'Bring tea,' demanded Ram Singh, 'with nutmeg and cinnamon in it.'

The old man is making peace, thought Ajit; he must be regretting his hasty words of yesterday.

It did indeed seem as if Ram Singh was anxious that Ajit should be right in his remarks about his marriage and that, having tentatively agreed to my coming to India, he wished that Ajit should not suffer more than was necessary from his 'mistake'. He spent some time in counselling his son on the proper management of his affairs, both financial and matrimonial, and he lavished as much thought in lecturing him on the care of his wife as most English fathers would have done in advising their sons on the care of a pedigree dog.

While they drank tea, Ram Singh dealt with the details of the duties of a householder, ranging from the keeping of household account books to the saying of prayers twice daily; and as he went on his temper improved. It was apparent to Ajit that he feared a scandal most of all, and once the chances of that had become slender he was willing to co-operate with his son, to a degree.

When at last Ajit was dismissed, Ram Singh's anger had evaporated and only a distinct coolness showed that his son was not yet restored to parental favour.

Mrs Singh was summoned to her husband's room and informed of the marriage. She looked suitably surprised, murmured that Ajit was a sensible boy and that his father should be complimented upon his wisdom in not being too hard on him, at which Ram Singh cleared his throat and looked embarrassed.

'May I give daughter-in-law a wedding present? And may I tell sisters-in-laws about the marriage?'

'No,' roared Ram Singh, so that Mrs Singh jumped.

'No present?'

Ram Singh shook his head irritably, and dismissed the present with a wave of his hand: 'You can give a present if you wish – but on no account is anybody to be told about this misalliance. Nobody must know of it – it will cause trouble enough without people speculating about it now. I shall speak to Bhim about it, after which the matter will not be mentioned either in my presence or in my absence.'

'Ji, hun,' said Mrs Singh.

'I have only agreed to it, because I do not want my son to go away to England again and perhaps never come back.'

'Ji, hun,' said Mrs Singh, rising to her feet.

'I don't know what the younger generation is coming to – defying their parents as they do.'

'Ji,' said Mrs Singh as she moved towards the door. 'Would you like some more aspirins?'

'No,' snapped Ram Singh, and added as an afterthought: 'One sari will be sufficient present.'

'Ji, hun,' said Mrs Singh.

Chapter Sixteen

In spite of the silence imposed by Ram Singh upon his family with regard to Ajit's marriage, there was an undercurrent of sly whispers amongst the ladies present at the tea party. When Mrs Singh approached a group, the conversation ceased or the subject was changed.

Ajit also felt that his private affairs were the subject of gossip, so he sought the company of Shushila and the other children playing in the courtyard, and left the entertaining of the younger men to Bhim.

It is likely, he thought, that Bimla has heard of father's negotiations with Kasher Chand Rana and has confided her hopes to her girl friends, and it has caused some speculative gossip. In any case, it was well known that the two mothers had been friends in their youth and had declared that their children should marry each other. He had felt all eyes upon him when he made his bow to Bimla, who was gorgeously dressed for the occasion. Her jade-green shirt and trousers were silk and the matching veil was embroidered in gold. She turned languorous, brown eyes upon him and her voice was unusually soft, but Ajit felt cold at the idea of marrying her, and he excused himself and left her to his cousins, who were happy to take his place and flutter round her with tea and sweetmeats. Moths round the candle, thought Ajit.

The tea party was soon forgotten by Ajit as a minor unpleasant experience, in the rush of visits he had to make to old friends. He spent a considerable time playing with Shushila and in talking to his mother; his father avoided him as much as possible.

On the morning after the tea party, he accompanied his mother to the bazaar. She could easily have asked merchants to bring goods to the house for her to see, but Mrs Singh preferred to go to the bazaar herself. She was still near enough to her days in purdah to feel an exhilarating freedom in walking in public, and a certain wickedness in having her face unveiled and her head uncovered.

She and Ajit wandered in and out of sari shops together. Mrs Singh made several purchases of pieces of cloth for blouses. She bought no saris, however, and Ajit remarked on this as she usually bought sari and blouse piece together.

She said with a smile that she had plenty of saris.

When they returned home they washed the dust off their feet and Mrs Singh asked Ajit to carry her purchases to her room. He did so, and laid them carefully on a side table.

Mrs Singh took her keys from her waist, unlocked the storeroom which led off her bedroom, and vanished inside. Ajit sat down and switched on the fan. He was daydreaming when his mother came back loaded with multicoloured silks.

Taking a pale-blue blouse piece from amongst those she had just bought, she lifted from the pile of silk a length of almost exactly matching colour, ornamented at one end with silver embroidery.

'One,' she muttered, her forehead lined, as she peered at the colours to make sure they matched.

She did the same with a length of red silk, heavily patterned with geometrical designs in yellow and green, and then she added a third of yellow with a border of brown flowers and touches of gold embroidery.

'Help me to fold them up,' she commanded.

Ajit did so, and she lifted the neat pile and put it into his arms.

'For my daughter-in-law,' she said.

A lump rose in Ajit's throat as he received the first wedding present from his family. Eleven saris might have been expected as the usual gift;

but, as his wife was not being recognised by his family, his mother was obviously giving from her own wardrobe three of the best saris she had.

She turned to lock up the storeroom, placidly chatting at the same time about the fashion in which Peggie should wear the garments; and Ajit was filled with gratitude towards his simple, but astute, mother, who had not once upbraided him but had heaped kindness upon kindness.

He put down the saris and, with a sharp movement, went to her, and bowed to touch her feet. She lifted him and smiled and patted him.

'My son,' was all she said, but it expressed all her devotion and all her desire for the real happiness of her child. However much she feared for him in his strange adventure, she was doing her best not to make it harder for him than it already was.

'Mother,' he said, 'Peggie will honour you, and I think she will always remember that her Indian mother was sympathetic towards her when she was new to this country.'

The bedroom door creaked, and they both jumped.

'Respected Mother,' said a silken voice, and Nulini slid into the room, 'if you are agreeable, I will call on Bimla this afternoon.'

Mrs Singh hooked her key holder back on to the waistband of her petticoat, and said: 'Yes, go. Take Ayah with you – Shushi can go too, if she has done her lessons.'

Nulini was dismissed, but she lingered, leaning against the door, her sari swaying in the draught. Ajit, who had stood silently behind his mother, noted her daringly short blouse, which hardly covered the generous curve of her breast and left her waist naked. He wondered that his mother did not demand that she should wear longer blouses – perhaps she hoped that Nulini's modern dress would attract Bhim to her. In any case, there was no one else in the house who could be enchanted by a slim, bare waistline. She rarely met any men from outside the family and was invariably chaperoned wherever she went – it was doubtful if she had at any time been alone with a man other than her husband. His thoughts rambled on: 'I suppose Mother is wise in not criticising her and spoiling the affection which seems to have grown up between them – Nulini probably realises that she is lucky to have as much freedom as she has and that she owes it to Mother's understanding of her.'

'What a fine blue silk you have there, Mother. I have not seen it before – it would look well on you,' remarked Nulini, eyeing the sari covetously.

Mrs Singh looked guilty and said: 'Yes, I have not worn it for years. Now go on your visit,' and she turned away to open the window.

Behind his mother's back, Nulini made a little moue with her mouth at Ajit, and then went out as quietly as she had come, leaving Ajit thoroughly shocked. Sisters-in-law, he wrote to me indignantly, should hardly look at their brothers-in-law, and in many houses they still covered their faces at the approach of their husband's brothers.

Mrs Singh sighed. 'Perhaps Paickie will also be a good friend to Nulini – and to Bimla. Bimla has a great capacity for friendship.' She sat down on a mattress and tucked her legs under her slowly, as if they ached.

Ajit knew perfectly well what his mother was thinking about, and said: 'I am sorry about Bimla, Mother.'

'Arree, don't worry about her – she is not in love with you.'

Ajit laughed, and picked up the saris.

'Shall I bring you some cool water to drink?' he asked.

She nodded assent.

He brought the water for her, and found her gazing abstractedly into her mirror. She put down the mirror and took the glass from him.

'Your children will be very fair, Ajit?' she asked.

'They will be as fair as the women of Peshawar.'

'Indeed? Ramji, that is very fair – and lovely.'

Ajit smiled and left her. He went to his room, and sat down to write to me.

Nulini, escorted by a grumbling Ayah and a jubilant Shushila, went to call upon her friend and confidante, Bimla Chand Rana.

Bimla found Shushila some coloured shells with which to play, and sent Mrs Singh's Ayah to join her own Ayah in the shade of a nearby mango tree, then she sat down with her friend on the swing which hung from the veranda roof.

'And how are things with you?' asked Bimla, tossing back her long plaits. Nulini seemed to be more on edge than usual.

'I am so bored,' said Nulini, pulling irritably at the cushion under her.

'Why? You have a good young husband.'

'Hmm,' sniffed Nulini, 'I have told you many times that I might just as well be single. I wish I was back in my father's house.'

'You should say to Bhim that he must take you out – he is modern – why, you could even dance together, as long as Singh Sahib never found out.'

'How can I tell these matters to a husband I hardly ever see alone? He never comes to my room – anyway, Shushila shares it with me – and he has asked that I should not go to his room unless he sends for me, as it interrupts his studies. Studies! Books!' She almost spat out the last word.

'He will be a great man one day.'

'A great man? And what am I to do in the meantime, pray? So rarely he sends for me and when he does he has an abstracted air, as if he is thinking of something else. He gives me money and tells me to buy myself something pretty. I do not care about money – it will not buy me a son.'

She looked down at her flat stomach and tears came into her eyes. Her voice was bitter as she said: 'Singh Sahib should not have insisted upon his marrying yet – he does not want to be bothered with a wife or children. I could have been enjoying myself, dancing at the club at home or playing bridge – instead, I waste away sitting on the veranda and knitting.'

Bimla put her arm round Nulini. 'If I were you, I would make him take an interest in me,' she said stoutly.

'You are different – you are not afraid of anybody.'

'Just wait until I come to the house – I will change all this – Ajit will eat out of my hand. Together, we will make the brothers less stuffy.'

'Arree, Bimla, troubled with my own woes, I forgot,' and Nulini caught her friend's hand. 'Such an uproar there is over Ajit.'

'Why, what has happened?'

'He has married an English woman.'

Bimla was off the swing in a flash, her face contorted with dismay.

'You lie!'

'I do not. It is true.'

Rage enveloped Bimla. She grasped Nulini's wrist.

'How do you know?' she hissed.

'Let go, Bimla, you are hurting me.'

'How do you know?'

'I was told.'

'By whom?'

Nulini twisted away from Bimla, and shrank into a corner of the swing.

'I will not tell you.'

'Have you been trying to win Ajit – and he has told you this to get rid of you?'

'No, no, Bimla,' said Nulini indignantly, as she rubbed her wrist.

'Did Mrs Singh tell you?'

'No.'

'Then how do you know and how do you know it to be true?'

Nulini blenched. 'Someone whose word I can trust told me.'

Bimla's rage left her as quickly as it had come and curiosity mixed with vague suspicions took its place. A small flickering fear for her friend warned her not to press her further. She asked no further questions and accepted Nulini's word that she had spoken the truth.

'Put an English woman in my place,' she muttered. 'How can I face my friends in such a situation – the humiliation of it. Father must demand that Ajit put her away – why, everybody knows he is going to marry me – the humiliation!' And she burst into tears.

Chapter Seventeen

When I received from Ajit the letter in which he told me of the agreement reached with his father, I felt as humiliated as Bimla Chand Rana must have done when she found she had been superseded by me. I was most indignant at having to serve an apprenticeship before Ajit's parents would acknowledge my existence, and it was two or three days before calmer feelings prevailed and I thought comfortably that I should be living six hundred miles from them, so recognition did not amount to much. I could not know then what a comfort it was to be part of a tightly woven family in a country where any other protection from disaster was negligible.

On my next free day, the spring weather tempted me to pay a surprise visit to Angela, and I caught the mid-morning train down to Pentecost.

When I arrived at the farm, I was met at the door by the farmer's wife. Miss Delaney, she said with a faint air of disapproval, had gone for a walk with a Chinese gentleman, who was staying at the George and Crown. I assured her that Dr Wu was an old friend of ours, and her disapproval melted into curiosity. 'He's the first Chinese I ever saw,' she said. 'Is he living here for always? Would you like some lunch?'

I accepted the offer of lunch with alacrity and sat in the kitchen while she prepared the meal. As she beat eggs and peeled potatoes, I entertained her by telling her about the people who came from all over the world to study at Wetherport.

There was a peal of laughter from the direction of the front door, which was open.

'That'll be your sister.'

I nodded and walked down the hall to the front door.

Angela was sitting on a garden seat, and Dr Wu was doing an excellent imitation of Dr Gantry in a bad temper. I laughed and ran to Angela.

'Pegs,' cried Angela, flinging her arms around me in unusual exuberance, 'see who is also staying here.'

'Yes, dear,' I said. 'Dr Wu, I am really glad you decided to take a holiday.'

Dr Wu bowed. 'My holiday has been embellished by Miss Delaney's company. We met in the lane only yesterday.'

Wu smiled and walked on into the house, to give us time for a word together.

'Has Wu told you what has happened to him?'

'No.'

I told her what I had learned at the club and from him personally.

Angela stood stock still.

'I would never have guessed at such a tragedy,' she said. 'He has been so cheerful – what misery must be inside him? Poor man! All his dreams and beliefs lost . . .' She scuffed on the path with her shoe. 'Thanks for telling me.'

The farmer's wife came to the door: 'Lunch, Miss,' she called.

I slipped my arm into Angela's and we went together into the house.

At half past eight that night I put the key into the lock of our front door and turned it wearily. Entering, I flung my hat on to the hallstand as I had done ever since my school days. Mother called: 'Hullo, is that you, dear?' as she always did, and I was grateful for the routine sanity of it.

'Hullo, Mum,' I called. I was very tired and I wanted Ajit. The world had been a topsy-turvy place during the past month. There had been the hurried preparations for my marriage, then the exquisite peace of my honeymoon, to be followed by the rushing back and forth for passports, permits, passages and all the impedimenta of travel, the uncertainty about Ajit, the finishing up of my work at the club. It all added up to an enormous expenditure of nervous energy.

I went into the kitchen, sat down thankfully on a primrose-yellow chair, and rested in the gentle stream of Mother's inconsequential chatter.

Three weeks later I abandoned the safe refuge of our old, Victorian house, and the parents who had, if anything, sheltered me too much from the rigours of life, and embarked for India.

It was then I discovered that the pain of departure is a real pain, a physical racking as if part of one is being torn away. As the three beloved figures waving from the dockside grew smaller and smaller and the tugs moved the great ship out into midstream, even the thought of Ajit's waiting for me could not ease the cruel wrench, and I clung to the ship's rail feeling that I would collapse if I let go.

During the upheavals of the war, I had been blessed by being allowed to stay at home, and the fact that my present banishment was self-imposed did not make the leaving less painful. Until the night came down and there was nothing to be seen except the foam falling away from the ship's bows, I stood in anguish by the rail; and then a kindly stewardess came to inquire if I was Mrs Singh, and when I said I was, she said she had put in my cabin a bouquet of flowers sent by a Dr Wu.

I went downstairs. A bouquet of daffodils lay on the dressing-table in my cabin and attached to it was a note. I opened it and read:

'Deep is the water in the Peach-blossom spring,
Deeper still is our hearts' feeling
When good friends are leaving.'
Best wishes for your happiness.

It was signed simply 'Wu', the name by which he had always been known to me.

Chapter Eighteen

Shahpur station is big, but when our train drew into the platform at the end of a hot May day it was crammed to capacity with a shouting, milling crowd and with immense piles of luggage, amongst which strode the railway police with their rifles slung over their shoulders.

A thin, red-shirted, red-turbaned porter piled on to his head our tin trunk, two pigskin trunks and a bedding roll, took a suitcase in each hand, and then motioned us to lead the way to the ticket barrier. Ajit, tickets in hand, pushed a way for me through the crowd, and I followed, clutching my unaccustomed sari closely round me.

Ajit had been waiting for me on the wharf when my ship docked at Bombay. I had dressed myself in the sari he had given to me at our engagement and when I took a last peep at myself in the cabin mirror, I had been surprised. The restful voyage, together with better food than I had tasted since before the war, had helped my figure and cleared my complexion, and the scarlet sari became me. Ajit had bounded up the gangway as soon as he was permitted to do so, caught my hands and looked into my face, while porters and passengers fought around us. Words did not come easily to either of us, but we both knew a wave of feeling. I knew I had come home.

'You – you look wonderful,' gasped Ajit at last.

'It's wonderful to be with you,' I said, slipping my arm into his and clinging close to him, as we became engulfed in deckhands and customs officers.

We managed to get the luggage through the customs quickly enough to enable us to catch the day train up to Shahpur; and I sat through the day in a semi-daze compounded of intense heat, great happiness and a terrifying flow of new experiences. So I walked out of Shahpur station following Ajit closely, while my new fellow countrymen looked at me with great curiosity.

Immediately outside the station we were buttonholed by a rogue in a red fez. He was carrying a long whip and he thrust his bearded face into Ajit's and shouted: 'Tonga, Sahib? Where to?'

'Pandipura. How much?'

A dismal expression was promptly assumed by the tongawallah. 'Arree, Sahib,' he whined. 'Pandipura is a long way, fully seven miles over poor roads. It will cost four rupees.'

'Three rupees,' countered Ajit, although he was swaying with weariness, having spent the previous night travelling to Bombay; his khaki shirt was black with sweat. I kept very close to him and clutched my handbag firmly.

Other tongawallahs were closing in upon us, attracted possibly by foreign suitcases on the head of the porter, who stood patiently near us, his eyes averted from me.

I pulled my sari well over my head and face, to avoid the stares of the passers by, and concentrated on the conversation. My weeks of study had not been in vain. Provided the sentences were short, I understood the gist of the tongawallah's speech. Ajit was answering him in Hindi, which the man apparently understood.

The tongawallah saw his rivals bearing down upon us and struck a hasty bargain at three rupees and four annas. The porter heaved some of the luggage into the high-wheeled horse carriage, and reverently laid my pigskin cases on one side of the driver's seat. Then he straightened his back, spat into the dusty, cowdung-strewn courtyard, rubbed his hands on his loincloth and held one out for his tip. Ajit paid him and he salaamed low.

The tongawallah saw the salaam and immediately became more obsequious. He must have realised that Ajit's tip was generous and thought that we were people of importance. He let down the steps at the back of the carriage, wiped the seats with the sweat rag from round his neck, and held the door open.

I put my hand into Ajit's and was helped inside. Out of the corner of my eye I saw the tongawallah gape as he saw my white hand, and his eyes shifted to my sandalled feet. It had dawned on him that one of his passengers was a Memsahib, and to him that meant that Ajit must be at least the son of a Raja – only a man as rich as a feudal lord could afford to keep a white wife.

Ajit climbed in and the tongawallah absent-mindedly folded up the steps, shut the door, walked round to the front of the carriage and laboriously climbed on to the driver's seat. He gave his horse a flick with a whip, and we were off.

The name of the owner-driver of the tonga, with his registration number, was painted on the back of the carriage, and as Ajit helped me to settle myself on the narrow seat, I asked him: 'Is Mohamed Ali a Muslim name?'

'Yes,' he said, looking surprised at the question.

'I thought all Muslims had gone to Pakistan.'

'No, no, there are more Muslims still left in India than are in Pakistan.'

'And are they safe? Do you still have riots?'

'Hindu-Muslim riots are becoming rare now. The police do their best to stop any disturbance before it becomes a riot.' He mopped his brow with an already sodden handkerchief. 'Ten thousand Muslims live in the middle of Shahpur, surrounded by Hindus, and I think Mohamed Ali would tell you that he does not take any more precautions for the safety of his family than a good father in India has always done.'

I was impressed. I knew of the religious and economic contentions between Hindus and Muslims – and I knew also that in West Pakistan very few Hindus were left.

The carriage was clattering over the cobblestones of the station yard, the driver shouting to people to get out of the way; beggars, fruit vendors and children scattered in all directions. The driver leaned down and said something rude to a turbaned taxi driver, who was trying to manoeuvre his vehicle through the yard gates. The taxi driver retorted angrily.

Ajit saw the incident, and said: 'Most of the taxi drivers here are Sikh refugees from West Pakistan, and they naturally hate the tongawallahs who are their competitors as well as being Muslims.' He grinned, as with a fine flow of language the taxi driver got through the gate and passed under the nose of Mohamed Ali's horse. 'Most of their fights are verbal,' he added.

As the tonga plunged into a narrow side street, I glimpsed a forest of mill chimneys sticking into the sky. Then we were ploughing through the cloth bazaar.

I leaned my head against the awning support and gazed in bewilderment at the packed street. A human flood eddied and flowed against the carriage wheels. The pavements were packed with people and crowds walked in the middle of the street. Each shop entrance was the centre of a small whirlpool of purchasers; and even the verandas overhanging the streets bore a burden of lounging women and children.

Our tongawallah frequently exploded into speech, as children ran nearly under the horse's hooves or a cyclist cut across the animal's nose, causing it to snort with fright. Once we had to stop while a string of camels, walking with the aloof air of mannequins at a fashion show, swayed across the road and vanished down a side street.

I laughed at their enormous dignity and said: 'It's a little different from Regent Street.'

Ajit rubbed the sweat from his forehead. 'It is,' he said. 'I hope you will be able to manage here, darling. I wish we could have settled in the north instead of in this stinking hole – but Pandipura is a little cleaner and quieter than Shahpur itself. The noise here is dreadful.'

The noise was indeed worse than the heat or the overcrowding; car horns vied with the shouting of vendors; the harassed clang-clang of temple bells competed with blaring radios; and bicycle bells and camel bells seemed to ring in my head.

'I'll get used to it,' I said, with more determination than conviction.

'I won't,' said Ajit gloomily. 'The whole town ought to have been razed to the ground two hundred years ago and then rebuilt. It's so squalid.'

'We've plenty of squalor in England,' I said, 'and at least people here look aboundingly alive and their diversity is amazing. Just look at that old man over there,' and I pointed to a countryman, dressed in the traditional white jacket and loincloth and red turban. He had one arm round the shoulders of a boy about twelve, who was supporting him as he walked. The old man also carried a staff to aid him in his slow progress through the crowd. The expression on his face, as he looked down at the boy and addressed him, was one of great tenderness; every wrinkle was softened and even the bushy, white eyebrows had a gentle curve. The boy's face had a clear, innocent look long since missing from Western faces.

Seeing that I was not horrified by the dirt and the turmoil, but only sympathetically interested in the people swarming about the tonga, Ajit lost some of his gloom and after a quick glance to see that the tongawallah was minding his own business, he took my hand and squeezed it, and as we jogged along he pointed out whatever he thought might interest me.

We passed a marble building smothered in intricate carvings. Its metal door gleamed dully in the fading light, and, though crammed between narrow, dirty shops, its beauty was obvious.

'What is that building?'

'It's a Jain temple built hundreds of years ago – the door is solid silver.'

'If the property round it was cleared away, it would look exquisite,' I said.

Ajit laughed. 'You will find that throughout this town beauty is buried beneath rubbish and dirt. Cotton and chemicals and the money they make are all that matters here.'

'That is not true. Somebody keeps the temple – its steps had been swept.'

'You are too observant,' Ajit said. Then he changed the subject and told me about our flat. He said it was a good flat by Indian standards, one of a block of eight built by the Government to house some of the staff of a new University. Except for the University itself, there was no other building for nearly a mile in any direction.

'I do not know why they built these accommodations in such an isolated place – unless they want to encourage building in that area.'

We passed out of the town and bumped along a dirt road. The tonga moved more and more slowly and, finally, after a particularly hard bump, it came to a stop.

'Sahib,' came a plaintive voice from the direction of the driver's seat, 'this is the Pandipura road. How far along is your bungalow?'

'At least three more miles. Drive on.'

'I must light my lamps, Sahib,' said Mohamed Ali, and sighing copiously he got down and lit the oil lamps on either side of the carriage. 'By the Beard of the Prophet, this is a very bad road.'

The tonga started off again and creaked its way through the near darkness. There was a breeze and its coolness was welcome. Far off, I could hear drums being beaten in an exciting rhythm.

At the end of twenty minutes the tonga stopped again.

'Sahib,' said the mournful voice, 'the horse can go no further. The road is too bad.'

Ajit leaned out. 'This road is no worse than any other road outside the city,' he said sharply. 'Get a move on.' And he sat back in his seat; but the tonga did not move.

'Arree, Sahib, this is the worst of roads and the horse is getting lame; if the horse is lamed how can I work? – my children will starve.'

'Don't be foolish,' snapped Ajit. 'The horse has travelled over worse roads than this.'

Resignedly, Mohamed Ali gave the horse a light flick with the whip. The horse stirred uneasily but did not move forward. It was now quite dark and the jackals were beginning to howl among the bushes, which reared man-high at the side of the narrow path.

'See,' said the driver, triumph in his voice. 'The poor animal is exhausted. I must go down and walk with him.' And he got down and went to the horse's head, but still the carriage did not move.

'And Sahib,' the voice floated ghostlike out of the darkness, 'the harness is strained. Supposing it snaps with the jolting – how can a poor man like me expect to buy new? Truly this is an unlucky day for me.' The voice trailed off.

The drums sounded menacing and there was a horrid smell about the carriage; later I was to know that smell well. It was the stink of a jackal. One must have been quite near us. Why, in heaven's name, could we not move?

I had followed the main theme of the conversation, and said to Ajit: 'Why not offer to pay a little towards the cost of the harness if it breaks?' I drew my sari closer round me, as a protection against the insects which bumped into me as they flew towards the oil lamps.

'All right,' said Ajit to Mohamed. 'If the harness breaks we will pay eight annas towards its repair.'

'If the Sahib would give a few more annas, I could feed the horse well tonight and could risk working him hard now, since with a good feed he would recover by morning.'

Such solicitude for the ill-used bundle of bones he called a horse struck Ajit as funny and he laughed.

'How much?' he asked.

'Another four annas, Sahib, would mean a good feed for him tonight.'

'That makes four rupees altogether,' said Ajit ruefully. 'I agree.'

Mohamed Ali climbed back on to the driver's seat with remarkable alacrity, gave the horse a merciless thwack with the whip, and the carriage lurched forward. I clung to Ajit, to save myself being thrown out, and began to laugh. Ajit clutched me, and gasped: 'Play-actor – all that trouble to get twelve annas.'

'Such a waste of time,' I said, trying to look sober.

'Oh, no,' said Ajit, 'he earned twelve annas.'

So I had my first lesson in bargaining in a country where time is plentiful and cheap.

Ajit had told me on the train that he had obtained a boy servant for me. He had had great difficulty in getting one, as most labour was taken up by the mills; and his parents had not been prepared to send one from their house because they wished the marriage to be kept secret. He had, however, talked to the headman of the nearest village, and, knowing that Ajit was working at the power house and not wishing to antagonise a man who, if offended, might cause some of his people working on the power-house building to be dismissed, he had sent Ajit to the grain bazaar to see his brother, who dealt in lentils.

The brother was a wily-looking individual; he had none of the upright, honest air of his country brother, but he had recommended a boy who had just been dismissed by Shah Vakil.

'Why was he dismissed?' asked Ajit.

The grain dealer ran his fingers through some lentils lying in a sack by his side. 'The Vakil said he was a thief, Sahib, but in my opinion, that Shah Vakil's law practice is shrinking and he wished to get rid of the servant without loss of face.' The lentil dealer spat on to the pavement. 'The boy is honest, Sahib, and he can cook. He is an agriculturist by caste – a Patel – but, Sahib, you cannot expect to get a servant of your own caste in this town,' and he shrugged his shoulders hopelessly.

The Sahib agreed with all the grain dealer had said, so Babu became our servant, and Ajit had been coaching him in his duties for a couple of weeks before my arrival.

Now, as the tonga tore along the narrow track, swaying perilously from side to side, Ajit said irritably that Babu should have put the front lights on in the flat, so that we could find our way. All the other tenants were spending the hot weather in the hills, so there was no other light to guide us. 'Big building on the left?' shouted Mohamed Ali, reining in.

'That's it,' said Ajit, with a sigh of relief.

The tonga stopped and a hungry, weary couple made their descent. We had been travelling since early morning – but for me this lonely spot was the end of twenty-one days of journeying.

'Babu, come and help Memsahib,' yelled Ajit, 'and take the luggage.'

The walls echoed back the cry and no one came. Outside the ring of light from the tonga lamps, the darkness encircled us like a wall. I moved closer to Ajit while he paid the driver, and they got down the luggage and dumped it into the sand.

'Babu, chelo!'

But Babu did not come, and there was not a glimmer of light from the flats. The tongawallah whipped up his horse, quickly turned the carriage in the clearing near the house and started back to town.

Ajit struck a match and we picked our way through odd bricks and builder's rubble, round to the entrance of the flat, which was on the ground floor and had a separate entrance.

'Babu,' shouted Ajit with real annoyance in his voice.

Only the echo answered.

'He must have fallen asleep,' said Ajit.

A flight of stone steps led up to a small veranda. Ajit ran up the steps ahead of me, but pulled up short at the top.

I too could see that the front door was open, and I too realised that in such a deserted spot any servant left alone would surely have bolted it shut. There was no light within.

Ajit backed quickly down the steps.

'Peggie,' he said softly, 'just wait here quietly while I see that all is well.'

Chapter Nineteen

I stood in the lonely dark and was dreadfully afraid. Far, too far, away, I could hear the jingle of the harness bells on the receding tonga.

Ajit bent down and picked up a brick, then glided up the steps with it poised for action. He paused on the top step and then moved swiftly to the entrance, and, standing on one side of the doorway, so that his body was shielded from any missile discharged from within, reached round into the room and switched on the light.

The light sent a pariah dog speeding away with fright, but I felt better now that I could see; and I picked up a brick and followed Ajit.

He had meanwhile peeped into the room, seen that it was empty, and crossed quickly to a second room which led off it; it was also empty. He turned to the other door leading off the main room and went through to the kitchen, and then to the bathroom and storeroom. Both were empty. In the kitchen a charcoal fire still glowed faintly in a tiny stove on the floor, and round it were grouped open cooking pots full of food. The back door was bolted.

He was puzzled. I stepped up behind him and he whirled round, brick raised to smash down on the intruder's face.

'It is only I,' I said. 'Don't look so grim.'

Relieved, he lowered the brick and said: 'It was not good that you followed me.' He looked round. 'I cannot understand. Babu has cooked – everything is in order – but where is the boy? Unwise to leave the front door open like that – dogs might have eaten our dinner.' He laughed nervously, and put the brick down on to the floor.

'I will bring in the luggage.'

'I'll come and help.'

'You are to stay here,' he commanded.

I started to object, but the look on his face was that of a man who expected to be obeyed, and I found myself acquiescing.

'OK, Chief.'

He grinned and pinched my cheek, but he shot the bolts of the kitchen door as he went out so that I could not follow. I heard him cross the living-room and then a muffled exclamation. I ran to the bolted door.

'Ajit, what is it?'

'All is well. It is Babu. Babu, what have you been doing?'

'Sahib,' said a feeble voice. 'Arree, Sahib.'

Ajit came and unbolted the door, and I nearly fell through in my haste.

'Good heavens!' I exclaimed.

A figure stood at the front door. It was clothed from head to foot in thick mud, out of which stared a pair of weeping, bloodshot eyes. A horrible odour rolled into the room and wrapped itself round us. Mud splodged on to the veranda, and there was a trail of it leading into the darkness.

'What has happened?' I gasped. 'He can't come in while he is like that.'

'He can't,' said Ajit, his eyes twinkling.

'Tell him to sit on the steps for a minute. My God, how he stinks.'

'Betho,' said Ajit, pointing to the steps, and Babu still weeping loudly sat down with a plop.

I flew back into the kitchen to fetch some water, but could not find a bucket. There was, however, a large earthenware jar on a stone stand. It was already full of water, so I staggered out on to the veranda with it.

'Close your eyes. I'm going to pour water over you,' I said, feeling that drastic action was necessary to clear the main coating of mud; and I tipped the water over his head.

Unthinkingly I had spoken in English. Babu had not, of course, understood, and I had acted too quicky for Ajit to intervene.

The boy leaped up with a shriek, as I cascaded carefully cooled drinking water over him. Gurgling and choking he fled down the steps and stood in the darkness, howling like a young animal, so that the pariah dogs, startled from the hollows in the sand where they slept, barked alarmedly.

'Babu, Babu,' shouted Ajit over the lamentations, trying hard to contain his laughter. 'Come here. You must have a bath. Come now. Memsahib will not pour any more water.'

Snuffling and rubbing the mud out of his eyes, Babu came slowly back to the veranda. The water had had some effect. His face and shoulders had emerged from their covering, and he proved to be a dark, low-foreheaded lad of about fifteen.

I said penitently to Ajit that I was sorry I had frightened the boy. 'What shall I do? I had no idea the water was so cold.'

'There is a bucket in the storeroom. Fill it with water from the tap – the tap water will be warm from the sun – and bring it here with an old cup and any soap you can find. I will stay here and calm him.'

I hurried to do as I was bidden, and when I returned with a bucket of water, Babu had stopped crying and was talking to Ajit in a slow, sulky voice.

Ajit stopped him and commanded: 'Go to the foot of the steps. Take off your shirt and have a bath.'

Babu looked at me resentfully, took the bucket from me, scooped up the water with his hand and washed out his mouth. After spitting over the veranda rail, he carried the bucket down the steps and a moment later the splashing of water announced that the bath was in progress.

'How will he take a bath out there?' I asked.

Ajit smiled. 'It will be somewhat cold, but he will use the cup to pour water over himself, then he will lather himself with soap, and rinse it off by pouring more water. Give him another bucket of water – and an old shirt and pyjamas of mine to wear. I think he has no clothes other than the ones he was wearing – I promised him two suits of clothes as part of his wages – I must order them.'

'Won't that be very costly?' I asked, as I delved in the cupboard for clean clothes. The cupboard was in chaos – clothes, blueprints, detective novels and bars of soap, mixed with crumpled bed-linen and my letters to Ajit.

'No,' said Ajit, 'it means only two each of shirts, cotton pants and vests.'

He fetched another pail of water and took it outside, with the garments I had found.

When he came back I was sitting on the floor in the kitchen, trying to coax the charcoal stove into burning again.

'What happened to Babu?'

Ajit fetched some more nuggets of charcoal from an old kerosene tin in a corner, before answering. 'I shall tell you – don't trouble with the fire – Babu will make it burn when he comes in, but these coals will keep it from dying in the meantime.' He sat down on the floor beside me and put his arm round my shoulder. He looked very tired, his eyes black-ringed.

'Babu has a friend who is a shepherd,' he said. 'This man came to ask Babu for one or two bilis – the brown cigarettes village people smoke – and as dinner was ready, Babu sat on the veranda with him and they smoked, while the goats grazed around the house – at this time of year fodder is so scarce that they graze one herd during the day and another on the same ground during the night – anyway, the shepherd had a goat lying away under the trees at the back of the house, and it had just given birth to three kids. Two kids being the normal yield, Babu's interest was aroused, and, forgetting that our door was open, they walked off to have a look.'

He paused to look down at me. Hunger had made me weak and I had laid my head on his shoulder. I did not really care about Babu as long as he was not hurt; all I wanted to hear was the rich cadences of Ajit's voice and to feel him close to me.

Ajit sighed. 'Babu saw the lights of the tonga flash as it turned, realised what it was and started to run back to the flat, hoping to get in before we spotted his absence – but he forgot about the sewage pond, and in the darkness he plunged into it. It is not deep – but the banks are slippery and it would be hard to get out of it.'

I smiled, roused myself and stretched. 'Poor Babu,' I said, 'I think I should heat and serve this food – we are both hungry, and Babu must be exhausted.'

'Babu exhausted? He is a village boy – very tough. Besides, my Queen, you do not know how to make the bread.'

'That is true – I don't know.' I had heard about the bread-making which is the bane of every Indian household, but I had not been able to find anyone in Wetherport to give me a cooking lesson.

We resigned ourselves to being hungry a little longer. I felt as if I had been pummelled by new experiences and I resumed thankfully my former position with my head on Ajit's shoulder, while he whispered into my ear that he loved me.

It was thus that a clean, damp Babu first saw us properly, as he stepped noiselessly into the kitchen, his master's old shirt flapping round his knees. He looked at me with great curiosity, and then cast his eyes down.

'Goddess Rhada's sister, namaste,' he said softly, putting his hands together in an attitude of prayer.

I sprang away from my husband. 'Namaste, Babu,' I said gravely, and feeling uncertain of my Gujerati I asked Ajit to tell him to serve dinner. 'We shall all feel better when we have eaten.'

Ajit broke into Hindi, which Babu apparently followed quite easily; and, none the worse for his adventure, he moved stolidly about the kitchen collecting trays and brass cups, while the charcoal in the stove caught alight again.

'No drinking water, Sahib,' he said mournfully. 'I boiled it specially for Memsahib this morning, and now she has thrown it away.'

Ajit looked anxious, and then said: 'Make another fire and boil some more water; you can give me unboiled water.' He explained to me that being English I was more likely to get dysentery than he was, so tonight I would have to drink tea, since there was no means of cooling the newly boiled water quickly.

'Babu, Memsahib will show you how to make tea as it is done in her country.'

I acquiesced, and Ajit led me first to the bathroom to wash my hands – it contained only a small sink and an additional tap set shoulder high in the wall, and was neither very clean nor tidy. The towel was grey, so I wiped my hands on a clean handkerchief. We went back into the front room. Except for four straight chairs and a table, it was bare. Ajit closed the kitchen door and turned on the ceiling fan. We stood under its welcome coolness; and Ajit kissed me as I had dreamed of being kissed for many weeks.

There was a final clatter of cooking pots from the kitchen. Babu shouted: 'Khana heh, Sahib.'

We let go of each other, chuckling like conspirators.

'Food's ready,' said Ajit, and we sat down at the bare table, our weariness relegated to the background, each knowing that we had found again the sweet intimacy of our days in England.

Although I was so hungry, I viewed the coming meal with trepidation. I had tried to eat curries aboard ship but the mass of spice had nauseated me, and since then I had eaten English food both in the ship and on the train. This was my first Indian meal with Ajit, and I feared I would not be able to eat it.

I gathered up courage, as Babu, moving fast for once, came in with two large trays and set one before each of us. He paused anxiously. There is no doubt that he had cooked the food and arranged the trays with the greatest care, but he was not a professional cook and could not be sure whether his efforts would please me.

'He is probably wondering if he can possibly please a Memsahib,' said Ajit, sniffing appreciatively at the good odours coming from his tray. He motioned Babu back to the kitchen. The boy sighed and shot back to his breadmaking.

The tray in front of me was of well-polished brass and on it were three small, brass cups, each of which held a different curry. There was also a saucer with slices of raw onion, tomato and green chillie in it. A small heap of hot rice lay on the tray itself and by it a wafer-thin, hollow ball of pastry.

'Bread,' said Ajit in explanation of the latter, as he tore apart his own little ball and with a piece of it deftly lifted some curry from one of the brass cups and popped it into his mouth. 'Babu,' he shouted cheerfully, his round face beaming, 'Babu, bring Memsahib a spoon.'

Memsahib was, however, trying to emulate her husband and managed to convey a little food to her mouth.

I do not know how to describe the bliss of that first mouthful of food in my new home. To my astonishment it had a delicate flavour compounded of potatoes, peas and tomatoes. No burning chillies seared my throat, no heavy, fatty taste cloyed my mouth. It was very different from the curries of the ship, and, as I delved into the other little cups, I remarked on this difference.

'They probably had Goanese cooks on board ship. They tend to make food very hot and rich. This cooking is nearly the same as that of my home – it is North Indian food. I also told Babu not to put many chillies.'

'This is going to be fun,' I said, more relieved than words can express. 'If I can eat, I can face anything.'

'I'm not going to starve you, darling,' said Ajit, rather taken aback. 'Even if you are not allowed to eat flesh here, you will not starve.'

'Not allowed to eat flesh! – you always ate meat in England.'

'We are living, my Rani, in a Jain community and they are against the taking of life. They tolerate us here only if we become vegetarians. That means no fish or eggs either.' He paused to shout to Babu for more bread. 'All the families normally living in this building are Jains, and since I am not from this province they asked the Government Agent, when they learned I was coming, to make it a condition of my tenancy that I would be a vegetarian.'

'This is going to make life awkward,' I remarked as I licked my fingers.

'I know. It means a purely Indian diet for you – I had to agree, as this is the only vacant flat within two miles of the power-house site.' He went on hopefully: 'If Babu would agree to its being brought into the kitchen, we could buy some meat at present, from the Muslim bazaar, and you could cook it, as the other tenants have gone up to the hills for the summer. They all work in a Government College near here and get months of leave.' He added regretfully: 'We shall get exactly three weeks.'

I giggled at the idea of asking Babu's permission to hold meat-eating orgies. 'Don't worry, darling,' I said. 'If all vegetarian food is as good as this, I shall not come to harm. If other wives can manage, I am sure I should be able to.'

Ajit blew me a kiss across the table.

When we could eat no more, Ajit produced cigarettes, and Babu took away the trays. I looked out of the barred window. The moon was high, lighting up a bleak, flat landscape. It looked cool.

'Could we walk outside?'

'Of course,' said Ajit. He went into the kitchen and told Babu to bring in the luggage, which had lain undisturbed in the sand where we had dumped it, and to wash the mud off the veranda.

'Come along,' he said.

We went out through the front door, carefully avoiding the smelly mud which Babu had deposited, down the moonlit steps and across the builder's rubble which had been left in front of the flats, to the track along which we had driven earlier. We paced up and down.

The scene was wild and lonely, but the silence was soothing after our hectic day. Only the drums still throbbed far away, although there was little sign of habitation other than our own; the track on which we walked continued across the plain, winding in and out of clumps of bushes and trees, and it alone hinted at the presence of others. In the sky above there was no mist or cloud and the stars seemed close enough to touch. On the wind came the smell of ripened crops, dusty sweet. My weariness fell away from me.

'Why are the drums being beaten?' I asked.

'It is the season of marriages.'

'I have come at the right time.'

'You have indeed, my love; the drums are beating for the farewell of the bride to her parents as she leaves to go to her husband's house.'

He bent and kissed me lightly. Arm in arm we went slowly back to the flat, and the happiness on Ajit's face as we passed through the shaft of light from the window was a full reward to me for coming to India.

Chapter Twenty

I lay in the curve of Ajit's arm and watched the sparrows swinging on the window bars in the morning sunlight; their steady cheeping reminded me of my own cosy bedroom at Wetherport, so different from the almost empty stone room in which I lay. No curtains, no pictures, no cushions, no dressing-table spread with silver brushes, nothing of beauty in the whole room, except the sleeping man beside me: but I felt drowsily content, with my husband's arm as my pillow and a cheap cotton sheet to cover me.

I had left my watch in the living-room and had no idea of the time. Ajit had taken only twenty-four hour's leave when coming to meet me and had to return to work that day, so I eased myself gently away from him and got up. He stirred but did not wake. I covered him with the sheet and kissed him; then put on my dressing gown and went into the other room, shutting the door quietly behind me.

My watch said six o'clock.

I wandered into the kitchen, and looked round a little helplessly. Through the open door of the adjacent storeroom I could see Babu spreadeagled on a mat laid beside four large grain bins. He wore only his master's old pyjama trousers and his naked chest looked as thin as a feathered pullet's. Followed by the sound of his snores, I crossed to the back door and pulled back the heavy brass bolts. The snoring ceased, but after a pause it was vigorously renewed. I chuckled to myself.

The door opened on to a new world. There was no compound wall, and stretched before me was what appeared to be a desert. Right to the horizon the sand stretched, almost without undulation. There was a little foliage; round bushes of cacti flourished, and the sewage pond, in which Babu had taken his unexpected bath, was marked by a circle of remarkably green grass and shrubs. I saw that an open ditch led from the building to the pond and this was also fringed with greenery. An unpleasant odour of old soap drifted up from the water, and I was relieved that the lavatory, at least, was connected with a closed cesspool.

To my right, prickly cacti had been arranged as a hedge and from behind this came the sound that was to be the constant accompaniment of my life in India – a steady creak-creak as a tethered ox walked up and down to draw water from a well to irrigate the land. I could just see over the hedge a man standing on the lip of the well and tipping the filled water-skin, so that it discharged its contents into the irrigation channel below him; when the skin had emptied I saw the ox's horns as it turned to walk back up to the well so as to let the skin fall again into the water far below.

An occasional mango or neem tree was silhouetted against the brilliant blue sky, and under one of the trees sat a shepherd boy dressed in a red turban, white frilly jacket and loincloth. He was surrounded by goats munching cactus leaves, and, as I leaned against the door jamb, he took out a flute and began to play. Above his head, in the mango tree, there was a flash of grey bodies amongst the leaves. Monkeys, I thought, with childish delight!

A snuffling at my feet made me jump. A dog, like a greyhound dyed brown, was sniffing round me, ready to take flight at any moment. I bent to pat him, but he cowered down, and I saw to my horror that he was covered with swollen ticks. I hastily withdrew my hand and retreated to the kitchen.

'Babu,' I called softly.

Babu just snored.

I wanted some tea, but had no idea how to light the charcoal stove. I prowled round the kitchen. It was a bare room, stone-walled and stone-floored, as was the rest of the flat. A built-in cupboard with a mesh door presumably held food. On some shelves in an alcove was a collection of brass trays, cups and cooking pots, such as I had seen at dinner, together with some thick china cups and saucers. On a stone stand was the earthenware water pot, the contents of which I had emptied over Babu; a water tap dripped in one corner and in the floor beneath it was a grid over an open drain. The floor looked as if it had been recently scrubbed.

'How on earth does one wash dishes?' I wondered. 'No sink, not even an enamel bowl, and no means of getting hot water quickly. Instead of walking, I should have watched Babu last night.'

Feeling very incompetent about housekeeping, I decided that Babu must be awakened, which I did by shaking him by the shoulder. I think he had not been asleep for some time but had been watching me furtively. He gave a most realistic jump, however, and ceased his snoring.

'Rhadabahin,' he said politely, as he rubbed the sleep from his eyes. He rose and yawned hugely, opened a creaky tin trunk, and took out a twig and a comb. I did not wish to disturb his normal morning routine – time enough for that – so I decided not to ask for tea but to await events.

Events were very slow.

He filled a bucket with water, took it outside the back door and, with much splashing and snorting, bathed himself. He squatted on his heels and while the sun dried him, he took out the twig and fluffed one end of it. Using it as a toothbrush, he cleaned his teeth. He scrubbed and spat into the sand and scrubbed again. He polished and rubbed until I began to give up hope about breakfast, but eventually the toilet was completed by a flick of the comb through his hair, and he lit a bili and sat for five minutes more, slowly inhaling the smoke.

I decided to take a bath myself and went to the bathroom. In the hurry of the previous evening, I had not noticed that, apart from the sink and the extra tap in the wall, it contained a bucket, a two-inch-high wooden stool and a couple of shelves which were littered with old bits of soap and rusty razor blades. An aged towel was looped over one of the bars of the window and a crow was sitting on it. He flew out at my entrance.

Not wishing to disturb Ajit by looking for a clean towel, I splashed myself all over with water and smoothed it off with my hands as best I could, realising with a sense of shock that the last time I had taken a bath had been on the train from Bombay. I wrapped myself in my dressing gown again and combed my hair with a broken comb which I found among the razor blades.

When I returned to the kitchen, Babu was stuffing newspaper into the lower half of a stove filled with charcoal, and I said hopefully in Gujerati: 'Food?'

Babu nodded, picked up the stove with a pair of pincers and took it outside the back door, where he laid a match to it. He fanned it with a straw fan and soon had a good fire burning, which he then transferred with his pincers back to the kitchen. Water was put on to boil.

There was a shout from outside. 'Dudhwallah,' and a pail clanked down upon the step. Babu picked up an aluminium pan, and the milkman squatted on his heels and carefully measured thin, blue milk into it.

The milkman was fat and his face was creased with laughter lines. His handlebar whiskers stuck out in a black fluff, nearly burying a pug nose. A cap which had once been white was kept in place by his cauliflower ears, and a thin shirt over a dirty loincloth completed his costume. He smelled of cows.

He took a quick look at me, as I stood in the middle of the kitchen, and lowered his eyes politely – but in that second the price of milk went up by two annas a pound.

He said in a subdued voice to Babu: 'An English woman? Your Sahib is a Hindu, isn't he?'

'Yes,' said Babu, as he put the lid on the pan. 'Sahib is Indian; Memsahib is English. She came yesterday.'

'He must be very rich to be able to keep an English woman,' remarked the milkman as he clamped the lid back on to his can.

'He gets Rs.700 a month and does not take bribes,' said Babu carelessly.

In order to hide my laughter, I hastily bent down over the fire and lifted the lid of the water-filled saucepan. What would Ajit say if he knew his servant was so well acquainted with his affairs?

Babu was continuing: 'Sahib is an engineer working on the new electric house,' he said proudly. 'He went to school for many years, and Lulbhai – you know, the peon at the electric-house office – says that when he is older he will be a powerful sahib.'

The milkman was impressed and looked as if he would like to ask more questions, but I was too near and he was not sure whether I could understand or not, so he hung his can on the handlebar of his bicycle and wheeled the machine away on to the track which led to the city.

The noise of the milk pail had aroused Ajit and he called me. I went to him eagerly.

'Put a cup of hot water into the bathroom,' he ordered without preamble, as he sat up in bed, 'and unpack my shaving things – and I'll need a towel and a big mug.'

I was shocked at the unexpected stream of abrupt orders, given without previous greeting. They struck me like a series of blows on the face. For a second I stood holding on to the door, trying to steady myself.

'Darling,' I said shakily, but my voice was hardly audible and the object of my affection had lain down again and covered his face with the sheet.

My first reaction was a desire to say: 'Damn you. Get them yourself or ask for them civilly.' Then I thought of our happiness of the night before and that I did not understand the customs of the country, so I crept away feeling very bewildered. Obediently I took some hot water from the pot on the fire. Babu had now lit a second fire, which was blazing underneath the milk pan, and the kitchen resembled an inferno, with a presiding devil whose floured hands whisked black pans, brass pots and food through the air with magical speed.

I placed the mug of water on the bathroom shelf and returned with hesitant feet to Ajit, who had climbed out of bed and opened the front door, only to be driven back by the smell of the mud which Babu had not washed away properly the previous evening. He yelled: 'Babu!'

'Sahib.'

A flood of Hindi poured from Ajit on the subject of servants who did not do their work properly. This was answered by placating shouts from Babu. The words came so fast that I could not follow.

'Dear Lord,' I thought, 'if they quarrel like this Babu will leave. What is the matter with Ajit this morning?'

'Don't be angry with him, darling,' I said. 'He could not see in the dark.'

'Angry?' he said. 'I'm not in the least angry. Get me a clean pair of trousers and a shirt.'

I bit my lip at the rough tone, but thinking it best to give no hint that I was hurt, I said as I went to the clothing cupboard: 'It's a lovely morning.'

'You wait,' said Ajit darkly, as he disappeared towards the bathroom and then reappeared flourishing a shaving brush. 'It will soon heat up.' He stood in the doorway of the sitting-room and lathered his chin. 'This evening when it cools we will go to the bazaar. You must learn to buy – otherwise Babu will cheat you.'

As he turned to go back to the bathroom he saw my face in the light of the window.

'What's the matter, my Rani?' he asked most gently.

Tears threatened to disarm me, and Babu looked at me as he came past laden with cups and saucers.

Shyness and a quiet pride made me force a smile and say: 'Nothing.' To change the subject I asked: 'How do you take a bath in the bathroom?'

'Come and see,' he said, and led the way. I paused a moment to show Babu how to set out cups and saucers correctly on the table, and then followed.

As I advanced to the bathroom door, a hand came round and flung out a pair of pyjamas. I caught them before they hit me in the face. I peeped through the door. Ajit was sitting on the wooden stool, which he had placed under the tap, and water was pouring down over him as he lathered himself with kitchen soap and sang at the top of his voice, while the dirty water made a gurgling accompaniment as it flowed across the floor and down the open drain in one corner.

The singing stopped abruptly. 'Shut the door,' he shouted through the streaming water. 'You're making a draught.'

I shut it abruptly and leaned against the other side. I was trembling from head to foot, partly with suppressed rage and partly with fear. I fumbled for my handkerchief and blew my nose sharply; the abuser renewed his song and apparently had not a care in the world.

Muttering maledictions against men before breakfast, I went to look for clean linen trousers.

Chapter Twenty-one

Ajit ate his breakfast quickly and almost in silence. I could not eat much, although the parathas, a kind of fried bread, were good. I was fuming over Ajit's rudeness, and away down inside me a feeling of panic was stirring. I was so terribly alone in this deserted place to which he had brought me, and I had only him on whom to depend to guide me into a new life. The sharp tones of his voice echoed in my head and drowned the whispers of his usual kindliness.

He licked the last of the chutney off his fingers and suggested that I leave the housekeeping entirely to Babu for the day. It would give me time to unpack and to rest.

I assented listlessly and went out on to the veranda.

He called for water and having gulped down a couple of glasses full, he strode down the steps and mounted an old bicycle which Babu had brought out. He said: 'Take care of yourself. Don't go far from the house. I'll return at one o'clock,' and off he went, the bicycle rattling protests, along an almost invisible track through the cacti.

I watched him out of sight. Already the desert was white in the glare of the sun. In all its great expanse nothing moved except the ox which I could hear walking up and down as it drew up water. Two vultures sat on a rotten tree stump, looking as if they were carved out of the wood. The goats and the goatherd slept under a tree.

The tears welled up in me. What had I done to incur such disapproval? What had I done?

I sat down on the steps, put my head on my knees and cried like a baby. I cried for Mother and I cried for Bessie, to take pity on my helpless loneliness. I cried aloud since Babu was clearing up at the back of the house and there was no one else to hear. But I had not counted on the sharpness of country people's ears. After a few minutes I became aware of a hasty confabulation towards the back of the building. It was carried on in quite loud voices – evidently the speakers thought I would not understand – and at first I could not do so, but as I listened a woman's voice came clearly: 'Who weeps? – has someone died?'

'Memsahib weeps,' said Babu uneasily.

'Memsahib?' queried a woman's voice.

'Yes, Sahib brought home his new bride yesterday.'

'Ah,' the woman gave a sigh of understanding. 'All brides weep at first. Mother-in-law is there to comfort her?'

'No, Memsahib came alone.'

'Ramji,' said the woman slowly, 'these big Sahibs do not understand the suffering of a woman newly taken from her family. Another woman should be here – a sister-in-law to make jokes with her.'

'Truly,' chimed in a male falsetto, 'she must be lonely.'

I had hastily smothered my sobs on hearing the voices, and listened with growing amusement as I was discussed.

'From which province is Memsahib?' asked the woman.

'She is from England.'

'From England? Is she white?'

'Yes.'

'Ramji! She is English and yet she weeps,' exclaimed the falsetto. 'In all my twenty years as watchman in the Civil Lines, I never saw an English woman weep.'

'Foolish one,' said the woman. 'Even monkeys weep.'

There was a sound of footsteps coming round the building, so I dried my eyes and composed myself for the benefit of visitors.

A woman walked round to the front steps, and I goggled at her. I had never seen such a perfect figure or such an exquisite, heart-shaped face. She wore a tight multicoloured blouse, which, although it had short sleeves, had no back and was kept in place by strings tied round the neck and waist. A red cotton skirt swung about her hips and a light veil hung from her head down her back.

Large almond eyes beneath sweeping eyebrows observed me in a friendly fashion.

'Namaste,' I said cautiously to this vision, thinking at the same time what a sensation she would make if she walked down the Strand. Every man in London would scamper after her.

The woman put down the earthenware pot which she had been carrying on her head. She smiled, showing small, even teeth, and inclined her head in acknowledgement of my greeting.

'Curd?' she said, pointing to the contents of the pot.

Babu, who had come up behind her, said a trifle sourly that he made it daily for the Sahib and that there was no need to buy. I refused to buy, therefore, but asked if she would like to have a glass of water before continuing her journey. She assented and I asked Babu to bring drinking water.

While the water was coming, she talked to me. I did not understand all she said but understood enough to discover that she was the daughter of the headman of a village a couple of miles away, her name was Kamala and she was going to the city to sell her curd.

I asked if she was married.

She giggled and said she was not.

Babu came back with a dripping glass. She squatted on her heels and let Babu pour the water into her cupped hands, from which she drank. Very little was spilt.

She stood up, swung her pot on to her head, and with a reluctant 'A-jo', she went on her way to town.

So I made my first friend in India; and I grew to love her and many of the other women of the villages round about – much to the disgust of the middle-class ladies, when they returned to the flats above ours. In their opinion, village women were not people with whom one made friends.

The owner of the falsetto voice had evidently gone round the back of the building and up the main staircase to the other flats. He now came round the front.

Wrapped in a shawl and carrying a staff, he bowed before me obsequiously and said in broken English: 'Me Udharbhai Watchman. Yesterday night sick malaria not come to flats.'

I considered this telegramlike communication and sought for the Gujerati word for 'well'. It came to me and I asked if he was now quite well. He did not understand my bad pronunciation and I asked again in English. He still did not understand, so he grinned all over his unshaven face, said 'OK' rather doubtfully and pottered off into the bush, where I afterwards found he had a small mud house, in which he lived with his mother, who was reputed to be a hundred years old.

Without being asked to do so, Babu brought me a cup of tea, sweet and scented. Evidently Kamala's remark that a new bride should be comforted had impressed itself on his mind.

He held the cup out to me tentatively, as if coaxing a young animal to eat. I exclaimed with pleasure and took the cup from him. Realising that I was pleased, his lips parted to show a set of teeth stained red with betel nut.

As I drank, the exhaustion of crying and the fears of the morning receded. I began to think constructively about my future life with Ajit.

Meanwhile, Babu produced a bunch of soft rushes tied together, and swept the rooms. He squatted on his haunches and shuffled along under the bed and table as he swept with the side of his broom. He swept with slow, steady strokes and sang a little song about Lord Krishna.

Soothed, I got up from the steps and walked through the flat. Although it was not dirty, it was in a dreadful muddle. The shelves were strewn with every bit of junk a bachelor could have collected in a lifetime. The bed, as yet unmade, was a jumble of sheets. In every corner lay suitcases and trunks, the contents sticking out where I had hastily rifled them that morning, and on the veranda the bedding roll still lay; and the steps certainly needed further washing, as Ajit had said earlier, although the mud had dried.

'Bachelors,' I thought grimly, as I wiped my eyes and then took a pinafore from one of my trunks.

Ajit had bought only the barest essentials for the house, pending my arrival, and nothing had been done to make it into a home. I left Babu to sweep and wash, and firmly opened the cupboard door to reveal the chaos within.

'Young woman – not so young woman,' I addressed myself as I unearthed a mass of crumpled shirts and undarned socks, 'your husband has not known much comfort during the past weeks. He has started a new and responsible job in a strange province, apart from arranging for the arrival of his wife, and it is your duty to make him both comfortable and happy – whether you have to do it in Wetherport or in a bally desert – and even if he is a pig in the mornings.'

At one side of a shelf, in a space cleared for it, I found a package wrapped in silk. Unrolling it I discovered a battered envelope and in the envelope a much-thumbed photograph of myself. I wrapped it up again carefully and replaced it on the shelf. I was smiling softly.

Chapter Twenty-two

A sweat-soaked Ajit came home for lunch. I heard the hiss of the bicycle tyres through the sand and opened the door for him as he staggered up the veranda steps. He came through the door and sat down in the nearest chair without saying a word, exhaustion apparent in every line of him.

'It's hot,' he said at last, and then as the coolness of the room had its effect, he looked about him and added: 'You have made the room look nice.'

'Do you like it?' I asked, anxious for approval.

'Indeed I do. I am sorry that I had to leave you this morning.' He mopped himself with a towel which I had brought for him. 'I had only one day of leave.'

He pulled me to him and kissed me and I realised that whatever the trouble of the morning had been, it was now past. I chatted about how we would arrange the silver ornaments and the pictures which I had brought from England. Perhaps we could buy some curtains, a wardrobe, and a desk in which to keep his papers.

'We could buy cloth for curtains when we go to the bazaar this evening,' said Ajit.

'You should wear your sari to the bazaar,' he went on, as Babu came in with the lentil soup and rice. He took his place at the table and then got up again suddenly: 'I forgot,' he said, 'Mother gave me a present for you.' He went to a trunk in the bedroom, which I had not yet had time to explore, and brought out the saris which his mother had given to him earlier.

I unfolded them, and was enchanted by their colours and texture.

'I must write and thank your mother.'

Ajit looked embarrassed. 'Father – er – does not know about the present – and he would open the letter.'

'Oh,' I said regretfully. 'Then you must thank her on your next visit.'

'I will,' he said, depression in his voice.

To change the subject, I asked him how his work was progressing, but the depression merely changed to irritation.

'Too many people are making money out of the power house. Only this morning a dealer offered me Rs.500 to pass an installation which I know will break down in no time.' He ground his teeth and waved his spoon in the air. 'I refused. So I have made an enemy who will go to the Minister and tittle-tattle about my corruption.'

I was shocked, and he saw the concern on my face.

'Don't be afraid, darling. I know how to deal with these matters. The Minister is a friend of my father's, and he knows the calibre of our family.'

'Is there much corruption?'

'No more than in many countries in the West – but it makes me angry.'

He finished his meal, went and washed his face and mouth, kissed me tenderly and went back to work, leaving me with much to think about. My respect for my husband increased considerably.

After he had gone, I washed the sari that I had worn the previous day, and watched fascinatedly as it dried on the veranda rail in a few minutes.

I put on one of the saris which Ajit's mother had sent. There was no mirror in the flat, but when I stood by Babu, who was sitting smoking in a shady corner of the veranda, there was no gleam of amusement in his eyes so I supposed that I had tied it correctly. I prowled contentedly round the flat, occasionally tripping over the front folds of my sari.

In the kitchen, I opened the small store cupboard and immediately recoiled with disgust. Evidently Babu's knowledge of housekeeping did not extend to cupboards. Old tins and bottles lay about in profusion; half a dozen different containers, ranging from an old cigarette tin to a cracked saucer, held dirty bits of fat; a forgotten cup of curd had gained an amazing growth of mould; an old kerosene tin held flour in which I could see black insects burrowing. When I moved the kerosene tin, a family of large, leggy beetles ran for cover, and I stifled a shriek as one ran across my hand.

'Babu,' I shouted.

There was no response.

I went to the veranda. Babu was curled up asleep in a corner.

He resented bitterly the interruption of his afternoon sleep, but I was adamant and made him get up and come to the kitchen. I pointed to the insects in the flour.

He grinned fatuously.

I had a strong desire to slap him.

He made some unintelligible remark, yawned and strolled to the storeroom, from which he fetched a tray. He set the tray on the floor and emptied the flour on to it. Still yawning, he carried it outside and set it in the sun. I followed.

The heat hit me as I stepped into the sunlight. It burned my bare feet intolerably and clutched my body like a vice. Gasping, I covered my head with my sari and narrowed my eyes against the glare, but curiosity kept me by the tray.

The insects crawled out of the flour and off the tray, burying themselves in the sand. I nodded and went back on to the veranda. After a few minutes Babu brought the tray to me. I ran my fingers through the flour and found no sign of life. Wheat was so severely rationed that I dared not throw the flour away, so I motioned Babu to bring the tray indoors.

'We will now make the tin and the cupboard clean,' I said. 'Make a fire and boil water.'

Looking thoroughly sulky at the loss of his afternoon sleep, Babu said that the water in the tap would be hot from the sun. I made him bring me a bucketful and found it was as hot as my hands could reasonably bear.

I put on my pinafore, cleared out the cupboard and scrubbed it, telling Babu to throw away the accumulation of rubbish. I noticed, however, that he secreted the bits of fat in a corner of the storeroom. I presumed he would take them home to his mother and made no comment, but made a mental note that when I gave him a holiday I would present him with a new tin of fat as a gift for his mother.

While I was finishing the cleaning, I told Babu to prepare Sahib's tea, at the same time cautioning him to look through everything he used and if he found insects or dust he was to tell me.

He did as he was bidden, sighing all the time like a morning breeze. I think he believed me to be mad and was most put out at my criticism of his housekeeping.

When Ajit came home and I told him about it, he roared with laughter. 'Darling, you must daily look at all the food. Keep it also behind locks, because otherwise Babu's family will eat as well as the insects.' He squeezed my hand affectionately. 'You will soon learn everything.'

'Babu,' he shouted.

'Sahib,' came a subdued voice from the kitchen. Babu appeared, wiping his hands on the towel he wore round his neck.

'What have you been doing with my stores, letting insects as big as buffaloes graze on them?'

'Sahib, they were few – the Memsahib does not understand how quickly they come.'

'No insects in future, Babu, do you hear me – and don't let me find the Memsahib having to make your kitchen clean in future – what do I pay you for, hey?'

'Sahib,' said Babu, his lips pouting.

'Memsahib will look daily at the cupboards.'

'Ji, hun,' came the polite assent.

It was getting cooler, so we ate our tea quickly, and after Ajit had given my sari a few hitches to make the hemline straight, we started for the bazaar.

As we walked along the path that led through the thorns to the bus stop a mile away, Ajit swung the cotton shopping bag cheerfully, and a comfortable feeling of comradeship enveloped us.

'Step carefully over those big cracks in the earth,' he said. 'Snakes sometimes sleep in them.'

I stepped very carefully thereafter, although my mind was not occupied by thoughts of snakes.

'Why were you so angry with me this morning?' I asked.

Ajit stopped and looked at me amazedly. 'Angry? Me? I have no anger for you, my darling – only love.'

'You must have been angry,' I said stubbornly, determined to get to the root of the matter. I gave him a nudge to start him walking again. 'You shouted at me, and asked for things most rudely. You never even said "good morning" or gave me so much as a peck of a kiss. Altogether, young man, you were a perfect pig.'

Ajit looked most distressed; then suddenly he laughed.

'It is no laughing matter,' I said. 'I was hurt.'

He slipped his arm through mine. 'I am a wretch in the morning – but I did not mean to be rude. Here I am at home and I do not modulate my voice as is done in England. We all shout at each other – but not in anger – a loud voice does not mean anger.'

'Hmm,' I said. 'You ordered me about as if I was a slave – bring this – bring that – without a single courtesy.'

'Arree, I forgot you were English – an Indian wife would feel that her husband did not love her unless he kept her near him and allowed her to wait on him.'

'In that case, you are forgiven – and may give me the kiss I did not have this morning,' and I lifted my face to his.

He looked about hastily and, satisfied that there was no one in that barren place to see us, he kissed me heartily.

'You are to tell me,' he instructed, 'when I say words which sound hurtful. My English is not good – and I may not understand always the inference of what I say. Promise this.'

'I promise.'

He took out his handkerchief and dabbed the sweat from my face. 'I do not wish to make your life harder than necessary,' he said. 'You have much to endure.'

Chapter Twenty-three

The bus, borne along by a cloud of dust, rattled into the centre square of the town and drew up by a large bus shelter. We descended, while the driver removed his turban and used the end of it to wipe the sweat from his face.

'It is very quiet,' said Ajit, looking round the almost-deserted square. Then he spotted a Thanedar and six policemen standing near. 'Arree, trouble,' he exclaimed. 'See the rifles.'

I looked apprehensively to where he pointed. It was true. All the police were armed with rifles.

'Inspector Sahib,' said Ajit to that dignitary, who had just finished telling the cringing driver of our bus that he was late. 'Has there been some disturbance in the city?'

The Inspector flicked the dust off the brass badge pinned on the pocket of his shirt. When the words 'Shahpur Bus Company' were again legible, he twiddled his moustache ends, stuck out his chest to show his importance, and examined earnestly the top of the only tree in the square. 'A little trouble, I believe,' he said in sing-song English. 'But I am not one to spread rumours. Rumours are the prerogative of Hindus and Muslims.'

Ajit's lips tightened. I looked at the Inspector with interest. He was the first Anglo-Indian I had seen. I hated him on sight. His rudeness was unpardonable.

'What has happened?' asked Ajit patiently.

'A Muslim tongawallah was beaten up on the Pandipura road last night. The Muslims say it was done by Hindus. They are quite capable of it.'

'That is not sufficient to cause the police to be armed.'

The Inspector transferred his interest from the tree top momentarily to me and then examined his patent-leather shoes.

'A Sikh taxi driver's house was set on fire and Muslims were seen running away from it. The house was gutted. The police are looking for the culprits now.'

'I see,' said Ajit, and propelled me across the square towards the main bazaar.

'We will keep well inside the Hindu bazaars,' he said. 'A riot can start so quickly. It may be that the raid on the Sikh's house was retaliation for the beating up of the tongawallah, and the police are being careful to see that the Sikhs don't start any more trouble.'

I nodded. I had heard in England and on the boat coming over of the horrors of the partition riots, and for the first time in my life I was glad to see an armed policeman.

The vegetable bazaar seemed to be functioning normally. It was packed with people, among whom unattended cows and goats nosed their way. Along the pavement sat village women dressed like Kamala. They had round baskets of vegetables set in front of them and they shouted hopefully to likely customers. Each woman had a small, heavy stick by her side, with which she hit the wandering cows if they tried to steal from her basket; she had also a pair of scales which she held up before the purchaser, manipulating them with skilful fingers so as to give light weight to the unsuspecting. Almost all the women had heart-shaped faces and at least one in every three would have been considered a beauty in England. I wondered why Ajit had bothered to bring a wife from England when such beauties were scattered everywhere.

In the bazaar itself, the police were armed only with lathis, and I watched them idly while Ajit bargained. It was apparent that the people feared them. Women lifted their baskets up and retreated a little as they ambled past. There was none of the easy aplomb of an English policeman on his beat. No one spoke to them.

The vegetable women made jokes about my fair hair, and Ajit said ruefully that I had caused a price boom in the market. When bargaining for fruit with a man who had a small shop facing the market, the man said flatly that for someone who had an English wife Ajit drove too hard a bargain.

At last we were finished, and I had received my first lesson in shopping in a market where there was no fixed price for any product. I wondered if I would ever gain enough patience to bargain for every vegetable I bought. Ajit assured me that I should eventually regard it as an amusing game of skill.

We were fortunate in catching a bus immediately we arrived at the square, but by the time we reached the end of the bus route it was dark.

'I forgot to bring a torch,' said Ajit, annoyance in his voice.

A voice from the neem tree which marked the end of the route said: 'Sahib.'

I jumped with fright.

Babu emerged from the shadows. He had brought the torch.

'How thoughtful of him,' I said to Ajit.

'He probably wanted to visit someone down here and sought for an excuse to leave the house,' said Ajit sourly. The bazaar had frayed his temper.

Babu took the shopping bags and Ajit the torch.

We came to a tiny restaurant – no more than a thatched roof supported on poles, with a couple of old iron chairs set under it and the owner's cooking utensils and other small belongings stacked in a corner which had been made by draping sacking from the roof.

Ajit stopped to buy a pan to chew. The panwallah carefully wrapped the tobacco, lime and spices into a green leaf, at the same time chatting to Ajit who was evidently a regular customer. Ajit asked him to make up a very small pan for me, which I took and trustfully put into my mouth, only to spit it out again with a fine disregard for good manners.

'It was so bitter,' I moaned, wiping my mouth with a handkerchief.

The panwallah grinned, and Babu looked regretful at such waste.

The panwallah's wife was squatting before the fire, slapping dough into rounds between her hands, preparatory to cooking it on an iron plate. She said something to her husband.

The man looked worried and spoke rapidly to Ajit, while Ajit chewed his pan and nodded now and then.

'What did he say?' I asked curiously.

'He warned me that a dacoit leader was believed to have come from Kathiawar to the Criminal Tribe village near our house. He said I should be careful that you are not kidnapped.'

'Kidnapped?' I laughed. 'Surely not in these days.'

'Robbery is more likely. This dacoit, Vallabhai, must have come so near to a big town for a special reason. He must know of some travellers passing through or an isolated wealthy house to rob. You must keep the doors locked while I am away, however, and I will tell Chowkidar that he must stay near the flats.'

It sounded like an excerpt from a comic opera, and I could not feel frightened about it; but I promised to keep the doors bolted.

Babu had, of course, heard the warning, and he said mournfully: 'Sahib, tell Memsahib to put away her silver ornaments, not leave them on a shelf. Silver will bring Vallabhai to our dwelling like a vulture to a dead camel.'

Ajit translated. I was amused.

'I am not going to bury our pretty things when the flat badly needs something to make it look more pleasant.' I glanced at Babu. 'Babu is quick to notice. I have only had time today just to unpack – never mind arrange the silver. There is nothing very valuable, anyway.'

Ajit said to Babu that what we had was of little value, and Vallabhai would never know what our house contained.

Babu sulked.

That night while we slept Babu packed his creaky tin trunk with his few clothes, his sacred picture of the Lord Krishna, a tin of cooking fat, a tin of tea, most of our precious wheat ration, and seven rupees and five annas of the housekeeping money. Some time in the early morning he let himself out of the back door, and, with his trunk balanced on his head, he loped away back to his village. Either my mania about insects or fear of Vallabhai or Ajit's complaints about bad washing of the veranda or, perhaps, just a desire to see his mother, had proved too much for him, and away he went, never to be seen by us again.

Chapter Twenty-four

Nulini had visited Bimla Chand Rana on the same day on which Mrs Singh gave Ajit the three saris for me. When she returned home she left Bimla seated on a cushion under a mango tree in her father's courtyard stabbing murderously at a piece of embroidery. Bimla's face was contorted with rage. So, she thought, Ajit has married an English woman, a dirty, casteless English woman. She cursed him with curses that scandalised her long-suffering and bewildered Ayah.

'Do not use such words,' said Ayah. 'They are unbecoming to Rana Sahib's daughter.'

'I know what is becoming,' screamed Bimla, her high Punjabi temper in full vent, and she shoved her needle in and out of the cloth as if it was Ajit she was impaling. 'Go away!'

Ayah had no inkling of what had caused her charge's outburst, and she went and sat a few yards away while she thought about it.

'I, Bimla Chand Rana,' muttered Bimla, as she savagely bit her embroidery silk at the end of a line of cross stitch, 'the handsomest woman in the district, to be bypassed by that pudding head of an Ajit in favour of a vulgar Western female!'

She threw her embroidery at a squirrel, who scuttled up the tree in fright, and sat and sulked. She did not wish to betray Nulini, so she did not go to her father, feeling sure that Ram Singh would be communicating with Kasher Chand Rana about the marriage; but the day came when her Ayah said that Ajit was leaving for Shahpur, and still she had heard nothing from her father. Finally, she could endure the suspense no longer, so one morning she put on her best veil and a new shirt and strode to her father's room, Ayah fluttering after her and longing to know what was amiss.

Swallowing hard, she knocked and entered. Her father was alone, working on his private account book. Taking an old servant's privilege, Ayah slipped into the room as well.

Kasher Chand Rana looked up nervously and pushed his spectacles further up his nose. Both his wife and daughter had high tempers and shrill voices, and there were times when he expressed the opinion that a dumb woman would be a priceless pearl. Mercifully, both women had also a full allowance of Punjabi charm and just enough self-control not to shriek at him in public. He was, therefore, under the illusion that nobody knew that he was third in command in his house. Unfortunately, his servants kept his friends' servants well informed and he was famous as a thoroughly henpecked husband.

He clasped his small, clawlike hands before him and lifted up a face on which trepidation was clearly written.

'Well, daughter?'

The story poured out. Kasher Chand Rana was surprised but not angry. In the background Ayah punctuated the recital with horrified exclamations.

'It is not Dr Singh's fault,' he said. 'It is Ajit's. We must tell your mother – she will not like it.' He sighed and twiddled his wispy moustache. 'And your grandmother, I suppose – what will she say?' He sighed again at the horrid prospect before him. 'How did you find out?'

Reluctantly Bimla told of Nulini's visit.

'How did she know? It may be only a rumour.'

Bimla's loyalty to Nulini made it impossible for her to say how Nulini probably got her information, so she said: 'I don't know. You should go and see Dr Singh.'

'I will inquire,' he said.

'Go now – please, Father,' demanded Bimla.

'Yes, yes, child,' said her father resignedly, and he got up from his chair and shuffled about looking for his slippers. Ayah found them and put them on his feet. 'I will go now – although it is already hot.'

Satisfied, Bimla left him. Ayah brought him water, while he was waiting for his carriage.

'Ayah, no one must know of this yet.'

'Sahib,' she said reproachfully, 'I have served you faithfully for forty years.'

'I have malaria, Ayah. My hands are shaking. And I shall have to start marriage negotiations all over again. It is trying, very trying. And where did Nulini Singh get this gossip – it may well be gossip, Ayah.'

'It is truth, I think, Sahib. Nulini Singh is likely to know the truth.'

'Why?'

Ayah shrank away.

'I demand to know,' said Chand Rana sharply.

Ayah whispered into his ear.

He looked shocked. 'Ridiculous,' he said. 'How dare you say such a thing – you are not to purvey such damaging gossip in my house – I am surprised at you.'

'I have seen him look at her with love, Sahib,' said Ayah defensively.

'Absolutely ridiculous,' said Chand Rana. 'Probably her husband told her.'

The carriage came.

Kasher Chand Rana spent half an hour discussing politics and drinking tea, before he could gather courage enough to ask Ram Singh about his son's marriage, and just as he broached the subject Mrs Singh came into the room followed by Thakkur bearing a special sweetmeat which she desired Kasher Chand Rana to try. The servant retired, but Mrs Singh showed no signs of going away again, so he was forced to speak in front of her and to nibble the confection with which she presented him.

He mentioned that he had heard a rumour, a most extraordinary rumour which he felt was unlikely to be true, but as his own family was involved, would Ram Singh be so good as to confirm or deny it?

Ram Singh could not imagine how Chand Rana had heard about the marriage, but it was the only source of rumour which could possibly have driven him to visit his friend in the middle of the hottest afternoon of the year.

'My friend – er – this distresses me very much – er – I cherish your friendship very much – I – er . . .'

'I understand,' said Chand Rana glumly and absentmindedly took another sweet.

Mrs Singh covered her face with her sari and the study was silent. It was a difficult moment for them all.

At last Ram Singh said: 'I am sure you will have no difficulty in finding another husband for Bimla. However, if you would care to consider another boy from our family, my brother has a son of the same age as Bimla – a fine young man, who will inherit a share in his father's silk mill. He is a handsome boy, nearly six feet tall and of good proportions. If you would . . . if I might suggest . . .', and he looked at his friend slyly, 'I would be very pleased to act as mediator.'

Chand Rana, who had been imagining the screaming fury of his wife when he broke the news of Ajit's marriage to her, was immediately interested. It would be something with which to placate her.

'Six feet tall, did you say?' he asked hopefully, 'and of what kind of nature?'

Ram Singh knew all about the distaff side of his friend's family, and he said: 'Of a most determined nature. He was very disappointed when it appeared that Ajit would marry Bimla. He has seen her here – and I think he would be delighted to have the honour of marrying her. My brothers also would find pleasure in an alliance with your respected family.'

The two men grinned at each other, and behind her veil Mrs Singh giggled with relief.

Chand Rana nodded his bald head. 'Will you arrange a meeting with your respected brother?'

'Certainly.'

They talked a little longer and then Khan was sent to fetch Chand Rana's carriage. Ram Singh accompanied his friend to the front door and paused on the threshold. A little anxiously, he said: 'My friend, at this time, the marriage of my son is a source of anxiety to me and we have decided not to make it known for the time being. May I count on your discretion in this matter?'

'Of course – and I will instruct my family not to mention it until you announce it.'

Kasher Chand Rana told Bimla as gently as he could that Ajit had indeed married someone else. Bimla wept and Mrs Chand Rana's voice reached new heights of shrillness as she held forth on the stupidity of the man that her parents had made her marry.

Kasher Chand Rana waited patiently until Bimla's tears of frustration ceased and his wife's upbraiding had been reduced to a recitation of the foolish things he had done in the past, and then he mentioned casually that he had heard that a most handsome young man was secretly in love with his pretty daughter.

The pretty daughter pushed her ruffled hair back from her face, and with a thread of excitement in her voice demanded to know his name.

Her father settled himself more comfortably on the mattress on which he had deposited himself, and added dryly that the young man would one day be very rich.

His wife's voice snapped off as sharply as if she had been turned off like a radio, and she became very attentive.

'The young man is very handsome indeed,' said Kasher Chand Rana.

The women forgot about Ajit and clamoured to know more.

He refused to say who it was, but promised to make further inquiries, and in the meantime they were to keep Ajit's marriage a secret, for the sake of Dr Singh, who was, after all, their very good friend.

'If a rumour of this marriage comes to me from any corner,' he said threateningly, 'I shall know who started the gossip – and I shall stop all negotiations regarding Bimla's prospects with the young man of whom I have heard.'

At such a dreadful threat, both Mrs Chand Rana and Bimla quailed and promised faithfully that neither of them would mention the subject, and Bimla went back to her embroidery which lay under the mango tree. There she sat down to dream of an admirer as beautiful as a Rajput prince; and her Ayah marvelled at the unaccustomed peace.

Chapter Twenty-five

Babu's departure was a blow to me, but Ajit took it more philosophically.

'They all do it sooner or later,' he said. 'I expect he has just gone home.'

'Gone home – without notice?'

'Without giving notice,' he said, sitting on the edge of the bed and rumpling his hair wearily.

'We must manage for a few days,' he added, 'until I can find another boy. Just make the simplest of food.'

I bit my lips. I had seen very little of Babu's activities in the kitchen, and had no idea as yet how to cook even simple Indian food. Without at least eggs, English food seemed out of the question.

'I'll light a cooking fire for you, before I take my bath,' Ajit said.

He looked so harassed that I bent and kissed him, and told him not to worry, that I would manage. I knew that the amount of work he was doing was growing with the power house and that the Chief Engineer was down with malaria; his load was enough, without domestic difficulties being added to it.

I improvised a breakfast and sent him off to work looking quite happy, but I felt far from happy myself.

The cooking fire had gone out, so I washed the dishes by scrubbing them with sand and rinsing them under the tap, as I had seen Babu do. The water, unconfined by any sink, splashed over the floor and over my sandals. I kicked off the sandals and thereafter went barefooted. I tore up an old sheet and mopped up the water.

My legs ached from squatting on my heels as I washed the dishes, but the rest of the house was full of sand and dust, so I took Babu's bunch of rushes and swept the floors in a kneeling position. The ache extended to my back.

With a stiffer rush broom I scrubbed the bathroom floor, again squatting on my heels. The water from the tap was already warm from the sun.

Leaving a trail of wet footprints across the rooms, I went back to the kitchen. Heat was already invading the house, and my hair was wet with perspiration. My cotton frock was already dust laden and the hem was soaked from my scrubbing efforts in the bathroom. I went to the water cooler for a drink, but it was empty. I remembered then that Babu boiled water in the evening and let it cool overnight; he had evidently not done so the previous evening. I set the clay vessel under the tap and filled it.

To hoist a two-gallon pot from floor level to shoulder height requires some skill. I lifted the pot by the rim, but it was too heavy for me, and I had just decided that I must empty it, put it back on to the stand and then ladle water into it, when the pot settled the question by bursting at the bottom and flooding the newly cleaned kitchen.

'Damn,' I said.

After wringing the water out of the skirt of my dress, I painstakingly swept the pools on the floor down the drain in the corner of the room.

It was getting late, and Ajit would soon be home for lunch, so I hastily piled charcoal into the cooking stove and lit some newspaper under it, then lifted the stove with the tongs and placed it outside the back door so that the wind could fan the charcoal into flame. The wind merely blew the charred paper out of the stove, through the kitchen door and on to the damp floor.

I tried not to cry, but the tears came. How I longed for even an old-fashioned English kitchen range.

More paper was stuffed into the recalcitrant stove. I lit it and it blew out again, and more charred newsprint was added to that already stuck on the kitchen floor.

I sobbed quietly and prepared to try again. I was kneeling on the sand outside the kitchen door, tearing up yet another newspaper, when I realised that someone in that lonely place was watching me. Slowly I looked round.

Almost immediately behind me stood a tall, thin man dressed in the red turban, white jacket and loincloth of a countryman. He lacked, however, a countryman's moustache and the face was hard, seamed and very dark. The thin lips were curled in cynical amusement, and, as he stepped up beside me, he fingered a wooden-handled dagger, half concealed in his silver belt.

I jumped up and backed towards the door, but the man lifted his hand from the dagger and made a conciliatory gesture. Slowly he laid his staff against the wall. His eyes, which were almond-shaped and light like a goat's, looked me up and down insolently, as he squatted down in front of the stove.

I stood ready for flight while he lifted half the charcoal off the fire and at the same time addressed me. Although his language was something akin to Gujerati I did not understand it, and he glanced up at me with a keen, hard glance. I was again reminded of a goat.

He half-smiled. I doubt if he had ever seen such a dishevelled Memsahib as me.

Pronouncing the words carefully, he said: 'Bring kerosene.'

'Of course. Why had I not thought of it before? Comforted by the English words, I ran to the storeroom and after sniffing at several bottles found one with kerosene in it. I took it to him and he sprinkled it over the charcoal and lit it. Deftly he set the stove so that it caught the wind and in a few seconds a fire was roaring. He picked up the pincers and handed them to me, so that I could lift the stove into the kitchen. For a second his fingers touched mine. His face was close to me, and my words of thanks died on my lips. I saw the peculiarly light eyes flicker, and sudden fear gripped me. He made a half step towards me.

With the pincers I snatched up the blazing fire and whipped it between us. In that moment I was more afraid than I had ever been in my life.

'Namaste, Memsahib,' said Udharbhai, as he rounded the corner of the building.

The stranger moved smoothly away from me, picked up his staff, raised his hand in salute, and then, mopping his face with his sweat rag, he passed Udharbhai and swung swiftly down the path to the Criminal Tribe village.

Udharbhai watched him go.

'Who is he, Chowkidar Sahib?' I asked Udharbhai, my voice trembling.

'He is a stranger, Memsahib. The Mem must door lock. Strangers no safe.'

'I will,' I said feelingly, and I took the stove indoors and shot the bolt.

I did not tell Ajit about the stranger, because he had warned me to keep indoors as much as possible and would surely upbraid me. As it was, he was delighted with the lentil soup and boiled rice which I had made and hugged me till my aching back throbbed with pain.

Ajit again consulted the village headman about finding another servant, but the headman was ashamed that the boy his brother had recommended had left so quickly, and he was diffident about recommending anyone else. Ajit asked his friends, but they also were finding it hard to get servants. 'The mills take them all,' they sighed. I suggested that we advertise in the local newspaper, but Ajit pointed out that it would be unwise to take into our home a boy not personally vouched for by someone we knew. 'He might open the door to robbers,' said Ajit.

So I learned to keep house by myself, and since there was no one to teach me, although Ajit did his best, I learned the hard way. The fact that we were so far from a bazaar made it even more difficult for me.

Once a week I walked two miles through broiling heat to the ration shop to buy our wheat and rice. I took this home, spread it on a tray and spent several hours painstakingly picking out all the stones and other debris. Then I walked back to the miller, who lived next door to the ration shop, and handed him the precious wheat ration for grinding. I dared not entrust this task to anyone else since they would surely steal part of the ration. It was Kamala, however, who showed me how to avoid being swindled in another fashion. She happened to be in the mill one day and she showed me how to feel the flour from time to time, as it poured out of the grinder into the bag, in order to be certain that I was given wheat flour, instead of some inferior flour from a cheap grain already placed in the machine.

At first, Ajit accompanied me to the bazaar, but as he was on his feet all day, to go into town in the evening became a burden. Further, the city had now relapsed into its usual calm and the police put away their rifles and returned to their traffic direction. Every other day, therefore, I made the trip to town for vegetables and fruit. I soon learned to bargain – but it took hours, and the walk from the bus stop to the flat seemed to get longer as the days passed and the heat and humidity increased.

No washerman was prepared to come so far out of town to collect our laundry, so I learned to wash the clothes, sitting on my heels in the bathroom and pounding the garments on the stone floor; and I got used to wielding an iron while sweat rolled off me.

Life seemed to be an endless circuit of work to be done and heavy loads to be carried; pain in my back and legs from doing all my tasks while squatting on my heels became my constant companion. I searched in vain in the bazaars for dishpans and brooms with handles – no one had ever heard of such peculiar things. Then dysentery struck at me, and with it came a lassitude that made a walk across a room seem too great a task to be undertaken.

Ajit had not been able to show me how to make chupaties properly. It was an art which eluded both of us, with the result that as long as the rice ration lasted, we ate rice with our meals. When that was finished, we made different kinds of fried breads although these were too rich for daily consumption. Kamala showed me how to make village chupaties, but this heavy, indigestible bread was meant for men who worked all day in the fields and was not very palatable to us.

One afternoon, sickened at the idea of again eating rice for dinner, I tucked myself into a sari and went to the city.

The heat was a raging animal that clawed at my hair and clung to my legs so that it was hard to drag one after the other, and I was exhausted by the time I crawled into the bus, but I was determined to buy some European bread, which I knew was sold free of ration coupons in the Muslim bazaar if one was prepared to pay enough for it.

The Muslim baker, whose shop was on the edge of the bazaar, knew me because I had bought biscuits and cake from him once or twice before, and when I said I wanted bread but had no coupons, he merely looked resigned, gave me two loaves and charged me double the usual price.

The loaves smelled delicious and I took up the parcel lovingly and turned towards the door. The door seemed to recede from me, the floor spun under my feet and I fainted.

I heard a man's voice in the distance shouting: 'Ma ji, Ma ji.' Far away, there was a heavy flip-flap of sandals, I was lifted up, and a long time afterwards there was the feel of water on my face.

'Allah be praised,' said a voice in my ear.

I opened my eyes. Three faces floated before me – a bearded man's, a fat female's swathed in dirty veiling, and the Madonna herself.

I shut my eyes again – I was so tired. Someone chafed my hands.

Wearily I forced my eyes open. I could not remember where I was, but I did not care much. If only I could sleep.

Above me was a low, dark ceiling, smothered with cobwebs.

The woman clucked with satisfaction and exclaimed over the light colour of my eyes.

I lifted myself on one elbow. The Madonna became a young girl with a face so innocent that it was not surprising that I had mistaken her for the Mother of God. She was heavy with child, her shirt pulling tightly over her swollen figure.

An old lady was rubbing my hands, her bracelets and earrings jingling as she worked. She smiled like the sun when she saw that I was recovering, her pan-stained teeth gleaming blackly in the poor light.

The man with the beard was, of course, the baker and he retreated to the shop immediately I raised myself up.

I was lying on some sacks in a grain storeroom, and I hastily swung my feet to the floor and made as if to get up, but the two women restrained me firmly.

With their hands upon me, I remembered that I was a Hindu woman in the Muslim quarter, that my value in the white slave market was enormous and that no one knew where I was.

I pushed the women aside and jumped to my feet, but the room dissolved around me and I must have fainted again.

Chapter Twenty-six

When Ajit arrived home from work and saw the big padlock on the front door, he realised at once I must be out. I had never failed before to be at home when he returned from his work, and while he unlocked and entered he was already anxious about my absence. He guessed that I had gone into the city – and he remembered the smouldering unrest there. He prowled into the kitchen – no sign of cooking – I must have been gone for some time. His throat went dry, as he remembered the panwallah's warning about the presence of dacoits from the east; it would be easy to kidnap a woman walking by herself in the bush. A sweat of fright redamped his shirt.

He went to the veranda to peer down the track to the city, and reproached himself bitterly for failing to accompany me to the bazaar. There was no sign of me along the path. He looked at his watch – the next bus from the city was just due to arrive at the Pandipura terminus, and, as I might be in it, he decided to wait for fifteen minutes before setting out in search of me – it would take that long for me to walk from the bus stop to a point where he would be able to see my approach from the veranda.

Far away, down the track, two moving clouds of dust appeared above the thorns.

'Bullock carts – or tongas,' thought Ajit. 'I can ask if they have seen a white woman anywhere along the track – or perhaps she has hired herself a tonga.' His fear turned to annoyance – I should have told him I was going out. Irritably, he kicked off his sandals.

To fill in the time until the tongas should approach nearer, he prepared a cooking fire for me, and got out the vegetables and spices from the store cupboard ready for the preparation of the evening meal. If only electricity was cheaper, he thought, he could buy an electric stove and I would be saved so much labour. But our electricity bill was already heavy, for light and the running of the fan. Only when the power house was complete could we hope for cheaper power.

The first vehicle, a tonga, arrived quicker than he had expected; and when he heard its bells, he ran down the steps so fast that his next-door neighbours, the three Misses Shah, who were descending from it, were quite overwhelmed by such an enthusiastic reception on their return from holiday.

When he saw who had arrived, all his fear for me returned and his anger was quenched. Courtesy demanded, however, that he should help the ladies, so he advanced and called as cheerful a greeting as he could.

He was immediately enveloped in a whirl of gaily coloured saris and flying pigtails. How was he? How was his wife? They had had a wonderful rest in the hills; dear papa and mama were happily settled up there. Had he any change with which to tip the tongawallah? Would he mind lifting that trunk out of the way of the wheels?

It was not surprising that he failed to hear the jingling of the second vehicle – another tonga; and he jumped when a horse neighed close to him and a vaguely familiar voice called: 'Sahib.'

To the disgust of the eldest Miss Shah, her best tin trunk was dropped into the sand as if it was a bomb, and their neighbour leaped to the back of the second tonga.

'Peggie,' he cried, 'Peggie, are you all right? Ramji, you do look white. What has happened?'

I was laden with newspaper parcels and I dimpled wickedly at Ajit's discomfiture, as I waited for Mohamed Ali to open the door.

'Of course I'm all right, love,' I said. 'Just help me down and pay this man – he has been very kind.' I handed out to Ajit a large parcel and said cryptically: 'Forbidden fruit – be very careful how you handle it.'

Mystified, he laid it and the other parcels in the sand and helped me down. I was still rather unsteady and clung to him for support, while the Misses Shah, silenced for once, watched with interest.

Ajit produced four rupees from his pocket and handed them to the driver.

Mohamed Ali's beard twitched as if he was smiling and he salaamed, then he shouted to the other tongawallah to be careful while he turned. I hastily grabbed my precious parcels before they were trampled by the horses, and looked expectantly at the other ladies.

Ajit introduced them, and in perfect English they chorused their welcome to Shahpur.

They were plain women, their hair drawn stiffly back from their faces into long pigtails. No flowers were tucked into the pigtails and no jewellery relieved the solidarity of their square faces; and yet they had charm. Unlike most Indian women, they looked at me straightly. No side glances or coquetry for them; plain honesty had written itself into their expressions.

I assured them that I was most pleased to have such pleasant neighbours, and I motioned to Ajit to move their luggage on to their veranda, while I invited them into our flat for tea before they unpacked.

After a polite flutter of refusals, they were persuaded into our living-room where they hopped about like budgerigars from one English ornament to another, while I put the water to boil and brought in cups and saucers. I still felt dizzy and occasionally the floor heaved under my feet, but I was enjoying the sudden feminine invasion very much.

They declared the English method of making tea far superior to their own and smacked their lips appreciatively as they sipped, although I doubt if they really liked it.

Finally, armed with a water pot of cooled water from our kitchen and some boiled milk, they departed to unpack, and I was alone with Ajit.

He also had enjoyed the fresh company, but occasionally I saw him glance at me anxiously over his teacup, and now the flat was quiet again, he asked: 'What happened, old girl?'

I told him, and finished up by saying: 'I thought they were trying to keep me by force and I was terrified, but they were only making tea for me and wanted me to rest until it was ready. They brought me English fruit cake and a cup of spiced tea, and sat on the floor of the granary and talked so sweetly while I ate.

'They afterwards sent for a tongawallah, who is a relation, and it turned out to be the same man who brought us here. He recognised me. The old mother said that it was he who was beaten up, that he had been attacked while driving back from our flat. He believed the attack was made by thieves from the Criminal Tribe village – unfortunately the rumour went round the bazaar that the Sikhs had done it, so some young rowdies burned down a Sikh house. The police made a lot of trouble about it.'

'Thank God you are safe,' said Ajit fervently. 'Anything could have happened in such a situation.'

'I was perfectly safe. No two women could have been more ingenuous.

The baker seemed upset at their telling me about the attack on Mohamed Ali – just annoyance over the chattering of women, I suspect – ' and I looked at Ajit with a twinkle in my eye.

Ajit did not laugh. He said: 'You are now to get into bed and I will cook a dinner. The dysentery and hard work have damaged you – tomorrow I will obtain a doctor.'

And in spite of protests, to bed I went. It was a blessed relief to lie down and I must have fallen into a light sleep, because it seemed no time before Ajit was standing in front of me with a hot dish of rice and lentils.

He looked tired, but when we had eaten together sitting cross-legged on the bed, he felt better and said he would walk for a few minutes in the breeze outside. I agreed and lay back on the bed. He lit his pipe and went outside.

The eldest Miss Shah must have been sitting on the steps of her flat because I heard her ask: 'Where is Mrs Singh?'

'She is sleeping,' said Ajit, in English. 'She is not very well.'

'Can I help her?' asked Miss Shah.

Ajit hesitated and said: 'I think not, thank you. The transition from one kind of food to another has upset her.'

'I will come and see her in the morning,' said Miss Shah.

My heart warmed to my new neighbour.

Ajit had told me about the three sisters, whose acquaintance he had made during his first week in the flat. When the University closed for the summer months, they went away to visit their parents at a small hill station. The family were refugees from West Pakistan. The girls had no brothers or uncles to help them, and the two elder sisters maintained their parents and the youngest sister by lecturing in English. A small cottage in the hills was all that remained of their ancestral property after the partition of India, and there they had established their aged parents, who would have found the heat of Shahpur hard to bear.

Although the sisters lived in Shahpur without the protection of a male relative, they were respected by their neighbours and few scandalous stories had been invented about them.

Ajit came in, kissed me and took the dishes away to wash. I knew that to him the washing of kitchen vessels was a humiliating task, beneath the dignity of a member of his caste and family, and I loved him for doing it.

Afterwards, as I was still awake, he brought pen and paper to my bed and sat cross-legged by my feet while he wrote his weekly salutations to his mother, adding that I was far from well. I protested that he should not bother her with such news, that I would be well by morning, but he insisted that his parents should know something of the struggle I was having.

I must have fallen asleep in the middle of the argument, because the next thing that I remember was awakening to broad daylight and the sound of peasant voices in the kitchen.

The long sleep had done me good, and I got out of bed and wrapped a shawl round me. I saw that a mat had been spread in a corner of the bedroom and a rumpled sheet on it indicated that Ajit had slept on the floor rather than disturb me by getting into the bed.

In the kitchen Ajit was talking to Kamala and a bent, old woman. It appeared that they had just come to an agreement, because Kamala said: 'All right,' with some satisfaction.

A fire was burning and a closed pot on it gave out a bubbling sound. Beside the little stove, on the floor, was a plate of buttered toast and a vessel of hot milk.

'Darling,' I said, a catch in my voice.

Ajit turned. 'Hey, Rani, you are supposed to stay in bed.'

I smiled at him and at Kamala. 'I feel better. What are you talking about to Kamala?'

'I saw her passing early this morning and told her you were ill, so she brought this woman – she is a sweeper and has agreed to sweep the house, wash the vessels, clean the grain and take it to the miller, and make your lunchtime cooking fire. Kamala says that now Miss Shah is back, a sweeper will come daily to clean the lavatory and remove the rubbish, and a washerman will come to collect in a day or two, when the other families get back.'

I was so pleased, and it was arranged that the old woman would return later. Apparently she worked in this manner for several families in the block of flats, and she would go to Miss Shah's first.

I lifted the lid of the pan on the fire. Two eggs were bouncing merrily in it. Ajit had discovered the forbidden fruit with which I had returned the previous evening. I had put the parcel in the cupboard and forgotten about them in the arrival of the Misses Shah. I closed the lid quickly, before Kamala and my new servant saw the eggs. I did not want to lose a friend and a servant at one stroke.

The two women went away, and Ajit made me sit on the kitchen stool while he served me with egg, toast and tea, after which he ate himself. His consideration for me was touching, and I could not eat until I had given him a hug that would have put a grizzly bear to shame.

He asked me where I obtained the eggs, and I told him that while I was drinking tea in the baker's granary a man had come in bringing a great basketful, and I had found my mouth watering and had been unable to resist the temptation to purchase some from the baker. He had offered to supply me regularly.

Ajit looked perplexed. He feared that if it was discovered that we had eggs in the house we would lose our tenancy and have difficulty finding other accommodation.

'I could dry the shells, grind them and throw them out with the ashes from the stoves,' I suggested.

'I suppose that would be all right,' he said reluctantly.

I sent him off to work that day with assurances that I was much better, but in truth my legs felt as if they would dissolve under me at any moment and the dysentery was threatening a fresh onslaught.

The eldest Miss Shah called before going to the college, to inquire how I was, and I assured her I was better. I told her ruefully about my inadequacy as a cook, and she offered to teach me. She cooked daily a meal at ten in the morning and another at about nine at night, so for over a week, as soon as Ajit had gone to work, I went into her kitchen and watched her cook. I learned much which I put to good use, but she did not know the dishes of Ajit's province nor was she able to make good chupaties.

'Dear Mother always made the bread when she was with us, and I have never learned the art. As I have not much time in which to cook we manage by eating rice.'

I nodded sympathetically.

'I find,' I said, 'that all food turns bad within a couple of hours of cooking. Is there any way of keeping food fresh from one meal to another? It would be such a help if I could prepare food in advance sometimes.'

Miss Shah looked disgusted at the idea of keeping food and said: 'Indeed, no. All food must be prepared freshly for each meal, including bread. It is dangerous to eat old food.'

Reluctantly I agreed with her. Only the previous evening I had put some lentil soup into a covered bowl in the hope that it would stay good until morning, and had found upon getting up that it was rotten throughout. Refrigeration would be the only safe way in which to keep food fresh – and a refrigerator was beyond the dreams of avarice.

Letters from my parents had been awaiting my arrival, but it was on the day of Miss Shah's visit that the postman brought me the first letter from Angela. I tore open the envelope before the postman's slippers had given a final flip-flap on the bottom step of the veranda.

After saying that she was glad I had arrived safely and how much she missed me, she wrote: 'Wu has been very kind. He has called several times bringing flowers, which amuses me very much. Father does not like him at all – keeps saying he wishes the fellow would go away – and yet he is so courteous that Father cannot snub him. Personally I find him refreshingly charming – he is a realist and a poet.'

I remembered the careful arrangement of the room Ajit and I had shared at the inn on the first night of our marriage. A poet and a realist had combined to arrange it. I scanned the letter again. I was pleased that Wu's friendship with Angela was progressing, but as for Father – poor Father must be afraid of losing another daughter to an oriental.

Having a woman to help me, dirty and inefficient as she was, proved a great comfort, but lead weights dragged at my legs and the dysentery did not lessen. Even to cook and to go to the city to shop became nightmares of effort, and I did not protest when a few days later Ajit brought a doctor home with him.

'This is Dr Venketraman,' he said as he ushered into the living-room a tall, black man.

I bade the doctor seat himself, which he did after placing his bag carefully on the table. 'And now, Madam,' he said as he removed an outsized pair of horn-rimmed spectacles from his nose, 'how can I help you?'

His dark face creased with polite solicitude and his extraordinarily black eyes ranged over me as I explained my symptoms.

He diagnosed dysentery, asked us to send our non-existent servant to his dispensary for medicines, and decreed a diet of curd and rice.

'What a queer man,' I said, as Ajit shut the door behind him. 'Is he a Negro?'

'No. He is from the south. Many of them are dark and curly-haired.' He put his arm round my waist and kissed me. 'I will fetch the medicine after dinner.'

For weeks the doctor and I waged war against dysentery. Sometimes it left me for a few days only to come again with greater vigour. I grew thinner and weaker, while Ajit became more and more worried.

The other tenants of the flats returned from their holidays and, without exception, curiosity drove the ladies to call upon me, regardless of whether they were elderly, orthodox and disapproving or young and highly experimental. They all knew different cures for dysentery but none of them cured. Many of the ladies, as the dampness of the rainy season approached and the mosquitoes came out of hiding, went down with malaria, but I was spared this as I did not fear to take modern drugs.

The unremitting kindness of people round me, from Kamala, who often shopped for me in the city and charged me only a small percentage on the goods she bought, to the Misses Shah, who brought me books and company, was overwhelming. Ajit, harassed at the power house by the slowness and inefficiency of the men under him and by his own limited experience, never murmured about the lateness of his meals or the general discomfort of his home. Night after night he massaged my aching legs when he must have been exhausted himself from much standing in the summer heat, and as he rubbed he told me funny stories of the day's doings. I laughed to please him and to see the smile of relief in his eyes when he heard me chuckle.

So, through the cruel Indian summer, we clung to each other and wondered how long we could endure without breaking.

Chapter Twenty-seven

Just before the monsoon broke, when the weather had become intolerably humid, a peon in a white uniform and a scarlet sash presented himself at Ajit's office. He brought a letter from Chundabhai Patel, announcing his return to Shahpur from England and asking us to take dinner with him.

Ajit scribbled an acceptance, as I was a little better and he thought I would enjoy meeting an old friend. He suspected that Chundabhai would be more than glad to see us, as it was likely that he would be finding it difficult to readjust himself to Indian life, despite the ease which his father's wealth purchased for him.

Chundabhai was a Vaisya by caste and a Jain by religion; that is, he was of a lower caste than Ajit and his religious beliefs demanded that he should take no life and in consequence be a strict vegetarian. The last time we saw him in England was when he was sitting in a Manchester eating-house, famous for its steak and kidney pies, ordering a second helping of this delectable dish. On the table before him was a tankard of beer, and by his side sat his red-headed sweetheart, Sheila. In Shahpur there would be no beer, since prohibition reigned, and no Sheila, because he had been married since he was fifteen.

We were both excited at the prospect of visiting someone other than the families who lived in our isolated block of flats, and both of us longed to talk to an old friend.

'I will hire a tonga to take us,' Ajit said. 'Even if you were well, the heat at present is too great for walking.'

On the morning of the day of the dinner party Chundabhai's peon again presented himself and announced that Chundabhai would be sending a car for us, as he felt that the long journey to the other side of the city would be arduous, if we travelled by bus.

With trembling hands, I dressed myself carefully for the occasion, and Ajit declared that I looked like Sita herself. Make-up could not hide the drawn look of my face, but I did not oil my hair that day and instead let it curl softly round my face. I loathed the daily oil bath that the hot, dry climate made necessary, and was glad to abandon the practice for one day.

When Chundabhai's car arrived, the Misses Shah came out on to their veranda to wave us farewell; they were nearly as excited as we were and looked forward to enjoying our visit at second-hand, as soon as we could return and tell them about it.

We drove across the city through the narrow, busy streets and then out into a district where houses bigger than most dwellings in England were set apart from each other amid groves of trees. We were swept through high gates where a khaki-clad watchman sat staff in hand like a petty king, up a long drive lined with trees and eventually came to a stop before a wide flight of steps.

A peon opened the car door, and I looked out at a fairytale palace with pure white walls, marble verandas and teak doors. It was surrounded by shade trees through which the setting sun hardly penetrated. It was cool as I stepped out of the car, heavenly cool.

We followed a bearer through the porticoed frontage, through double doors flung wide open and into an immense circular hall, round the sides of which curved a staircase leading to a series of galleries above. In the centre of the hall a fountain played in a pool covered with water-lilies.

Ajit grinned at me slyly when he saw the wonderment on my face as we mounted the stairs, passing as we ascended a series of niches in the wall in which sat stone gods carved in meticulous detail. From above came the sound of a very loud voice shouting in Gujerati. It was not an angry voice – but certainly Chundabhai had not lost his vocal cords since we last saw him.

We entered a large, square room, where about a dozen ladies and gentlemen were seated on settees and drinking tomato-juice cocktails. In the middle of a pink Chinese carpet stood Chundabhai talking to four ladies of most sophisticated appearance. Chundabhai looked like a straining village ox amongst delicate ivory figurines; but there was nothing oxlike in the shrewd, hazel eyes glowing in the bullet head which crowned his mountain of a body. He was garbed in the handwoven cotton shirt and loincloth beloved of Congressmen, and his broad feet were slipped loosely into leather sandals.

At our entrance he stopped in the middle of a sentence, excused himself and strode across the floor to us.

'Welcome, welcome,' he boomed as he folded his hands together in salute. 'Singh, it is good to see you again – and Mrs Singh – how beautiful you look in a sari,' and he whispered impishly, 'Some men have all the luck. You must meet my wife.'

At the top of his voice he called his wife, and a voice at his elbow said: 'I am here.' A tiny, hard-faced woman came forward. She looked rather grim, but she was an accomplished hostess and carried me off to meet the other ladies present.

Ajit had told me that it was well known that Mrs Patel did not approve of her husband and, in fact, it was hard to find anything of which she did approve. There were no children of the marriage, and the story went that examination by specialists had showed that Chundabhai was at fault, which did not make his wife more tolerant of him; and they quarrelled frequently. Chundabhai had lingered abroad longer than he need, I knew, and I could see bitterness between his wife and him.

With frigid courtesy Mrs Patel conducted me round the room, which in its furnishings was a graceful mixture of Indian and English styles, and introduced me in a formal fashion to the other ladies.

Two young women dressed in the briefest of blouses and the most transparent of saris, having eyed me up and down rather insolently during Mrs Patel's introduction, made room for me on the red upholstered settee on which they were reclining. I sank down thankfully, still panting a little from the climb up the staircase.

The girls by whom I sat proved to be less sophisticated than their dress indicated. Their English was good and they were soon confiding to me that Chundabhai's dinners were always a bore, firstly, because his wife was such a spoilsport and, secondly, because no meat or alcohol were served. I was amused by their complaints and, having accepted a glass of tomato juice brought to me on a silver tray by a bearer, I sat back and prepared to enjoy myself.

The young ladies bent their flowerladen heads close to my ears and asked confidentially if I ate meat.

'No,' I said, having been previously primed on this point by Ajit, 'neither my husband nor I eat meat.'

Disappointed they drew back from me, only to lean forward again and whisper: 'Do you drink?'

To comfort them and gain their confidence, I said: 'I enjoy a glass of wine.'

Morbid interest sprang into their eyes.

'Do you drink whisky?' they asked in chorus.

'No. Not many English ladies do – and here you have prohibition – so I am reduced to tomato juice.'

They sniggered. 'Aha, you do not know the secret,' exclaimed one, wagging her forefinger. 'Plenty of drinks are available – if you know where to look – but first you must go to the Civil Surgeon and be registered as an addict.'

'An addict?'

'Yes, then you can get a legal drink ration. After that you can buy on the black-market – and if you are found drunk you can always say that you drank all your ration in one day.' The lilting voice was full of laughter, and the speaker leaned closer to me to whisper into my ear a very improper story of the drunkenness of one of the ladies present. 'She employs two ayahs for the sole purpose of putting her to bed when she is drunk,' she finished up.

I was feeling very embarrassed at the malicious gossip poured into my ears, when a bearer announced to my relief that dinner was ready, and the guests rose and moved through an archway which had hitherto been curtained.

When I passed under the archway, I exclaimed with delight. I found myself on a large veranda round which the treetops swayed in the wind. A gold sovereign of a moon lit up the marble balustrade and floor. In the centre of the veranda, a dinner table had been set, and we ranged ourselves informally round it.

The servants under the direction of a bearer in a turban brought each guest a beaten silver tray on which lay the usual cups of curry and heaps of chutney, rice and puris. It looked most inviting and the guests ate with enjoyment, although one of my new acquaintances pulled a face at me across the table and mouthed the words: 'No meat.'

I was still clumsy at eating with my hands and I looked round my tray for a spoon but there was none. Cautiously I tore a puri, being careful to use only my right hand, and began to eat, but I dropped a morsel of curry on the cloth. Blushing with embarrassment, I tried to remember the Gujerati word for spoon so that I could ask a servant for one, but it evaded me. I could not remember it either in that language or in Hindi.

After a minute of quiet struggling on my part, a voice rolled down the table: 'Mrs Singh, can I order anything that you would like to eat? Our curries are peculiar, I know.'

I jumped. I had forgotten the watchful eye of my host, beside whom Ajit was sitting.

Feeling my cheeks burning with blushes, I said: 'Patel Sahib, the curries are delicious but I am clumsy at eating with my hands. Would you kindly ask the bearer for a spoon.'

At this there was a burst of good-natured merriment from everybody, and the lady and gentleman sitting next to me both turned and said reproachfully: 'You should have told us. We would have asked for a spoon for you.'

The concern on their faces was almost ludicrous, and they spent the rest of the time at table making me feel at home, while Chundabhai kept sending the bearer to me with dishes that he thought I might like. Occasionally he shouted a cheerful query at me or teased the couple looking after me, who proved to be husband and wife. The husband was an astronomer and his wife, though not so well qualified, worked with him. The husband had educated his wife after marriage, and I was impressed with the earnestness with which she must have studied, just as I was daily impressed by the patient application of the Shah sisters.

I listened with interest to an account of the astronomer's work given by his wife. It was much interrupted, she said, by visits of important people, political leaders and Government officials.

'These people,' said the little wife with a laugh, 'they come expecting to see weird instruments making big noise. They are disappointed if my husband is not always looking through telescope – if he do the calculation or sit and think they imagine he not work. They think this man play with paper and pencil and waste good Government money. Jobs we must have and our student they must keep their scholarships, so we no disappoint our visitors. We make excellent assembly of noisy instruments with which visitors can play.' She waved her hands and shrugged her shoulders. 'Then we work at evening when no visitors come and it is quiet.'

I laughed heartily at this recital, although the husband looked somewhat disapproving. I could well imagine Members of the Opposition in England bouncing out of their parliamentary seats to ask why Government funds were being wasted on astronomers who spent their time doodling, it seemed, or sitting in an easy chair doing nothing.

After dinner two servants brought a brass ewer filled with water, and a basin and towels. Each guest washed his hands by holding them over a bowl while a servant poured water over them.

It was while waiting to perform this ceremony that I found myself standing next to Chundabhai, a little apart from the other guests. He was staring through me, quite oblivious of his surroundings.

I said: 'It must seem strange to be catapulted back into India after so long in England.'

He jumped, looked at me gently and said: 'Indeed, Peggie, it is very strange – although this is my home and these are my people – and my true life is here.'

I thought of Sheila Ferguson and perhaps he did at the same time for he said quickly: 'I cannot expect to have everything in life – I have so much.'

I remembered Sheila's adorable roundness and her irrepressible laughter in comparison with Mrs Patel's frozen disappointment in life. If he had cared to invoke the old Hindu law, he could have replaced his wife by sending her elsewhere to live, and marrying Sheila as his second wife.

'Chundy, you are very good,' I said impulsively.

He grinned at me wickedly: 'My coat of virtue is thin,' he said. 'Go forward, Mrs Singh, and wash your hands – a brass bowl is at least a change from porcelain.'

Chundabhai moved over to a knot of male guests and began to tell one of his interminable funny stories. From the expressions on the faces of the guests it was obvious to me that they had heard the story before, but as a rich man's jokes are always funny they laughed uproariously, and Chundabhai beamed once more.

Mrs Patel came over to say a few words to me. She gave the impression of long since having lost all warmth of feeling for other people. When I considered her in conjuction with her husband I pitied her. Her marriage, I thought, would have been arranged by her father when she was about fourteen; it had been, I knew, the union of two great families of chemical manufacturers, and would have appeared a good match to an outsider. But even at fifteen Chundabhai must have been big and awkward; his tremendous desire to try everything, to explore, to take to himself all that life could give a rich man's son, must have frightened still more a terrified, purdah-bred fourteen-year-old. She must have feared his huge hands and the cold clarity of the brain that dictated their movements, and she must have shrunk away mentally and physically. And then to have no child would humiliate her in the eyes of her friends and complete her misery. Chundabhai needed someone tough and passionate like Sheila, not a shy young girl who had become a frigid, disillusioned woman.

The object of my reverie asked me how I liked India and whether my Hindi was sufficient to enable me to talk to my mother-in-law and sisters-in-law.

I said I was very happy in India, although I was having the normal difficulties of a newcomer. Absent-mindedly I added: 'As yet I have not met Ajit's family.'

Mrs Patel's eyebrows shot up and I realised my mistake too late. The implications of my remark were manifold.

'I came straight from Bombay to Shahpur, as Ajit had to take up a post here,' I said hastily.

'Doubtless one of your sisters-in-law came to help you start your new home?'

I could feel my face reddening. Damn Ajit's family, I thought.

'No,' I said sharply, 'my sister-in-law was not free to come.'

At that moment there was a stir as the guests prepared to leave, and I immediately got up from my chair. Mrs Patel realised that she had embarrassed me and said politely: 'Please call on me if I can be of help.'

I thanked her, and in the turmoil of farewells my face had a chance to recover its former whiteness; but a bitterness cankered in me as I thought of the indifference of Ajit's family. I had done them no harm but they were making me suffer a dozen steady pinpricks. A little help and advice from one of them would have saved me a lot of suffering.

In the car going home, Ajit mentioned that Chundabhai had asked him to have a look at the recording instruments in his works, and this might mean later a place as consultant and consequently more money for saris and blouses. I smiled and kissed him.

'As a Government servant, will you be allowed to be a consultant?'

'Probably not – but I am looking at this from a long-term point of view – I have a five-year contract with the Government at present – and after that possibly there will be other openings elsewhere. I do not want you to spend your life sweating in Shahpur. We shall see.'

'I like Shahpur,' I said. 'I like Pandipura – and the desert – and the wild animals – and the country people.'

Ajit looked down at me in astonishment. 'Do you really?'

'Yes,' I said.

'Well, I'm damned,' he said incredulously.

The next day, however, I was not interested in saris or Shahpur or anything else. The rich meal which I had foolishly eaten at Chundabhai's made me ill again, and after struggling to get Ajit's breakfast I crept back on to my bed.

Ajit promised to send the power-house peon for the doctor.

Chapter Twenty-eight

The last of the monsoon rain was dripping off the roofs of Delhi when a bored Bimla decided to call on Nulini. When she arrived at Ram Singh's house, however, she found that her friend had gone to a purdah party.

'Ma ji is at home,' Thakkur informed her, having explained about Nulini's absence.

'I will come in and see her for a few minutes.'

Thakkur escorted her through the house to the inner courtyard, her Ayah trotting behind them and noting that Khan was sitting with his hands folded in his lap, by the door leading to the courtyard. He scrambled to his feet and salaamed as Bimla passed.

Mrs Singh was sitting in a basket chair in the driest corner of the veranda. She held a letter in her hand and had just finished reading it; her generously curved mouth drooped and she was nodding her head disconsolately from side to side.

She greeted Bimla rather absent-mindedly, invited her to sit down on the chair beside her and then continued to stare silently at the letter.

She suddenly realised that she had a guest, and abruptly thanked Bimla for the invitation to her wedding, which, accompanied by a personal note from Bimla's father, had arrived that day; after which effort at conversation she again relapsed into silence.

Bimla made herself comfortable in her chair and wondered what bad news was contained in the letter. Mrs Singh was certainly far from being her usual gracious self. Although there was a great difference in age between the two women, there was an odd intimacy between them. After her hot-tempered mother, Bimla found Mrs Singh a sweet and loving confidante who listened to her childish woes as her mother never had the patience to do; and to Mrs Singh, Bimla had always been a prospective daughter-in-law whose beauty and honesty would one day grace her house. After a gloomy minute or two, therefore, Bimla ventured to ask if Mrs Singh had any news of Ajit – Bimla was now fully engrossed by her new fiancé and could think of Ajit with comfortable condescension.

Silently Mrs Singh handed the letter to Bimla.

Bimla glanced over it.

Ajit sent his best respects to his mother and father. His work was progressing satisfactorily. Peggie was still ill. A kind neighbour was helping to take care of her. And that was all.

Bimla returned the letter without comment, and for some time they surveyed the garden glittering with raindrops.

'It is a hard family,' said Mrs Singh at last, 'that will not send a member to one who is sick. And these neighbours – who are they? The Gods only know what stupid things they will do – she might die.'

'You have been very patient . . .' Bimla began cautiously, but her remark was cut off as Shushila bounced up the steps, her sandals covered with mud and her hands full of wet, white flowers.

'Mummy, Mummy,' she cried, 'I want to go to the bazaar with

Thakkur. He says in two days it is Ruksha Bandhan.' She dumped the flowers in her mother's lap, and went on importantly, 'I must prepare for it. All must be ready for Ajit and Bhim.'

Her mother smiled sadly. In their caste at this most important Festival all the young men renewed their vows to protect their womenfolk with their lives, and such protection could be claimed by any other woman if she placed a bracelet on the wrist of a young warrior.

'Hullo, Bimla,' said Shushila, her mind full of thoughts of the Festival, as she rubbed her cheek impatiently against her mother's shoulder, and then went on to announce that she must go immediately and buy two bright, tinsel bracelets to place on her brothers' arms. Would Mother also please give her some vermilion and could Maharaj give her some raw rice, so that she could make good caste marks for them? She would then have two mighty warriors to protect her. And would Maharaj make lots of sweetmeats, and please could they all go to the pictures together in the evening?

Finally, as her mother made no answer, she asked: 'Are you cross, Mummy?' and Thakkur, standing in the mud outside, eyed his mistress curiously.

'No, Shushi,' she said as she straightened the child's Turkish trousers and shirt. 'Unfortunately Ajit will not be able to come for Ruksha Bandhan this year.'

Shushila was shocked. 'But, Mummy,' she wailed, 'it's the first time I could play bracelets with him – he is naughty,' and she stamped her foot. The plump face crinkled up and tears threatened.

'Well – ' said her mother uncertainly, 'Bhim will certainly be here – and you could buy two bracelets, in case Ajit is able to come after all.' Her voice trailed away. She did not know what to tell Shushila. Although it was a choice titbit for gossip, the secret of Ajit's marriage had been well kept, both by the Singhs and the Chand Ranas. For once, Kasher Chand Rana had asserted himself in his own house, and had said grimly that his wife and daughter must be silent on the subject, otherwise Bimla would lose her second chance of a marriage. Ram Singh, Mrs Singh and Bhim had told no one, and though a faint rumour seemed to have gone round the neighbourhood it had apparently died.

Once she had recovered from the shock of the news of Ajit's marriage, Bimla had enjoyed herself, as Kasher Chand Rana, being wiser than his daughter realised, had allowed Ajit's handsome cousin to court his future wife. The boy really loved her and courted her with remarkable skill, with the result that Bimla had suddenly become quite dovelike.

Bimla's Ayah had presented a problem to Kasher, as her tongue was very likely to wag. He had, therefore, sent for her and with the air of a conspirator, had explained that for Bimla's sake nothing must at present be said about Ajit's affairs. Ayah could, however, be most helpful if she would let it be known in the course of casual gossip that, on meeting again, Bimla and Ajit had not felt suited to each other, and as the parents wished only for their children's happiness, a fresh suitor had been found. Delighted at being asked a favour by her master, the old Ayah had fulfilled the commission with an ability born of long practice in the art of gossip.

'Go with Thakkur,' said Mrs Singh to Shushila, 'and choose two pretty bracelets. I will also give you some annas to buy glass bracelets for yourself. Look,' she went on, trying to sound gay as she lifted up one fat wrist on which only two gold bracelets remained, 'look, you haven't a single glass bracelet left to match your dress.'

Shushila giggled. 'I broke the last one fighting with cousin Ranji,' she said.

Her mother opened her handbag and took out a rupee. Shushila joyfully snatched it away and ran down the steps to join Thakkur.

Bimla had been silent during Shushila's presence, except for acknowledging the child's greeting. Now she said: 'What a fine handbag that is.'

Mrs Singh nodded and clicked it shut. 'Yes, Ajit brought it from England.'

Ajit had told her that Peggie had helped to choose it. Now Mrs Singh looked at it again. Someone had really given consideration to her requirements. The bag was white and finished in such a way as to be washable and, although elegant in design, it had many pockets and sections, such as are loved by housewives.

Idly she opened the bag again and her slender fingers poked about in it. Bimla saw her expression change suddenly. She poked more purposefully and then drew out a small card. She turned it over slowly in her hand, and Bimla got up from her chair and came over to see what she had found.

The card had silver flowers embossed upon it and also something written in ink. Mrs Singh could not read the English words, so she handed the card to Bimla. 'What does it say?'

Bimla read out: 'To dearest Mother, with much love, Ajit and Peggie.' She translated it into Hindi.

'Hey, Ramji,' exclaimed Mrs Singh. It was not the kind of message which an Indian daughter-in-law would have penned, but the kindly meaning of it was undoubted.

'Dearest Mother,' repeated Mrs Singh thoughtfully and pursed her lips.

Bimla stared at the message which her rival had written without realising that she was to be ostracised by her dearest Mother. She thought of my lying sick in Shahpur, and she realised that if I had not come into Ajit's life, she would have had to marry him instead of the handsome, romantic boy who was soon to be her husband. She kept silent, however, and Mrs Singh began to speak slowly and reflectively as if talking to herself. 'I am a woman from a small village. When I first came to Delhi to be married my ways were the ways of village people, and my mother-in-law taught me with great patience the ways of the city. We were in purdah and such confinement was new to me – but still we had to know how to make welcome the wives of the English and the wives of the powerful.' Mrs Singh laughed softly. 'I remember she had a special tea set for casteless visitors – it was kept in a special cupboard by itself, so that our vessels should not be polluted. So much she taught me – and I? Arree, what have I done for my daughter-in-law?'

'She is not of your caste,' said Bimla.

'Caste? What is that in these days? My son suffers because his wife suffers. Hey, Ram, what a mess!'

Khan, who had remained placidly seated out of earshot while he waited for his master, now rose and salaamed. Ram Singh swept on to the veranda, inclining his head in acknowledgement of the salaam. He saw his wife and Bimla and came forward to greet them.

Both women hastily covered their heads with their veils. Ram Singh motioned them to remain seated, put down the copy of the Upanishads which he had been carrying, and sat down in the basket chair. 'No tea yet?' he asked querulously.

'It will be coming soon,' Mrs Singh said, and at that moment Thakkur appeared from the direction of the kitchen bearing a tray. He set the tray on a table in front of Mrs Singh and departed, and Ram Singh leaned forward and took a pakaurhi which he stabbed irritably into the chutney.

'I shall have to go up to Simla,' he said. 'There is a land dispute on which I have been asked to give an opinion. Would you like to come too?'

Mrs Singh looked as if she had made up her mind suddenly.

'No. If you are agreeable to it, I should like to visit Jaipur sister while you are away. She has not been well for some time.'

'Sister ill? Is it serious?'

'Oh, no,' said Mrs Singh hastily. 'Just the hot weather has given her fever.'

'If it had not been for this dispute, I could have come with you . . .'

'Oh, no, no,' exclaimed Mrs Singh, 'there is no need for you to come with me. I will take Thakkur.'

'Well, I suggest that you go on the day after Ruksha Bandhan – I shall have to travel on the same day. The change will do you good – you are looking tired.' He took another pakaurhi and munched it more contentedly. 'By all means take Thakkur – have another pakaurhi, Bimla, they are good – how's Rana Sahib?' and he handed her the dish.

Bimla said: 'Quite well, thank you,' and took a pakaurhi. She had retired into the background upon the arrival of Ram Singh, her head covered and her eyes cast discreetly down while she laughed to herself. She had a suspicion that Mrs Singh's destination would not be Jaipur but Shahpur. Of course she would take Thakkur on such an expedition – Thakkur who would have died for her if need be. As a boy, he had come from Mrs Singh's own village and served three generations of Singhs. He loved them all, but his true loyalty was to Mrs Singh. He would certainly disapprove of such an adventure – but he would do as Mrs Singh bade him.

Ram Singh leaned back in his chair and twiddled his moustaches.

'Then it is settled. Nulini and Bhim will take care of Shushila – I do not wish that she should take a journey so soon after the monsoon – too much polluted water about – she might catch typhoid.'

Mrs Singh nodded.

'I will take Khan to Simla – after that he is to go home to be married.' He rambled on, teasing Bimla about her forthcoming marriage and saying that next hot season both families should make an expedition to Nan-y-Tal, since they had not been away this year. She answered shyly that her respected father would no doubt be delighted. She did not, however, hear Ram Singh's rejoinder – her attention had been caught by a movement behind Ram Singh.

Khan had again risen and salaamed. Nulini, returning from her purdah party, came through the house door and on to the veranda. Khan had kept his head down as he salaamed, so he did not see the expression that flashed across Nulini's face – but Bimla saw it.

As she looked down on the servant, her face had become unutterably sad, and then she smiled with a tenderness that Bimla had seen before only on the face of her own fiancé. When passing, her sari brushed Khan's salaaming hands, and when he squatted down again he put his hands against his lips.

The incident was over in a second, and Nulini was advancing towards her, hands together in salute, while the Singhs' Ayah made her appearance through the same door and grumbled that her sandals were soaked and it was too wet for any sensible soul to go visiting. Bimla pulled herself together and greeted her friend, although her heart was beating like a wedding drum. O Lord, so that was how Nulini knew about Ajit's marriage, she thought. A trusted servant could have overheard Ram

Singh lecturing his son – and if the terrible suspicions which filled her mind were true, it was quite likely that Khan had told Nulini.

Bhim was going to pay dearly for his neglect of his scatterbrained wife, Bimla thought. Poor Nulini! She knew that her friend missed the club life which her father had permitted her to enjoy when single. She must have found the Singh household singularly dull, and this, added to Bhim's preoccupation with his work and her lack of a child, must have made her intensely lonely. Mrs Singh had the house to run, Shushila had her lessons and her games with her cousins, but Nulini had nothing to do all day except for a few simple tasks set her by her mother-in-law. She must have turned in despair, driven by the unsatisfied needs of body and mind, to the only love she could find – that of a servant. It was the age-old tragedy all over again – a wife cut off as usual from any other male society had sought a lover in the kitchen – although in this case it seemed more than lust. Bimla visualised again the tender smile and Khan kissing his hands – Ram have mercy on them – they really loved each other.

After exchanging a few politenesses, a very shaky Bimla took leave of the Singhs. She shivered although the weather was warm and sticky, and asked for her own Ayah to be brought from the kitchen. Ram Singh insisted that she should go home in the car and she had to wait a little while until it was brought round to the front door by Khan.

They climbed in, Khan shut the door, got in himself and drove them through the puddly streets. Bimla looked at the back of his proud head and straight shoulders. A warrior from the hills, she guessed, who had come down to the plains to earn some ready money to assist in a family crisis. No wonder Nulini had fallen in love.

But in the Name of God, what would they do to Nulini when her adultery was found out? And it would be found out. Some other eyes as sharp as Bimla's own would notice, and gradually a hasty whisper to someone else would become a crawling rumour, which would grow and grow until it strangled both Khan and Nulini.

Supposing Nulini was thrown out of her father-in-law's house – what then? Probably her father would not take back an adulterous woman, perhaps carrying a bastard child. There was no way, thought Bimla frantically, in which a middle-class woman without a degree could earn a living – except in a brothel. Bimla did not know much about prostitution other than that the women invariably died of revolting diseases; and she reeled as she thought of her friend, silly but not wicked, screaming out her death agony in some back alley.

And Khan? What of him? He would be beaten half to death – as he deserved, thought Bimla savagely – and then thrown into the street, to find his way back to his native mountains as best he could, since he would find it difficult to obtain another job without a reference. He could not help Nulini – supposing even that he was able to take her home, high into the Himalayas, she would die after a few weeks of harsh life as a mountain woman – would die as certainly as if she had remained in Delhi.

Bimla's sly old Ayah asked if she was well.

'Of course I am,' said Bimla testily, as the car drew up in her father's driveway.

Khan got down and opened the door for her. She cast a fleeting glance at him through her veil. He was a sturdy specimen of manhood, though small. The slightly Mongolian cast of feature was not unpleasing and the expression was genial. Bimla wondered what it would be like to be kissed by such a man – and then hastily flung the thought from her as being most unmaidenly. She flinched, however, at the idea of such excellence being beaten into utter ugliness.

Ayah must have looked at him too, because she said as they walked up the front steps: 'If I were Singh Sahib, I would not employ a man such as that in a house where I had a young daughter-in-law. A man of more mature years would be a better choice.'

'What do you mean, Ayah?'

Ayah looked even more cunning than usual: 'Nothing, nothing,' she said. 'You are too young to understand such matters.'

'I am twenty-five and about to marry.'

'Tut, tut, my pretty. Do not be angered. I only made a remark.' And Ayah folded her lips virtuously, picked up the slippers which Bimla had kicked into two different corners of the hall, and went away, leaving Bimla full of dread that Nulini's secret was already out.

Chapter Twenty-nine

At lunchtime, two days after Ruksha Bandhan, as Ajit sat on my bed eating the thick village bread and lentil soup which had been prepared for him by our old sweeper woman, the postman handed him through the window an unusually bulky letter. There was also a letter for me from Mother.

As I had been largely confined to bed for over a fortnight Ajit had moved the bedstead into the living-room, and in this new position I had some hope of seeing, without getting up, what was going on in my neglected home.

Ajit had suspected that the doctor was deliberately not hurrying about curing me, since by his standards we were rich and well able to pay his bills. He had threatened to find another doctor unless I was cured within a fortnight, and whether it was the threat or a fortuitous combination of circumstances, I do not know, but I had become slowly better and for four days there had been no recurrence of the dysentery. I was very weak, however, and had no strength left with which to fight any other disease I might easily catch in such damp weather.

The monsoon had been unusually heavy for the district, and everywhere the earth steamed and gave birth to crops, insects and germs. I had been astonished to see the endless stretches of sand round our house become clothed in a few weeks with a closely patterned carpet of wild flowers and grass, and I longed to go out and walk and drink in the loveliness of it. But I was too weak and had to be content with the bunches of tiny flowers which Ajit stopped to gather for me on his way back from the power house.

Occasionally, I saw a snake slide silently along the path in front of the house, and Ajit warned me that if I found one in the house I was to leave it undisturbed, shut the door of the room in which it lay, and ask Kamala or the watchman to get someone to kill it; non-violence did not extend to snakes.

Typhoid and malaria were frequent visitors to the villages, and, according to Miss Shah, some cases of cholera in the city had made a harassed Director of Health order mass injections, to avoid a repetition of the epidemic of the previous year.

I dragged myself into a sitting position and pushed my damp hair away from my face. My head buzzed, but I asked as cheerfully as I could: 'What have you got there?'

Ajit gulped down the last piece of bread, picked up the letter again and turned it over and over in his hand. The address had been laboriously written in English. He tore open the envelope – and a glittering bundle fell out.

I could see that the bundle consisted of a piece of tinsel, to which was attached shiny red and green paper fringed with gold; a few grains of rice were clinging to the tinsel and there was also a folded paper stained pink and much finger marked. In addition, there was a letter.

'Ruksha Bandhan,' Ajit exclaimed immediately he saw the collection from the envelope. His hands shook as he unfolded the letter.

'It's Shushila,' he said softly, and, after a pause to scan the letter, he added: 'Father did not even ask if I would be free to come home for Ruksha Bandhan.' His mouth quivered, as he reread the letter.

'Darling, what is it?' I asked, slipping my arms round him.

He dropped the letter on to the table and explained the ceremony to me, its importance to his caste and Shushila's disappointment at his absence. Normally, he would have gone home for the ceremony as a matter of course, but this year he knew he was not very welcome and he had hoped that his father would write and tell him to come. His father had not written.

I took the tinsel bracelet and, kneeling up on the bed, I tied the emblem round his wrist. 'Now,' I said gaily, hoping to divert his thoughts, 'you are my warrior and will protect me.'

He looked down at me and I must have seemed a helpless, tousled wretch to him. His eyes went moist.

'My dear,' he said, lifting me close to him, 'I have not been able to protect you from anything. You are so sick – and I dreamed of making you so happy.' He wept, his head resting against mine.

I stroked the smooth black head and tried not to cry myself. 'My love, don't cry. You have made me very happy – do you hear me – very happy. I would not change my present life for anybody else's. All I need is to get well – and I will get well, never fear.'

I crooned the words to him and because I spoke the truth he was convinced and a little comforted. In the depth of my being I was happy. I loved my husband and I was content in this strange, isolated flat, despite the crushing amount of work and the lack of any semblance of Western culture.

Since our misunderstanding on the morning after my arrival in Pandipura, Ajit had been careful to remember that I was a stranger to his customs and outlook, and we had spent many evening hours discussing religion, politics, love, domestic customs and so on, until gradually I began to understand at least a few of the complexities of Indian life and became less easily irritated by the slowness with which everything moved and the inefficiency with which even the smallest service was performed.

My heart went out to Ajit whose job it was to help to build a modern power house in a country where tomorrow is still a better day for working than today, where workmen's hands are more used to milking cows than fixing circuits and where persistent undernourishment and malaria make those hands soon tired. And yet the power house was going up. I had seen it myself, one day when I felt stronger and had sat on the back of Ajit's bicycle while he pedalled me to it over the scrub land.

Occasionally some of his colleagues came to our flat for a game of bridge, which they played sitting on a mat spread on the veranda, and I heard their bitter complaints of the inefficiency here, the corruption there. Their complaints may have been well justified, but the fact remained that Mother India was building her children something better than they had ever seen before, and there was no doubt in my mind that very soon the water-drawing ox at the back of our flat would be replaced by an electric pump lifting water from a much deeper well, so that the villagers who owned it would be able to irrigate a larger area with less backbreaking work, and the food in the village would be that much increased.

There were plenty of men like Ajit, who, although their tongues were acid-dipped when talking about the shortcomings of their country, worked like demons, so that electric power might be provided and industry and agriculture might flourish in a district which otherwise was destined to become an unpeopled waste.

The man in my arms ceased to weep and lay rested. Usually buoyantly optimistic, he occasionally plunged into the depths of depression, and this seemed a particularly bad bout. I thought of all the small hardships he had had to endure, in addition to re-accustoming himself to his own country and teaching me how to live in it. I held him close.

'Darling,' I said, 'I think you forget the wonders you have performed since I came here. You have held down an important post although you are so young; you have struggled back and forth to work on that awful old bike in appalling heat; you have hardly known what it is to come home to a properly prepared meal; you have cooked and taught me how to cook when you must have been weak with hunger and weariness – and you have even had to wash and iron your own clothes. All this, from a man who has been waited upon all his life, is quite a wonderful achievement to me.'

I lifted his face and kissed him: 'Now the dysentery is gone, I'll soon get strong – you will see.'

He smiled. 'When you are stronger I will send you up to the hills.'

'Oh, no,' I said, appalled at the idea of going six hundred miles away to a hill station without him. 'No – I couldn't leave you – I just couldn't.'

'You are a strange girl. Most women would jump at the opportunity of a holiday in a fashionable hill station.'

'I would die of misery without you.'

He pinched my cheek, his eyes twinkled and he said: 'In that case, after I have been here six months I will take the ten days' leave which I shall have accumulated and we will go together to Bombay – it's at least a trifle cooler and the sea air may help you. We will have a honeymoon – yes? – and thus avoid a funeral pyre.'

'That would be wonderful.'

'I need a holiday myself.'

He did. I realised with some fear that his face was lined and thin. Poor food was having a deleterious effect on him too. Milk diluted to a blue thinness by the milkman, no butter, meat or fish, few eggs now I was too sick to fetch them, improperly cooked vegetables and bread – what chance had either of us on such a diet? I must get up, I thought, I must get up and I must learn to provide properly balanced meals. But from whom should I learn? The lecturers and teachers amongst whom we lived could not afford to eat very well, and most of them were undernourished, eating too much starch and too few proteins. Even the villagers looked better fed than they. I must ask Kamala how she prepared her father's food and find out what made her so strong. Unfortunately Mrs Patel was a very unapproachable person and had, in any case, gone to visit her parents in Kathiawar, so I could not get advice from her.

In the absence of his wife, Chundabhai had called on us several times and his visits were a delight. He always brought fruit and lettuces from his garden, and sat for an hour cracking jokes in his roaring voice, until his chauffeur came to remind him of his next engagement. Then he would depart in a cloud of sand, the big voice getting fainter and fainter as the car threaded its way through the narrow path.

'I must go back to work,' said Ajit, easing himself away from me. He seemed comforted, and kissed me lovingly before he left.

When he had gone, I lay staring at the dirty vessels on the table. The flies were already collecting on them. Suddenly I began to weep. To muffle the noise of the sobs that came from me I turned my face into the pillow.

'O Lord,' I prayed, 'if you really exist, help me to get well. If I can get strong, I can learn to do everything here. Help me, O God, to help my husband.'

But Lord Krishna looked down from his shelf near the kitchen door and smiled his same ivory smile and fingered his ivory flute with his ivory fingers; and from a print of one of Raphael's pictures which hung by my bed, the Holy Child smiled equally enigmatically. Ajit believed that they were two manifestations of the same great God, and I was prepared to believe him, but they were of little comfort to me.

I wept myself to sleep.

Now, although always warned by Ajit to keep the outside doors bolted, I never did so during daylight hours. Even the advent of the frightening stranger who had lit my fire had not been able to persuade me that there was anything outside that would harm me. The bleak land was always so quiet, and I loved to see the shifting light and shade on the sand. I used to take as much of my work as possible on to the veranda, and from there, as I cleaned grain or mended shirts, I could watch the crows and other birds go about their noisy business. A myriad of strange multicoloured insects, from locusts to tiny spiders like red velvet pin-cushions, lived in and around the veranda, and whenever I had time to spare I would squat on my heels and watch them work. With the coming of the monsoon their number had multiplied, and to keep out the larger and more dangerous ones, such as scorpions – and also snakes – Ajit had got a carpenter from the power-house site to screw a bar of wood across the threshold, so that when the door was shut nothing very big could crawl in. It was still necessary, however, to deter ants from entering. They were worthy adversaries and endless kettles of boiling water and sprays of insecticide stopped their coming only temporarily – they always returned to the attack.

There were plenty of animals to watch, too – baboons, wild ponies, jackals, wild cats and dogs, and, of course, cows, buffaloes, camels and goats which came to graze on the sparse herbage. With the domestic animals came the herdsmen and boys. I think it was knowing them that made me feel so safe. At first I was an intruder into their world, like the other people in the flats, but after a while they came to know that I would always give them water if they asked, and that I never made a cup of tea without sharing it with some small boy or girl. I was never angry if by chance a goat strayed into my living-room or a very small boy scrambled up my steps. My washing frequently blew off the veranda and when they brought it back to me they found I could speak their language a little, so they stayed to talk and thus they got to know me. The other flat dwellers swore that the village people would steal from me, but, although my open doors would have made it simple for them to do so and Kamala came and went freely, nothing was ever stolen.

Before I had become too weak to do so, I had wandered round the nearest villages, avoiding, however, the Criminal Tribe village about which Kamala had warned me repeatedly. This was a village started by the Government in an effort to transform a tribe that had lived for centuries by raiding into a peaceful farming community. The Government seemed to be having some success with their experiment, but the local inhabitants were still deeply distrustful of these ex-raiders. Most of the villages were a close huddle of huts, with an occasional small brick house. Narrow alleys filled with rubbish turned and twisted between the dwellings, and as I walked, stopping occasionally to stroke a baby goat tethered near a doorway, dogs barked and snapped at my heels.

People stared at me, but they soon found out from whence I came and almost invariably I was offered water or buttermilk to drink. Inside the huts, I saw, cleanliness and neatness reigned. The thalis and cooking pots were ranged neatly in niches in the wall, spare clothing was hung tidily over a clothes line across the hut and the floor was swept smooth. The thick mud walls gave some measure of protection in the heat of the day; but life went on mostly in the little space in front of the hut, where sometimes a rough wooden bed would be placed on which people could sit. During the monsoon, however, life in the villages must have been most miserable, as the water dripped through inadequate roofs and the cooking fires had to be brought indoors.

The village women heard from Kamala of the strange way of living of the Memsahib. They also heard that I was sick and although they were too shy to walk up the veranda steps to inquire after my health, they peeped through the window, smiled at me as I lay on my bed and wished me soon well.

I had other visitors – beggars and holy men, for whom I kept a pot of annas, and to each supplicant I gave two annas; a few of them came every week to collect this small dole but most of them travelled onward to unknown destinations. I kept also any food left over from the last meal and any old clothes we had, and these also I gave. Ours was the only well for several miles from the city and so I offered water to all who knocked at our door; this made the Brahmin lady who lived on the floor above point out that Ajit was a caste Hindu and his water pots should not be polluted by those of lower castes or by untouchables. When I told Ajit about her complaint, he just laughed and told me to scrub the vessels they touched very thoroughly as many beggars were diseased.

Although I hardly realised it at the time, I was slowly becoming part of India. Each friend I made, each custom I learned to understand and tolerate, was a thread which bound me closer to her and made me part of her multicoloured pattern. Just as in times past she had absorbed invader after invader, she was absorbing me, tolerating my idiosyncrasies and asking only toleration in return. The desperate mental loneliness which had afflicted me at first grew less as the good teachers living round me strove to understand me and meet me half-way in my struggles in a strange society. We did not always approve of each other, my neighbours and I, but we recognised each other's virtues and hesitated to condemn what appeared to be vices.

And so I slept with my door open to the hot desert wind, feeling perfectly safe amongst the people and animals who knew me. I slept so deeply that it was the eldest Miss Shah, and not I, who heard the taxi draw up. She immediately abandoned her vina practice and went outside to see who had been so extravagant as to hire a taxi, and it was she who directed a very fed-up Thakkur to Singh Sahib's flat.

Thakkur's disapproval of this journey was clearly observable in his long face and dragging step. At Jaipur, on the way to Shahpur, his mistress, his honoured Ma ji, had poured into his ear a confused story of how Ajit Sahib had married an English lady, about which his master was not pleased – and who would be pleased at such a marriage? Thakkur wanted to know. Anyway, Ma ji did not want her husband to be worried by anyone telling of this visit to her son. Thakkur was not, therefore, to write home about it. Ma ji and Thakkur would stay about two weeks in the house of the foreign lady.

Thakkur felt that he was the centre of some great intrigue when at Jaipur he posted a postcard to his master from his mistress. He read the card before putting it into the box, and discovered that he and his mistress were supposed to have arrived safely at the house of his mistress's sister at Jaipur, that sister was recovering from an illness and that they would stay about a fortnight. He was so glum for the remainder of the journey that although he remembered to buy a tray of food for Ma ji, he forgot to eat himself, and as he climbed the veranda steps in front of Mrs Singh, his feet were faltering.

The door was open and the house was very still. The lowering sun cast long rays straight through the entrance on to the bed. Thakkur gasped. As he told Ayah later, he saw stretched like a corpse on the bed the whitest lady imaginable. Even the hair spread on the pillow looked white in the sharp light.

He drew back for Mrs Singh to see.

She peered at her daughter-in-law and then glided over to the bed, signalling Thakkur to enter. Her keen eyes must have seen the traces of tears on my face, for she bent down and with one delicate finger brushed a tear away.

At the same moment Thakkur caught his foot on the ledge laid across the threshold to keep out snakes, and tumbled headlong into the room scattering luggage right and left.

I was up in a flash; the room seemed full of people made huge by the setting sun behind them.

'Ajit,' I shrieked in absolute terror, 'Ajit! Dacoits! Robbers!'

Chapter Thirty

Mrs Singh drained her teacup, her chubby face still creased with laughter over the fright she had given me. I was laughing too. The mother-in-law whose goodwill I so much desired was much less fearsome than I had imagined. She sat on one of our bamboo chairs, her legs tucked up under her, while in the kitchen the sweeper crept about in awed silence and succeeded in cleaning the lunch trays without her usual efforts at orchestral percussion between floor and brassware.

I had myself crawled out of bed and made the tea, as it was certain that Mrs Singh would not drink tea made by an untouchable – I was agreeably surprised when she took it from me. I had also served Thakkur, who, after moving the luggage into the bedroom, was sitting on the veranda viewing, with great disfavour, the heatwaves dancing across the landscape.

Mrs Singh at first spoke rapidly to me; but I did not understand, so she made her subsequent sentences short and said them slowly.

'You have been ill?' she asked.

'I have had dysentery for some weeks,' I said, wondering at the same time how I was to gather enough strength to cook an evening meal for the visitors – mercifully Kamala had brought some fresh vegetables.

My mind fidgeted over domestic difficulties, as Mrs Singh subjected me to a long scrutiny. She could not really know how a white woman would look when sick, but the lines on my face must have told her of a rapid loss of weight because she nodded and said: 'You are thin.' She put down her cup, and added, 'I know how to treat dysentery.'

'The dysentery is gone – but my legs are weak.'

'Do you eat vegetarian food?'

'Yes,' I said, ignoring the eggs which I had consumed from time to time. 'Yes, I do – although I cannot yet cook such food very well.'

Mrs Singh laughed. 'Your servant will cook,' she said.

I gathered together my Hindi and tried to explain the acute servant shortage, but was finding my vocabulary hopelessly inadequate, when there was a soft tap at the open door. The eldest Miss Shah entered, making shy salutations to us.

'I came,' she said, 'to inquire how you are.'

I smiled within myself. The sisters' curiosity was insatiable; the crisp, unwrinkled sari in which the eldest sister was garbed proclaimed that she had hastily changed into a clean sari and had come to find out who my visitor was. So few happenings stirred the sisters' lives that my arrival had been a great event to them; and all my doings and my visitors were the subject, I was sure, of evening-long discussions between them and our other neighbours. They criticised the shortness of the summer frocks which I wore when doing housework, the frequent visits of Chundabhai Patel and my friendships with the villagers. I had heard, however, that their comments were not at all unkind and that when a particularly fantastic rumour of my immorality – fantastic to an extent only possible in India – reached them, they came quickly to my defence and corrected the too-vivid imagination of the offending neighbour. As all the neighbours also gossiped to me, most stories reached me eventually, and I followed the old Yorkshire adage of 'hearing all, seeing all and saying nought'.

Miss Shah's eyes gleamed with interest when I introduced her to Mrs Singh and she was delighted to act as interpreter.

The sweeper fluttered by the kitchen door to indicate that she had finished her work, and although I was loath to let her go I knew that she must cook for her own family and I therefore dismissed her. She covered her face with her veil and went out the back door.

Ajit's bicycle wheels made a soft slurring sound through the sand and I usually heard his approach but that day he got a puncture in one tyre and had to walk home. The first indication of his presence, therefore, was when a joyful voice suddenly shouted through the window: 'Mother!' He vanished; there was a cry of 'Thakkur, Namaste,' and Ajit was through the door in a bound and kneeling at his mother's feet, babbling incoherently to her.

In that moment I realised to the full what being estranged from his family meant to Ajit. I saw the ropes of affection which bound mother and son – and I felt very alone – but I vowed that never again should he suffer such alienation if it could be avoided.

Mrs Singh raised her son up.

'Arree, Ajit, have you been ill too?' she asked, anxiously surveying his face.

'No, Mother. It is Peggie who has been so ill.'

He looked round the room, and, seeing the teacups, he relaxed. Some hospitality had been offered. I slipped off the bed and found some tea still hot in a pan on the dying fire. I filled a cup and brought it to Ajit.

Miss Shah saw that it was time for her to go. As she slipped on her sandals, which she had removed at the door before entering, I thanked her for translating for me.

'Don't mention it,' she said in her best English. 'It is a pleasure to me.'

The evening that followed was a turning point in my life. Mrs Singh was the first Indian lady I had met whose life had not been greatly affected by Western influence. My neighbours had all attended University and were widely read in English; Ajit and Chundabhai were more English than Indian in their habits; but Mrs Singh still kept most of the rules of her caste, although she was wise enough to waive them when she found it necessary. As she talked, I realised that many of her caste rules were only those of cleanliness and that if I adopted them I might avoid further illness. I listened to all that she had to say, and determined that I would discard her advice only if, after much consideration, I felt that it was founded on superstition alone.

She was full of the wisdom and fun of a country-bred woman, and as I studied the open, cheerful face and the small, gesticulating hands, I saw that she had the same trustworthiness as Ajit. When her face was in repose it had the calm of self-reliance, rather than the patient resignation I had seen on my neighbours' faces.

After sitting for a few minutes with mother and son, when Miss Shah had gone, I excused myself and went into the kitchen. I wanted to give them time to talk together, and also I had to prepare an evening meal. I leaned my head against the kitchen cupboard door to steady myself. Suddenly Mrs Singh's voice was raised: 'Where is my daughter-in-law?'

Ajit had watched me leave the room, anxiety clearly written on his face.

'She is in the kitchen,' he said.

'In the kitchen! She must not work – she must rest and eat to gain health again.' Turning to the door, she shouted: 'Thakkur.'

Thakkur, who was nodding quietly in the first gust of the cool evening wind, leaped up from the steps on which he had been sitting and found himself appointed cook, starting immediately.

Since he had expected to cook for his mistress during the visit, it was not such a blow as might be imagined, and he installed himself in the kitchen without comment, while I was borne protesting back to bed.

I whispered to Ajit that I felt very embarrassed that I was dressed only in a faded wrapper and, as his mother was present, I would like to make myself neat and put on a sari. He was delighted at the suggestion of my wearing a sari, and Mrs Singh clapped her hands when he told her; so I tottered to the bathroom, bathed myself as best I could and put on one of the saris which Mrs Singh had sent to me.

When I returned, she made me stand in the middle of the room while she pattered round me, straightening a fold here and there – and then she noticed that my wrists and neck were bare.

'What is this?' she cried, giving Ajit a disapproving look. 'No necklace – no ear-rings – no bracelets? What kind of a husband are you, to allow your wife to be seen without suitable jewellery?'

Ajit bowed his head and accepted the rebuke, omitting to say that he had not been earning for long, that the doctor's bills had been heavy and, moreover, I had not received the customary wedding presents.

Hot in defence of my husband, in an extraordinary mixture of Hindi and Gujerati, I said: 'I have a fine gold bracelet – and – and a loving husband is the finest jewel – I need no other.'

Ajit drew his breath apprehensively, feeling sure that my heated retort would offend his mother.

Mrs Singh, however, laughed. 'You speak the truth,' she said. 'It is good, though, to own jewellery – it is your insurance against hard times – it belongs to you without dispute. Ajit must buy you some as soon as possible – and add to it throughout your life.' She paused, then took a ruby ring off her finger. 'See,' she said, 'I will begin the collection,' and she took my hand and slipped the ring on to one finger.

I did not know what to say or even whether it was correct to accept such a present, which to my Western eyes was a valuable one; and I looked at Ajit for guidance.

He nodded his head slightly. I should accept.

There is no word in Hindi for 'thank you', so I did what I would have done in the case of an English mother-in-law: I bent and kissed her and said 'thank you' in English.

She looked quite stunned at such presumption. Ajit broke into explanations, to which she listened attentively. 'It is a charming custom,' she said firmly.

Tension slackened.

All this time Mrs Singh had been in her travelling clothes, although she had washed her hands and feet upon arrival, and I asked if she would like to take a bath before dinner.

She assented, so Ajit took her luggage into the bedroom and undid some of the locks for her, while I made another unsteady pilgrimage to get out clean towels and new soap.

While Mrs Singh made her toilet, I asked Ajit whether we should return the bed to the bedroom for Mrs Singh and ourselves sleep on mats on the floor in the living-room.

'She might like to sleep in the same room as us, but, of course, we will give her the bed.'

'Sleep in the same room!' I exclaimed.

Ajit grinned and pulled my ears teasingly.

'Oh, you English women with your stiff ideas of privacy! Family guests often share rooms with their hosts – they might feel lonely and lost in the middle of the night otherwise.'

I opened my mouth to protest, but before I could say anything, Ajit added: 'I expect Mother will like to have the bedroom to herself – so that she can make puja.'

'Say her prayers?'

'Yes,' said Ajit. 'Now she is getting old, she will take more trouble over her religious observances.'

'She can't be fifty years old yet,' I said.

'Fifty is old in this country.'

I made a face. 'I doubt if I shall be able to take to prayers and contemplation when I'm fifty,' I said. 'I shall probably want to play bridge, wear red saris and paint my face.'

Ajit looked serious and sat down by me on the bed. He put his arm round me – I was not much of an armful – and said: 'And you will be able to do so, Rani. I shall always earn enough to indulge you in such simple pleasures; and if I die, I will leave enough money for you to make life as you please.' He rubbed his nose delicately against my cheek, savouring my perfume, as he went on: 'I ask only that you should say your prayers with me each day, so that we do not forget God, and that you give in charity either a little of your time or a little money.'

'You are never to die,' I said passionately, clutching one brown hand.

He promised dryly that he would not die just yet, and then sent me to see how his mother was managing.

I found her sitting cross-legged on the floor in front of a mirror on a stand, which Thakkur had evidently unpacked for her. She was rubbing oil into her freshly washed hair. I stood and admired the black, glossy waterfall of hair which touched the floor at the back, while I asked if I could help her.

She said promptly that I should rest and not walk about, but I lingered and she asked me to get a fresh sari for her out of the open tin trunk; when I had lifted out a neat bundle of pink cotton, she told me to go back to bed.

When she was dressed, she went into the kitchen, and I could hear her finding fault with everything that Thakkur had done. He was not cooking enough; he must cook lentil soup without spices for daughter-in-law; where had he put the lemon pickle which they had brought? – really, he was always mislaying things.

I heard her opening our grain bins and the shirr-shirr of the falling grain as she ran it through her fingers.

'The quality of the grain ration here is deplorable,' she said. 'Why does not my son buy good grain on the black-market?'

Thakkur murmured something about the Sahib always having been extremely honest.

'Am I not honest?' asked the lady tartly. 'Yet I always buy on the black.'

'Ji, hun, ji, hun, most honest,' assented Thakkur hastily.

Mrs Singh came within my line of vision as she crossed to the water pots. Standing on tiptoe, she took down the brass water-ladle from its hook, dipped it into one of the pots and filled a brass goblet.

She sipped.

'This water is not boiled,' she said. 'Paickie must have boiled water.'

My heart sank. I had daily asked the sweeper to boil water for drinking and daily she had said that she had done so; but apparently she had lied. Miss Shah had, in any case, assured me that although the water was very salt the well was new and its contents pure.

Before eating herself, Mrs Singh supervised the arrangement of my tray and watched me eat a bowl of tasteless lentils, some rice and curd.

As I ate, she lectured me on the necessity of boiling every ounce of water that I drank and washing all fruit with water containing permanganate of potash.

'Eat the fruit with a little salt sprinkled on it,' she advised. 'The salt kills little animals in it.'

She was vague about what kind of little animals, but I promised to do as she said.

'But, Mother,' protested Ajit, laughing at his mother's vehement tones, 'I have eaten and drunk the same things as Peggie and I am not ill.'

His mother sniffed. 'Foolish man, you were born here. All English people suffer when they come. They insist on living in their English style and then wonder why they become ill. They should adopt our ways, eating no flesh, taking curd daily and remembering our caste practices. Do you wash your mouth out after every meal?' she suddenly shot at me.

'No,' I said humbly.

'Then do so, child. Also take a bath and change your clothes on coming from the bazaar. Keep specially some clean clothes to wear when cooking. Do not allow sandalled feet in your kitchen.'

On she went, giving out laws of cleanliness that would have done credit to a London surgeon, while I ate and listened hard.

I could see from the trepidation in Ajit's expression that he feared I would be offended at his mother's peremptory tones; he knew I was not used to submitting myself to the authority of an older woman.

He need not have feared; I guessed that Mrs Singh had not arranged her visit without opposition from the family, and that she had not, therefore, come from curiosity or to criticise. It was much more likely that she had come to help us and to heal the breach in the family.

I listened, therefore, and learned much. Ajit and I, I argued to myself, would spend most of our lives away from his family, and I could discard that part of the advice which seemed mere superstition and put to use the sensible part.

Thakkur brought trays of food for Ajit and Mrs Singh. It smelled delicious, and I said so hopefully – but Mrs Singh was adamant that rice, lentils and curd were all that I could have that night.

Ajit had previously asked after his family as a whole, but now he asked his mother cautiously if his father could not have spared time to visit us too.

Mrs Singh immediately looked so guilty and shifted about so uncomfortably, that Ajit guessed that she had somehow managed to come secretly, and he changed the subject; but there was a glint of amusement in his eyes.

To my relief, Mrs Singh elected to sleep alone in the bedroom, and Thakkur lifted our bed into it, opened her bedding roll and spread her own clean sheets and pillows.

We made ourselves comfortable on a couple of mats in the living-room. Thakkur also took a mat and curled up on the veranda. As no thief was likely to venture in while he lay there, we left the front door open so that we could have the benefit of the night breeze.

The floor was hard to one unaccustomed to lying on it, and I did not sleep much. Thakkur also had a bad night, because every time he went to sleep the pariah dogs crawled on their bellies up the veranda steps and sniffed at him from head to toe. One or two poked their noses through the door, but I quickly shooed them away.

Thakkur rose at five, cursing all dogs and uncivilised Gujerati builders who failed to build compound walls round houses. He was not up before Mrs Singh. She was already taking her bath preparatory to saying her prayers.

I fell asleep.

Awakened by the clank of the milkman's pail and the shouts of the drovers of a passing camel train, Ajit was surprised to find the visiting half of the household already busy. When he stirred I woke up; but all that Mrs Singh would allow me to do was to say my prayers and take a bath.

I was troubled that my visitors were having to work, but Ajit pacified me by saying that in any case Mrs Singh would not take food cooked by me, so Thakkur would have to cook for her, and it was not much more trouble for him to cook for us as well. To Thakkur the work of our little house would be nothing, he assured me. I was to rest and enjoy myself.

He moved my mat and pillow on to the veranda, and I lay down thankfully. Now was my chance to get well.

Ajit realised that on that day his home would be run like his father's house, so he took his bath leisurely and sat and talked with Mrs Singh and me, until at nine o'clock Thakkur presented us with a full meal of rice, lentils, vegetables, curd and bread – bread so light I said the fairies must have made it. Ajit promptly translated this remark for Thakkur's benefit and the old man's dismal face showed the faintest suggestion of a smile.

Again I had to be content with rice, lentils and curd, with the addition of one piece of bread.

Ajit explained that this meal was meant to last him until evening; there would be no lunch, although something good would probably arrive for nibbling with my tea, and there would be a good evening meal, to all of which Mrs Singh nodded agreement as she sat cross-legged on a chair like a jolly, feminine Buddha.

As the day progressed, I learned just how much work a good Indian servant could do. The sweeper came and washed the dishes and swept the floor; but Thakkur, without fuss or hurry, cooked, cleaned grain and had it ground, and went to the city to buy vegetables. He returned with finer vegetables than I had ever been able to buy, and as he spread them out on the newly scrubbed storeroom floor I was amazed at their succulence. When I admired them, he gave me the first real grin he had been able to muster since he arrived.

Mrs Singh spent hours talking to me, and it was remarkable what we managed to say to each other with the aid of a dictionary. Once or twice, I drew pictures on my writing pad to illustrate clearly what I meant; and Mrs Singh laughed at the little drawings until her ear-rings rattled.

The youngest Miss Shah, a bundle of agonised shyness, came to inquire after my health, and at the same time the Brahmin lady from upstairs slipped in through the back door, keeping her face closely covered until Thakkur had moved away. She kept purdah from preference, her husband being quite willing that she should go out if she wished. From the demeanour of the two women in front of my mother-in-law, I realised that I had omitted many forms of outward respect to Mrs Singh. After they had gone and she had expressed her approbation of such well-behaved acquaintances, I asked her forgiveness if my Western ways seemed very disrespectful to her.

She smiled affectionately upon me and said that she had been surprised how much I had learned of Indian ways; I asked her if she would teach me the usual forms of behaviour before certain people and she readily agreed. 'There is no strict etiquette, as the English have,' she said.

I was feeling better. When Ajit saw me that evening, he was pleased and his own spirits went up. As I reclined on my mat in the moonlight like some Indian Cleopatra and Mrs Singh sat cross-legged on a cushion, he regaled us with funny stories, all of which seemed to begin: 'There was once a Sikh . . .'

Mrs Singh stayed with us for a fortnight and during the whole time she never made me feel jealous or left out of proceedings. There was no doubt that she loved Ajit deeply, but her thoughts always seemed to be for us as a pair. She made me feel that I was part of Ajit and, therefore, to be cared for equally with him. No word of criticism ever passed her lips and yet she managed to teach me how to put my house in order. I begged that Thakkur should give me some cooking lessons, which the old man happily did, and before they left I could at last make good bread.

When Thakkur found that I could not sit cross-legged without pain, he suggested to Mrs Singh that he should buy from the bazaar a cheap table and a 'piece of the cloth that does not burn', so that the stoves could be put on the table and I could cook standing up.

Ajit reproached himself for not having thought of this before, and Thakkur was despatched to the carpenters' bazaar with instructions to buy a strong table and a piece of asbestos.

I also had a private conference with Thakkur, with the result that he came back with a proper, long-handled English broom and a similar mop, things which I had not been able to find in the bazaar. At Mrs Singh's suggestion, he also bought a big water boiler. Thakkur carried none of these purchases himself, but engaged no less than three coolies for the purpose. The table and boiler were, of course, too heavy to be carried in any way except on the head, and it was beneath the dignity of a member of the warrior caste, such as Thakkur, to be seen carrying brooms.

Apart from teaching me the simplest method of running a house, Mrs Singh taught me to make puja, that is, to say my prayers while accompanying them with small offerings of spice and oil thrown on to the first fire of the day. The ivory Lord Krishna had incense sticks burned in front of him, and Mrs Singh, when she heard that the Raphael print was a picture of the Lord Jesus, asked me if I would like to place incense sticks in front of that as well; to please her I placed them there also. God is God, no matter what his manifestation, and this was one way of acknowledging his existence.

The preoccupation of Indians with matters of the spirit was strange to me after the lukewarm interest of my fellow countrymen. The fact, however, that death sits grinning on the shoulder of every man in a country of famines and huge natural disasters, makes an interest in the next world imperative if one is to avoid being always afraid. An Indian peasant's burden of suffering is so terrible that he tends to draw away from the agony of the present and to dream of a rebirth into a higher, more privileged caste or of his return to his Maker.

Various political parties were trying to convince people that their current lives could be made much more bearable, by their own efforts; but it was a slow and difficult task, and to most men life was still something to be borne patiently until death gave release from it.

New ideas were, however, stirring among the young; I occasionally saw newspaper reports of local leaders of dynamic personality who had succeeded in obtaining cooperative action, and practical results had followed, such as a village road built or a new type of well bored.

As I lit the incense sticks and said my mantras, I vowed that when I was well and had a reliable servant, I would help in one of these new movements.

'Do not meddle with customs you do not understand,' my conscience warned me.

'I will first learn to understand,' I muttered to myself. 'I will be humble; first learn and then teach.'

Chapter Thirty-one

At last Mrs Singh's bedding roll had to be buckled up and farewells said. A tonga was ordered to come from the city to take us to the station.

Before they left, Ajit managed to extract from Thakkur the details of Mrs Singh's arrangements for her visit. Thakkur ventured to say that the Big Sahib should have come too; he would have enjoyed the visit. The little Memsahib was not at all like the Memsahibs he had met before Independence; she was like an Indian lady but more peaceable.

Ajit laughed when he told me this. At least I had gained one adherent in his father's house, he teased. He did not tip Thakkur in the ordinary way, but bought him some good, white-papered cigarettes and slipped a ten-rupee note into the tin.

I was sufficiently recovered to drive into the city with Ajit to see the visitors off. At the station, I placed round my mother-in-law's neck a farewell garland of flowers, and it was with real sorrow that I waved goodbye.

'I will send a servant to you soon,' shouted Mrs Singh, as she leaned out of the purdah compartment in which she had elected to travel for safety's sake.

'Namaste, namaste, Sahib, Memsahib,' called Thakkur from the servants' compartment, his face contorted into a smile. 'Come soon to Delhi – come soon.'

Come soon! How could we visit until Ajit's father gave permission? Though we did not know it, at that moment he was in no mood to even look at his foreign daughter-in-law.

We took a tonga home, since my legs were still not too strong; and against the jingling of its bells we did not at first hear the shouts of the Misses Shah, who, when we arrived, were all standing on our veranda instead of on their own.

In front of our flat was a coolie cart in which reposed a very large wooden box; two coolies, one woman and one man, were squatting on their heels nearby smoking bilis, while in a tiny hammock made by a piece of veiling attached to the shaft of the cart, a baby lay whimpering.

'What can it be?' I asked. 'Have you ordered something?'

'I haven't ordered anything. I would not do so, without consulting you first,' said Ajit, a trace of indignation in his voice.

As we descended from the tonga and paid the tongawallah, a man who had presumably been knocking on our door fluttered down the steps. He peered at us through silver-rimmed spectacles and his nail-brush moustache quivered like a rabbit's nose. In one hand he held a fountain pen and in the other a piece of paper.

'Singh Sahib?' he queried.

'Yes.'

'Sign here, please,' and the pen was pushed into Ajit's hand.

'Wait a minute,' said Ajit. 'Who are you and what is this?'

The little man drew himself up and thrust out his chin. 'Shahpur Electrical Supply Company associated with the Bombay Marine Electric Company one refrigerator Class A ex our Bombay associates,' he recited without taking breath.

'Ramji,' exclaimed Ajit, appalled. 'I have not ordered a refrigerator.'

'I forgot,' said the representative of the Shahpur Electrical etcetera. 'I have a letter to deliver to you also.' He drew out a crumpled envelope from his shirt pocket and handed it to Ajit, while the eyes of the Misses Shah nearly popped out of their heads as they murmured: 'A refrigerator? A letter?'

Ajit ripped open the envelope and, holding the letter close to his eyes in order to see in the waning light, he read it.

I fidgeted with impatience.

A slow grin spread over his face and became a great laugh.

'Well, I am surprised,' he said, a very sweet expression on his face.

'Tell me, tell me,' I implored like a child.

'It's a wedding present,' said Ajit, 'from Chundabhai. Take the letter and read it.'

'A wedding present?' chorused the Misses Shah, as I read. 'Whoever heard of a refrigerator for a wedding present? Most extraordinary! Quite unorthodox!'

I read: 'Dear Ajit Sahib, I am sorry that this fridge has been so long in coming to you, but it took some time to get it shipped from Bombay. Nevertheless, it comes to you and to Peggie with all good wishes for a long and happy married life from my wife and me. I feel that it will probably give Peggie more pleasure than a pile of saris – and somebody has to make ice cream soufflés for me! Kindest regards and good wishes, Yours, Chundabhai.'

Feeling dazed, I slowly folded the letter up. I had forgotten that such things as refrigerators existed.

'It's a tremendous present,' I said. 'Should we really accept it?'

'Of course we are going to accept it,' Ajit said. 'Chundy is my oldest college friend, and he is simply rolling in money – if he had sent saris or silver it would have been quite expensive. He is so good-natured that he probably spent weeks cogitating over what to give us – and by Heaven, he could not have thought of anything more helpful than this.'

'Fresh milk,' I said, a sob in my throat, 'no more rancid butter – meals prepared ahead of time – only one journey a week to buy vegetables. Oh, darling, what a present!'

Ajit put his arm round me and hugged me. The Misses Shah giggled and the coolies stirred out of their lethargy. He dropped me as if I was a newly-made piece of bread red-hot from the tava, and took the delivery note and signed it. The coolies got up reluctantly and with much puffing, blowing and complaining, heaved the box up the steps and into the living-room. They then opened the wooden packing case under the direction of the representative.

The refrigerator was large, with a commodious freezing section. Its white, polished glory looked incongruous in the stone-floored, colour-washed Indian room; but to me it was a marvellous release from labour.

'How could he guess what it would mean to us?' I asked, as I ran my fingers tremulously along the immaculate metal shelves and the enamelled boxes.

'He was in England for six years,' said Ajit, as he tipped the coolies.

I hastily fetched water for both the coolies and the representative and they departed. It is doubtful if the coolies knew what they had unpacked.

The Misses Shah, although they knew the purpose of a refrigerator, had never had the opportunity before of examining one closely, and they stole round it as if it was an unexploded time bomb.

'Will it really keep food from rotting?' asked the eldest lady.

'Not yet,' said Ajit. 'An electric power line is being run out here soon, and when the refrigerator is plugged in, food will keep for days in it.'

'Wonderful,' they chorused.

'It has no lock,' remarked the second Miss Shah. 'How will you avoid a servant's stealing from it?'

I was nonplussed, and looked at Ajit.

'We shall keep it in this room,' he said firmly. 'We can lock the room when we go out.'

My first reaction was that I could not have a refrigerator in the living-room, but on consideration I realised that it was the only place in which to put it, to avoid pilferage when a servant occupied the kitchen.

The Misses Shah declined tea, being quite unable to refrain from speeding up the stairs to our other neighbours to tell them of the extraordinary arrival.

The younger neighbours, being educated, had few taboos, and merely called in a body the next day to inspect the wonderful machine; but a few old parents wagged their heads in horror at the thought of eating food which had been kept for days. It was against the laws of nature and of caste.

We did not care what anybody thought. We were blissfully happy as together we cooked our dinner, after Ajit and the watchman had managed to ease Chundabhai's magnificent present into a corner. When we had eaten, Ajit dragged the bed to the front door and we sat on it together, enjoying the coolness and the songs of the insects.

I saw that from Ajit's shirt pocket a letter protruded, and I asked him from whom it was. He immediately drew it out.

'I'm sorry,' he said. 'I picked it up from under the door as we came in this evening. It is for you.'

I straightened myself, took the letter, saw it was from Mother and opened it. It was a long and garbled letter, full of bits of local news. Towards the end she wrote: 'You will be pleased to know, dear, that James's practice has grown so much that he is taking an additional partner in – his mother is very proud of him. Naturally your dear father and I hope that he will marry Angela – though they do not see as much of each other as they used to do.

'Angela is very quiet these days. She does not go out much – not like her usual self at all – I get quite worried about the amount of work the child is doing. Sometimes she goes on far into the night – says she is writing another paper. Dr Wu has called several times, and talks to her about her work – far above my poor head, I fear. Such a nicely behaved young man, but Father gets furious about his visits. I can't imagine why – he does not stand a chance with Angela now that James is doing so well – Angela has such a matter-of-fact outlook on life and would not prefer a penniless oriental student to the most successful solicitor in town . . .'

There were several paragraphs more, but my mind did not absorb their contents. How little Mother and Father knew about their daughters. I could imagine Father's fears of another oriental son-in-law, and yet I sensed that Wu could give Angela all that she needed most to make her flower into a warm-hearted, contented woman. James might have been able to help her, but his chances had been spoiled by his brother.

'Bad news?'

'No.' My voice was hesitant.

'What is it, Rani?'

I snuggled my face into his neck.

'It is nothing.'

'Something is.'

'It's Wu.'

'Wu?'

'Yes. He is courting Angela and my parents don't like it.'

Ajit's laughter was deep and rich. 'Good old Wu,' he said.

'I want him to marry her,' I said.

'Well, why not? He is my good friend.'

'My parents don't realise how excellent a man he is; they would like her to marry James.'

'Ah, yes. I remember James – he would not be good for Angela.'

I looked up at him. 'You realise also what Angela needs?'

'I know, my dear. She is very like you.'

'Like me?'

'Yes – only you are afraid of the world and of people and shrink away from them – you need always to have a little protection to which to retire, while Angela plunges into life, and nearly drowns.'

'How do you know she nearly drowns?'

'Her trials are written on her forehead.'

Then he smiled at me. 'I think Wu will win her,' he said.

'I hope so.'

'This James looked very cold fish to me,' remarked Ajit, as he flicked a moth off my pillow.

'He is a kindly man,' I said, 'and he might understand Angela quite well – but I want her to start afresh with Wu. James is thinking only of his career at present.'

'I will pray that he continues to succeed in it, so that Wu has time to acquire a beautiful wife,' said Ajit mischievously.

'And what will Lord Krishna say about such a weird prayer?'

'He will know what to do – he is an expert on affairs of the heart – did he not have sixteen thousand wives and thus found the Indian race?'

Chapter Thirty-two

Late one evening, a few days before his wife's return from Shahpur, Ram Singh came home from Simla. He found that his house had been kept in good order under Nulini's guidance and that Shushila was her usual bouncing self.

'Papa,' she shouted joyfully, 'Nulini has shown me how to play caron properly – I will beat you next time we play.'

Her father pulled her ears lovingly. 'We will play tomorrow,' he promised.

When he sat down to eat, he remembered to praise the pickles that Nulini had made earlier in the year, and he told Bhim that his wife was learning to keep house very well. Bhim smiled absent-mindedly at the compliment and asked about the result of his father's investigation into the land dispute at Simla.

They sat and chatted for some time after the meal was finished, relishing the legal intricacies of the dispute. Bhim asked if he might examine Ram Singh's notes on the subject and the elder man agreed. He took out from his brief case a large, untidy file, which he handed to his son, after which he went away to take his bath, say his prayers and go to bed. He asked Khan to find his Gita for him, which the servant did, and then he dismissed him for the night.

The cooking fires in the servants' quarters flickered out, Khan turned restlessly on his cot outside his master's room, Shushila slept and the house was still for the night.

Hours later, Dr Singh awoke feeling ravenously hungry. He called Khan, but the man did not answer.

Ram Singh reluctantly got out of bed, gave his dhoti a characteristic hitch and again shouted for Khan. There was no reply. He wrapped a shawl round himself and went to the door of his room. Khan was not in his cot, so he went in search of Ayah, who slept at the door of his wife's room.

Ayah slept the light sleep of the old, and at the sound of his footfall she sat up and screamed, clutching her sari tightly round her.

'Noisy one,' said Ram Singh petulantly. 'I don't know where Khan has gone, and I'm hungry. Find me something to eat.'

'Ji, hun,' said Ayah, delighted to be singled out for a special service, and she leaned over the edge of her cot and scrabbled beneath it with one gnarled hand, feeling for her spectacles.

'Here,' said Ram Singh, lifting them off the window sill.

She hastily relieved him of their weight and with fumbling hands hooked them round her ears, after which, like a pair of pariah dogs, she and Ram Singh slunk silently along the inner veranda to the kitchen. The kitchen, however, was as barren of food as the desert itself. Nulini had locked up everything before Cook Maharaj had departed to the servants' quarters. Not so much as a humble rôti was to be seen.

Ram Singh looked dismally round him. Each cupboard exhibited a neat padlock on its door. Each cooking pot sat on its shelf emptily upside down. He turned and looked at the storeroom doors. The room in which most foodstuffs were kept was locked up. The grain storeroom padlock, however, hung loosely down from its chain. He shivered – the kitchen was quite chilly.

'Ayah.'

'Ji.' She saw that Ram Singh was shivering. 'Sahib, why do you come to the kitchen? I will bring food to you in your room.'

'I don't know why I came,' said Ram Singh, like a cross, small boy. 'The grain storeroom is open. See if there is any parched flour – that will do.'

'Sahib,' protested Ayah, 'that is only for beggars or for pilgrims.'

'I am hungry – where does Maharaj keep the cashew nuts, I wonder,' growled Ram Singh, and Ayah scuttled across the kitchen while her master followed her with greater dignity.

Ayah pulled the heavy door open and peered into the dark store.

'Sahib,' she shrieked suddenly, pushing her spectacles up the bridge of her nose. 'Sahib.'

Ram Singh covered the kitchen in a couple of strides. 'Hey, Ram,' he exclaimed in horror, and then shouted in a paroxysm of rage. 'Come out!'

On a pile of sacks in a corner of the storeroom and just visible in the moonlight from the window, lay a man dressed only in a loincloth. Although apparently paralysed by fear, he had raised himself on his elbow and half lay over a woman, as if to protect her from view; but her bare legs were clearly visible, the sari pulled up from them, and the sharp, terrified gasps of her breath could be heard in the silence which followed Ram Singh's command.

'Come out,' repeated Ram Singh, ice beginning to overlay the rage in his voice.

The man swung himself carefully off the sacks, still keeping his body between the woman and Ram Singh. The woman's legs vanished, as she drew them up under her sari.

'Khan!' exclaimed Ram Singh.

The hill man hung his head and said nothing.

'I will not have women brought into my house,' shouted his enraged master. 'In a month you are to be married – and yet you have to bring some beggar off the streets.' He stopped abruptly. His eyes had got used to the gloom of the storeroom, and he saw for the first time part of the sari which the woman was wearing. It was no beggar's sari. It was red – red silk.

'Ramji,' he gasped and pointed at it.

Ayah looked where the finger pointed. 'Arree,' she wailed at the top of her voice.

Ram Singh covered the distance between the door and his delinquent servant in a second, pushed the man aside and grabbed the trembling heap that was the woman. Roughly he pulled her off the sacking and by the power of his grip on her shoulder kept her from sinking to her knees.

'Nulini,' he said in a horrified whisper.

She stood with her eyes cast down, her sari fallen to her waist. She was blouseless – the tiny scrap of red silk still lay on the sacking – and the large, exquisitely formed breasts were naked. In the soft hollow between the breasts lay the gold necklace that Ram Singh had himself given her at her wedding time. He lifted his free hand as if to snatch it off her, but something held him back and he flung her down on to the sacking, where she lay motionless.

Khan fell on to his knees. 'Sahib,' he beseeched. 'The fault is mine. The little lady is but a weak woman and I tempted her. She is unharmed, Sahib, quite unharmed, I swear it.'

He caught at Ram Singh's feet and kissed them; for the first time in his life Ram Singh kicked a servant, but Khan seemed hardly to feel it. He lay prostrate before his master, the muscular back awaiting further blows.

'Sahibji,' he said. 'Punish me as you will, but do not tell Bhim Sahib. Let your respected daughter go back to him – she is untouched. I swear it, I swear it. She is most innocent, Sahib – the fault is all mine.'

In speechless rage, Ram Singh bent and struck his defenceless servant again and again with his clenched fists, while Ayah moaned in the background.

'The fault is mine,' said a calm voice behind them.

Ram Singh straightened up and turned round sharply. Bhim stood in the doorway. He had presumably been wakened by Ayah's shriek and had followed the sound of voices echoing through the house. His hair was rumpled and his garments creased from sleep, but his step was firm and he held himself in a dignified manner as he crossed the storeroom to his wife, who lay still on the sacking, her face hidden and her shoulders heaving as she wept silently.

'Nulini,' he said stiffly, 'cover yourself and come with me.'

There was no reply. Khan raised himself to his knees and hid his face in his hands.

'Nulini.'

Nulini shrank closer to the sacking.

'Come, child,' said Bhim, his voice soft as if he were really coaxing a child, 'I will not beat you.'

'Don't bother with her,' said her father-in-law angrily. 'Tomorrow she leaves this house. She can go back to her parents, if she dare face them, or she can join those whose profession she has already emulated.'

Bhim did not answer immediately. He put his arm round his wife and raised her to her feet. She stood passively, her eyes shadowed by their lashes, while he carefully draped the sari over her shuddering form and over her head, so that she was shielded from Ayah's fascinated gaze.

'Father,' he said slowly, 'Nulini has done wrong and I am sure she realises it. Yet I know that it is in part my fault. I have not always remembered my responsibilities to her.'

'You have been a good husband,' said Ram Singh tartly as he arranged his shawl round himself. 'Tomorrow she goes.'

Bhim drew himself up. 'She is my wife. If she goes, I go.'

'Don't be ridiculous,' said Ram Singh.

'Does not the scripture say that if a wife errs the husband must be punished for it?'

'It does,' said his father coldly. He looked Nulini up and down as if she was something unclean. 'Do with her as you will.' His anger boiled up uncontrollably 'Father a bastard if you wish.

'And as for you,' he said, glaring at the supplicating Khan. 'Get out of this house and out of this province. Never let me see your face again. Get out!'

There was a loud hammering on the kitchen door. The watchman, attracted by the sound of voices, shouted: 'Kon heh? Kon heh?'

'It is I,' bawled the exasperated Ram Singh. 'Go away.'

'Sahibji,' said the watchman obsequiously, and padded away.

'Ayah, open the door and let this untouchable out,' said Ram Singh, his voice trembling.

Ayah had been watching the proceedings with rapt attention. 'Miss Nulini has the key, Sahib,' she said.

Nulini did not move, so Bhim bent down and unhooked the key ring from the waist of her petticoat. He flung it at Ayah's feet, and, mumbling that the present generation was not fit to live, she picked up the keys and moved to the door.

Silently Khan rose to his feet. Ram Singh caught him a staggering blow across the face with the flat of his hand, and the man stumbled. He made no sign that he had felt the blow, but straightened himself and walked with head erect past his master. He did not even glance at Ayah as he glided lightly on his bare feet out of the door, his dhoti gleaming white in the moonlight and his sacred thread making a dark line across his chest.

Ayah shut and locked the door, and then hooked the key ring into her sari.

Ram Singh saw the last movement, and resented that Ayah had put herself in the place of a deposed member of the family.

'Give me the keys,' he said, his moustache bristling. 'Say no word to anybody of what has happened tonight or by Ram himself I will make you suffer.' He glared at Ayah, whose heart gave a little leap of fright as she handed him the keys.

Bhim put his arm round Nulini and began to propel her across the floor towards the inner veranda, when suddenly there was a sound of running feet and a heavy pounding on the door.

'Sahib, Sahib,' yelled the panic-stricken voice of the watchman, 'Sahib, come quickly.'

'What is it? What is it?' shouted Ram Singh as he fumbled for the key and put it into the lock.

'Arree, Sahib, Khan has fallen down the well. I tried to save him but he slipped from my fingers.'

Ram Singh flung open the door and ran outside; from the servants' quarters Cook Maharaj was already racing for the well, while frightened, sleepy voices behind him asked if it was a Muslim raid or was there a thief in the compound?

Nulini moaned and then fainted. Bhim laid her back on to the sacking and said to Ayah: 'Take care of her – good care.' He then ran out of the house towards the well.

In the light of the moon people ran about confusedly, shouting for a rope, for someone who could swim.

'Maharaj! Pratap!' called Bhim. 'Let me down with the water-skin – I can swim.' He snatched a torch from the gardener's hand.

'My son,' cried Ram Singh, fear for his eldest boy obliterating every other feeling.

'I shall be safe, Father,' said Bhim, and seized the flaccid water-skin. Maharaj and Pratap let it down slowly, muttering that they hoped the rope would stand the weight. Ayah, not being able to bear being left out of the excitement, had deserted Nulini who lay in a faint in the storeroom, and was now peering down the well.

There was no sound of splashing; only the creak of the wheel broke the tense silence.

Just above the water line Bhim yelled to those above to stop letting him down. He flashed the torch around the dank, green walls and across the still water. He could see nothing of Khan. He clung to the rope for another minute, swaying perilously, but nothing stirred, and he called to be pulled up.

'Only a man who wanted to drown could have drowned so quickly,' he said to his father, as, aided by Pratap, he eased himself over the lip of the well. Cook Maharaj dropped the rope and assisted him to his feet while the rest of the servants and their families stood in stupefied silence.

'It appears that Khan has drowned,' Ram Singh told them. 'There is nothing that we can do tonight. In the morning we will get the body out and Pratap shall go and fetch the Thanedar from the police station. Chowkidar, continue on your rounds and the rest of you go back to bed.'

'Arree-ee,' a little sigh went through the knot of people, and one or two women began to weep softly. Khan had been popular in the compound, and it was with sad faces that his fellow servants reluctantly turned and went back to their homes, the womenfolk keeping close to their men in fear of the nearness of death.

Bhim spotted Ayah amongst the crowd. 'Get back to my wife,' he yelled at her furiously. Ayah fled.

Father and son walked slowly back into the house, both heavy with thought. They went through the kitchen, Ram Singh locking the back door, saw that Ayah had apparently moved Nulini from the storeroom, and walked along the veranda together.

Was Ram Singh remembering Khan's patient service through many months? Did he feel that he had driven the man to his death? Nobody knows. But the next day Ram Singh obtained from his clerk the name of Khan's father and of his village so that he could send news of the man's death – and with the letter he enclosed his wages for six months to come

– the clerk showed to Ayah the note of the amount written in the housekeeping book.

And of what was Bhim thinking? His was a difficult position in which to be; and because he was a conscientious man he probably reproached himself bitterly for not taking more care of his wife; but that he was prepared to stand by her was made abundantly clear just as he and his father were passing Shushila's and Nulini's sleeping-room.

The silence of the house was broken by a muffled cry. 'Give it to me,' panted Ayah's voice, as if she spoke with difficulty. There was a sound of scuffling and of laboured breath, as if two people were fighting.

'What now?' exclaimed Ram Singh, and leaped towards the apartment with an agility surprising for a man of his years. He was, however, not quicker than Bhim, who tore apart the curtains of the doorway and stood for a second paralysed by what he saw.

'Nulini!' he exclaimed in a hoarse whisper, fearing to wake his little sister, who still slumbered on her cot at the far side of the room.

'Ayah,' cried Ram Singh.

Locked together like wrestlers, Nulini and Ayah fought for possession of a small dagger. The younger woman held the weapon in her right hand and was attempting to drive it down upon herself, but Ayah had caught her wrist with one hand and forced it back, while she held the girl's body in a bony grip close to her own, so that Nulini could not strike without first killing or wounding the old nurse.

Bhim shot forward and snatched the dagger from his half-naked wife. Nulini wrenched herself away from Ayah and stood swaying unseeingly in the middle of the room, her hair loose down her back with a few withered flowers still tangled in it. Naked to the waist, she looked like the ill-used captive of some ancient Muslim conqueror.

'She was about to stab herself,' panted Ayah quite unnecessarily, while she tucked her sari into the waistband of her petticoat and readjusted her spectacles which were hanging from one ear.

'Hey, Ram!' exclaimed the harassed father, nodding his head helplessly from side to side.

Bhim tucked the dagger into the waist of his dhoti and then silently supported his fainting, unprotesting wife out on to the veranda. Ram Singh and Ayah followed him, while Shushila still slept on.

Nulini looked ghastly in the moonlight, blood oozing down her face from a scratch.

'Father,' said Bhim urgently. 'Let me deal with this matter. There will be no scandal, I promise you – if you can shut the mouth of Ayah.'

Ram Singh's anger had evaporated, and he looked old and sad. 'Do what you will,' he said shortly, and turned on his heel, and with trembling steps sought the seclusion of his own room.

Bhim picked up his wife and carried her to his room – a strange room to her, which she had hardly entered since her marriage. Impelled by curiosity, more than a desire to help, Ayah trailed along after her swiftly-moving young master.

Bhim sat down upon his cot, his wife upon his knee, took his shawl from amongst the rumpled sheets and wrapped it round Nulini, who had maintained a dazed silence seeming hardly aware of what was happening to her. He rocked her back and forth as if she was a baby, whispering encouragement to her, while Ayah, uncertain what to do, fluttered nervously in the doorway.

'Bring a glass of water, Ayah,' said Bhim.

She went and fetched the water from the kitchen, handing the glass to him with silent disapproval. She was full of indignation that Bhim thought it necessary that she should be instructed to keep her mouth shut. Keep her mouth shut, indeed – as if she was going to betray the honour of the family. It was Nulini who had done the betraying, and what the girl needed in Ayah's opinion was to be thrown out on the street, not nursed and soothed by her husband.

Bhim forced a little water through Nulini's lips. It ran partly down her face, but it brought her back to her senses, and she moved as if to jump off her husband's lap. Bhim held her firmly, however, continuing to rock her and whisper in her ear. She turned her face into his shoulder and suddenly great sobs shook her; she clenched one hand and beat a tattoo on Bhim's shoulder.

'You don't care – you don't care – not about me – not about Khan.' Her voice rose. 'Why did you drive him to his death? you and Father-in-law.' She wailed in mourning, and continued to reproach her patient husband in between sobs.

Bhim went a sickly grey. 'You may go,' he said frigidly to Ayah, and very reluctantly Ayah went. She remembered that Ram Singh was hungry and trotted along to his room, calling quietly at the open door: 'Sahib, Sahib.' There was no reply, so she entered, tentatively ready to retreat: 'Sahib, shall I bring you something to eat?'

Ram Singh was sitting on his divan and staring into space, his shawl wrapped round his shoulders and head. He seemed at first hardly aware of his old questioner, but when she repeated the query, he said coldly without looking at her: 'No.'

Ayah turned to go back to her bed, only to be brought to a halt by Ram Singh's saying in the same frigid tone: 'Woman, if you speak a word of this night's happenings to anyone, I will beat you to death – to death.'

Ayah shrank away. Small as Ram Singh was, he had a terrifying presence.

'Ji, hun,' she said, 'I shall say nothing.'

And she kept her promise for years, until time had made the events of little interest to any but the family.

Chapter Thirty-three

Ram Singh's clerk drove his master and Shushila to the railway station to meet Mrs Singh. The clerk had silently shouldered a lot of extra work during the previous few days. It was he who directed the operation of recovering Khan's body and he who kept the police constables from wandering all over the house and making themselves a nuisance in the kitchen, while Ram Singh dealt courteously with the Police Inspector. The Inspector had come to make routine inquiries and was made so comfortable that he remained for the day, taking meals with Ram Singh. He was quite satisfied that in a house such as Ram Singh's nothing untoward could have occurred – the lip of the well was low and easily stumbled over in the darkness. He suggested that Ram Singh should have the wall built higher and keep the well covered at all times, and he was flattered when Ram Singh said that he welcomed such ingenious suggestions.

It was the clerk who arranged the funeral, buying a stretcher for the body, cloth in which to wind it and ghee and wood for the funeral pyre. He did not himself touch the body; some strange old women, like witches, came from the nearest village and wound the faithful lover and arranged him on the stretcher.

Khan did not lack mourners at his funeral. The servants went, and many of the people he knew in the village followed in straggling procession down to the burning ghat where his body was consigned to the flames.

Bhim did his best to keep from Nulini the sounds of the disturbance caused by the police and the rescuers; but it was impossible, even with the windows shut, not to be able to follow the whole operation from the shouts outside. She lay on his bed, staring wide-eyed at the ceiling, while he sat and chafed her limp hands. When a half-triumphant wail announced the bringing of the body out of the well, she was suddenly sick, retching helplessly on an empty stomach, while Bhim held her and Ayah ran to and fro with bowls and cloths. When the sickness eased, Bhim, who had not slept during the night while he sat with his tossing wife, went to his father and asked permission to send for a doctor.

Ram Singh refused flatly. He evidently feared what a doctor might be told of the night's happenings, and he assured Bhim that Nulini would get over her hysterics in a day or two. She ought to be grateful, he said, that she had such a forgiving husband.

In the early evening when the funeral procession had gone its noisy way under the window, Nulini became feverish, muttering and turning restlessly on the bed. Bhim sent Ayah to his mother's storeroom for blankets, and when they came he packed them over Nulini. In the absence of Cook Maharaj at the funeral, he himself went to the kitchen and cracked ice from the big block which was delivered daily, filled an ice bag and placed it on Nulini's forehead, but she writhed so much that it was hard to keep it there.

'I wish Mother was here,' he said to Ayah.

'She comes tomorrow,' said Ayah, pity for the boy making her gentle-voiced for once.

Shushila, on her way to the station with her father, knew nothing of Khan's death, her father himself having taken her over to her uncles' house immediately she had eaten her breakfast on the morning after the tragedy, on the excuse that sister Nulini was not very well and it would be dull for a little girl if she had no one with whom to play.

Shushila, therefore, gave her mother a tremendous welcome, complete with a garland which she had chosen herself in the bazaar on the way to the station.

Thakkur sat with the clerk in the front of the returning car and, of course, asked where Khan was, and the clerk told him in an undertone of the accidental drowning, while Shushila babbled happily to Mrs Singh.

'Nulini has fever,' Thakkur heard her say. 'It is a pity because she has given me her badminton racket and was going to teach me how to play.'

'Nulini ill?' exclaimed Mrs Singh, full of concern.

'She is not well,' said Ram Singh, 'I shall tell you more about it at home.'

'When she is better, Bhim is going to take her to Simla for a holiday,' said Shushila. 'I asked if I could go too – he says I can go next time – not this time.

'He's going to learn to play badminton too, so that we can all play together,' she added. 'Can I buy some shuttlecocks, Mummy?'

'Of course, dear.'

Ram Singh asked how Mrs Singh's sister was progressing and Thakkur held his breath while Mrs Singh said calmly that she was now quite well and sent her namastes to her brother-in-law.

As soon as they arrived home, Ram Singh drew his wife into his study and shut the door behind them. 'Before even giving her a glass of water,' remarked Ayah indignantly.

He must have told her about Khan and Nulini, because without even waiting to wash her feet and hands, she hurried to Shushila's room, while Ram Singh stumped up the stairs to his prayer room, looking like a small thundercloud.

'Sahib and Ma ji must have disagreed,' thought Ayah, as she hurried after her mistress. 'Nulini Bahu is in Chota Sahib's room,' she informed Mrs Singh, a little breathlessly.

'Is she very sick?' Mrs Singh asked, as she changed direction and headed for Bhim's room, her sari end wafted out behind her in the breeze of her passing.

'Temperature is down, Ma ji.'

They reached Bhim's room.

'Wait here, Ayah,' said Mrs Singh, pointing to a spot out of earshot, and disconsolately Ayah sat down on the stone floor and waited. Mrs Singh lifted the door curtain, and Ayah could see Bhim sitting at work at his desk, while Nulini lay quietly on his cot, which he had moved close to the desk. The boy rose, and the curtain dropped.

Nobody ever knew what passed between Mrs Singh and the young couple, but having nursed one daughter-in-law back to health, she silently nursed the other one, and about ten days later she saw Nulini and Bhim off to Simla.

Ram Singh did not speak to his elder son before he left. Apparently Bhim's quiet acceptance of his wife's infidelity was too much for the old man, and the thought that his first grandchild was likely to be a servant's bastard must have burned in him.

Both parents looked old and tired. The beautiful, big house which had been built to hold lots of grandchildren was silent and empty. Even Shushila, robbed of her playmate, was quieter and spent more time at her uncles' house playing with her cousins.

The warm, damp days of the monsoon went slowly by like monotonous drips from a tap, and the first cool breath of autumn rippled softly along the verandas.

'Soon it will be Diwali,' shouted Shushila, 'lovely, lovely Diwali.'

Thakkur was serving his master with lemon water when the sound of her cheerful shouting to Pratap echoed through the garden. He saw Ram

Singh's moustache twitch as if the mouth beneath was trembling, and Mrs Singh cleared her throat nervously. He might well look dismal, thought Thakkur, with one son under a cloud at Shahpur and the other sent to Simla out of season as if he was also in disgrace. Thakkur did not know why Bhim should be in disgrace, but he had marked the unusual lack of communication between father and son and the departure to a hill station at the wrong time of year. What was the use of Diwali, Festival of Light, ruminated Thakkur, a time of family reunion, when there was no family to reunite?

He pottered off to the kitchen and when, later, he returned to clear away the glasses, Mrs Singh was saying rather diffidently: 'Father, can we not have a real family party here for Diwali?'

'Who is there to ask?' asked Ram Singh sulkily, not having noticed Thakkur's approach.

'You have sons,' said Mrs Singh reproachfully.

'They have brought me nothing but sorrow and worry,' said Ram Singh, full of self-pity.

Thakkur mopped up imaginary spots of lemon from the side table; it always amused him how Mrs Singh managed her husband, and he did not wish to miss any more of the conversation than he had to. The couple were sitting on a sheet-covered mattress enjoying the mild late afternoon sun, and Mrs Singh moved closer to her husband. She patted his hand just as if she was a young wife, as Thakkur remarked later, and said: 'Is it not our duty to guide our children lovingly and not to leave them to struggle alone in the world? This is surely our duty and should be our pleasure while we are here.'

Ram Singh said nothing but did not withdraw his hand. She smiled impishly at him, and Thakkur found some more imaginary spots to mop up.

'I have a story to tell you,' she said. 'Before I tell you, however, you must promise me something.' Her voice had a gay inflection.

Ram Singh showed faint interest.

'Yes. The promise I ask . . .' and she looked at him with her fine eyes in such a way that he had to smile at her. 'The promise that I ask is that if I make you happier with my story, you will buy me a present, and if I make you unhappy you will not upbraid me.'

'Humph,' said Ram Singh grumpily. 'There might as well be one happy person in the house – I will buy you a wrist watch.'

'Oh, how lovely,' breathed Mrs Singh.

Her husband bridled a little, rather enjoying the impression he had made. In fact, Mrs Singh looked so hugely satisfied at his offer that in the end he laughed.

'Well,' said Mrs Singh, taking a big breath. 'There was once a young man of great ability, whose father desired that he should enter the family silk business. The boy was unfortunately not very obedient and swore that he would never be any use as a merchant; instead he wanted to be a lawyer. His father was furious and said that the young man would come to a bad end . . .'

Reluctantly Thakkur drifted unnoticed back to the kitchen. Ma ji had more courage than ten men. He would never, if he were a woman, be brave enough to tell the Burra Sahib that he himself had been an unfilial son of great strength of character, and that his sons had merely inherited their father's propensity for independent thought. Thakkur could remember being told, when he first came to the Singh household, about the fierce family row that had occurred when Singh Sahib had demanded further education so that he could become a lawyer. He had won his point, the second and third brothers had entered the silk trade, and the old father had lived to see all his sons flourishing.

Ma ji was a woman of strength, too. No wonder her sons demanded to go their own way. He hoped very much that Ma ji would prevail upon the Burra Sahib to bring the family together. Thakkur had served the family for so many years that he felt a part of it, and it distressed him very much to see the courtyard empty and the dining-room next to the kitchen barely used.

It was queer how Bhim Sahib had suddenly taken his wife away to Simla. He never would understand how they had suddenly become such a loving couple. They never seemed to bother much about each other before, although he had to admit that Miss Nulini was quick to serve her husband whenever he asked anything of her. Now it was just as if they were newly married and could not be enough in each other's company. Bhim Sahib had hardly left his wife throughout her illness, and even Cook Maharaj had noticed his solicitude for her when they set out on their journey. Ayah knew something, Thakkur was sure – she looked so secretive. Well, there was only one kind of secret women ever kept and that was when a new baby was expected, and they were always so cheerfully secretive about it, that it was never a secret for long. He grinned to himself as he thought he had reached the core of the mystery; no doubt the tailor would soon be called in to stitch small garments.

But it was eleven months before the sewing machines whirred on the back veranda, so Thakkur never found out what caused Bhim Sahib's sudden interest in his wife.

Thakkur sat in the shade of the house and smoked a bili while Cook Maharaj prepared dinner – such a small dinner. The house was, indeed, far too empty. He wondered if Khan haunted it – and shivered at the thought. Strange how he fell down the well – as if he did not know where it was, after being so many months in the house. There were rumours about him. Chowkidar said that on the night of his death Burra Sahib had found the hill man stealing and had turned him out. Thakkur could not imagine Khan stealing – he would have trusted him with his life. He had been a very quiet man but in Thakkur's opinion he was no thief. Anyway, if he had stolen, no doubt in his next life he would be born a sweeper as punishment.

Thakkur watched Mrs Singh's wrist for several days. Would there be a suitable Diwali celebration? Would the boys be coming home? He had nearly given up hope, when one day Ayah told him that Burrah Sahib had bought Ma ji a fine, new watch, the best she had seen for a long time.

Thakkur was ironing a sari for Mrs Singh, and slowly he put down his charcoal-heated iron, looked up from his position on the floor of the kitchen and began to smile, his face nearly cracking with the unaccustomed effort. He gathered up the sari and made Ayah help him fold it, while the grin gradually expanded across his face. He picked the ironing cloth up off the floor, giving a peculiar snort as he did; then he suddenly threw back his head and laughed aloud, the cackles echoing round the kitchen and making Cook Maharaj and the little kitchen boy look up from their work in astonishment.

'I don't see what there is to laugh at,' said Ayah testily. 'Come to think of it,' she added sourly, 'it's the first time I've seen you do anything but moan for years past.'

'Be patient, my old fox – here, take the sari for Ma ji – this is going to be the best Diwali for years.'

'I don't know what you mean – and I am not an old fox – and I will not be spoken to like that.' Her voice rose shrilly. 'And why Ma ji always gets you to iron her saris instead of me, I can't understand,' she added, full of suppressed resentment at Thakkur's privileged place in Ma ji's affections.

'Now, now, Ayah,' said Cook Maharaj. 'He meant no harm. We could all do with a bit of a celebration – although I don't know what it has to do with watches. There hasn't been a really good do since Ajit Sahib's sacred thread ceremony – and how many years ago is that?'

'Hmm,' sniffed Ayah. 'Some people seem to enjoy extra work – and right busy you'll be if there's a big Diwali party.'

'It'll be big all right,' said Thakkur, his face relapsing into its usual mournful lines.

'Good,' said Cook Maharaj. 'I shall make carrot hulwa for Ajit Sahib and suji hulwa for Bhim Sahib – it's his favourite – and something special for our Shushila.' His kind, round face beamed, as he kneaded the dough in the pannikin before him. 'And I must ask Ma ji about savouries for Burra Sahib.'

Chapter Thirty-four

Our flat seemed very empty after Mrs Singh had returned home. I had enjoyed her visit more than I could have believed possible; her calmness had soothed my harassed nerves and her advice had smoothed away many of my physical woes. Ajit also took heart from his mother's visit and he often talked about her and about his childhood spent in his grandfather's house – the same house in which his uncles now lived. His grandfather had been a terrifying domestic despot, who, for business reasons, had cultivated the goodwill of the English civil servants in the district, with the result that his patient, orthodox wife and her daughter-in-law had found the comfortable untidiness of their purdah apartments invaded at times by casteless, staring white women. His grandmother, Ajit told me with a chuckle, plied the strange ladies with sweetmeats and tea, but refused to eat a crumb in their presence or touch the special tea set kept for such visitors. I was, therefore, not the first English woman that Mrs Singh had observed at close quarters, although I was the first wife with whom she had carried on much conversation – she had been far too shy to speak in the presence of her mother-in-law's visitors. She was, however, relieved to find that I was not very much like these visitors – I was much less formal.

In between my household tasks, I often stopped to talk to Kamala as she squatted in the shade at the back of the flat and made cow dung cakes for her cooking fires, from the dung which she collected in a basket beforehand. Kamala was full of excitement, as in the following spring she was to be married to a man from another village, with whom she had fallen in love when he came to her own village with a marriage party. The fathers had been prevailed upon by the young people to open marriage negotiations and, as they were of the same sub-caste, the arrangements had been concluded most amicably.

'Supposing he had been of the wrong caste, Kamala?'

'Then Father would have found somebody else,' said Kamala with calm acceptance, as she slapped her cow dung cakes between her slender, aristocratic-looking hands.

I was sitting on the back step one day, talking to her and at the same time feeding a kid with cactus leaves from a nearby bush – to the amusement of the goatherd – when the postman cycled up.

'So many letters, Memsahib,' he said as he handed me three. I smiled. He was reminding me that he worked hard for us, so that his Diwali tip would be generous.

Only one letter was addressed to me personally. It was from Father, who hoped I was well, informed me that he was having some success with his chrysanthemums, had been made Chairman of a Red Cross Committee, and that the country was going to the dogs. I felt a tug of homesickness and for a moment the tangy smell of chrysanthemums obliterated the odour of the desert.

The other letters were for Ajit, one from Delhi addressed in a firm Italian hand of slender up strokes and heavy down ones, and one from Simla in the crabbed, hasty writing of a note maker. I propped them against a silver candlestick in the living-room and returned to the kitchen to cook the dinner.

'Letters for you, love,' I called, when I heard Ajit's step on the veranda, and, wiping my hands on my pinafore, I went to kiss him.

He was looking at the letter in the Italian hand. 'Father,' he said softly, and quickly slit the envelope.

I felt as awed as if he had said God had written, and sat down on the edge of a basket chair to hear what had caused such an event.

Ajit sat down by the table and read in silence, and when he came to the end he put his head down upon the table and burst into tears.

Horrified, I ran to him and put my arm round his shoulders, begging him at the same time to tell me what had happened.

He buried his damp face in my pinafore, sobbed a moment or two and then with a beaming smile looked up at me and said: 'It is joy. I cry for joy.'

'Your father has written kindly?'

Ajit hugged me round the waist. 'He has written that we are both to come home for Diwali. He has announced our marriage, and desires to make the acquaintance of his new daughter.'

'My darling,' I exclaimed, 'I am so happy – so very happy, for your sake.'

'Life is kind,' said Ajit, hugging me tighter. 'You are well – the house blossoms under your feet – and now we have again a family.'

'What about the other letter?' I asked, laughing at his poetic flights.

'Oh, yes. It's from Bhim. What's he doing in Simla at this time of year?' he queried as he examined the postmark.

'Open it and see.'

He opened the letter. There was only one sheet of paper, closely covered with Hindi characters. Ajit translated it as he read: 'Dear Brother, Nulini and I have come here for a rest, as she has had fever – Bannerji is looking after my practice during my absence. Mother writes that you are coming home for Diwali, and Nulini and I expect to return in time to welcome Peggie and you. Father announced your marriage. Mother says Uncles were amazed and she has been inundated with visitors who have come to ask about Peggie. There is great interest, although I believe no animosity.

'Nulini is becoming strong again, and she is teaching me to dance. I did not know that she liked to dance. On our return to Delhi we shall join a small club, so that we can dance and play a game of bridge occasionally.

'When you come to Delhi, I shall consult you about buying a radio and a pickup. I have never really listened to Western music – Nulini says I am missing much enjoyment.

'We both send namastes to Peggie and you.'

Ajit looked at me out of the corner of his eye and grinned. 'There is more to this letter than meets the eyes,' he said. 'What on earth has driven Bhim to learn to dance?'

'Ha,' I said wickedly, 'what about your learning to dance – I didn't know that one could dance in India.'

He looked at me appalled. 'No!'

'Yes,' I said ruthlessly. 'You could dance a little when you were in England. We'll start again tonight – and you can take me to a dance when we go to Delhi.'

'Oh, no,' he wailed in mock misery.

We had a most entertaining evening while he renewed his knowledge of the waltz.

Ajit was dizzy with excitement during the days that followed. He nearly burst with happiness. So obvious was it, that the eldest Miss Shah inquired if I was going to have a baby.

'Not just yet,' I said.

When I lay ill, she had asked me if my parents-in-law had accepted me, because it was strange that no one had come to my aid from the family. I had asked her not to talk about the matter to anybody else and had then told her what had happened. Knowing the situation, she had rejoiced with me at Mrs Singh's visit, and now I expected that she would share my pleasure again; but instead she looked very troubled. At last she said: 'Are you not afraid of being poisoned?'

'Poisoned? Good heavens, why should I be?'

Miss Shah said uneasily: 'It is not an unknown way of getting rid of an unwanted daughter-in-law.'

'Ridiculous,' I said.

But as the train to Delhi carried us through the bleak country of Rajasthan, the clattering wheels chanted: 'Poison, poison, poison,' until I wanted to scream. As it slowed down to enter Delhi junction, it said: 'Could be poisoned and burned in a night, burned in a night, burned in a night.'

At the station before Delhi junction there was a general exodus from our carriage and nobody else got in; Ajit and I were left in possession. I sat quietly as the train jerked forward again. We had long since rolled up our bedding and packed away the books we had bought to while away the thirty-hour journey, and nothing remained to be done, except listen to the chant of the wheels.

My face must have shown something of my sickening doubts, for Ajit looked at me and asked: 'Are you all right, Rani?'

I could not answer. Unreasonable fear clamped my throat shut.

Ajit looked alarmed: 'Dearest, what is it?'

I found my voice. 'Ajit, I'm so frightened.'

'Why should you be frightened?' He put his arm round me comfortingly.

'It's something Miss Shah said,' I said hesitatingly. I felt I must lay this terrifying ghost. Common sense told me I was being ridiculous – and yet I did not really know how bitter were the feelings of my father-in-law. Dreadful crimes had been committed at the time of the partitioning of the country, and how could I be sure that an equal anger might not descend on me?

'Well, and what did Miss Gossip say?'

I told him.

'Women!' he exclaimed, 'and some in particular.'

The typically Lancashire exclamation which he had picked up made me giggle, in spite of my fears.

'Do you honestly believe that my father would murder my wife?'

'I don't know,' I said defensively. 'How can I know what people will do – anything could happen in such a strange country.'

'You deserve to be spanked,' said Ajit grimly. 'To begin with, if Father really wished to get rid of you, there are a thousand more easy and less incriminating ways than poisoning you in his own house.' He shook me playfully, and went on: 'Secondly, although I know this is to you a queer, rickety old country, we do not as a rule spend our time poisoning people, even if we dislike them. There are probably not many more murders per head of population here than there are in England –

and not even Father could escape official inquiry into the sudden death in his home of a perfectly healthy young woman.'

I felt ashamed.

He continued: 'Miss Shah is romancing. Perhaps such things did happen long ago – I cannot say – but she has no right to fill your head with such rubbish. Why did you not ask me about it before?'

'I did not know how you would take it.'

He was hurt. 'Rani,' he said very gently. 'I have told you before that you must never be afraid to confide in me. I love you and you could not do anything which would break that love.' He bent his head and kissed me; the kiss became a deep and long one. 'Love you, love you, love you,' recited the wheels.

'Porter, Sahib?' asked a very intrigued man, as he put his head through the carriage window.

We laughed and jumped apart. Ajit looked out of the window nearest to him. 'I can see them,' he shouted. I straightened my travel-stained sari, took up my handbag and shawl and picked my way after Ajit through the luggage strewn on the floor. The porter wrenched open the door, we gave him hasty instructions, took his number and stepped down on to the platform. Then we were running hand in hand towards the little couple, who looked so fragile and lonely in the milling crowd.

I let go of Ajit's hand and allowed him to approach first. He took dust from their feet, while Shushila, whom I had not noticed previously, danced up to me. 'Are you my new sister?' she asked.

I smiled. 'If you are Shushila, I am.'

'Mummy, Mummy,' she shouted, 'I have found sister – see.'

Ajit had drilled me well for this meeting. My sari veiled my head and most of my face. I kept my eyes a little down and made my best namaste to my parents. I was a foot taller than Ram Singh, but he had an awe-inspiring dignity as he looked at me coldly for a moment. Then the big moustache twitched and he smiled, as he said in perfect English: 'You are welcome, daughter.'

'Thank you,' I said.

'Allow me to take your shawl,' he said, just as Father would have done. The quiet, Western courtesy, remembered presumably specially for my benefit, to make me feel more at ease, touched my heart, and I handed the shawl to him with a frank smile, looking shyly into his eyes as I might well have done if he had been an elderly Englishman. He seemed to like it and straightened himself, smoothed his whiskers and called Shushila. Meanwhile, Mrs Singh turned from Ajit to ask me if I was now quite well and not too tired. I assured her that I was now comparatively strong and whispered that it was due to her great kindness.

She giggled like a girl, but did not reply; possibly she had not yet told her husband of her visit to Shahpur, and I resolved not to betray her by an idle word.

We went through the vast halls of the station to the world outside, where I pulled up short. I had forgotten that it was Diwali.

The city was bathed in light. It burst upon my senses as if the sparkle of a huge catherine wheel had enveloped me. Lights were everywhere, outlining every building; arc lamps added grace to new buildings, tiny separate lights outlined the older establishments and left their ugliness in darkness, lights in the gutters and on the pavements kindled from carefully collected scraps of paper, by beggars and refugees; but best of all, thousands of tiny oil lamps outlining Ajit's home, as we drove up to it.

Every balustrade, every window sill, had its row of lamps; intricate patterns in the brightest colours had been painted on the wide entrance steps; several small children were chasing each other backwards and forwards across the veranda, and through the windows came a buzz of conversation from their elders. Somewhere someone was plucking at a stringed instrument and the plaintive notes reverberated through my head, as I descended from the car after Mrs Singh, and stood hesitating at the foot of the steps looking up at the family before me. I hesitated only a moment, but it was sufficient to photograph upon my memory a picture which would stay with me always; long after the family had scattered I would remember them as I saw them then.

At the top of the steps stood a tall, glittering woman and by her side an equally tall, handsome man. It was my first glimpse of Bimla, who was to give me an intimate friendship; the man by her side was her new husband. Behind her stood Ayah and Thakkur, whose affection I was to enjoy through many years; they were craning their necks to catch a glimpse of the new daughter-in-law. Bimla had her arm round the shoulders of a slender, veiled woman – Nulini, I guessed correctly. Half-way down the steps was a big, shy-looking man, bending down to catch Shushila, who ran up to him. 'Bhim,' she cried. 'Brother Bhim, we have brought sister.'

Finally, at the foot of the steps was the father, who, once having made up his mind to accept me into his family, was to enrich Ajit's and my life by his learning and wisdom, and a few steps further up was the mother, to whom I would turn in times of stress as automatically as if she was my own mother.

The moment came and went. The photograph remained.

The group broke into movement. Bhim rushed down the steps, Shushila tucked under one arm and protesting loudly.

'Ajit!'

'Bhim! – How well you look – and how happy, you old scoundrel.'

'I am happy,' he replied simply. He smiled at me, but I was not introduced – I was a member of the family and needed no introduction. Nulini and Bimla started down the steps towards me, as Ajit, talking gaily to his mother and his brother, ascended towards Bimla's husband and a bevy of aunts, uncles and cousins, who came pouring out of the house. I prepared to follow Ajit, but Ram Singh stepped back until he was level with me. He viewed his house with approbation, and gesturing towards it, he asked: 'Do you know why we light up our houses like this?'

'No, Sir,' I said respectfully.

'We believe that Lakshmi, the Goddess of Fortune, will come to the house which is most brightly lit up.'

'May she enter your house,' I said.

Ram Singh looked round at his family chattering on the steps; he saw the children of his brothers playing on his verandas; he heard the merry voices of his kinsmen enjoying his hospitality; and he looked up at his wife, who had turned round on the top step, to see why we were not following her in.

She smiled down at her husband and I saw him look up at her with the same sweet expression that Ajit had for me. He turned and looked at me, making a gay little gesture towards Mrs Singh. 'I think Lakshmi has been in my house for many years,' he said roguishly, his moustaches twitching and his heavy eyebrows curving upwards over the eyes which were narrowed in merriment.

I laughed. 'I feel sure she has,' I said.

Ajit ran down the steps again, and I put my hand into his. 'Come and meet your family,' he said.

THE MONEYLENDERS OF SHAHPUR

To Dianne, with love.

You are worried when you hear that she is born;
Picking husbands makes you anxious and forlorn;
When she marries, will her husband be a churl?
It is tough to be the father of a girl.

At her birth she steals away her mother's heart;
Loving friends, when she is older, fall apart;
Even married she is apt to bring a stain:
Having daughters is a business full of pain.

The Panchatantra,
trans. by Arthur W. Ryder from the
Kashmiri version 1199 AD.

Prologue

'They'll think I'm mad,' muttered Dr John Bennett to himself, as he waited for the station porter to load his luggage into a tonga. 'To come back to India, when so many Indians are trying to settle in the West. It won't make sense to them, even though I was born and brought up here.' He smiled wryly to himself. 'Mad dogs and Englishmen . . .'

For over a year now, he had been thinking seriously of returning to India. He was bored by his job as lecturer in Asian Studies. He was tired of Liverpool, its cold, its dampness, its depression; he longed for sunshine. Suddenly, he could stand it no longer. He had his Air Force pension and some savings; he had no family. At the end of the 1949/50 university year, he packed up his books and joyfully took a boat out to India.

Now he stood unsteadily at the top of the imposing steps of Shahpur station, a thirty-four-year-old Englishman, whose war wounds in his legs ached abominably, and wondered if he would still be welcome; India had, after all, fought very hard to rid itself of the British, and it had had its freedom for only two years.

People pushed and shoved past, their luggage perilously poised on the heads of porters. Where once there would have been a number of white faces amongst them, now there was none. Amid the crowds of Hindus and Muslims, a fair sprinkling of Jains stood out, distinguished by their plain white clothes and their more sedate movements.

Looking across the railway lines, he could see the Chemical Works which his father had managed until his death. He observed from the neon sign that its name had been altered to the Star of Asia Chemical Company, and a large addition had been built. The smell of sulphur and other chemicals from it far outweighed the more traditional odours of horse manure and open drains.

He shifted his weight off his wounded legs and on to the two sticks with which he supported himself. God, how the heat made his wounds throb – but at least here he would not have to stand on them while he lectured, he consoled himself. He would try to find his old friend, Dr Ferozeshah, and get him to prescribe a pain reliever for him.

A dignified, elderly Jain came slowly up the steps, his quiet, saintly face lit by a smile, the palms of his hands held together in greeting.

'John, I am pleased to see you. I'm sorry I'm late. Your letter arrived only an hour ago.'

He paused for breath, and then looked aghast at John's sticks. 'You've not been cured?' he asked, a quaver in his voice.

John was sharply reminded that Jains regard physical disability as a punishment for misdemeanours in previous lives, and his heart sank a little.

'No,' he replied, as he watched his father's old friend trying to overcome his repugnance. 'But I can manage quite well with my sticks – and on a bicycle.'

The older man recovered some of his composure.

'I am very relieved to hear that,' he said, looking again uneasily at the offending legs, then averting his gaze to look round the station yard. 'We must get a tonga.'

'I have one,' said John, as he slipped a coin into the eager palm of the hovering porter.

They moved slowly to the little carriage, which was weighed down with a trunk, a bedding roll and three suitcases.

'Thank you for coming to meet me, Dr Mehta.'

'I was most happy to come,' replied Dr Mehta with conviction. 'Since the death of your dear father and mother in that dreadful aeroplane accident, I have felt as a parent to you – and I hope you will regard me as such.'

John warmed to the kindly old man, and he felt sad that someone so gentle should have aged so much. The once upright figure was bent and thin, the face fine drawn. The voice which he remembered so well from many a lecture on English literature had lost its richness and was faded.

'You are very good,' he said.

He struggled into the carriage after Dr Mehta, using a firm grip on either side of the door at the back to swing his awkward legs up and over the difficult steps. He cursed under his breath as he hit his knee.

'And how is little Anasuyabehn?' he inquired, as Dr Mehta and he settled themselves on the side seats. 'She was about to be married last time you mentioned her in your letters.'

Dr Mehta arranged his white dhoti neatly round his legs before he answered. His ascetic-looking face registered an uneasy frown. Finally, he said, 'Her betrothed died, so she is not yet married – being motherless makes life a little more difficult for her than it should be – but I shall arrange another marriage for her soon. She must have time to recover.' He did not mention a grave shortage of suitable young men in his caste or that he had left his child's marriage rather late, because he found it hard to part with her.

John nodded politely.

'She's getting into touch with your father's old servant, Ranjit. We felt sure you would like to have him to serve you. He went back to his village after your father died.'

John was delighted. 'I'd like to have him very much,' he said. Ranjit was a Hindu, and he remembered the happy hours he had spent nestled against the strong, kindly peasant, listening to his harsh country dialect as he told him tales of the great Arjun, and of Ram and his faithful Sita. He also remembered suddenly his gentle, easy-going Ayah who had taken him with her to pray in Jain temples; he could almost feel again his offering of flowers clutched in his hand.

The carriage jogged along the narrow streets. Women were standing in queues to draw water from street taps, to carry up to their families who lived over the open-fronted shops. From behind white saris or red veils they peeked shyly at the strange Englishman.

In the Moneylenders' Quarter, the sweepers were busy brushing the pavements with small rush brooms. They worked their way phlegmatically in and out amongst the beggars, who sat on their heels with their backs against the high compound walls surrounding the moneylenders' communal family homes.

The carriage swept through the ancient Red Gate and John caught a glimpse of the temple to which his ayah used to take him when he was a little boy. It had a double row of lepers lining its imposing steps from top to bottom. Then, within a few minutes, they were engulfed by the overwhelming perfume of the Hindu flower bazaar.

The bazaar marked the end of the city. Dr Mehta raised his hand to point towards a group of fine, modern buildings, fronted by well-kept flower gardens.

'Our new Government University,' he announced with pride. 'You can just see our original college – which you'll remember – through the trees.'

Indeed, John assured him, he did remember – he had been happy when he had attended it. Many of his fellow scholars had been the sons of merchants and moneylenders from the Jain community, sent to the college to obtain a good command of English.

He had always been interested in Jains. They were so determined not to kill anything, not even an insect or one of the souls they believed inhabited the air or crowded into root vegetables and unripe fruit. Their desire not to commit violence meant that they could not use any implement, be it plough or typewriter; so they were usually moneylenders or merchants, though there were many monks and nuns amongst them and a fair number of scholars like Dr Mehta.

'My bungalow is one of those facing the campus, along that lane over there,' said Dr Mehta. He clutched the side of the carriage as it bumped suddenly off the gravel road and into the rutted lane he had just indicated. Then as it began to trundle more safely along, he asked, 'I'm not sure, my dear John, what your plans are . . .?'

John's voice was a little defensive, as he replied, 'My *History of India* is selling so well in the States, and in Britain and India, that I thought I might follow it with a history of the Gujerat – approaching it, perhaps, through the story of the Marwari Gate temple here in Shahpur.'

Dr Mehta nodded, and directed the driver to his bungalow.

'An old bachelor like me doesn't need a great deal,' John said. He did not know how to explain to Dr Mehta his desperate need to rest and be quiet. England had been as alien to him as to any other immigrant; his upbringing in India had not prepared him for the difference in its way of life. The struggle to earn a living when crippled had also been exhausting.

After the war, he had expected to marry the girl to whom he had become engaged before being taken prisoner, but she had looked with undisguised distaste at his torn legs and viewed with horror his tentative proposal that they should live in India. She had left him sitting in a wheelchair in a military hospital and, a month later, had married someone else. This unhappy experience had tended to make him brusque and defensive with women and he had never proposed to anyone else. He never considered that in spite of his damaged legs he was still a fine-looking man, with his brush of black hair lightly touched with grey, and blue eyes which normally twinkled cheerfully from under straight, bushy eyebrows; he had never really examined himself in a mirror for years.

As they descended from the carriage, Dr Mehta murmured gentle agreement with John's plans. The driver began to unload the luggage and dump it into the sand.

The compound gate was opened by an excited boy servant. Behind him, fidgeting nervously, was Dr Mehta's sister, who kept house for him, an old lady in white widow's garb, her cunning face creased with anxiety about her English visitor, whom she remembered as a precocious, ever curious young man.

Anasuyabehn, small, plump and passive, stood half behind her aunt, peeking at John through thick fluttering eyelashes.

John whistled under his breath. It always defeated him how Jain women could look, at the same time, so prim and so seductive. No one looking at a Jain, he thought, could guess at the passions raging beneath their placid exteriors.

Smiling, both women advanced timidly, putting the palms of their hands together in salute.

As John bowed and said how pleased he was to see them again, he was thinking that if he were Dr Mehta, with a twenty-four-year-old daughter like Anasuyabehn, he would marry her off fast, before she got entangled with someone unscrupulous.

Chapter One

The office of the Vice-[illegible] of Ishapur [illegible] was extremely [illegible]. It seemed [illegible] white walls of the Arts [illegible] were floating back [illegible] that September [illegible] absorbed all the heat [illegible] and K. had then [illegible] concentrated in the Vice-[illegible] curiously pleasant room [illegible] the seemingly aimless [illegible] in front of the building.

[illegible]

Chapter One

The office of the Vice-Chancellor of Shahpur University was extremely hot. It seemed as if the white walls of the Arts and Science Building had, that September morning, absorbed all the heat of the surrounding desert, and it had then become concentrated in the Vice-Chancellor's usually pleasant room overlooking the carefully cultivated gardens in front of the building.

The Vice-Chancellor, Dr Yashvant Prasad, drummed his fingers irritably on his desk and tried to concentrate his attention on the papers before him, but the fan kept fluttering them and finally he closed the file and handed it to the Dean, Dr Mehta, who was standing by the desk.

The Dean's gnarled brown hands shook a little as he took the file from his superior. Today was a fast day and he felt suddenly very weak and weary and thought wistfully of his retirement, still twelve months away.

He flicked over the pages of the file, which was neatly labelled *Dr Tilak, Zoology*, and said, 'Dr Tilak should arrive this afternoon. I'm giving him two rooms in the students' hostel for the present.'

'That will do very well,' agreed the Vice-Chancellor.

'There's a small room next to the Botany Museum which has water laid on, and I have arranged for him to have it as a laboratory.' The Dean paled a little. He had long considered the requirements of Dr Tilak, the first staff member to be recruited for the new Department of Zoology. Would he, for instance, pin dead insects on to boards, as they had done in the Bombay Museum? Would he dissect animals? Perhaps, knowing how sacred life was in the Gujerat, he would teach with the aid of pictures and diagrams. Dean Mehta fervently hoped so, as he continued, 'I – er am not sure what his research involves, but doubtless a little money will be forthcoming for equipment for him?'

'I doubt it,' said the Vice-Chancellor glumly. 'It was difficult enough to squeeze his salary out of the provincial government.' He chewed his lower lip thoughtfully. 'I'll try again,' he promised.

Several flies were buzzing round the office, so the Vice-Chancellor banged the bell on his desk and called to the peon outside the door to shut the window.

The peon, a thin wraith of a man clad in crumpled khaki, slipped down from his stool and trailed languidly across to the window, skilfully palming his small brown cigarette as he passed the Vice-Chancellor's desk. He banged the window shut and returned to his stool.

The Vice-Chancellor leaned back in his wooden revolving chair and fretfully pulled at his long straight nose. He thought longingly of his native Delhi and wondered why he had ever agreed to come to the Gujerat to head this struggling university at Shahpur. He had, he thought despondently, only two fellow mathematicians on the staff – poor company for a Harvard man like himself.

The peon brought him a cup of lukewarm, oversweet tea, and, momentarily forgetting the Dean's presence, the Vice-Chancellor viciously swatted a fly about to descend upon it. Flies all winter, roasting heat all summer; then the humidity before the rains, then the rains themselves with their following of cholera, typhoid and typhus. When the rains stopped there were clouds of mosquitoes carrying malaria to contend with. Really, Shahpur was only fit to live in for about two months of the year.

The Dean tucked the file on Dr Tilak under his arm and said anxiously, 'I hope that a Maratha like Dr Tilak will fit comfortably into our Gujerati ways.'

'I am from Delhi and I am managing to do so,' responded the Vice-Chancellor tartly.

'Ah, yes, indeed, my dear sir,' said the Dean, realizing his slip immediately. 'You are, however, *so* understanding.'

The Vice-Chancellor bridled and said jokingly, 'Well, well, at least the British left us a common language, so that it makes no difference that Dr Tilak's native tongue is Marathi, yours is Gujerati and mine is Hindi.'

'Oh, yes,' agreed Dr Mehta hastily. But his mind revolted at the idea that an alien tongue united his beloved Gujerat with the cocksure southerners and the stupid northerners. His thoughts began to wander.

Although he was a professor of English, knew the plays of Shakespeare nearly by heart and had bookshelves crammed with the latest works in English, his heart lay in his little glass-fronted bookcase amongst his sacred Jain writings, laboriously collected over the years, some of them manuscripts written in Gujerati or Prakrit or Magadhi. Before this bookcase he would sometimes put a little offering of rice; and he would carefully take the writings out and dust them at the appropriate festival.

Vice-Chancellor Prasad glanced up at the Dean's thin, lined face, clean-shaven except for a moustache, with its drooping eyelids and calm, firm mouth. The Dean saw the glance and came back to earth immediately. He pulled his watch out of his trouser pocket; it was a fine gold one which had belonged to his father, and he flicked the lid open carefully.

'Dr Bennett is coming to see me for a few minutes at about twelve o'clock. He wants to go over the Marwari Gate temple; so if you will excuse me I'll go now.'

'Certainly. I should like to see Dr Tilak as soon as he arrives – I'm particularly anxious that our new Department should start off properly.'

'I, too,' replied the Dean with more fervour than he felt. He had advised against a Department of Zoology and he had an uneasy feeling that Dr Tilak could find himself on a collision course with Jain members of the staff.

That same morning, a very bored Anasuyabehn Mehta had been to the library to change her books. Domesticated and obedient as she was, she trusted implicitly her father's promise to arrange another marriage for her. But in the meantime, she seemed to be living in an empty limbo, too old to associate with other single girls, yet without the advantages of matrimony.

Her aunt frowned at her as she entered and put the library books down in a corner. 'Go and wash yourself, child, before entering the kitchen,' she instructed. Then she turned to chide the boy servant for putting too much charcoal on the fire. 'Savitri is waiting on the roof,' she shouted, as Anasuyabehn trailed off to the bathroom.

Her friend, Savitri, knew her well enough to wait a little longer, thought Anasuyabehn, as she filled the bath bucket. Before commencing to wash herself, however, she went to the bottom of the stairs and called to Savitri that she would be up in a few minutes.

Savitri, comfortable in the shade of a tree taller than the bungalow, shouted that she had not to be back at work for an hour.

Anasuyabehn quickly bathed, washed her hair and changed her petticoat, blouse and sari. Then, taking a towel and rubbing her hair as she went, she climbed the stairs to the roof, promising herself that she would go down to help Aunt in the kitchen after a few minutes' gossip with her friend.

Savitri lived such a full and interesting life, she thought enviously. She actually earned her living as a chemist. She herself had never been able to persuade her father to allow her to work.

'Have you had lunch?' she asked Savitri. Her voice was solicitous and deferential. It rejuvenated the other girl's self-esteem, which always sank when she saw Anasuyabehn.

She turned her thin, heavily bespectacled face towards her friend and said she had eaten. She thought mournfully that she had a university degree and competed successfully in the world's hardest labour market; but when she and Anasuyabehn walked together in the evening it was at

Anasuyabehn that young men cast longing glances. Savitri's needle-sharp wit might enliven a party, but it was to Anasuyabehn's shy acquiescing answers that men really listened – negative, obedient Anasuyabehn – so obedient, thought Savitri grimly, that it was just as well that she had few opportunities to meet young men alone. Savitri herself had haughtily repelled her father's offers to find her a husband and yet she craved for a man of her own.

She sighed, and watched without interest as a tonga loaded with luggage rumbled down the lane beneath her.

A thin, sharp shriek of 'Niece!' up the stairs broke into their conversation and reminded them suddenly that a caustic-tongued old lady awaited Anasuyabehn's ministrations.

The girls grimaced at each other.

'I wish I were married,' they said in chorus and then dissolved into laughter. They were still laughing and joking when two gentlemen walked down the lane.

Chapter Two

John Bennett had found the peace he sought in a high-ceilinged, stone-floored room in the house of a retired teacher, a few doors away from Dr Mehta's home. The room was light and airy and austerely furnished with a wooden couch for sitting and sleeping, a big desk and a chair, and a table from which to eat; there was also a large cupboard for his books and other possessions. On a veranda behind the room, Ranjit camped contentedly among the cooking pots; and on another veranda, to the front of the room, were comfortable basket chairs.

Since his arrival, John had immersed himself in his new history and was almost happy. Though he could not trace any of his former English friends, he had met some Indian ones again and found that none of them held any rancour against him for being English. He had visited his old friend, Dr Ferozeshah, at his surgery, where he was introduced to his head nurse, an English lady of quiet, professional demeanour, Miss Armstrong; Ferozeshah told him that she had previously served in a medical mission north of Shahpur.

As time went by, he was able to discard one of his walking sticks, though his legs still caused him pain occasionally.

While Savitri and Anasuyabehn chatted on the roof of Dean Mehta's bungalow, John took the record of Beethoven's Fifth Symphony off his record player and dusted it carefully.

He opened the cupboard and laid the record on the top shelf, put the record player on a lower shelf, and closed and locked the door.

'Ranjit,' he called, as he began to unbutton his shirt, preparatory to changing.

'Ji?' responded his servant. He put down the tray of wheat he had been cleaning and creaked slowly to his feet. Though elderly, he was a powerful-looking peasant. He had come to Shahpur from United Provinces forty years before, when only a boy. Except when the Bennett family was on leave in England, he had never left them. He had made a close study of Shahpur and was well known for his profound knowledge of exactly where to place a bribe to hurry officialdom or obtain a favour.

'Put those papers into my briefcase, while I change my shirt. I've an appointment with Dean Mehta.'

Ranjit wiped his seamed face with the dish towel draped over his shoulder and, with surprisingly deft movements, he packed the briefcase. He turned a toothless smile upon John. 'Will you be in for lunch?' he asked.

John buckled his belt, and, balancing himself by holding on to various pieces of furniture, he went to the bathroom in search of a comb.

'Yes,' he decided, as he combed vigorously at his hair, which never would lie down properly. 'I won't go to look at the temple until tomorrow.'

When he was ready to leave, Ranjit preceded him through the shady compound, in order to open the gate for him.

'Sahib, there's a tonga here.'

John presumed that the occupants of the carriage had come to visit his landlord. He viewed with interest, however, the tall, slim man who sprang down into the dusty lane. An elderly woman and a thin young girl still in the carriage peeped at him from behind their veiling saris.

'Excuse me,' said the man in good English. 'Can you tell me where to find Dr Mehta, the Dean?'

'Certainly. His house is the eighth one from here, down that way,' replied John, indicating the way the tonga had come.

'I'm really looking for his office.'

John looked thoughtfully at the man. Definitely not a student, he decided.

'I'm going to his office now,' he said. 'Would you like to come with me?'

The young man glanced up at the two ladies, who were whispering to each other, and seemed undecided. The tongawallah, on his high perch, started to fidget and began to mutter about people who made him wait forever and lose business. It was apparent that, at any moment, he would demand an increase in the agreed fare.

'I don't know what arrangements have been made for us. Mother is tired after our long journey.'

John's perplexity must have shown on his face, because he added, 'I'm Tilak from Bombay. I'm to teach Zoology here. In which department do you teach?'

'I'm not a member of the University staff,' John replied. 'But Dr Mehta mentioned that you were coming. I hope you'll like it here.' He extended his hand to the newcomer.

Though Tilak's fingers looked slim and delicate, his grip on John's hand was firm. 'Thanks,' he said.

'Perhaps the ladies would like to rest in my room,' John suggested. 'My servant would look after them, while we go to see the Dean.'

The offer was accepted with alacrity. With Ranjit's help and with much puffing and blowing, Mrs Tilak and her daughter were installed in John's room. John left to Ranjit the task of offering refreshments to the ladies. He had no idea of their caste or orthodoxy. If they were very orthodox, they would refuse all refreshment, in spite of the fact that Ranjit was himself a Brahmin.

Dr Tilak and he walked down the line of flat-roofed houses and bungalows before turning into the path which led to the Arts and Science Building. Tilak looked about him in a brisk, almost military manner which proclaimed his Maratha forebears, in marked contrast to the stolid, slower movements of Gujeratis. He seemed excitable and full of life, and remarked enthusiastically upon the green lawns and little flowerbeds which had been conjured up out of near desert.

Tilak had the beauty of face and form, thought John, which had made Indians famous for their looks, though he was gaunt and very dark-skinned. Though he did not know who John was, he was respectful to him, and he soon drew from him some details of his writings, in particular, about his new book on the history of the Marwari Gate temple and the surrounding district.

But Tilak's expression lost some of its exuberance, as they chatted. Finally, he said, 'I wonder what these Jains will think of my subject?'

'Why? I expect there is a demand for Zoology courses here. Otherwise, it would not have occurred to the University to appoint you.'

'There's a demand – probably from Hindus. However, it may not have occurred to anyone that I'll require small mammals to dissect for the benefit of my students – and fish to dissect for my own research.' He turned to John, his face very earnest, 'One can never be sure with Jains.'

John smiled at the ominous tone in which he pronounced his last sentence. His eyes twinkled, as he replied, 'The Vice-Chancellor is a graduate of Harvard – I'm sure he'll understand the requirements of modern research. We have some old diehards here. A few staff fought against the establishment of a Science Faculty. Dean Mehta is, himself, quite orthodox in his personal life – but I've never noticed his trying to impose his views on anyone else.'

Tilak relaxed a little and was about to make some further remark, when his attention was caught by a flutter of pink on the roof of the Dean's bungalow, which they were approaching.

John, also, had noticed Anasuyabehn on the roof, her pink sari almost obscured by her long, black hair which she was drying in the sunlight. She was generally a very retiring girl and, presumably, imagined that she could not be seen from below or she would undoubtedly have dried her hair indoors; her Western education had failed to rob her of her modesty or dignity. Now, she stood, in all innocence, shaking out her wonderful tresses, and laughing and chattering with her friend, Savitri, who was seated on the low parapet which guarded the edge of the roof.

John thought what a contrast the two women made. Anasuyabehn had an inborn winsomeness, and, as she raised her arms to rub her hair, her fine figure was readily apparent; yet her laughing face and cheerful voice had all the ingenuousness of the carefully protected woman. She was no beauty; but he knew that when she felt at ease with people, she could be quite charming.

Savitri – well, Savitri was Savitri. Thin as a camel after a desert journey, hair cut short and permanently waved last time she had been in Bombay, large, horn-rimmed spectacles; an assertive woman, whose violent efforts to be modern sometimes had results which left her acquaintances gasping. Yet she and Anasuyabehn were old friends, products of the same school and the same college – but different parents, thought John. Though Savitri's parents were Hindus, their home was almost completely European, while in Dean Mehta's house, despite his study of English, many of the old Jain ways still lingered.

As he and Tilak came level with the bungalow, Anasuyabehn approached the parapet, and, parting her waterfall of hair with her hands, she looked out across the compound straight at Tilak.

Tilak stopped in his tracks, fascinated by the gentle, fair face, made stronger looking by sweeping black brows, and by the marvellous hair rippling down past the girl's knees. In that unguarded moment she did, indeed, look very different from her usual modest self. Behind her, the leaves of an overhanging tree rustled and cast a dappled shade over her, guarding her from the searching rays of the sun.

She stood for a moment, as if captivated, and then, suddenly realizing her dishevelled state and the impropriety of staring at a man, she whipped away across the roof to the staircase.

Tilak continued to stare at the spot where she had stood, as if the shabby, white parapet had mesmerized him.

'Heavens,' he breathed in English, and then blinked and turned his face away, as he realized that he was being insolently scrutinized by Savitri, who was still seated on the low wall.

Embarrassed by this merciless examination, he turned to John and said in his stilted English, 'What were you saying about the Vice-Chancellor and the Dean?'

John was also acquainted with Savitri. He gravely lifted his stick in salute to her. She smiled acknowledgment and he turned his attention again to Tilak.

Though Tilak had reopened the conversation, it was obvious that he was not really listening to John's reply. His face was rapt as they walked along, the eyelids narrowed, the lips parted, and John felt uncomfortably that this lean, attractive newcomer was probably far too emotional to slip quietly into the life of the University. An intense man, thought John, with a difficult subject to teach, in a district where the life of every crawling bug is sacred.

In the middle of a story being told to him by John of how local villagers refused to spray a locust invasion, because of their beliefs, Tilak asked suddenly, 'Whose was the bungalow where the two girls were up on the roof?'

As they climbed the steps of the Arts and Science Building, he looked up at John, impatient for his answer.

A quizzical gleam in his eye, John glanced back at Tilak. 'It was Dean Mehta's bungalow. Why?'

Tilak flushed at the query and did not reply at once. Then, with a burst of inspiration, he said, 'It is helpful to know exactly where various members of the University staff live, and so on.'

In the hall, he saw the name of the Dean on a door facing him, and he promptly changed the subject, a slight grimness in his voice. 'Well, here I go. Now we shall see what effect Zoology creates in a Jain world!'

But Dr Tilak was received with quiet courtesy by Dean Mehta and his fears were allayed. The Head Peon was instructed to help him remove his mother and sister and luggage from John's room and he left to do this, while John arranged with the Dean to visit the Marwari Gate temple with him the following morning.

Chapter Three

The Marwari Gate temple had been built by an emperor as a sacrifice for the sins of his teeth. John had visited it on a number of occasions, but this time he wanted to arrange to see some of its sacred manuscripts.

The next morning, with clean handkerchiefs held politely over their noses, he and Dr Mehta followed their amiable guide, a monk, through the courtyard and into the halls and sanctuary. He marvelled again at the lacelike carving of canopies, roofs and figures of Tirthankaras, all in white marble.

It was explained to him that some of the manuscripts he wished to see were kept in the Treasure House and no stranger could be admitted to that. He was allowed, however, to examine the outside of the Treasure House. It was covered with finely engraved silver. The engravings told the story of the fourteen dreams of Trisala, the mother of Mahavira who was the founder of Jainism. John asked if he might make sketches of these.

The monk was reluctant to agree to this, and called several others to consult them. John remembered again that a limp is considered punishment for past sins, and, from the conversation, he thought he would be turned down because of this.

They finally agreed, however, and John arranged to visit them again in a few days' time.

Dean Mehta wished to remain at the temple with his religious teacher, so John wandered off by himself.

A few minutes' walk brought him to the flower bazaar and to the big, frowsy cinemas; the latter were tawdry with electric lights and hand-painted posters showing languid, suffering film heroines.

Near one of the cinemas, he stopped to buy some hot sweetmeats from a man clad only in a loincloth, who had a tiny stall tucked into the angle of a wall.

While he slowly ate his sticky sweets out of the palm leaf in which they had been wrapped, he watched an artist in the cinema entrance painting a poster to advertise the next film. Crowds of people pushed impatiently around him. A beggar woman, clutching a naked, swollen-bellied child, squatted at his feet and whined hopefully. He put a coin into the child's hand and the woman blessed him, while the starving child stared unseeingly over its mother's shoulder, giving no sign of life, except to clutch the coin firmly in its mouselike hand.

Although such sights were familiar to him from childhood, a sudden wave of pity swept over him as the woman crept away. With an irritable gesture, he threw away the dripping palm leaf, and made to move out into the crowd.

'Bennett Sahib!' exclaimed a cheerful, feminine and very English voice. 'How could you?'

Startled, he looked round.

Diana Armstrong, Dr Ferozeshah's head nurse, was standing half behind him. Down her rumpled khaki skirt was a spreading splash of sugar syrup, where the palm leaf had struck her. Her freckled face, brick-red with heat, was crinkled up with laughter. Her red hair was plastered down against her head by perspiration and her khaki shirt was equally soaked and clung to her slim figure.

John's first thought was that he had never seen a more bedraggled-looking Englishwoman. Then he hastily collected his wits. She was, after all, his doctor's head nurse.

'Miss Armstrong!' he exclaimed. 'I am so sorry.'

He looked around him helplessly.

'Can I get you a tonga in which to return home? Or perhaps the restaurant across the road would find us something to wipe it with.'

'The restaurant, I think,' replied Miss Armstrong. Her voice had suddenly lost its laughter and was rather quavery. 'I think I'd be grateful for a cup of tea as well.'

John looked at her sharply. The flush was ebbing from her face and he saw the blue smudges of fatigue under the clear green eyes. Poor woman, he thought. Why on earth does she work as she does, for an Indian doctor who probably pays her in annas?

He put his free hand under one of her elbows and, marshalling his stick, he guided her firmly across the street to the restaurant and into the gloom of a family cubicle at the back of it. He took her little black nurse's bag from her and sat down. He knew her quite well as Dr Ferozeshah's efficient shadow, but had never wished to know anything more of her, except to wonder idly how she came to work for Ferozeshah; and he was now quite surprised at his own temerity. She was, however, English like himself and obviously not feeling too well. He would not admit to himself that he wanted to speak English to somebody English.

'Tea,' he told the white-shirted, barefoot waiter, who was goggling at the rare sight of an English couple in his humble café. 'English tea with sugar and milk separate – boiling water for the tea. And a clean cloth to wipe the Memsahib's dress.' He pointed to the sugar stain.

'Would you like something to eat?' he asked. 'They make nice kabobs here.'

She smiled, showing uneven, very white teeth. 'No, thank you,' she said. 'Just tea.' She leaned back and closed her eyes for a moment, looking, in her exhaustion, soft and vulnerable.

The waiter departed, not too sure how to make English tea, but hoping the cook would know. He brought a cloth to sponge the skirt, and Miss Armstrong removed the worst of the stickiness.

'It doesn't matter,' she said. 'I'm a wreck anyway.'

John was inclined to agree with her but had sufficient diplomacy to stop himself saying so. He just twiddled his cold pipe which he had taken out of his pocket, and wondered what to talk about.

Miss Armstrong leaned her head against the wall of the cubicle and hoped she would not faint. She had certainly walked too far and too fast that morning. This John Bennett, though he was something of an oddity, was very kind and she was overwhelmed with gratitude at his bringing her into the restaurant and his concern at her spoiled skirt. She wished suddenly that she was beautiful, charming and amusing so that she could really entertain him with witty conversation. The ceiling gave a sudden swoop and was obliterated by a cloud of darkness for a second.

'I think you had better sip some water.' His voice came from far away, though he was bending over her and holding a glass, clinking with ice, to her lips.

She sipped gratefully and the faintness receded. John's lined, red face, topped by its unruly brush of dark hair, came into focus.

'Thank you,' she said with a wobbly smile, 'I am all right now.'

'Perhaps you're working too hard,' ventured John. 'Surely Ferozeshah doesn't expect you to work all the hours God sends?'

'Oh, no. He's very reasonable – though he works like a machine himself.'

She leaned forward and put her elbows on the stained, battered table, and ran her fingers across her eyes. Her shirt was open at the neck. John found himself a little flustered by a glimpse of lace barely masking full, incredibly white breasts. It had been a long time, he thought depressedly.

Unconscious of the stir she had caused in her companion, Miss Armstrong relaxed in the welcome gloom of the restaurant. The dark, varnished wood partitions and the smoke-blackened ceiling gave it an air of shabby, homely comfort.

'There's so much to do here – for a nurse,' she said, a note of compassion in her voice.

John sought uneasily for a further source of conversation. Finally, to bridge the growing gap of silence, he asked abruptly, 'Were you visiting someone sick, just now?'

'No – this is my spare time. I don't have to be in the operating room until eleven, today. However, some of the big Jains here are trying to do a real survey of the city. They want to find out how many people live in each district, what water supplies they have, what parks or playgrounds for children. It's an awfully difficult job. I've been counting refugees from Pakistan camped out on the pavements round here.'

John's bushy eyebrows shot up in surprise.

'That's a departure – for Jains. They've always believed that suffering is brought upon oneself. I didn't realize they cared how the other half lived. What's the idea?'

'To raise funds to provide some amenities in the worst slums.'

Miss Armstrong rubbed absent-mindedly at a water ring on the table. She looked up at John's strong, calm face.

'Humph,' grunted John. 'Times they are a-changing!' His wide, thin mouth broke into a grin. 'Jains are usually more interested in protecting animals than humans – charity is simply giving to monks and beggars.'

'I know,' replied his companion. 'That's why I want to help them.'

She removed her elbows from the table, so that the waiter could put down the tea tray. When he had gone, she seized the teapot in a small, strong hand and poured out the tea.

John took the proffered cup and himself added sugar and milk, while Miss Armstrong sipped eagerly at the black brew in her own cup. She sighed. 'That's better. Mind if I smoke?'

'Not at all. Do you mind if I smoke a pipe?'

Miss Armstrong dug a packet of Capstan out of her shirt pocket. After he had given her a light, she began to look a little less flushed and her skin took on its more normal appearance.

'Cream velvet powdered with freckles,' reflected John in some surprise. 'She can't be much over thirty.'

He told himself hastily to stop thinking like a naive youth, and he dragged his mind back to the prosaic subject of the proposed map. 'I know Shahpur quite well,' he told her. 'I was actually born here, and I think I could draw a map of most of it. I'm sure that a proper one doesn't exist, particularly since the influx of refugees – they've built all kinds of shanties – I've watched them go up.' He laughed a little grimly. 'I bet the postmen are the only ones who really know Shahpur.'

'You're right.'

'It would save a lot of time, if you had a map – and, believe me, I could fill in a great deal of detail – mosques, temples, ruins, fountains – what few gardens there are . . .'

'Would you *really* draw one?' Miss Armstrong asked eagerly. Her face was alight, the mouth a trifle open to show the tip of a tongue as narrow as a cat's. 'Could I tell Lallubhai – he's the Chairman – about your offer?'

'Certainly,' replied John, and wondered what possessed him to undertake such a monumental piece of work. 'Do you want a wall-sized map – or sections?'

She looked doubtful and then quickly glanced at her watch. 'I'm not sure. Look, I've got to be in the operating room by eleven.' She picked up her bag. 'Could we meet somewhere to talk about it?'

John was immediately appalled at this complication. There was not a single European restaurant in the city. He could not very well ask her to his room. A vision of Ranjit's horrified face floated before him – an English Memsahib in his room would probably ruin her reputation. He had no idea where she lived or with whom. What a fool he was to get involved.

He fumbled with his pipe, matches and stick, at the same time trying to open the swing door of the cubicle for her. She waited patiently while he sorted himself out and thought of an answer to her question.

'Perhaps you should first talk to your Chairman, Mr Lallubhai,' he temporized, as he finally managed to push the door open with his elbow. 'If a student or artist would volunteer, I'd be glad of a little help. Any map I draw is not going to be technically perfect, but it'll save your Committee a lot of work.' He paused outside the cubicle, and then asked, 'I wonder if Mr Lallubhai has thought of asking the City Engineer for a look at his maps. He'll have some showing drains, waterpipes . . .'

Miss Armstrong's little white teeth flashed in a quick smile. 'I'm sure none of the Committee has thought of it. I'll suggest it. I'll write to you – your address is in Dr Ferozeshah's file.'

As they moved through the crowded restaurant, customers paused in their conversation to watch them pass. At the bottom of the narrow entrance steps, they were besieged by beggars. Miss Armstrong ignored them. She looked up at John, and said, 'You're a brick to offer to help – it's a big job – are you sure you want to do it?'

She looked anxiously at him, and he could not say to her that he wished he had not volunteered, and said instead, 'I shall enjoy it – it will be a change for me. Now, can I get you a tonga?'

She was dismissed and, in spite of his affirmative reply, felt unaccountably a little hurt.

'No, thank you,' she muttered, 'I'll walk. Goodbye – and thank you.'

She turned stiffly on her heavy, flat-heeled shoes, and in a moment was lost in the jostling crowd.

John waved at a passing tonga, and the driver drew into the pavement.

'University Road,' said John, 'How much?'

'Eight annas, Sahib,' said the driver outrageously.

'Four annas and not a pice more.'

'Sahib,' the voice was full of reproach.

'Four annas.'

'Six annas,' said the driver, 'and not a pice less,' and he lifted his whip to start his horse, to indicate that he would rather go without a fare than reduce his price further.

'All right,' said John, and clambered in through the door at the back of the carriage. A little boy, who had been sitting by the driver, scrambled down, ran round the tonga and locked the door after John.

John smiled at the boy and gave him an anna. But behind the smile he felt cross. In two days two new people had entered his life, if one counted that Miss Armstrong had previously been only a pair of hands passing papers to Dr Ferozeshah. They both seemed to be people who would disrupt the peace of his life; Dr Tilak appeared likely to seek his advice quite often and Diana had momentarily disturbed his usual composure.

Since his dismissal by his fiancée, he had tried to avoid women, swearing that he would never let himself be hurt again. Almost every time he walked, he was reminded of the repugnance in his fiancée's eyes, when she saw how crippled he was; and then he would damn all women.

He told himself not to be ridiculous. Nevertheless, by the time he was deposited at his compound gate, he had worked himself into a thoroughly bad temper. When Ranjit saw him, he scampered out to his own veranda, from which he did not stir until he had listened to the typewriter pounding steadily for more than half an hour.

Later, when he crept into the room to ask the Sahib what he would like for dinner, he was surprised to find him leaning his head disconsolately against the typewriter, looking as miserable as he had when first he returned to Shahpur.

'Sahib?' queried Ranjit, his wizened face full of concern. 'Are you well?'

The Sahib did not raise his head from its hard resting place, but he smiled up at Ranjit out of the corners of his eyes, and with a jolt Ranjit was reminded of the small boy John had once been who wept and raged his frustrations out of himself.

'I am all right now, Ranjit. Sometimes I get fed up because I don't walk very well.'

Ranjit scratched his jaw, and wondered if that was the only trouble. He decided, however, that this was not the time to probe further, and said, 'Your legs improve daily, Sahib. Don't get depressed.' Then in a cheerful managing voice, he asked, 'What would you like for dinner? I have some good lady's fingers, succulent and green.'

'I'd rather have them smooth and white,' said John with sudden spirit, while Ranjit looked at him aghast.

Chapter Four

It was about three weeks later that John was again reminded of an uneasy sense of unwanted change in his life.

Ranjit came in to tidy his room and, seeing that he was not working, sat down on the floor to gossip.

He regaled John with a detailed description of the contents of Tilak's baggage, Mrs Tilak's disgruntlement at the poor lodgings provided for her son by the University, Dr Tilak's hot temper and, by comparison, the quiet character of his sister, Damyanti. Mrs Tilak was a widow, he said, and she and her daughter normally lived with her elder brother-in-law in Bombay.

John lay resting on his wooden couch and laughed at Ranjit. He lay on his back, with one muscular arm curled round his head, and Ranjit, as he watched him, thought that he must be much taller than he seemed when standing. When on his feet, he tended to stoop and put a lot of weight on his stick. A strong man, however, and very virtuous, though, in Ranjit's opinion, he was too young to live in quite the sagelike manner that he did.

'It defeats me, Ranjit,' remarked John, 'how you manage to find out all these things.'

'Sahib,' replied Ranjit primly, 'I do but listen to the conversation of others. Ramji told me himself that Mrs Tilak upbraided him personally because, she said, the lavatories were filthy, and, you know, Sahib, that he does his best to clean them.'

John thought of Ramji's apathetic efforts at cleaning, and snorted.

'And anyway, Sahib, what else does one expect a lavatory to be except very dirty?'

'Ours is clean,' said John, yawning and stretching like a cat.

'You clean it yourself, Sahib,' said Ranjit disapprovingly.

'If I left it to you and Ramji it never would be clean.'

He rolled over to face Ranjit and his eyes were suddenly a little flinty.

'Why should one not clean one's lavatory, may I ask? Gandhiji set everyone a good example by taking a sweeper's broom and doing a sweeper's work.'

'I am a Brahmin, Sahib, and well versed in the scriptures.'

'You cook for me.'

'True, Sahib – but times are changing and I must change with them,' said Ranjit huffily, fingering the little shikka on his head. His grey hair was thinning rapidly, but he cultivated carefully this precious tuft of hair by which God, in due course, would pull him up to Heaven.

John abandoned what he knew to be a useless argument and swung his legs down to the floor.

'Let's look at the account book,' he said. 'It's time we did.'

Ranjit heaved a sigh and produced from his shirt pocket a much thumbed notebook, in which were entered in Gujerati characters the various expenditures of their small household. John ran an experienced eye down the list, to make sure that not overmuch of any one item was being used; occasionally, Ranjit's hospitality to his family extended to gifts of tea or sugar out of John's store, as well as free meals.

Meanwhile, Ranjit took out of his shirt pocket a dirty screw of newspaper and from this extracted three rupee notes and a handful of small change, which he carefully counted out on to the floor in front of the couch. John checked the amount with the book and found it balanced. Satisfied, he returned the housekeeping book to Ranjit, heaved himself up and unlocked the almira, took out his cash box and went back to the couch.

Without thinking, he sat down cross-legged and was surprised that he could arrange himself in that position without pain. Ranjit held out an incredibly wrinkled brown hand and John counted his wages into it. He then gave him money for a week's supply of food and fuel.

The servant folded the notes up carefully and stowed them away in a grubby handkerchief, after which he sat looking rather gloomily at a small line of ants marching across the floor, until John asked him, 'What's the matter, Ranjit?'

'Sahib, you have thousands of rupees in the bank and yet you live like a monk. It is not fitting, Sahib, for an Englishman to live so. You should have a pukka bungalow with a compound – and a mali to cultivate the garden – and a kitchen boy to help me.'

'Ranjit,' said John with a sigh, 'you should be in the Secret Service. Do you by any chance know the exact amount of my bank balance?'

Ranjit flushed under the implied reproof, though he answered steadily, 'Yes, Sahib. Rs. 40,581, As. 3.' He cleared his throat, and went on, 'Further, Sahib, you will soon get another letter from Wayne Sahib, your book man in America, with more money; and you have two wealthy students to coach here – more money!'

John leaned back against the wall and roared with laughter.

'You know more about my finances than I do,' he said.

'The Statement from the bank lies on your desk,' replied Ranjit blandly.

The idea of launching out on to a sea of housekeeping appalled John; he liked his present existence. It was comparatively uncomplicated, he had plenty of learned men for company, and for a change he could take an occasional trip to Abu or Delhi or Bombay, without having to worry about the cost of it. Already Tilak and Miss Armstrong had stirred in him a faint premonition of unwanted change, and here was Ranjit lecturing him about rearranging his life. A sharp reproof rose to his lips, but he stifled it hastily – Ranjit cared more about his wellbeing than anyone else.

'I'll think about it,' he told Ranjit gravely, and dismissed him.

He sat down at his desk and commenced reading the notes he had made on the Marwari Gate temple.

The evening was approaching and there was a comfortable clatter of saucepans from Ranjit on the veranda. Behind it John could hear the wind whining among the bungalows and University buildings. He rose and stretched. Balancing himself by holding on to the furniture, he went to the door and opened it. The sky was flushed with sunset, the pinkness dulled by the threat of storm in it.

His landlord's grandchildren were playing, as usual, in the compound, and the smallest child was in the act of unlatching the compound gate. As he watched, it managed to heave the gate open and peep through it, and then ventured outside. John called to it to come back but it did not, so he got his stick and walked as quickly as he could to the gate.

The toddler was sitting in the middle of the lane cooing to itself, while a small black carriage, drawn by a single horse, bowled smartly towards it.

As he went to retrieve the child, he shouted a warning to the driver. He pulled the youngster to its feet and, with a pat on its behind, sent it back through the gate. He paused himself, because the awkward bending had hurt his legs. The mangy horse drew up by him, and its owner leaned down from beside the driver.

Mahadev Desai smiled and bowed. 'Good evening, John. Can I give you a lift anywhere? Nice to see you.'

John surveyed the plump speaker through the dust engendered by the carriage. He had known Mahadev casually for most of his life. He was the son of a powerful moneylender and jeweller; but today he wore, like any fairly prosperous businessman, a plain white cotton shirt, jacket and trousers. A white Gandhi cap surmounted a moonlike, though not unhandsome, face. Shrewd eyes stared unblinkingly, while he awaited John's answer. Behind him, sat his younger brother and sister-in-law, who murmured 'Namaste' in greeting.

'No, thanks,' replied John. 'I called to you, because I wasn't sure if your driver had seen my landlord's grandchild – the little tike had strayed into the lane.'

'I saw him, Sahib,' the driver interjected hastily, lest he be blamed for carelessness.

John nodded, and inquired after Mahadev and his family. The cadences of the man's voice, he thought, had not changed over the years. He knew the nervous respect with which Mahadev was treated in the city. The Desai Society in which he lived was nearly in the centre of the old town, and from it, financial tentacles stretched out into the mills and homes of half the city, even as far as Delhi and out to Europe, it was said. Nobody held more mortgages and family jewellery in pledge. Nobody could put pressure on a hapless debtor faster than the Desais, or produce a bigger bribe when needed. Their knowledge of invective, that priceless asset of any Indian moneylender, had not been lost as their business became enormously expanded. John had heard Mahadev himself, before he had taken charge of their business in France, screaming in the bazaar at some unfortunate businessman, while a crowd gathered to see the fun, and the police vanished.

Desai was speaking to him.

'I am going to catch the Delhi Mail, after calling on Dean Mehta,' he confided in a slightly pompous whisper.

'Indeed,' said John absent-mindedly, his thoughts already wandering back to his book. 'A pleasant journey.'

'Thank you,' replied Desai graciously. 'A-jo.'

'Goodbye,' said John, stepping back as the driver, in response to a gesture from Desai, whipped up the horse.

John went slowly back into the bungalow. The children had gone in for their evening meal. The wind still whined its threat of a dust storm.

He went back to his desk and looked again at his sketches of the Dreams of Trisala, so often meditated upon by Jain women. He saw instead the ivory-coloured face of Mahadev.

The wife of one of his father's old friends on campus had told him that the well-known moneylender was considering remarriage; as one of the richer men in Shahpur he was of interest. His first wife, she said, had died in childbirth and, soon after her death, he had been sent by his father to Paris, presumably in connection with their business in fine jewellery. Rumour had it that he had opened an elegant jewellery shop there, where they sold silver filigree and other Indian-designed ornaments. By all accounts, this venture had thrived well.

Now Mahadev was home again and, perhaps because of his hairstyle, looked rather Westernized. He was not so influenced, however, that he had lost the ancient instinct of a moneylender to hide his wealth; he was still dressed quite humbly and drove a half-starved horse.

John smiled to himself, as he remembered Ranjit's description of why Mahadev Desai was being encouraged to look for another wife.

'It is well known, Sahib,' Ranjit had said, 'that the older Desais fear greatly that Mahadev may take a French woman to wife – France is next to England, isn't it, Sahib? And there has already been enough trouble in the Desai Society.

'The Society was quite happy when ruled by Mahadev's mother and father, and his little daughter blossomed in spite of the lack of a mother. But when the old lady died and that shrew of a younger sister-in-law became the eldest lady, then, Sahib, trouble seemed to spread from house to house inside their compound. The cousin brothers went away because their wives would no longer stand the ceaseless nagging. Then the wretched woman complained to all the neighbours that she was worked to death, because there was no other woman in the house – though they do have a number of servants, Sahib.'

Ranjit had stopped to blow his nose into a corner of his handkerchief which was not knotted round the housekeeping money, and had then gone on disparagingly, 'Trust them to think of the most economical thing to do – they are persuading Mahadev that he must marry again.'

Chapter Five

As Mahadev continued on his way to visit Dean Mehta, he mused on the charms of his possible future wife.

He wished to marry for reasons other than economy. He had discovered, to his cost, that a well-to-do Indian jeweller, alone in Paris, could be quite popular amongst women; and their bare legs and tight dresses had been a constant temptation, to which he had, too often, succumbed.

He thought that an educated Indian wife might keep him out of further mischief; he could take her on his travels. He also passionately desired a son. He was fond of his little daughter, but, all too soon, she would grow to marriageable age and leave him, whereas a son would be a joy to him all his life.

For different reasons, the older Desais were of the same mind. Mahadev had hardly distributed the gifts he had brought from France several weeks before, when, with sly hints, the matter was broached. Girls of suitable caste and orthodoxy were suggested; Mahadev found fault with all of them.

'It looks as if our French investment will flourish,' he reminded his father, 'so it is important that I should have a wife able to mix with French ladies.'

'French women!' exclaimed his father. 'She'll live in this house. She doesn't have to go with you to Paris.'

Mahadev felt the perspiration trickling down his back. He did not know how to explain to his father the witchery of the women he had seen in France. The amount of sin he had accumulated during his visit appalled him; somewhere, sometime, it would have to be expiated.

'It's the custom in France to travel with one's wife,' he lied in desperation. 'It's expected of one.'

His father digested this information in silence. He was aware of the pitfalls of travel. There was the temptation to eat meat, for example.

As if reading his thoughts, Mahadev said, with a burst of inspiration, 'It's extremely difficult to eat properly without someone to cook for me.'

'Ah,' exclaimed his father, satisfied at last. 'Most of the girls whom your uncles mentioned can read and write. They'd be docile enough and do whatever you asked.'

Mahadev mentally dismissed the whole solemn, dull collection of them. He had seen a woman walking, with her boy servant, near the University. He had known her for years by sight. He remembered her long plait of hair swinging softly over pretty, rounded shoulders, her delicate ivory skin, her demurely lowered eyelids. Swallowing hard, he inquired of his father, 'Did Dean Mehta's daughter ever get married? Her father's with the University – you may remember him.'

Old Desai looked at him. 'She's not one of our people.'

'I know,' replied his son, rather crestfallen. 'But she *is* a Jain.'

Desai Senior pursed his thin lips, and considered the merits of the match. Finally, he said uneasily, 'She's not a lucky woman – she's been bereaved even before being married – and her horoscope may not be correct.'

Mahadev dared not show the irritation that he felt, neither could he describe the subtle seductiveness of Anasuyabehn or say that he had thought her beautiful long ago, when he was a young man and she was a quiet school girl travelling to and from her lessons. He had never questioned his father's choice of his first wife, who had been a good, obedient girl, but now Mahadev was no longer young – he was a rich, experienced man who hungered for a woman of his own choosing. He wanted Anasuyabehn, the sight of whom made him tremble. And of what use was being rich if one could not buy what one wanted?

The elder Desai listed a multitude of reasons regarding Anasuyabehn's unsuitability as a wife, but they only hardened Mahadev's determination to wed her.

'Perhaps eldest aunt from Baroda could inquire discreetly about the horoscope,' he said, trying to keep his face impassive.

His father looked at him penetratingly. Mahadev seemed set upon this woman, and he himself was very anxious to see him safely married. Mahadev was his favourite son; in comparison, his younger son was a dunderhead – and the boy's wife was an avaricious shrew. He wondered what kind of a temperament Anasuyabehn had; something about her evidently pleased his son.

'Have you spoken to this girl?'

'No, father.'

'Have you seen her?'

'Yes, father. Many times since childhood. She used to go to a school near the Red Gate and I would see her getting off the bus at the flower bazaar with the other girls.'

'Hm,' murmured his father, thinking that young men did not change much from generation to generation. 'I'll consult your uncles.'

The elder man waved his hand in dismissal, and Mahadev knew intuitively that he had won. He got up from the mattress on which he had been sitting, bowed and made for the door.

'Wait,' said his father, and Mahadev turned apprehensively.

'You realize that a man in your position can choose almost any girl in our caste – parents would happily approve of you.' He paused, and then went on, 'You should consider this carefully, for I do not know whether the Mehtas will be so happy. Dean Mehta presumably has had other offers for his daughter.'

Mahadev, secure in his family's financial empire, had never thought of being snubbed by Dean Mehta and he was nonplussed for a moment, and then said, 'Would Baroda aunt cause inquiry to be made on this point first?'

He is quite determined, thought his father fretfully. I should be firmer about it – and yet the other boy is very unhappy with his witch of a wife.

'Very well,' he said grudgingly. 'Here, take these photographs and have another look at them – you might change your mind about one of them – Baroda aunt's young sister-in-law looks quite nice.'

Mahadev reluctantly took from him the half dozen or so studio portraits of prospective wives, promised to consider them and made his escape.

A man of thirty-four, who had seen the world, he fumed, should surely be allowed to choose a wife; and yet, beneath his resentment at his marriage being arranged for him, lay the knowledge that his father was being extremely patient.

He wandered into the compound, round which were ranged dwellings dating back a hundred years or more. How crowded and dirty it looked! Its smoke-blackened stone verandas with their steps hollowed out by generations of feet, its rotting woodwork, its lack of paint, depressed him. Later on – he would not admit to himself that he meant when his father and his Partner Uncle died – he would build a new Society in a more salubrious neighbourhood, and leave this compound to his brother. Now that India had settled down after the horrors of 1947, others, less rich than he was, had moved out; he would, too. He sighed, and looked at his watch. Time to go into the office and relieve his brother.

In the gloomy, dusty office, his brother was haggling superbly with a rather cowed local landowner about a loan against his next crop. Mahadev went to stand quietly by him.

His father might consider Younger Brother dull and commonplace, but Mahadev was fond of him and felt he would make an excellent junior partner, completely reliable in all routine matters, and, as far as the family was concerned, painstakingly honest. It was a pity that his father was so hard on him.

Gradually, Mahadev was drawn into the argument, and in a very short time he was engrossed in squeezing a higher interest rate out of their client.

The would-be brides soon had an account book banged down upon their neatly photographed features – and were forgotten.

Chapter Six

Anasuyabehn's widowed aunt had made her home with her brother and his daughter because she had no sons and disliked the idea of living with one of her brothers-in-law. She had constantly berated the old scholar about his neglect of his daughter in respect of finding a husband for her. The only reply she had been able to obtain from him had been, 'We should wait a full two years from the time of her betrothed's death – it is not judicious to hurry the girl.'

As a result of this, Aunt had almost given up hope of ever seeing her niece married, since the older a girl became the harder it was to marry her off. Aunt felt that her own abilities as a matchmaker were simply withering away.

She had, therefore, been delighted when, by devious routes, it was made known to her that the Desais would make an offer for Anasuyabehn, if they could be sure of not being snubbed. This was an opportunity which could not be ignored, a real test of her matchmaking skills, which would benefit dear Anasuyabehn immeasurably. She consulted nobody, but assured the lady from whom this indication had come that such an offer would be well received. She was overwhelmed by the idea of being the instrument by which such a wealthy alliance could be brought about; it would crown all her previous successful efforts on behalf of other relations. After this, all her female relations with children to marry off would crowd about her, begging her favours on behalf of their offspring. Her thin, hooked nose quivered at the anticipation of her future importance in the family.

She conveniently forgot the difference in caste. She thought only of the Desai bank balance and willingly became the mediator between the two fathers. Two other offers for Anasuyabehn from the parents of poverty-stricken scholars were left to die from neglect on her part.

When she first broached the subject, Dean Mehta looked up from his book, said flatly, 'No,' and returned to his studies.

Undeterred, she continued to sit in front of him, chewing her thumb. He again glanced up, and added, 'I'll advertise for a husband for her in early spring.'

'The girl is already twenty-four years old.'

'I know, I know,' said the Dean testily, 'but Desai is not a Mehta.'

'He's near enough,' said his sister, 'and he's rich, healthy and in love with her. What more could we want in these changed times?'

'Does Anasuyabehn know Mahadev?' asked the Dean suspiciously. It would, he thought, be quite easy for her to carry on an intrigue without his knowledge – after all, she occasionally went shopping or to visit a friend by herself.

'No,' said Aunt decisively. 'Someone would have seen her and told me, if she had ever spoken to him.'

The Dean sat silently at his desk for a few minutes, staring out of the heavily-barred window and idly twiddling his fountain pen. He reviewed carefully all he knew of the recent history of the Desais, the hints he had heard of their holdings in many new enterprises, their influence amongst Government officials, Mahadev's travels. At last he said, 'Discuss the Desais with Anasuyabehn. She's old enough to be consulted.'

His sister hid her satisfaction at this reply, and merely said, 'All right.'

Her bare feet made a soft brushing sound on the stone floor as she shuffled off to the kitchen, ostensibly to consult Anasuyabehn.

The Dean continued to think about the Desais. Except on grounds of caste, there could be no reasonable objection to the match, and for years he had been preaching that Jainism had originally been a revolt of the Kshatriya military caste against their overbearing Brahmin priests; there was no caste among the original Jains. Young Desai was reasonably educated, had a good, though old, house and was certainly rich; his trips to Europe would have broadened his outlook and, indeed, these days, the family seemed to be financiers and jewellers rather than orthodox moneylenders.

It was said that Mahadev's father was ailing and his uncle was very old, so it would not be long before Mahadev became the head of his communal family. Further, in less than twelve months Dean Mehta would himself retire, and he dearly wished to give himself to a life of contemplation – to become a monk; he had for some years been quietly directing his life towards this goal by study, fasting, confession and the taking of those vows permitted to a layman. To have Anasuyabehn settled now might mean that he would see a grandchild before he severed all earthly relationships by taking his final vows.

He re-opened his book and composed his mind again for work.

'We'll see what Anasuyabehn has to say,' he decided.

Aunt, meanwhile, had sat in a corner of the kitchen and helped to prepare vegetables, while she considered what to say to Anasuyabehn.

The kitchen was quite modern. It had a water tap and beneath it, on the floor, had been built a low, stone enclosure to confine the splashes from it and guide spilled water down the open drain. The walls were whitewashed and, on a built-in shelf, glittered the brass cooking utensils. A watercooler reposed on a stand in a corner near the casement window, and huge double doors, which led on to a veranda, stood open to let in the morning freshness before the real heat of the day began.

'Take the new box of charcoal outside,' Anasuyabehn said to her little servant, 'and brush it.'

The boy picked up a small handbrush and the box and obediently went out into the compound, where he could be heard happily talking to a squirrel, as he gently went over each piece of charcoal with the brush to make sure that no insect was accidentally burned when the fire was lit.

Aunt seized the opportunity to say, 'I saw Mahadev Desai this morning.'

'He's been away a long time,' said Anasuyabehn. 'I don't suppose many people will be glad to see him. He drives even harder bargains than his elders, I'm told.'

She was sitting idly on her kitchen stool waiting for the boy to come in with the charcoal. A neat pile of prepared vegetables, flanked by a tin of cooking fat and her spice box lay on the well-scrubbed floor beside her. The empty charcoal stove was out on the veranda and soon the servant would light a cooking fire in it and bring it to her, carrying it gingerly with long pincers so that he did not get burned.

'Tut,' said Aunt. 'You listen to too much gossip.'

Who's talking? thought Anasuyabehn grimly.

'He's concerned mainly with the jewellery side now – opened a shop in a place near England.' As she snipped away at the vegetables, she tried to think of aspects of Mahadev which might appeal to a young woman, and added, 'He had a Western suit on this morning. I saw him driving through the cantonment, when I was on the bus – on my way to Mrs Patel's.'

'Did he?' murmured Anasuyabehn politely, and thought absently that she must buy some more glass bracelets next time a bracelet seller came round.

Aunt had no intention of discussing matrimony with Anasuyabehn, but she did want to obtain from her some words of approbation in respect of the Desais, which she could carefully misinterpret as assent to a proposal. Mistress of domestic intrigue, dedicated matchmaker, she had no intention of giving Anasuyabehn the opportunity of refusal, and she was certain that a man with the taint of moneylending about him would be refused. She, therefore, said no more that day, but during the weeks that followed Anasuyabehn was regaled with quite a number of stories of the nobility and kindness of Mahadev Desai.

Anasuyabehn should undoubtedly have realized what was in her aunt's mind, but she was entirely absorbed by ideas of marriage elsewhere. The memory of the beautiful, intense features of Dr Tilak staring up at her, as he walked past her home with Dr Bennett, had occupied her thoughts recently, and she only half listened to her aunt's chatter.

Aunt, meanwhile, luxuriated in the thought of bringing off such a superb alliance in spite of the difficulties of Anasuyabehn's advanced age and partly Christian education. If only her sons had lived, she thought sadly, how much more interesting life would have been to someone as skilled in matchmaking as herself; there would have been grandsons and granddaughters to marry off. Why the cholera should strike at her sons and leave her daughters was beyond her; and what trying daughters she had – always complaining because they had been married off to brothers who lived in Bombay, so far away from Shahpur. They were lucky, she thought bitterly – at least they ate twice a day, which was more than she had done in the first days of her marriage.

How good her brother had been, she reflected, to give her a home. Anasuyabehn, too, was a charming, respectful girl; Aunt would enjoy taking an interest in her children, though, of course, she would not see very much of them – once a girl was married she belonged to her husband's family, not to her father's family.

First, however, Anasuyabehn must have a husband.

If I can get my brother so enmeshed in marriage arrangements that it would be difficult for him to retreat with dignity, he also will press Anasuyabehn towards the marriage. And I must prepare Anasuyabehn, so that at least she does not immediately object when the offer comes.

Lucky women went to and fro between the parents' houses, and it was curious how, every time a visitor was expected at the Mehta house, Aunt thought of something which was required from town, and Anasuyabehn and her boy servant were dispatched to purchase it, whilst the horoscopes of the proposed bride and groom were discussed and compared.

Anasuyabehn was not a gossip; she had no reason to suspect anything. Even Savitri, her best friend, who might have told her, knew no one else amongst the Jain community and, busy with her work as a chemist in a cotton mill, heard nothing.

Skilfully the old lady spun threads of praise and flattery between the unsuspecting fathers – the wily old moneylender, who was busy trying to rid his family of most of the taint of moneylending and to gain instead a reputation as a jeweller and financier of integrity, and the absent-minded scholar, who, having inspected and spoken to Mahadev, liked him very much. There were times, not so long since, thought Dean Mehta ironically, when neither of them would have dreamed of speaking to the other, but many things were permissible nowadays – the walls between the castes were crumbling down, and Dean Mehta was quite prepared to give them a helping push.

Once Dean Mehta asked his sister, 'Is Anasuyabehn content about this marriage?'

'Oh, she has all the foolish ideas of a young girl – but she will appreciate a good man. She agrees that the family in this generation is becoming a most worthy one – and she has been most interested in my stories of Mahadev.'

'Ah,' said her brother, a little relieved. 'I'm content, as long as she has no antipathy to the match.'

'None at all, none at all,' said Aunt, with considerably more conviction than she really had. She hoped fervently that all her propaganda directed towards her unsuspecting niece was having sufficient effect to ensure an affirmative answer when the time came.

As she became further committed, the horrid thought of how other women of the family would snigger behind their hands at her, if she failed, began to haunt her – they might even suggest that she was, with advancing years, losing her skill, and that would be hard to bear. She put these thoughts firmly behind her; dear Anasuyabehn should have a wonderful marriage – and all through her aunt's sagacity.

Chapter Seven

The day on which Mahadev would make a formal visit to his prospective bride's family drew near. Unfortunately, his aunt had to return to Baroda to nurse a sick son, so it was understood that Mahadev would be accompanied by his brother and sister-in-law.

That morning, Anasuyabehn's aunt hinted to her that her father had a well-to-do and charming suitor in mind for her. Anasuyabehn, who had done little else but dream about the new, unmarried Professor of Zoology, ever since she had seen him from the roof of her father's bungalow, asked with interest, 'Who is he?'

'Ah-ha,' responded Aunt, all cheerful coyness. 'Your father will tell you in due course.'

Anasuyabehn could not think of any particularly eligible man who had swung into their orbit recently, other than Tilak, and she smiled happily.

Aunt had informed her brother that all was now arranged. The first gifts had been exchanged, and Aunt explained, 'I locked them in the almira, so that they will be a nice surprise for Anasuyabehn, when you tell her that the final arrangements have been made.'

The Dean smiled. He liked the idea of giving his daughter a pleasant surprise. He had been extremely busy, because the enrolment in his Faculty had increased markedly that term, and he had hardly exchanged a word with his daughter for weeks. He felt that he really must now talk to her about her marriage, though his sister, he was sure, would already have discussed everything with her. He opened his study door, and called, 'Daughter, come here.'

'Well,' he greeted her, as she entered a little apprehensively. 'This is a happy day for us, isn't it?'

'Yes, father,' she answered submissively, masking a tumult of anxiety in her heart.

Aunt shuffled in behind her and sank on to the couch.

Dean Mehta sat down in his desk chair and took his daughter's hand. 'Well, now, are we quite happy at the idea of leaving our old father and going to a fine, young husband?'

Anasuyabehn did not know how to reply, and raised her heavily kohled eyes to her father.

Finally she said, 'I don't want to leave you, father – but I know it *is* time I was married.'

'Good, good. You won't be going far from me, anyway.'

He contemplated his daughter benignly. A placid, obedient girl, educated and yet without the flighty ideas of some of the women students on the campus. He beamed at her with satisfaction, while she waited with as much patience as she could muster. Then she said, in reply to his remark, 'That will be nice, father.' After all, Tilak would probably remain for years at this university.

Dean Mehta dug his key chain out of his pocket and selected a key, which he handed to his sister, while he nodded his bald head in amiable agreement.

'Get the parcels out of the cupboard,' he instructed her, and Aunt creaked to her feet to do so. Anasuyabehn watched her with pleasant anticipation, willing to go along with their desire to tease her gently.

'The Desais have sent some beautiful gifts,' said her father, as he watched his sister bring out a number of bundles.

'The Desais?' Anasuyabehn looked at him with blank incomprehension.

Dean Mehta glanced quickly at her, startled by the surprise in her voice. She was looking at him as if she had suddenly discovered a corpse.

'Yes – Mahadev,' he said.

Anasuyabehn sank into the visitor's chair by her father's desk, dazed by the shock. Far away, she could hear her father's voice, but the only word she really heard was Mahadev. She was so aghast that it seemed to her that she never would take breath again; however, her aunt evidently turned the fan towards her, because she felt the breeze on her face. Gradually, the world took shape again. Out of the mist loomed her father's face, full of anxiety, and his voice boomed into her ears.

'Dear child,' he said, full of self-reproach. 'I kept you standing too long on this hot day. Let Aunt give you some water.'

Aunt had already poured a glassful from his carafe, and she held it to the girl's lips. For once, the old woman could not think of anything to say.

Anasuyabehn sipped obediently, and life flooded furiously back into her. All her aunt's gossip of the previous few weeks came back to her and fell neatly into place.

'Marry a moneylender?' she gasped scornfully. 'Oh, no, father. No!' The last word came out in a wail.

Dean Mehta looked at her in some astonishment.

'He's hardly a moneylender, child. He's a big financier. Desai Sahib and his associates put up no less than half the money for the new chemical works at Baroda. Anyway, I thought you wanted to marry Mahadev.'

'Why should I think of marrying him?' Anasuyabehn asked, through angry tears.

'Your aunt assured me that you wanted to.'

'When I spoke of him,' interposed her aunt hastily, 'you agreed what a nice family they were. You made no criticism whatever.'

'I never thought of marrying one of them,' retorted the girl. She dabbed her eyes with the end of her sari.

Dean Mehta looked at his sister, and demanded sharply, 'What've you been doing? Didn't you ask her?' He seemed suddenly fierce.

Aunt looked uncomfortable. Her mouth opened and shut, as she searched for a reply. She had not expected serious opposition from Anasuyabehn, once her father was committed to the match. She thought the girl would accept fairly contentedly the prospect of such a fine, rich bridegroom.

Anasuyabehn's faintness had passed and she glared at the old woman, whose white widow's sari served only to remind her of the troubles of early widowhood, the likely result if one married a man much older than oneself. Only a lifetime of training stopped her from screaming with rage at her aunt.

Aunt mustered her forces. She said indignantly, 'I've talked of little else for weeks. I told her all about the family and about the return of their eldest son. I was sure she understood.'

'Marriage never occurred to me,' Anasuyabehn defended herself, through gritted teeth. 'They're not the same caste. I just thought you were telling me the news – gossiping!' The last word came out loaded with rage.

'Sister!' Dean Mehta's voice was full of reproach. 'Now we are committed. You stupid woman!' Mentally he reviled himself for leaving so important a matter to her.

'It's a good match,' said Aunt defensively. 'Mahadev could marry anyone he chooses round these parts – and he chose Anasuyabehn.'

'*Chose* me?' exclaimed Anasuyabehn. Since she had never even spoken to Mahadev she had assumed that his father was arranging the marriage.

'Yes,' replied Aunt quickly. 'He's admired you for years. However, you were betrothed. But now he finds you are free, and dearly wants to marry you.'

'Oh,' said Anasuyabehn, surprise for a moment overcoming her anger.

The Dean, thoroughly exasperated by his sister, nevertheless saw his chance, and said to his bewildered daughter, who was agitatedly running her fingers through her hair, 'My daughter, your aunt is right. It is a good match in these troubled times.' He pursed his lips, and then went on, 'Certainly she should have talked it over thoroughly with you – I regret not asking you myself, but I've had so much on my mind lately – however, here we are committed to it, and before we do anything more, I want you to consider it carefully.'

Anasuyabehn looked at him helplessly. She felt, as her father pressed Mahadev's suit, that her last Court of Appeal was being closed to her, and she sat like a silent ghost while her father extolled Mahadev's virtues. When he produced an exquisite sari which had been brought, as a token of the engagement, by one of the ladies concerned in the negotiations, she sat with it half opened in her lap, and hardly heard his voice.

'Child, it was sad that your betrothed should die – I know you liked him. And, unfortunately, it made you look a little unlucky in the eyes of parents . . .' He tailed off.

'Mahadev is a handsome man,' put in the old woman, her voice almost wistful, only to be crushed by an icy look from Anasuyabehn.

'And a generous and thoughtful one,' added her father, cheering up a little, as he picked up a small box from his desk.

Mahadev had often been impressed by Anasuyabehn's quiet and

dignified demeanour when he had watched her in the streets; she walked with the perfect foot placement and timing of an elephant, he had many times told himself. Older and wiser than most bridegrooms, he greatly desired to win the favour of his wife-to-be. He had, therefore, insisted that the traditional bags of white and brown sugar be sent to her home, burying in them, instead of the usual two rupees, a small silver box with which to surprise her. It was this box which her father now handed to her.

Though she was very dejected, Anasuyabehn's curiosity was aroused by the unexpected token. She took the box from her father and opened it.

On a fluffy bed of cotton reposed a small nose ring consisting of a single diamond set in gold. Exquisitely cut, it flashed in the sunlight with a delicate blue radiance, a beautiful ornament which spoke, with fabulously expensive eloquence, of its donor's wealth, and of his interest in her as a person. With an odd quirk of humour, Anasuyabehn saw the mental agony with which a close-fisted, traditional moneylender must have parted with such a valuable gem. He must be in love to the point of insanity, she thought grimly.

Fascinated, she lifted the ornament out and laid it on the palm of her hand, a hand that began to tremble with a deep fear of the unknown. Here was proof positive that her suitor would not take a negative answer easily. The gift was really valuable and quite unnecessary at such a time.

Until her father had handed her the little box, she had taken it for granted that, somehow, she would be able to escape from the marriage agreement. But now fear seemed to creep out from the blue stone and wind itself round her heart. A man who loved passionately was not going to be fobbed off so easily – nor was his powerful family, who seemed to be bent on rising socially as a caste. She knew what it was to be in love, she admitted, in love with a strange Maratha from Bombay, and, as she met Tilak on various social occasions, she had begun to feel the white heat of it. What might a powerful man like Mahadev do, if he felt the same?

And deep down inside her was a little worm of added fear, nesting in her Gujerati respect for money, that, because of Mahadev's undisputed wealth, she might be tempted to be unfaithful to the new unnourished love which possessed her – though Tilak was not a bad match; a professor had everyone's respect and a steady, if not large, income.

She could feel fresh grief rising in her, in belated mourning for her original betrothed. If he had lived, she would have had a family by now and would never have lifted her eyes to Tilak – and Mahadev would have looked elsewhere for a wife. She had not cried at the time of her fiancé's death – one rarely does about someone seen only once; but now she wished deeply that his thin, tuberculosis-ridden body lay between her and the fires of passion and fear now consuming her.

I'll object, she thought, and her inward sense of weakness made her outwardly more belligerent. She gritted her teeth and glared furiously through her tears at her aunt.

Her father took her silence for reluctant acceptance, and said quite cheerfully, before her defiance could be expressed verbally, 'Well, daughter, now you can see how highly Mahadev thinks of you. I think well of him myself and I believe you would learn to, too. Come, let us make him happy and give him a marriage date.'

Toothless and shrivelled as a dry orange skin, her aunt squatted on the floor, nodding her head and smiling amiably.

'An astrologer should arrange it,' she said, taking out her betel box and scraping round in it for a suitable piece of nut to chew. 'Though first there should be some parties, so that my niece may meet her future husband.'

'I don't want to be married,' said Anasuyabehn in a small tight voice.

'Tut, tut,' said her aunt, grinning as she chewed.

'I'd rather be a nun.'

'You'll change your tune when you have a small son in your arms,' said the old lady, waving one scrawny arm to hitch her sari further over her shoulder.

'Father,' implored Anasuyabehn, tears pouring down her face. 'Must I?'

The Dean scratched his head in embarrassed silence. Finally, he said, 'Daughter, I have loved you too well and kept you by me too long. It will not be easy to find anyone else as well-to-do, so healthy or so influential.'

'I don't like him, Papa. I don't care about him being rich.' She sniffed back her tears. 'He's not the only man in the world.'

'Come, come, daughter,' he said. 'You have not yet even *met* your future husband. We'll have all the usual tea parties, as if you were just a young girl, and you may speak with him. Don't cry, child. I am sure you'll be a patient and dutiful wife and will be amply rewarded.'

Her aunt sniffed and looked at the ceiling; her own rewards in marriage had been few. It was unnatural, however, for a woman not to be married; and this is what came of leaving girls single too long – they became stubborn.

Anasuyabehn covered her face with her sari and, under its comforting darkness, she saw for a moment a dark, thin face looking up at her as if enchanted. The new Zoology man was a fine man to look upon. She gave a little, shivering sigh.

'Father, could you try for somebody else?'

'Who?'

'Perhaps someone in the University.'

'They're all married.'

Anasuyabehn tried to bring herself to the point of saying that the Professor of Zoology was not, but her courage failed her and she whispered, 'Not *all* of them.'

'Who isn't?' asked the Dean, his ire against his sister again beginning to rise.

Aunt cackled. 'I know,' she said. 'I've seen you with the other girls, making sheep's eyes.'

'Well, who?' queried the Dean again.

'The Zoology Professor!' laughed Aunt.

The Dean digested this information slowly. He had honestly not considered this young man, but the suggestion did not meet with much approval. Marathas were not popular in the Gujerat; thin, taut, warrior-descended, mentally agile, they were the very antithesis of Gujeratis; and this particular Maratha, with his demands for journals, for more lecture time, for a greater water supply, for a laboratory assistant, was already proving a bane to the worthy, but slow-moving Dean.

Meanwhile, Anasuyabehn stared unbelievingly at her aunt, marvelling at her powers of observation; she tended to think of her as part of the furniture, a necessary encumbrance, without life in herself.

Her fears redoubled.

Very quickly, Aunt loosed the deadliest shaft she possessed.

'A man who kills and cuts up animals,' she said.

Dean Mehta stared at her, horrified, his worst fears realized.

'No!' he exclaimed.

'Oh, yes. The mother of one of his students told me.'

'I must see him about it,' he muttered.

Making a great effort to be calm and firm, he turned to Anasuyabehn. 'A young man about whom we know so little would not be suitable, child. I would prefer you to marry a Gujerati, at least.'

Anasuyabehn nearly burst with rage at her aunt, and was about to explode verbally, when her little servant boy slid into the room.

'The young Desai Sahib is here,' he said to Dean Mehta. 'He's sitting on the front veranda.'

Anasuyabehn's rage gave way to panic; she sprang to her feet as if to fly.

Her father and aunt got up immediately, and her father said kindly, 'Don't be afraid, child. Would you like to see him?'

'No!' said Anasuyabehn fervently, while her aunt exploded, 'Tush, what are things coming to?'

'All right,' said the Dean a little testily, and, turning to the servant, he told him to bring Mahadev into the living-room.

Anasuyabehn fled to the kitchen veranda, picked up a basket tray full of millet which she had been cleaning earlier, and began feverishly to pick the small bits of stone and the insects out of it. When she was sure all the insects were out and carefully deposited over the side of the veranda, she tossed the grain up and down on the tray to bring to the edge any other impurities. She picked these out and then emptied the millet into a shopping bag.

'Bhai,' she called to the servant, 'take this to the miller.' Her voice still shook, but she had gained some comfort from her domestic task.

The boy shouted that he was making tea for the Sahib, and she waited quietly until he had finished and had taken the tea to the study.

He came slowly back to her, his bare feet dragging, and took the bag from her. He did not leave her at once. He stood first on one foot and then on the other, his grubby face as woebegone as Anasuyabehn's. In the moment or two he had been in the study his world had crumbled; from the conversation he knew that Anasuyabehn, whom he loved as much as his mother, far away in his native village, was going to marry the terrifying Mahadev Desai. He was only ten, and he could not visualize life in a house which held only a tart, old lady and an absent-minded old gentleman.

'Well?' asked Anasuyabehn.

'Bahin, are you really going to be married?'

Anasuyabehn nearly choked, as sobs rose in her and were hastily crushed down.

The boy looked frightened, and she took his hand and pulled him to her. 'I'm not sure,' she said. 'But you mustn't worry. Your work will be here just the same.'

He was not satisfied; a child's instinct to sense trouble was with him, and he feared change.

'Can I come with you to serve in Desai Sahib's house?'

'I don't know, boy. I will ask. Do you want to come?'

The boy fell to his knees and touched her feet. He would have lifted her foot and touched his head with it, but she restrained him. Such devotion from so small a person hurt her. 'My cup is full,' her heart cried. 'My cup is full.'

'There,' she said comfortingly. 'If the marriage is finally arranged, I'll ask the Sahib. Go and get the clean shopping bag, to put the flour in – and remember to feel the flour as it comes out of the chute. Last time you brought back half of someone else's rubbish which was already in the machine. The miller is a rogue.'

Her gay tone made the boy laugh. He crammed his round, black cap on to his head and was soon on his way.

Anasuyabehn sat stonily on the veranda. The first panic had ebbed from her and she felt tired and exhausted. Furthermore, she had no idea what to do. She was no fool; she knew that by worldly standards an alliance with the Desais was desirable; the difference in caste troubled her not at all – she had gone to school with many different castes – but the possible Bania orthodoxy of the Desais' home life did. It was an orthodoxy which forbade more than a minimum of communion between husband and wife, judged success in life by the amount of money buried in the floors of the house and regarded its acquisition as a religious duty.

Then there was Tilak, whose burning, narrowed eyes sought her out from among the other women at the tea parties and badminton parties given by the University staff, so that she blushed and had to put her sari up over her head to hide her confusion.

In angry revolt against her father's wishes, her tired mind sought frantically for a solution. She could become a nun, she considered desperately, and gain universal respect thereby – but the Jain religion offers little of true comfort for a woman.

She could run away – to what?

There is no place in India for a woman by herself, she thought bitterly, no honourable means of earning a living alone.

She remembered mournfully those brave Jains who sought release from the cycle of rebirth by starving themselves to death. She thought of her soft, round body tortured by hunger, reduced to an ugly bundle of suffering.

'I couldn't do it,' she acknowledged miserably. 'I want to live – life could be so sweet.'

She thought of Tilak and the weight of disapproval that would descend upon him, as a result of her aunt's remark about his dissecting. What an old troublemaker she was. She wept.

As her weariness gained on her, fear receded. Eventually, half asleep, she began to dream of a real lover, someone who thought her beautiful in mind and body, someone who would give her a son like himself, tall, slender, dynamic, and a little girl to dress in frilly, Western dresses. But the fact that Desai obviously thought of her as a very desirable woman was forgotten.

* * *

Desai had stayed half an hour, listening politely to his would-be father-in-law and hoping to catch a glimpse of his betrothed. At last, reluctantly he took his leave, and it was arranged that he would call again more formally, bringing his relations with him to meet Anasuyabehn. The Dean gave no hint that his daughter might repudiate the agreement, because he heartily hoped she would not. Orthodox he was in much that concerned himself alone, but he was intelligent enough to know that his grandchildren were going to live in an entirely different world, and he felt that that world, as far as India was concerned, was going to belong to those with capital and initiative. The Desais had both. He knew that many might criticize his choice of a husband for his daughter; yet his instincts told him that he was right. Moreover, he liked Mahadev personally; the man was neither ignorant nor stupid and he heartily respected his future father-in-law's learning.

John had heard all these things from devious quarters. It provided him with considerable quiet amusement to listen to the sweeper, to Ranjit, to the milkman, the vegetableman, the washerman, all the horde of people who daily came up his veranda steps and took a tremendous interest in those they served. It was John's opinion that it was impossible to eat something different for dinner without all the neighbours being informed by their servants of the details of it. To John, it was like a play which he watched as an audience. His own life was so plain, so austere, that he cared nothing if his neighbours knew all about it; he gathered from Ranjit that it met with their approval, even if Ranjit himself felt that his lifestyle should be a little more suited to his station.

As John sorted out his sketches of the Dreams of Trisala and prepared to write captions for them, for his book, he wondered idly how Mahadev would get on at the formal family meeting in Dean Mehta's house; and whether Tilak was aware that his name was being coupled with that of Anasuyabehn. Did Anasuyabehn herself realize the fact?

Chapter Eight

John soon dismissed Mahadev Desai from his mind. After finishing the captions for his sketches, he began to draft a description of the enclosing cloisters of the Marwari Gate temple, with their fifty-two small shrines, each of which seemed to be the work of a separate person.

He did not hear the students shouting goodbye to each other as they left the badminton courts and the cricket pitch, nor Ranjit gossiping with the milkman when he brought the evening milk.

When Ranjit brought his tea on a small, brass tray, he forgot to drink it; and Ranjit took one look at the dark head bent over the manuscript and at the scuttling fountain pen, and turned on the desk light. Then he retired to the kitchen veranda and took a nap, knowing well that on such a day dinner would not be required until late.

A sharp rap on the outside door, however, forced John to lay down his pen and call, 'Come in.' He fumed inwardly at the interruption.

His irritation quickly turned to pleasure when he saw who the caller was.

'Why, Tilak!' he exclaimed. 'Come in.' He waved a friendly hand towards the couch. 'Sit down. How are you?'

It was odd, he reflected, that this excitable, tense man had found his way into his affections so quickly. Perhaps it was because his ability to be one minute exalted and the next minute cast down was almost childlike and one automatically consoled him as if he were still a youngster.

As Tilak took the proffered seat, he looked unsmilingly at John. Then the door was flung open again by the wind, and a swish of sand flew across the stone floor. With a muttered exclamation, he jumped up to shut it. 'Sand storm coming,' he said, as he shot the great, brass bolt with unexpected force, as if to keep at bay something more than the whirling wind.

He plonked himself down again on the couch and sat there silently, pounding one clenched fist into the palm of the other. It was obvious that he was in a dreadful temper; his face was as grim as an idol of an avenging god.

John hastily abandoned all thought of his work, and asked, 'Anything the matter?'

'Everything,' said Tilak.

'Like to tell me about it?'

'Yes, indeed. I came to you . . .' he started and then stopped, realizing that he really did not know this monklike Englishman very well. The man was famous in the city and in the University, he told himself. Everybody spoke of him with admiration, and one of the first questions any member of the staff asked him was whether he had yet met him. Surely, he would understand. He looked at the face before him; a typical lantern-jawed English face, the skin made red and leathery by much exposure to the Indian sun, lines of pain etched deeply into it, yet with a long thin mouth as sensitive as his own and narrow, blue eyes, bloodshot with study, observing him sympathetically. Compared to Marathas, the English were not a handsome race, he ruminated with sudden pride. He sensed, however, that this eccentric Englishman had an integrity, a trustworthiness, which was rare enough anywhere, and he badly needed to talk to somebody outside the University.

John always seemed willing to give him time, time and a considered opinion when asked for it, so Tilak made a real effort to control his rage; but the words he wanted would not at first come to him in English.

John turned his chair so that he faced Tilak, took his pipe out of his pocket and resigned himself to listening. Quite often he found himself consulted by irate members of the University staff deeply provoked by the petty politics of the campus – as if I were some antiquated guru, he thought ruefully, guaranteed to give impartial advice. He knew that all he had to do was to listen for an hour and then suggest a little moderation on both sides, and the men concerned went away comforted. Most of the squabbles were incredibly petty and he got some amusement out of watching them resolve themselves.

John offered Tilak a cigarette from the little wooden box which lay on his desk, and it was accepted eagerly. He struck a match for his guest, and watched him puff like a steam engine until he was wreathed in a cloud of smoke.

Since Tilak did not seem to be able to get started, John eventually asked, 'Well, how are things?'

'Things are very well, thank you,' said Tilak, grinding his teeth, 'except that it seems that I am not to do the work which I came here to do.'

'Really?' exclaimed John, rather puzzled by the intensity of rage in Tilak's voice.

Tilak scowled, his fine face distorted with anger, and ground the end of his much abused cigarette into an ashtray.

'These fools! These lunatics,' he muttered. 'These religious maniacs!'

John surveyed the bent and shaking shoulders. He was almost afraid of such intensity of rage – it appeared unnecessary and unseemly to him. But when Tilak buried his face in his hands, and muttered that he might as well be dead as in Shahpur, John got up and went to sit beside him, not even noticing that he had managed several steps without the aid of his stick. He put a kindly hand on Tilak's shoulder.

The friendly gesture calmed Tilak. He began to speak more coherently.

'After weeks of dealing with new students,' he said, 'preparing lectures, attending endless tea parties, fighting for the supply of a few magazines – at last, I tell you – at last it seemed that I might have a few hours for my own research; I'm doing some work on the gills of fish. So, off I went to the Muslim fish bazaar, and arranged for a small supply of the particular fish I wanted – you'll know that fish are shipped up here from Bombay in salt-water tanks, live.'

'Well?'

'Well,' responded Tilak. 'I took some fish back to my laboratory. They were dead but fresh, so I began work. I had three fish on a slab beside me, ready to put into formaldehyde, and one dissected. Then there was a knock at the door and the Dean came in.

'"Ah, good day, Dr Tilak," he greeted me, all charm.'

'He is a very pleasant man,' said John, a little on the defensive immediately.

Tilak snorted.

'Humph,' he said. 'He came close to the table and peered at what I was doing.'

'"Whatever is this?" he quavered.

'"A fish," I said. "In fact, altogether four fishes."

'He went quite white and looked at me horror-stricken.

'"But, my dear sir, we cannot have this kind of thing in our University," he said.

'I didn't know what to say. I was not quite sure what part of my operations was disturbing him. He looked very shaken.

'"This is a Jain community, Dr Tilak, a Jain seat of learning. We cannot have life taken haphazardly right on our campus."

'I was so dismayed that I could only say stupidly, "They were dead by the time I got them here."

'He made a great effort to control himself, "I know that the sciences must be taught, but surely it can be done without taking life? Do you make a habit of this?"

'"I dissected a frog this morning for Zoology I," I said. Whereupon he was immediately violently sick all over my fish.'

John suppressed a desire to burst out laughing.

'What did you do?' he asked.

'I assisted him outside, and sent a servant across to his bungalow to get him clean garments. Anasuyabehn brought them herself. He did not address me further, and refused my help while changing in my office.

'After he was cleaned up, he went home, leaning on Anasuyabehn, while I walked behind him carrying his briefcase and the bundle of dirty clothes. I felt a complete fool.'

He got up and walked with three swift strides to the end of the room, turned and, with eloquent gestures of his hands, went on, 'When we got to the gate of his compound, he turned round and said, "I'll see the Vice-Chancellor tomorrow. In the meantime, please arrange to use only diagrams during your lectures."'

'What did you reply to that?' asked John, a twinkle showing in his eyes, despite Tilak's fury.

'I just said, "All right" and left them and went home. What could I say? While Anasuyabehn was there I couldn't quarrel with her father – such women as she are rare and I would not wish to trouble – and furthermore, he *is* the Dean, and I have only been here a few weeks.'

Tilak's rage was fizzling out and he looked haggard.

'When I went back to the lab this afternoon, there was a different padlock on it – and that seemed the final insult. I couldn't even get into my own laboratory. I'm tired, Bennett Sahib. No Hindu will take life wantonly – but the situation here is absurd.'

He sank his head again into his hands and groaned, the drama of which was lost, as the veranda door burst open, admitting three of Ranjit's grandchildren, who must have been visiting him. John knew them well. They liked to peep around the door and examine the white Sahib, unbeknown to him, they imagined.

Ranjit shouted to them from amongst his cooking pots to come back, but John held them with a smile.

'Tilak,' he said, 'stay and have your evening meal with me. We can send a message to your mother by the children, and we can talk about the Dean.'

Tilak looked relieved.

'Dean, Dean,' shouted the children like parrots.

John laughed, and explained to them what he wanted. Tilak wrote a note for them to carry to Mrs Tilak and gave them an anna each. They hitched up their ragged little pants and were away through the front door and were scudding through the gloom of the dusty lane, before an irate Ranjit was aware they had gone.

Chapter Nine

Anasuyabehn had been very frightened by the message from Tilak, asking for a clean set of clothes for her father. As she flew to the almira to get out the garments, she questioned the peon.

The man knew only that the Dean had vomited. A cold fear nagged at her that he might be seriously ill – he fasted so much.

She decided that she would herself take the clean clothes to the small corner of the University building in which the Zoology Department had been lodged.

Two silent, embarrassed men awaited her. The peon carried the clean clothes into Tilak's office, so that the Dean could change in privacy, and then sat down cross-legged outside the door, to wait. Except for him, she was alone with Tilak for the first time.

Although she had already met him at several parties, she felt very shy, and her eyes uneasily examined her toes peeping out of her sandals.

Tilak cleared his throat, and after two false starts managed to say, 'It's nothing very serious. Dr Mehta was a little upset.'

Anasuyabehn raised her eyes as far as Tilak's middle shirt button, became painfully aware of the fine, muscular body showing through the sweat-soaked shirt, and despairingly raised her eyes to the thin, black face at least a foot above her own.

'What upset him?' she asked.

The shy scrutiny to which he was being subjected was too much for poor Tilak. Unused to having many women about him, he was acutely aware of every detail of the small, plump person before him. He could not think how to reply; he was aware only of the turmoil caused in him by a pair of rather deepset eyes, carefully rimmed with kohl, looking anxiously at him. He had a frightening desire to touch her softly rounded cheek and tell her that all was well.

He turned abruptly and took a couple of steps away from her.

'I dissected a fish and a frog,' he said.

Anasuyabehn was shaken out of her shyness by this admission, and she asked with a faint trace of awe in her voice, 'Did you kill them?'

'Yes,' said Tilak defiantly. 'It's part of my work – it doesn't hurt them.'

'Oh,' said Anasuyabehn. 'I didn't attend the science courses at the convent – I don't know much about these things.'

She lifted her sari over her head, so that her long hair, now carefully plaited, was hidden. She held the sari a little over her face, so that neither the peon nor Tilak could see her trembling lips. She again examined her toes, while the peon smoked a cigarette hidden in his palm.

A shaken Dean emerged from the office. He accepted the support of his daughter's arm, and they walked slowly homeward, followed by Tilak carrying the neatly bundled dirty clothes.

She prevailed upon the Dean to rest in the big swing which hung on the veranda and brought him water and a bowl in which to cleanse his mouth, face and hands; she was grieved to see that his hands shook, as he washed himself.

She set her little servant to preparing rotis and herself completed the making of a light lentil soup, which task she had had to leave unfinished when called to the University.

The need to hurry with her household tasks steadied her; her heavy lower lip ceased to tremble. With quick, experienced hands, she relit the charcoal fire, selected spices and pounded them, and took out the shining brass talis ready for serving the meal, as if nothing had impinged on her quiet life with her father.

Only after the meal was over and her father had gone to lie down for a little while, could she retire to her own room and acknowledge the tumult within her. Her aunt had spent the last few days extolling the virtues of the Desais to her. She was sick of it and was thankful to lean her tired head against the cool stone wall by her bed. The old lady had, that morning, gone to visit another elderly gossip nearby, so presumably, by now, the whole neighbourhood would know that she, Anasuyabehn, was to marry a Desai. Anasuyabehn cursed softly and fluently, as only suppressed, orthodox women the world over can curse.

She allowed her mind to wander back over the past few weeks. Her lips curved tenderly. Her pulses pounded, as she remembered the boring tea parties through which she had sat patiently with the other women in the kitchen, in the hope of glimpsing a certain tall, soldierly figure.

The advent of a new, high-caste bachelor on the campus had, of course, caused quite a lot of interest among the few unmarried girls in the families of the staff. They all agreed that, if he had not been so dark, he would be handsome – and he was so *Western*, that magical word vaguely associated with delicious licence and peculiar freedoms.

And the wonder of today. To stand alone, quite close to him, and actually speak to him. One by one, as if they were gold, she went over the words of their little conversation. He kills animals, she reminded herself, and was shocked to discover that she did not care whether he did or not. She, who had once hotly defended a scorpion against the thwacks of a University gardener's spade, found suddenly that anything done by Dr Tilak must be right, regardless of what the scriptures propounded.

Her aunt returned from her visit and crawled on to the end of her niece's bed, to sit cross-legged and reflective for a moment. Out of courtesy to the older woman, Anasuyabehn moved to get up, but with a slight gesture of one gnarled hand, she was told to remain where she was. Rheumy eyes regarded her kindly.

'Your future husband is calling again in the late afternoon,' she informed Anasuyabehn. 'Put on your best sari – he wants to see you.'

Cold commonsense flooded back. Who was she to dream?

'Yes, Aunt,' she replied sadly, doing her best to hide the burning resentment she felt. She knew she had no right to complain. Parents decided who one married.

Aunt watched her, as she changed into a blouse to match her best sari. 'In my young days,' she said, 'things were much more formal. But, then, this is a late marriage.' She shifted the piece of betelnut in her mouth, and then added, 'I am glad you're seeing sense at last.'

She wiped her lined face with the end of her white sari, while Anasuyabehn, feeling very helpless, got her best sari out of the cupboard and unwrapped it. The bright orange silk spoke to her of many a wedding attended in it, and her depression increased.

'I ordered a basket of ladus,' said her aunt conversationally. 'Dadabhai will make and deliver them himself. One never knows how many people will come on these occasions, and one should have plenty to eat in the house. I bought extra vegetables last evening for pecawlis, and I was looking for the boy to prepare them. Where is he?'

'At the grain shop. He won't be long. I'll prepare some of the vegetables now, and put on my sari later.'

The habit of obedience to her elders was so strongly ingrained in her that her acquiescence and her offer to help to prepare the tea for her unwelcome suitor were automatic. Only much later did it occur to her that she could have refused to have anything to do with the visit.

She was still tying her sari when she heard the carriage draw up at the compound gate. There was the sound of strange voices mingled with those of her father and her servant. She hastily brought the end of her sari forward over her bosom and tucked it into her waistband; the soft folds failed to disguise completely the generous curves of her figure, and she wished heartily that she was fat to the point of ugliness.

She felt so afraid of the interview before her that she was tempted to shut herself in her room and refuse to come out, but Aunt came to inspect her and quickly swept her out towards the front veranda.

'You look very well,' she said approvingly. 'That dark green blouse shows off your pale complexion. Hurry up, now. Your future husband has to catch the Delhi Mail.'

'Oh,' said Anasuyabehn, 'I wondered why the visit was so late.'

To her nervous fears was added more resentment. So she was being sandwiched in between business, was she? Her lips closed tightly, and it was a very distressed young woman who followed her aunt out on to the shadowed veranda.

A woman was seated on the swing; she was very thin and her expensive, flowered sari drooped on her. Huge eyes looked insolently out at Anasuyabehn from a heavily-boned face. Her lips smiled, however, and she put the palms of her hands together in salutation.

A small fat man in spotless white, who was seated in a basket chair near her, sprang anxiously to his feet and also saluted her. The lady immediately frowned at him and he subsided obediently back into his chair.

Another man who had been observing her quietly from the shadows now rose and made his salute.

Anasuyabehn was terribly afraid and looked down at the floor as she put her palms together in greeting. Except for a crow squawking in a tree in the compound, there was complete silence; all eyes regarded her, and she knew what it must be like to be a slave on sale in a market.

The stillness was broken by a shrill giggle from the visiting lady.

Anasuyabehn bit her lips and slowly gained enough courage to look up at Mahadev.

Her first thought was that he was much bigger than she had envisioned him to be. In spite of his plumpness, he had a commanding presence. Though she had no knowledge of the business world, she understood suddenly why he might be successful in his work. There was a dignity about him which spoke of a man who would not tolerate any nonsense, and his bright, intelligent eyes gave indication of the quick wits which were essential to his caste. Today, however, he had put aside his business for an hour and was looking down at her with benign approval.

So great was her respect for male authority and her desire for male approbation, that she held down her fears and treated the moneylender like any other visitor.

Mahadev himself was very nervous. He was anxious to make a good impression, and that bitch of a sister-in-law with her arrogant laugh was too much altogether. He scowled at her, and she retired behind her veiling sari to sulk.

He turned back to his wife-to-be, and the scowl cleared from his face. From a distance, he had watched Anasuyabehn many times in the bazaars and on the campus, but seeing her closely he was enchanted. She had a skin like ivory and the innocent expression of a child. All sorts of ideas shot into his head. That piece of land they owned down by the river – he could build a house upon it – a house for his father, himself, his daughter and Anasuyabehn; a quiet haven by the water. And she should wear emeralds – he had some perfect stones which only needed cutting.

Behind his impassive expression, his quick brain was already circumventing for this charming little woman the ills which she must most fear, particularly the one now sitting on the swing. After his experiences in

France, he felt restless and anxious to shrug off the collar and lead of custom and try himself in the new world evolving in free India.

Anasuyabehn looked down at the floor again, and he was disappointed. He felt that the lid of a box had closed just as he was about to discover the contents.

'Let's all sit down,' said Mahadev, and Anasuyabehn and her aunt obediently sat down on basket chairs a little way from the Desais.

A painful silence ensued, which was providentially broken by the arrival of another carriage. Everyone, except Anasuyabehn, whose head was swimming with fresh fears that she might not be strong enough to fight the match, got up and went to the veranda rail, while the servant danced excitedly to the gate to let the new visitors in. They proved to be a stout, middle-aged couple accompanied by two wide-eyed schoolchildren.

'My respected father's cousin-brother,' announced Mahadev. 'Father and Uncle were unable to come owing to business. Father mentioned it to you last time you saw him, Doctor Sahib,' he said to Dr Mehta.

The Dean nodded, and room was made for extra chairs brought by the servant. Everyone again sat down and stared at Anasuyabehn.

Aunt ordered the servant to make tea, and the children cuddled close to their mother, who turned an amiable, lined face to Aunt.

'It's so hot still,' she said. 'It should have cooled a little by now.'

She accepted a glass of water brought by the servant, who carried a tray as big as himself from one visitor to another until all were served, and then vanished into the kitchen.

Aunt smiled at her, and inquired the names of the children. This launched the fond parent on the history of her offspring, their misdoings and shortcomings.

Anasuyabehn excused herself and went to help in the kitchen. Mahadev watched her go with regret; he would have dearly liked to talk to her.

Dean Mehta was, however, talking about making a visit to Abu during the summer and he had, perforce, to give his attention to him, while in the kitchen Anasuyabehn deep fried savouries for him and wished he would kindly fall in love with someone else.

She was very bewildered. Her first fierce hatred of her suitor had died on seeing him; he did not strike her as the kind of man she could hate, nor did she despise him or his power. She felt like a mouse in a Gujerati cage trap; her thoughts rushed round and round and saw no way of escape. It is harder to fight an enemy one does not hate, she thought. Curse Aunt and all her machinations. 'Oh, Tilak Sahib,' she muttered, 'could you not make a move to save me?'

Why should he? asked commonsense; he doesn't know what you feel for him.

'I'll stall as long as I can,' thought Anasuyabehn, and then winced as the boiling fat she was using spat and burned her wrist. 'Time might offer some escape.'

She handed a dish of savouries to the servant to take out to the visitors, and then put a saucepan of water and milk on to the roaring Primus, for more tea.

She was sitting on her little stool, watching the mixture, when Aunt brought the two lady visitors into the kitchen. Though she stood up respectfully, she looked surly; then the heavy eyelids were again lowered.

The cousin-brother's wife was startled by the resentment apparent in Anasuyabehn's quick glance; it was unexpected, since the family had been assured that Anasuyabehn felt very honoured at the match. She sighed softly. She hoped that this new addition to the family would not cause more trouble; the thin stick of malice standing by her was a big enough trial. Mahadev should have looked in his own caste for a wife – this girl was too well educated for comfort. Mahadev's father had, however, agreed, so the good lady extended an invitation to the sullen girl to make a formal visit to the Desai household, in company with her father and aunt.

Anasuyabehn did not reply, so her aunt spoke for her. They would come in a week's time. She shot a reproving look at her niece, who ignored it. They could arrange her life for her – let them get on with it. She saw no reason to give them much help. She needed time – time to draw Tilak's attention to her. But how?

The gentlemen could be heard pushing back their chairs to leave, so the ladies put their hands together in farewell and an unsmiling Anasuyabehn did likewise.

The Dean saw his guests to the gate and afterwards walked slowly up and down the compound. A good, respectable family, he thought. And to think that Anasuyabehn had allowed her thoughts to stray towards that bloodthirsty horror, Tilak. The Dean shuddered as he remembered the murdered fish.

'Tomorrow, I'll talk to Dr Jain of Mathematics,' he considered, 'and together we can see the Vice-Chancellor. By this time even he must have heard about it.'

Indeed, by dinner-time most of the staff was debating the matter, the story having been spread by the peon who had overheard Anasuyabehn's and Tilak's conversation while they waited for the Dean to change his clothes. The story had lost nothing in the telling. The younger members of the staff laughed gleefully at the Dean's predicament. Despite persistent propaganda from the Central Government in Delhi that locusts, vermin and invading armies might be dispatched without sin, the older staff held strongly to the view that all life was sacred.

Chapter Ten

That evening the heat was still so great in John's room that he and Tilak decided to sit on the veranda, despite the occasional gusts of wind carrying sand. John propped his front door open in hope of cooling the room a little.

As he settled himself carefully in his basket chair, he tried to assure Tilak that he should not take Dean Mehta's fussing over his fish and frog too seriously. 'It may take a little time, but there are other, more worldly people on campus who'll prevail – don't forget that they want a medical school here one of these days.'

Tilak thought this over and then said, 'It isn't the Dean's being sick that troubles me – anybody unaccustomed to seeing meat or corpses might react in the same way. It's his assumption that everybody thinks the same way that he does – he's supposed to be Western educated and is a university man – he should have room for other people's ideas.'

'I know, but ahimsa is pretty well embedded anywhere in India, and especially so in the Gujerat.'

'If it were village people who had complained, I could understand it,' said Tilak, twisting himself round in his creaking basket chair. 'The village people here are Gandhiji's own people, and their belief in ahimsa – non-killing – was reinforced by him. It would be very hard to persuade them to kill anything, under any circumstances.'

'I think that's correct,' replied John. He remembered, again, the story Ranjit had told him about Government officials who had, a couple of years previously, tried in vain to get the local farmers to spray the locusts in their fields. They had faced starvation before they gave in, too late to save that year's crop.

'You know, Tilak, the Gujerat furnished both money and brains for Gandhiji's cause.'

'We all did,' sniffed Tilak.

'Kana,' shrieked Ranjit from the kitchen veranda, much to John's relief. He realized that they were both getting irritable from hunger, and he got up immediately and ushered his friend into his room.

A cloud of moths was dancing round the lamp and in the circle of light reflected on the ceiling, so he told Ranjit to move the table into a corner where they would not be bothered by falling bodies.

When they were seated, Ranjit went to the kitchen and returned with a bowl, a jug of water and a towel, so that they could wash their hands. Then, with a clatter of brassware, he brought in two talis laden with food, and the two friends ate ravenously in spite of the heat. Lentil soup, vegetables, fresh Indian rotis and curd vanished remarkably quickly, and Tilak looked considerably better when he finally accepted a cardamom from a carved box proffered him by John.

John took a clove from the same box, and they tipped back their chairs and grinned quite cheerfully at each other.

'I didn't eat much lunch,' said Tilak, almost apologetically.

'You would hardly feel like it.' John lit his pipe. 'Would you like a cigarette?'

Tilak accepted a cigarette, lit it and drew slowly on it.

'To someone like myself,' John remarked reflectively, 'Mehta is typical of all India – keeps his own customs, but is tolerant of other people's – except when it is a matter of killing something.'

'He's far too reactionary to be typical.'

'Not in everything,' John protested. 'He doesn't seem even to press his daughter to comply – she actually finished her education at a Christian convent school – and then her engagement – that's not a bit orthodox.'

'I heard that the boy died,' Tilak replied idly, as he blew a smoke ring.

'Yes, but I wasn't thinking of him. I was thinking of her new fiancé.'

'Her new one?' Tilak was shocked. His thin hands gripped the arms of his chair.

'Yes, she's going to marry the Desais' elder son – you know, the family which seems to have a financial finger in any pie round here. They're really moneylenders, but on a big scale these days.'

Tilak asked in a breathless voice, 'When is she going to be married?'

'In a month or two, I suppose.' John glanced quickly at Tilak. The Maratha's face was immobile, the lips compressed, the black eyes staring into the darkness, as if he saw, unexpectedly, something frightening. 'Why?'

'Because I want to marry her myself,' Tilak almost snarled between his clenched teeth.

'Well, don't bite me, old chap,' said John humorously. 'I didn't know you were interested – seriously.'

Tilak stood up and went to the veranda rail. 'I am most interested,' he said sadly.

'I'm sorry,' John said sympathetically, and wished suddenly that he, too, could feel as strongly about a woman. Now, however, he looked at Tilak with some concern. The man had seated himself on the veranda rail and was feverishly cracking his finger joints, pulling first one finger and then the other as if he would dismember himself.

'I've no father to advise me, and my uncle would not understand,' he said. 'Bennett, what can I do?'

John shifted about in his chair.

'Do you *really* want to marry her?'

'Of course I do. It's time I married and I want to marry her.'

'She's a different caste and religion.'

'Don't be old-fashioned, Bennett Sahib. Plenty of people are marrying out of caste now.'

'Surely your family would object?'

'Uncle will – and so will mother, at first – but mother I can persuade.' He spoke with all the certainty of a spoiled younger son. 'It's Dean Mehta who is the stumbling block.'

'And the girl? What does she think?'

Tilak looked startled for a moment, and then said, 'I haven't asked her.'

'Well, perhaps you should find an opportunity to know her better, and then ask her. You'll have to be quick, though.'

Tilak gave up cracking his finger joints and gnawed one instead. 'I feel that it is all right with her – I've seen her a number of times.'

'Have you spoken to her?'

'Twice. The last time was when she brought clean clothes for her father this morning.'

John marvelled at the speed with which Tilak had made up his mind. Yet was it so very different among English people? One saw a girl and sought to know more of her and, after a while, one realized one was in love; yet probably that love was present from the first moment, unacknowledged.

'Look,' John said, 'I can't see, really, how you can forestall the marriage arranged for her, without a concerted effort on her part. Even then, I can't imagine how you're going to persuade the Dean to let her marry you – you're simply not popular with him, at present.'

'I'll do it, somehow.'

John whistled under his breath. 'Be careful, Tilak,' he warned him. 'It's not worth ruining your career.'

Tilak agreed, and then laughed sardonically. 'To have a wife and no food for her would be a disaster.'

'I saw Desai and some of his relations going to visit them, earlier this evening,' John told him, as he relit his pipe.

Tilak started to pace up and down, and John pushed his chair back, to give him more room. 'Don't do anything rash, old man.'

'Humph.' Tilak swung back to John's chair. 'I'll go home, Bennett Sahib. Come to visit me one day.'

'I will,' John promised, and escorted his friend down to the compound gate. 'Take care,' he said.

Tilak hardly heard him. He was already swinging swiftly down the dark lane, towards the hostel.

After he had vanished into the gloom, John stood for a moment holding the heavy compound gate ajar. It was not a pleasant night. A small crying wind was whipping up little whirls of dust. Families, who would usually be strolling up and down at this time, had obviously stayed at home because of the threat of a storm. Even the pariah dogs, who could ordinarily be heard rustling in the bushes or snarling at each other, seemed to have taken refuge. In spite of the puffs of wind, the heat was intolerably oppressive, and John took out his handkerchief to mop his forehead.

As he tucked the hanky back into his shirt pocket, he heard the sound of galloping horses approaching up the lane. Fools, he thought, to ride so fast in the darkness.

They were passing him almost before he could see them; four turbanned figures, their turban ends wrapped across their faces to protect them against the dust, naked feet thrust into high stirrups. He wondered who they were; there were few riding horses in the district, camels and oxen being the working animals. Horses were used for carriages.

Strangers, he guessed. Visitors of some kind, following the lane through until they would, eventually, strike the new road that had been built to connect more distant villages with Shahpur. It was a road which ran parallel with the railway and would, one day, be driven right through to Delhi.

Encumbered by a stick, it was not easy for him to shut the gate and shoot its great iron bolt. He felt tired and was thankful to reach his couch again, to lie down under the slowly turning ceiling fan.

Chapter Eleven

John rose early the next morning, with the intention of working steadily through the day. He felt restless, however, and found himself doodling idly in the dust deposited on his desk by the dust storm the previous night.

The storm had begun soon after Tilak had left. The wind had howled round the small bungalow, like a lonely ghost. It had stirred up a dust so thick that windows and doors had had to be shut tightly, to avoid near suffocation. This morning, every leaf on the trees in the compound had a thick coating of dust balanced precariously on it. Inside the building, a fine powder lay on every floor and ledge; food tasted gritty and hair and skin felt dry and uncomfortable.

'Ranjit!' John shouted. 'Come and clean this room – it's not fit for a dog. Get the chattya wetted, to cool the place.'

'Ji,' came a resigned response from the back veranda. Brass dishes clattered against the stone floor, as Ranjit stopped doing the washing up and found his duster. Then John heard him shriek across the compound to Ramji, the sweeper, to bring his broom; Ranjit himself would not touch a broom – he was high-caste.

Ranjit appeared at the veranda door and surveyed his fretful master. 'Sahib, do your legs hurt?' he inquired solicitously. 'When I go to the bazaar, shall I ask the Doctor Sahib to come?'

'It's not my legs this time, Ranjit; my brain won't work.' He pressed his hands over his eyes. 'I can walk fairly well now with only one stick. In fact, I think I'll go for a walk.'

Ranjit grunted agreement. So that he could dust, he piled all the books and papers on the desk into one tottering tower. Ramji came in silently and began to sweep, shuffling across the floor in a squatting position, the soft fronds of his broom making a sighing sound on the stone flags.

As Ranjit removed the cover from the typewriter and shook the dust off it, he remarked, 'That murder on the Mail train was a bad business.'

John was halfway into a clean shirt and his voice came muffled through the cotton cloth. 'What murder?'

Ranjit ran his duster along the window sill, and Ramji clucked as the dust fell where he had already swept.

'You haven't heard, Sahib?'

'I haven't been out today. How will I know if you haven't told me?' A flushed face emerged through the neck of the shirt. 'Who's been murdered?'

Ranjit paused in his work and twisted his moustache thoughtfully before he answered, 'An English lady travelling on the Delhi Mail.'

'Not Miss Armstrong?'

Surprised at the sharp concern in his master's voice, Ranjit hastened to reassure him. 'No, no, Sahib. That was not the name. She was going up from Bombay in the First Class – a stupid place to travel, Sahib. It's where thieves will go first – she should have gone in the Ladies' Compartment.'

John smiled, as he buttoned up his shirt. It was true that when trains were held up, the Ladies' Compartment, full of screaming women, all of whom would have sent their valuable jewellery ahead by post, was not usually tackled by thieves.

'Where did this happen?' he asked.

'About four miles up the line, Sahib. You know where the train curves into that cutting? – I think it's called Ambawadi.'

'A good spot,' said John.

'Yes,' said Ranjit, 'Harichandra says there were many of them, some on horseback, some travelling on the train, and they – '

'On horseback? I saw four men on horses pass, when I was seeing Dr Tilak out of the gate last night.'

Ranjit stopped dusting, and Ramji looked up and gaped at John.

'Did you, Sahib? It could have been some of the Sindhi refugees – some of them brought horses when they came, and have made a little business trading in them – but horses are not very commonly ridden here, Sahib, are they? They are mostly for pulling carriages.'

'Yes,' said John. 'Perhaps it was just some Sindhis taking horses to a customer.'

He ran his fingers through his hair to straighten it. 'Make something with puris for lunch,' he instructed. 'I'll go for a walk round the campus and maybe call on Dr Tilak.'

'Ji, hun,' agreed Ranjit. 'The campus will be the only place free of police today.'

'Do you think they'll scour round this district as well?'

'They will come bothering and badgering, no doubt, Sahib. Locusts!'

'Tut, Ranjit. They have to work fast, or the dacoits will be out of the province before they can say Jack Robinson.'

Ranjit opened the door and Ramji continued his sweeping across the front veranda. He grunted. 'Police – work?'

John laughed, and went out into the merciless sunshine. Although it was hot, the air smelled sweet after the storm, and he began to whistle cheerfully, as he wandered along the lane. From inside the houses he passed he could hear the lively chatter of women's voices and the thud-thud of spices being pounded. The dhobi, bent nearly double by the great bundle of washing on his back, saluted him. Children stopped their play to listen to his whistle, fascinated at the strange, sweet sound, and he called a cheerful 'Hullo' to those he knew. It was a pleasant morning and his spirits rose.

He found Tilak emerging from a lecture room, followed by a crowd of students who drifted down the corridor, their shirt tails wafting gently behind them. They were all talking at once, their voices as shrill as cockatoos'.

Tilak drew John into the welcome quiet of his small laboratory which, he informed him, he had found unlocked that morning. He bade him sit down on a stool, while he washed the chalk from his hands.

'My frog and fish seem to have sparked a great debate,' he remarked, as he dried his hands on an old duster. 'The families of some of the students are really orthodox, and their relations are making a fuss. They don't want their children to take such Courses.'

'O, Lord,' groaned John sympathetically.

Tilak flung the duster into a corner.

'The old folk want the impossible,' he said. 'They want their young men to get enough training to put them into the better paid Government jobs, without their usual way of life being upset. It's the same everywhere.'

'Surely, it's only amongst the Jains that you would find it. And you have to remember that they are really a very cultured people. Seeking work outside their traditional occupations is new to them.'

'A pack of village moneylenders,' snorted Tilak.

John laughed. 'Come, Tilak,' he said. 'It's not so bad. They'll get used to you. After all, you must have had a battle with your family to get permission to take up research.'

'No. Father went to Cambridge,' replied Tilak tartly. 'He did physics.'

John felt snubbed, but he managed to say, 'That must have made your path much easier.'

Tilak caught the slight sarcasm in his friend's voice, and repented his sharpness.

'It didn't,' he said with a rueful laugh. 'He was insisting all the time that I take physics.'

John relaxed and laughed, too. 'Do you want to do some work now?' he inquired. 'If so, I'll leave you.'

'I prepare my lectures at home. Like to walk over with me? I can offer you some coffee.'

John assented, and they went out together and walked through the flower gardens in front of the building.

On the lawns, water-sprinklers slowly revolved, with an opulence which always made passing villagers stop to gape, because they themselves were so short of water. Blackbirds hopped in and out of the gentle downpour and the flowers glittered with tiny droplets; their perfume in the desert air seemed strange and exotic to John.

Tilak interrupted his thoughts by saying, 'Mother and Damyanti went home to Bombay this morning. They caught the nine o'clock train.'

'Really?' exclaimed John.

'Yes. They missed the gaiety of Bombay – and the heat here was hard on mother. I suppose I must get myself a servant.'

'I can imagine their being homesick.'

'Can you? Is it that you are homesick for England?'

'No. When I was in prison, I used to be homesick for Shahpur!'

Tilak laughed, disbelievingly. 'That is not possible. I wish I had never seen the place. You were in prison?'

'I was a prisoner of war.'

'Ah,' said Tilak, highly interested. 'I once did three months for participation in a riot.'

'All the best people in India have been in jail.'

'True,' replied Tilak. 'How else would we have got Independence?'

They came on to the road which bordered the campus. Students were standing about in sullen groups, all apparently engrossed in shrill argument. On the verge, a group of villagers was squatting in a circle, resting for a while from their long walk to town. As they leaned towards each other and gave respectful attention to an old man haranguing them, their big, ruby-red turbans looked like great raspberries ripening in the sun. Their red-clad womenfolk sat placidly behind the men, gossiping amongst themselves, while their half-naked children, oblivious of the heat, darted about like minnows in a stream.

John paused and regarded the scene lovingly. So colourful, so sane.

'Arree!' shouted Tilak suddenly. He stumbled and clutched at one shoulder.

John jumped, and turned to him in astonishment. 'What happened?'

Tilak picked up a half brick. 'This,' he said grimly. 'It was thrown at me.'

John's eyebrows shot up. 'Good heavens!' He turned swiftly to look back along the road.

The groups of students were melting rapidly away; those who had bicycles had already mounted them and were pedalling hard into the distance.

The villagers had shot to their feet and were staring aghast at the two men. Except for squawking crows, there was a profound silence.

'Did you see who threw that brick?' John called to the nearest villager, a middle-aged man.

'No, Sahib.' His face looked like a dried raisin, and he fluttered work-roughened hands. John could well imagine the panicky fears of accusation going through the man's head; fears of arrest, of beatings, of a fine levied against his village. He would never open his mouth.

John turned back to Tilak, who stood looking down at the brick in his hand. With the other hand, he ruefully rubbed his back.

'Are you much hurt?' John asked, in some anxiety. 'Turn round. Let me see your back.'

'I'm only bruised, I believe,' Tilak answered, as he turned. 'My frog is avenged, I think.' He dropped the brick in the dusty road.

There was some blood on Tilak's shirt, so John said, 'Let's get back to your room, so that you can take off your shirt and I can see better what the damage is. Are you steady enough to walk?' He put his hand under Tilak's elbow, and they continued slowly towards the hostel. 'I don't think a villager threw that brick – they would not dare to,' John continued. 'It was a student, all right. We'll get the Dean to institute an inquiry – he'll find the young devil.'

'The Dean?' exploded Tilak. 'No, John. I'm grateful to the brick-thrower – he's made up my mind for me.' He stopped and faced John. 'I'd like to be alone,' he said, his expression sad and disillusioned. 'I'm not badly hurt.'

'Of course, if you wish it.' John bit his lower lip. 'Are you sure you'll be all right? Don't do anything rash, will you?'

'My friend, sometimes one must grasp life by its shirt tail. Otherwise, it flashes past before you realize it.' He raised his hand in salute and left John to ruminate over this cryptic remark, while he strode away towards the students' hostel and his empty rooms.

Chapter Twelve

When John approached the gate of his compound he was surprised to see Ranjit squatting outside it, when it was reasonable to suppose that he would be on the back veranda preparing lunch. John quickened his step, and, as he approached Ranjit, he observed an unusually tense, tight-lipped look about him.

'What's up?' he asked in Gujerati.

Ranjit stood up, and his clean, white loincloth gleamed in the sun, as he set his legs belligerently apart.

'A Memsahib has called and is waiting in your room,' said Ranjit, rank disapproval apparent in every line of him. Never, in all the time he had served the Sahib, had a Memsahib called. Why, the Sahib hardly ever visited English people himself.

'A Memsahib! Who is it?'

'Armstrong Memsahib.' Ranjit had an excellent knowledge of English names.

'Oh,' said John. 'She's come about the map, I suppose.'

'Map, Sahib?'

'Yes, Ranjit, I'm going to help her and Lallubhai Sahib prepare a special map of the city – showing drains and playgrounds and parks.'

'I see,' grunted Ranjit, relaxing a little. One never knew, however, what happened when a Memsahib was made free of a gentleman's home – Ranjit could not imagine a worse disaster.

John knew fairly precisely what was running through Ranjit's head and the gossip which would sweep through the campus, and yet, as he hurried across the compound, he was full of pleasurable anticipation. He forgot Tilak and his frog and thought only about talking to someone English; he found it hard to admit this need but knew it to be true.

He paused at the top of the veranda steps to rest his legs, then approached the door more slowly.

She was seated nervously on the edge of the chair by his desk, her face turned expectantly towards the door. He smiled as he approached her and shook her hand. Behind the smile there was great surprise.

He had previously seen her only in her nurse's uniform and again on the occasion of meeting her in the bazaar, when she had been garbed in grubby khaki. Today, her red hair shone with washing as it fluttered in the breeze of the fan, and, though her green eyes still had rings of fatigue round them, they were oddly appealing in a face no longer brick-red from exertion. Like many English women in hot climates, she wore little makeup, and the natural gold of her eyelashes and the delicate pink of her mouth reminded him of one of his mother's beautiful china figurines.

The same artist's eye which could note and transfer to sketch book the incredible detail of Jain sculpture saw and realized the implications of her plain white dress, obviously made at home from the cheapest mill cloth, and the plastic chuppells on her feet. Propped against her chair was a black umbrella, the cheapest way to protect herself against the ruthless sun.

God, thought John, Ferozeshah must pay her in annas. Yet, in spite of her obvious poverty, she made a pleasant picture, sitting in his working chair.

She explained shyly that Lallubhai and his Committee had come to the conclusion that the housing needs of the refugees were very urgent, so the previous evening they had asked her to convey their thanks to John and to discuss with him the map and the data already collected by the Committee. As she handed him a file of papers, she added her apologies for descending upon him so abruptly, but she had only one day a week free, and this happened to be it. 'I didn't want to delay it another week,' she went on. 'We have only four months before the rainy season and we hope that the maps will show up small open spaces, which we can begin to beg from landlords in order to put huts on them.'

John smiled and soon made her feel at ease, and she continued by saying that they had enlisted the help of the reluctant, overworked City Engineer, who had agreed to let them have access to his records, inasfar as they touched on the mapping of the city. The Mayor was already on the Committee, so civic co-operation was assured, as long as it did not get bogged down in the usual inertia of Indian officialdom.

John listened with pleasure to the rather deep voice, slightly tinged with a Gloucestershire accent, as she made each point clear. Occasionally, he asked a question. They had no hope, she said, of compiling a properly surveyed map, but, using John's and the City Engineer's maps as a base, they hoped to fill in most of the blanks sufficiently well to discover the more pressing needs of the population.

John considered all this for a minute or two. Then he said, 'They'll have to watch that the funds don't get misappropriated somewhere along the line.'

'Lallubhai is incorrupt,' said Miss Armstrong, 'and so are some of the others.'

'Yes. It's a very good Committee. Jains are like the little girl with a curl in the middle of her forehead. When they're good, they're very, very good, and when they're bad they're horrid.'

Miss Armstrong laughed.

'Could you stay to lunch?' asked John, and he was amused to see her go faintly pink as she answered that it was her free day, and all she had to do was to visit an old woman in Pandipura later in the day.

John went to confer with Ranjit, who was grinding spices on a flat stone, with a stone rolling pin. He still looked as sour as old milk but agreed that he could feed the lady, if she could take the north Indian food he usually prepared. John said that he was sure that she could eat it, provided he did not put too many chillies in it.

John returned to his guest and explained the situation to her, and she confirmed that she enjoyed Indian food.

'I eat a good many meals with the Ferozeshahs,' she said. 'Mrs Ferozeshah is a friend of mine – she was trained in Edinburgh as a nurse.'

'Ah, I wondered how you coped in a purely Indian hospital.'

Miss Armstrong blushed at the implications of the remark.

'Oh, I've never had any trouble,' she said. 'Dr Ferozeshah and his hospital have an excellent reputation, and he's always treated me very well. He's an FRCS, you know.'

'I know. He's lucky, though, to have a State Registered Nurse to help him.'

She beamed at him, and fingered the tiny brooch pinned to her dress; its enamel and gilt indicated her nurse's status.

'I find the work very worthwhile. Doctor does a lot of work in the City Hospital – and a good deal in the villages round about. You should see his doorstep at Divali – people come from miles around to bring him thankofferings of flower necklaces or fruit – he won't take anything else from poorer people.'

John was enjoying this feminine company more than he cared to admit, and wanted badly to know more about her. He chanced a direct question.

'Have you been with Ferozeshah long?'

'About two and a half years – I was with the Mission of Holiness before.'

John had never heard of such an institution, and said so.

'They have a tiny Mission about twenty miles north of here – almost in the desert. There were two American nurses, besides myself, and an elderly doctor.' She hesitated, and then said, 'They do excellent medical work . . .'

'A bit "holier than thou"?'

Miss Armstrong grinned mischievously.

'Very,' she said. 'I couldn't stand it any more, and yet I liked India and was in no hurry to go home. One day, when I'd come to Shahpur to buy shoes, I met Mrs Ferozeshah also trying on footwear. She saw my nurse's brooch and spoke to me, and ended up asking me to have tea at her house. She used to help her husband in his work, but now she has children she has not much time; and after another visit, when I met Dr Ferozeshah, I was offered my present post. The salary isn't much – a little more than he would pay an Indian nurse – but I can manage, and both of them are wonderfully kind to me, and I love their children, too.'

'You could nurse in England – and you must have friends there, also.'

'Yes, but the need there isn't so desperate. Maybe when I'm older and can't stand the heat so well, I'll go back home. My father would like to have me at home with him – he is a minister, a widower – and would like me to settle down at the parsonage and keep house for him.' She looked shyly out of the corners of her eyes at John. 'I simply couldn't face it,' she said with feeling. 'At least I'm alive here.'

'It can't be very entertaining for you, here, though. So few English people around.'

'On the contrary, I find I have quite a social life. The Ferozeshahs have introduced me to a number of their friends, and I get invitations to tennis parties and tea parties from all kinds of people. I feel very content. Nobody drives me in any way – I am free.' She unclasped her hands, which she had previously held tightly in her lap, and made a little opening gesture as if to show how her character had expanded in the wide latitude of Indian life.

John deliberated over this, and then said, 'You're right – I have the same feeling of freedom from social pressure. People aren't pressed so tightly into moulds here, are they?'

'No, they're certainly not.' She gave another of her low soft laughs. 'Is that why you stay here?' she asked.

'Me? I – er – well, after the war I just came back to the place I knew best.' Her question had confused him. He could feel an old depression creeping over him. 'To be honest, I felt after the war that we should be blown to hell pretty soon and, since there was not much I could do about it, I wanted to enjoy what time was left doing the work I like best. So I came home to Shahpur. After all, I was born here,' he finished up a little defensively.

The laughter went from Miss Armstrong's face and she stared unseeingly out of the window. His reminder of the menacing atomic shadow over the world brought back to her her reasons for taking up nursing. A desire to repair, to build in some small way in a destructive world, had become a dedication so that she had soon lost herself in her work. Now, she never thought further than a day or two ahead, and that mostly when she was arranging Dr Ferozeshah's tight schedule of visits, operating, and so on.

She glanced quickly at John. He had absent-mindedly taken out his pipe and was packing tobacco into it, and at the sight of this male refuge being prepared, she smiled.

'I'm told that your coming here has been very fruitful. I've read your book about the conquest of the Gujerat in the thirteenth century, and, frankly, I found it so gripping that I read it at a sitting.'

She wanted badly to cheer him up and see him laugh. Today they were alive and there was time enough to worry about other days when they arrived. She was delighted to have such a cultivated Englishman to whom to talk and wanted desperately to please him.

He was grateful to her for turning the conversation, and replied, quite cheerfully, 'Ala-ud-din the Bloody in 1297. He was nearly as thorough as present day conquerors.' And once launched, he kept her spellbound, while he told her tales of ancient Shahpur.

The door to the back veranda swung open. A frigid Ranjit, in clean shirt and dhoti, announced that lunch was ready.

Miss Armstrong ate neatly with her fingers, using pieces of bread as a spoon where necessary, as did John. Afterwards, he persuaded her to wait a little, in the hope that the heat would decrease, before she set out to see her patient in Pandipura; but it was still very hot when she announced that she must go, and firmly picked up her small, black bag. He looked at her uneasily.

'Would you like Ranjit to accompany you?' he asked. 'The police are supposed to be looking for the train robbers in this district.'

'I heard about it,' she said. 'But I shall be all right, thank you very much. The police know me and most of the villagers do, too.' She went to the door and opened the umbrella. 'Mr Lallubhai has promised to invite you to the next Committee meeting. I do hope you can come.'

'Certainly,' said John. 'Only too happy to help.'

He was rewarded by a quick smile from beneath the ugly umbrella, and he felt reluctant to let her go. The Indian countryside was not a place for a woman to walk alone, particularly when it was believed dacoits were in the district. He told himself that his disquietude was unwarranted, that she was obviously accustomed to going about by herself and that the robbers had probably made all haste back to Saurastra, their usual stronghold.

He saw her out of the gate and received again her thanks, then closed the gate and shot the bolt.

Back in his room, he surveyed with distaste its cell-like bareness; only the desk with its untidy piles of paper spoke of life and work. He sat down on his chair and thumbed idly through his notes, which represented months of research. Determinedly, he picked up his pen and began to write.

Chapter Thirteen

Tilak went slowly up the long, stone staircase which led to his rooms. His back hurt more than he had admitted to John, and his spirits had suffered an equal blow. He could still hardly believe that a student had stoned him.

He dropped his briefcase on to the cement floor of his living-room, shut the door quietly and locked it. His second room led off the first and had been used by his mother and Damyanti.

He peeled off his shirt and vest to examine the backs of them. They both had a little blood on them, so he took down the cracked piece of mirror which served him when shaving, to have a look at the wound.

By holding the mirror at an angle and peering over his shoulder he was able to see the nasty weal, raw in places, which the brick had caused. He put the mirror down on his worktable, on which the remains of a hasty breakfast still lay.

Deeply depressed, unsure of what to do, he crawled on to his unmade bed and lay there through the long, hot afternoon until darkness fell, his thoughts wandering miserably backwards and forwards over the events of the previous few days.

Footsteps in the passageway stopped at his door, and a white envelope shot under it and across the floor. He sat up quickly, winced when his back hurt him, and went to retrieve the missive.

In a polite note, Professor Jain regretted that a tea party, to which Tilak had been invited, had been cancelled, owing to unforeseen circumstances. 'Arree,' grunted Tilak. 'Poor frog – you are now called *unforeseen circumstances*.' Irritably he screwed up the note and flung it into a corner.

This letter reminded him of another, and he went to his briefcase and took it out. Delicately, he unfolded the two precious sheets of paper, and went back to his bed to sit down and read them again. The first page said:

Dear Dr Tilak, I am requested by the Committee of the Thomas Jones Foundation to inform you that they have considered your recent application and are pleased to grant you a Thomas Jones Fellowship, tenable at our laboratories in London from October 1st, 1951, for two years, after which consideration may be given to extension of this period by a further year. The scholarship consists of a grant of £700 per annum plus travelling expenses to and from England, and a small sum to cover visits to universities during your stay here. Kindly let me know when you expect to be able to take up the Fellowship.

Yours sincerely, Ian MacAngus, Secretary.

The second sheet was an informal and kindly epistle from Mr MacAngus, congratulating him and offering advice regarding travel and accommodation.

Tilak caressed the letters gently with his fingertips. The Head of the Foundation was Sir Andrew Diamond, a specialist in Tilak's field; and Tilak knew that, working under such a great man, he would expand his own knowledge and could hope for international recognition of his research.

Could he marry Anasuyabehn in a civil ceremony, get her a passport and whisk her out of the country, before her father could catch them? An elopement, that was the English word for it. The problem was that the Fellowship was not available until October and as yet it was only March; the Desai marriage was probably planned for sometime in the next two months.

'What the hell shall I do?' he fumed. 'What *can* I do?'

Would his uncle offer for her? No point in that; he would almost certainly be turned down politely, on the grounds that she was already betrothed. Alternatively, if he approached the Dean himself and begged a reconsideration of her present commitment, he would court an immediate rebuff. His dead frog would be enough to put the Dean off, never mind the problem of untangling himself from an agreed marriage. To add to the problem, there was always the argument that they were of different religions and different language groups.

While he stewed over the problem, he lit his Primus stove and made a cup of coffee. He took it over to the open window and sat down on the sill.

From the floor below rose the din of brass on brass as seven Brahmin students were served their dinner by the Brahmin servant they jointly employed to cook for them, and Tilak realized fretfully that the vegetable seller had not called on him that evening. This worthy, being the brother of the nightwatchman, was able to go through the hostel hawking vegetables, and he had never missed calling on Tilak before.

Perplexed, Tilak put down his cup and went out into the passage, in case he had failed to hear his knock and the man had left some vegetables outside his door. There was nothing. Three doors down, a wilting green leaf testified to his passing. Tilak's eyes hardened and he went quickly back into his room and banged the door shut.

The vegetable seller was a Muslim and it meant nothing to him that Tilak chopped up animals or fish for his research. It did, however, mean a great deal to him if some of the larger Jain families or groups of Jain students, who lived in or around the students' hostel, indicated that they would take their business elsewhere, if he continued to serve Dr Tilak on the second floor. Undoubtedly, the vegetable seller's memory would slip conveniently, and Dr Tilak would be forgotten. Tilak wondered if the milkman would also forget.

He surveyed the grain bins in the corner of his room and wondered if he should cook himself some rice and lentils. He decided that it was too much trouble. Instead, he took down a round brass tin from the shelf and extracted half a small loaf of bread from it. Dipping pieces of it into another cup of coffee, he wandered round the room eating it. Though the bread was very dry, the austere meal revived him and improved his ragged temper.

Tilak could hear the nightwatchman doing his first round, stumping his staff on the ground to warn thieves, snakes and scorpions of his coming. He went back to sit on the windowsill. The chatter of students returning from their evening walks subsided, and a later wave, returning from the cinemas, was also swallowed up by the great hostel, and still Tilak sat grappling with his problem – Anasuyabehn.

The parade to the communal bathrooms could be heard shuffling up and down the corridors and slowly sleep crept through the building. In that time, Tilak finally made up his mind.

Chapter Fourteen

While Tilak dozed the afternoon away and John worked, Diana Armstrong trudged through the blinding heat to Pandipura village. She wished she could have afforded a tonga, but she had already spent eight annas on one to John's house, and that was the limit if she were to be sure of eating for the rest of the month.

'You don't *have* to see this old girl at Pandipura,' she told herself, as she paused to wipe the sweat from her eyelids with her handkerchief. She had, however, volunteered to keep a watch on her, so, after a moment, she went on again.

The operation on the scrawny body had been a success, and it seemed as if the woman's excellent constitution would lead to her early recovery. They had not counted, however, on the stark fear of being cut open, nor on the fact that she had expected that such a cut would fester and that she would die.

Dr Ferozeshah had found her by the roadside near his house when taking his usual early morning walk. She and her niece had been on their way to the market with a basket of vegetables when the pain which had been bothering her for some days had suddenly flared up. The young girl was seated with the woman's head in her lap trying to soothe her. Though the old woman was doubled up with pain, it had taken the united efforts of the watchman's wife and Diana, hastily called by the doctor, to persuade her to come into the consulting room to be examined. Nothing would persuade her to remove her cotton skirts, so the doctor had to feel through them to find the source of the pain.

He diagnosed appendicitis and advised an immediate operation, which was enough to send the old woman nearly into hysterics. She tried to get off the examination table. Dr Ferozeshah, and the sharp agony within, persuaded her to lie down again, while he sent the watchman's son out to Pandipura to get her brother-in-law.

Once over her first panic, she gasped to Diana that she had been a widow for years and that her brother-in-law, with whom she lived, disliked her very much. It was better that she should die.

Diana suggested that this would be tantamount to suicide, since the doctor had the power to cure her. She took a cloth and wiped the sweat off the sick woman's face, and added, 'There may be work for you to do yet, respected mother. Grandsons or grandnephews to guide. Motherless children to look after.'

A gaggle of relations had come running, babbling with fear of the unknown. They had blenched when the doctor had explained what needed to be done. The brother-in-law, his small, bright eyes shifting uneasily from the doctor's feet to his face, had said, 'I remember, Sahib, that when the cholera raged, you and the city Doctor Sahib came to our village and put needles in us to save us. I do not forget this, Sahib – but a cut like that would fester and mean certain death. Why bother? A little opium may help her to get over the pain and recover.' He shrugged, as if to suggest that the woman's life was of little importance.

His sister-in-law had all this time been lying on the examination table, breathing heavily and trying not to moan. Suddenly she had spoken up.

'There is no particular reason why I should live,' she gasped, 'but let the Doctor Sahib assuage the pain in any way he can. If I don't recover, who will mourn me?' She turned her head and glared malevolently at her brother-in-law.

The brother-in-law spluttered about the cost.

'I shall not charge,' Dr Ferozeshah assured him, and before anybody could say anything more, he called the bearer to wheel the woman into the next room and told Diana to scrub up.

A cry of real fear burst from the forlorn little group behind the brother-in-law, but the doctor turned and said authoritatively, 'One of you stay here to cook for her. There is a veranda where you may sleep and cook, and a well in the yard. Bring in a little food to which she is accustomed.'

With much going to and fro and grumbling and fussing, it had all been arranged. After a few days, the invalid had been carried home on a stretcher borne by her nephews. She was cheerful and had undoubtedly enjoyed being made a fuss of and the unaccustomed rest in a real bed with a cotton mattress. Not so many of her caste practices had been flouted, and she hoped that prayer and suitable ablutions, when she was well, would appease her caste brethren.

Diana reached the village and stood for a minute in the shade of a tree by the well, to recuperate from the heat.

How very quiet everything was. Though it was long past the hour of afternoon naps, there was none of the usual shouting back and forth between housewives across the lanes, no sound of scolding mothers, no sound of goatherds playing their flutes – or a cloud of dust on the horizon to herald the return of the buffaloes to be milked. A few men sat on string beds outside their houses. They were talking quietly, heads close together, not arguing loudly with lots of gesturing, as they usually did. When a woman with a small child on her hip came out of one house, crossed the lane and went into another house, Diana relaxed. It must be the heat, she decided. She walked briskly down the main lane and then turned into another, in which her patient lived.

The woman's brother-in-law and his sons rose from their string bed outside the hut door and greeted her politely. Two women came out and led her inside to the old woman. They watched quietly, as Diana checked and changed the dressing, and took the woman's temperature and blood pressure. It was obvious to her that her patient was far from well; yet the wound appeared clean and healing. The silence of the waiting relatives oppressed her – Indians were not a silent people. Diana slowly put her thermometer back into its case. She wondered if something had happened to the village as a whole; had a fine been levied collectively for some misdemeanour? Or were they afraid of some infectious disease? Or had they lost a crop?

The hut in which she stood was clean, she noted, its earthen floor smooth and shining from a recent application of cow dung; the talis and other eating utensils twinkled on a shelf cut out of the earthen walls; the womenfolk's spare skirts and a couple of clean, unwound turbans hung neatly over a rope stretched across the hut, so as to divide it and give a little privacy; a figurine of the Elephant God, Ganesh, shone softly in a corner, a small offering of rice before it. Everything was as it should be, and yet she sensed that something was wrong.

The woman opened her eyes, knew her and tried to smile. Again, Diana took her wrist to check the faltering pulse. In slow, clear Gujerati, she teased the old lady that she would soon be up and making flower offerings in the temple in thanks for her recovery. Now she was going to give her a pill, something like opium, which would give her a good, long sleep, after which she should feel very much stronger.

'Radhabahin,' murmured the sick woman. 'Sister of God.' She trustingly swallowed the pill.

As Diana went outside to speak to the three men and the two older women who followed her, she was worried. She reiterated to the relations that the woman would live, if the family would help her. Perhaps the little niece could be delegated to sit with her, hold her hand, fan her, make her feel she was needed and respected.

'She's not easy to live with,' the brother-in-law said frankly.

Diana laughed, and responded, 'We all grow old and impatient, in time.'

The response was an absent-minded smile, instead of the light joke which she had expected. She snapped her little black bag closed and said she would return on the following day.

It's as if all their cheerful gossip has been turned off, by order, she thought crossly.

Across the way, she was almost relieved to see Miss Prasad, a volunteer who came each week to teach women to read. She was asking Jivraj, a member of the village council, if he could send a donkey to fetch her servant, who was sitting by the side of the track leading to the village, unable to walk because she had a thorn deeply embedded in her foot. After the lesson, Miss Prasad would like to retain the animal to take her servant home. She would see that it was returned the following day.

Jivraj was looking most uncomfortable. He was an old man and he walked with the support of a grandson, a quiet, wide-eyed boy, round whose shoulders he draped one arm. In his right hand he held a staff for further support. His short, frilly jacket hung loosely on him and his dhoti flapped against sticklike legs. Jivraj had faced many famines, many disasters, and Diana thought that life could hardly present him with a problem he could not solve; and, yet, the polite request for a donkey from a most respected lady had obviously put him out.

'All the donkeys are at work, Miss,' he was telling her. He dug his stick into the sand and looked around him doubtfully. 'They will be busy for several days.' Then relief dawned on the lined, tired face. 'My grandson can go and help her,' he said.

Miss Prasad's earnest face still showed some anxiety, but she agreed to this. His grandson helped the old man back to his seat on the string bed outside his house, and then skipped away to find the servant.

'Good afternoon,' Diana called as cheerfully as she could to Miss Prasad.

'Namaste,' responded Miss Prasad briskly, as she gestured to a growing group of women and children to follow her to the shade of a nearby neem tree. She set up a tiny blackboard, and, as Diana made her farewells to her patient's family, the women sat down cross-legged and began to chant the letters of the alphabet, as she wrote them on the board. Diana had seen her do this in many villages, and usually the women made a social event of the occasion and there was much laughter. Today, they kept their veils across their faces and sometimes their excellent memories slipped.

'I can't imagine what's up,' Diana thought irritably, as she waved to them in passing. 'But something is.'

Chapter Fifteen

Tilak waited patiently until the students' hostel had been perfectly quiet for over an hour. Then he moved swiftly.

He dug out a clean shirt and cotton trousers from his untidy cupboard. Taking a towel and a sliver of soap, he walked with his usual, quick, masterful stride down to the indescribably filthy bathrooms. He found a shower cabinet less disgusting than the others and made a hasty toilet. Back in his room, he put on his clean clothes and his chuppells and slipped his torch into his pocket.

Very quietly he opened the door of his room.

The passage was empty, except that at the far end a servant lay sleeping on a mat outside a door.

Tilak glided across the passage and down the ill-lit main stairs. Behind the last flight of stairs he found a narrow door, made originally for the entry of Untouchable cleaners. It creaked when he opened it and he waited for a second or two to make sure that the nightwatchman, sitting on his stool towards the front of the building, had not heard him. Then he slid silently through it and left it a trifle ajar for his return.

The moon had risen and cast a great shadow of the building. Tilak made full use of it. The ground was rough, undeveloped land, criss-crossed by tiny paths made by many student feet. He found one of these paths leading to the lane bordering the campus, and followed it. Once out of the shadow, he might be seen by a watchman, but he would be far enough away not to be recognized.

He began to breathe more easily. There was no curfew to prevent his taking a walk at night, but anyone observing him would undoubtedly gossip speculatively about his being out at such a late hour.

On the other side of the lane bordering the campus, grazing land stretched for at least a mile, and he could hear heavy beasts moving about and snuffling at the herbage. The herdsmen must be somewhere near, he thought, and he walked lightly, using the shadows of a few mango trees to mask his presence as much as possible.

He saw them before they saw him. They were crouched in a tight circle, their woollen blankets clutched around them against the night chill. When they heard him, they sprang to their feet and raised their staffs ready. Tilak lifted his hand in salute and passed on quickly; he did not know whether he was recognized or not.

He reached the row of bungalows in which many of the senior professors lived. Here he paused, beside a small Jain temple which lay a little to the rear of them. His head throbbed and his throat was dry. He had walked so fast that his breath came in short gasps.

He wanted the eighth bungalow from where he stood. He forced himself to think carefully. The Dean, he reasoned, would at this time of year probably be sleeping in the courtyard, the boy servant nearby; Anasuyabehn, with her sharp-eyed aunt, would be either on the inner veranda or on the roof. The problem was to get close enough to the girl to talk to her without waking her family. Would he have to get on to the roof? And thence, possibly down to the veranda? That, he decided, would be madness.

He began to move, rather uncertainly, down the field path that ran at the back of the bungalows. His heart sank when he realized that a bungalow emitting a great deal of light from its back window was that of the Dean.

'I'm crazy,' he muttered, and wondered if he should look for an opportunity to speak to Anasuyabehn when she went out to the bazaar or the library. 'But it could take days,' he told himself, 'and then she might have the servant with her.'

The lighted window was open and the thin curtains flapped sporadically in the night breeze. Was a late-working Dean behind the curtains? Or a sleepless old lady? Or Anasuyabehn?

The curtains solved the problem for him by suddenly billowing inward. Before they subsided, he caught a glimpse of Anasuyabehn sitting on an iron bed, reading. His mercurial spirits rose. What luck!

He crept forward to stand at the side of the window, so that he would not be silhouetted against the light. He had to find out if she were alone. When, eventually, the curtains obliged by flipping inward again, he could observe no one else, so he chanced anyone being in the corner outside his line of vision, and called softly, 'Bahin!'

The quiet voice calling 'Sister' through the window shocked Anasuyabehn. She dropped her book and jumped off the bed to slam the window shut before the impudent student or would-be thief had time for action, but again the voice came, 'Anasuyabehn!'

'Ramji!' she exclaimed, and gripped a window bar for support. With the other hand, she parted the curtains slightly. The shadow of a neem tree dappled the side of the house and she could see no one. 'Doctor Sahib,' she whispered.

'Put the light out,' whispered the disembodied voice hoarsely.

In her agitation she vacillated.

'Don't be frightened,' urged Tilak, his usual irritability apparent in his tone. 'There are excellent window bars between us.'

Shakily, she went across the room and switched the light off. Then she wrapped her sari closer round herself and returned. A small plump hand timidly drew one of the curtains back. 'Bhai,' she whispered. 'What are you doing here? Go home before you're caught.' Here was romance straight out of a Western novel, but it was too scary.

There was no reply to her question, so she gripped the window bars to peer out, and gave a frightened squeak as a masculine hand closed over one of hers. 'Brother,' she gasped again imploringly, as she tried to free her hand.

Tilak was entranced and held her firmly. He could just see her face glimmering in the moonlight, despite the tracery of the tree shadow, and behind her was the immense shadow of her loosed hair. Though the folds of her cotton sari covered her completely, she was blouseless and petticoatless. He could feel the heat of her body and smell her perfume. He nearly choked with desire and leaned close to the unyielding bars.

As he put his arm through the bars and then round her shoulders, she sobbed, 'Bhai, please, please go home. You'll be caught – and I've enough grief to bear without any more.' She burst into tears. Without thinking, she laid her wet face on the arm which gripped her, and Tilak came to his senses.

'Don't cry,' he said softly. 'I'm sorry I frightened you.'

He had come to find out if his feelings were in any way reciprocated. Now he knew by the trustful way in which she wept in his arms that love was there. All the ancient love stories seemed suddenly to be true. He was going to fight for this woman.

The words came tumbling from him. 'Rani,' he said. 'All I want to do is to marry you and take you to England and make you happy. I'm going to England to study – I can take you with me . . .'

'I'm to be married to Mahadev Desai,' she interposed, her voice lifeless. 'Tomorrow some relations will arrive – the first guests – and Aunt has already sent for the astrologer to name the day. Desais have already sent the last gifts before the marriage. I am inundated with silken saris and jewellery.'

The jackals howled at the moon and the insects sang, while Tilak silently digested this information. In the distance, the nightwatchman called to his relief man to take over.

'I have to be quick,' he told her. 'When is the marriage likely to be?' He slipped his hand under her hair and ran his fingers along her neck. She shivered, and said, 'Two or three weeks, probably.'

'You must prevaricate – bribe the astrologer. Pretend to be ill. Defer it somehow while I make arrangements.' She was trembling under his touch, but she did not draw back, and he thought that few would let him come so near, bars or no bars. She loves me, he rejoiced.

Her deepset eyes searched the gloom to see his dark face. 'Father is so upset by you. He'd never give permission.'

'Nothing's hopeless,' he assured her passionately. 'We're old enough to decide for ourselves. Would you like to marry me?'

Her teeth flashed, as she smiled up at him, and the heavens rang with pure joy for him, before she even breathed out, 'Oh, yes, of course.'

With a curious prescience, Tilak felt that this was the happiest moment of his life, and he savoured it.

The fresh watchman's staff was plunking down the front lane. 'I must go,' he said. 'Meet me tomorrow. Where?'

She sighed helplessly. Then she said, 'I'll try to be at the Marwari Gate temple about nine o'clock. But how shall we manage everything?'

'Never fear. I'll arrange it all.' He stepped back reluctantly and bent to kiss the hand holding one of the bars, and then he was gone.

Chapter Sixteen

The following morning, preparatory to going to the Marwari Gate temple, Tilak wrote a note on the blackboard of his lecture room, telling the students that the lectures for that day were cancelled.

He had spent most of the night going over his financial position, a record of which he kept in a battered account book. He had some savings and a little money in Government Bonds left him by his father, but it was not enough. He wondered which of his relations could be prevailed upon to lend him some more.

He was certain that his uncle would be pleased about his Fellowship and would stand surety with the passport people, so that he would not have to find the considerable deposit which would, otherwise, be demanded of him.

Suddenly, he stopped writing. How was he to get a passport for Anasuyabehn?

His uncle would certainly not connive with him in the abduction of a young woman. He had planned to marry her and then take her straight on to the boat or plane for England. This would not give time to have her name included on his own passport; and to obtain a separate passport would take even longer. Speed was of the essence if they were to avoid her family's wrath breaking over their heads, not to speak of the anger of the mighty Desai clan.

He was standing staring with glazed eyes at the blackboard, when Dr Yashvant Prasad, walking along the corridor, spotted him.

'Ah, Tilak,' he called. 'I was about to send my clerk to find you. Will you come into my office for a few minutes.'

Tilak turned sharply, trying vainly to think of an excuse to evade the interview.

'Ji hun,' he assented, and followed the Vice-Chancellor with lagging feet. 'My murdered frog,' he thought glumly and correctly.

As Tilak sat opposite him, Dr Prasad's pleasant voice meandered on. Tilak said, 'Yes, sir,' and 'No, sir', wherever it seemed appropriate, and thought of Anasuyabehn loitering alone by the temple. He prayed that she had sought seclusion inside the building.

'I propose,' said the Vice-Chancellor, putting his fingertips together, 'to speak personally to each Jain member of the staff and urge tolerance.'

'Thank you, sir,' responded Tilak, seething with worry under his polite exterior.

'I also propose to call on the more influential and forward-looking Jains in the city, to seek their help. I hope through them to reach the more orthodox groups with whom we do not so frequently come into touch. There is a very powerful family of Desais here, for example – if one could get people like that . . .'

'Desai?' queried Tilak, jerked back from thoughts of the Marwari Gate temple.

'Yes. Big financiers – they live in the centre of the city.'

'I've heard of them,' responded Tilak. It dawned on him that it was probably one of these Desais who was to marry Anasuyabehn. He thought bitterly that it would be too ironical to lose Anasuyabehn to a family which might be able to influence favourably his own position in the community.

The Vice-Chancellor was continuing.

'It will be slow work, I fear. In the meantime, Tilak, lock the laboratory door while doing your researches.' He smiled conspiratorially.

Tilak felt despairingly that if the Vice-Chancellor went on much longer, all his anger at the Dean, all his worry regarding Anasuyabehn and his frustration in respect of his work would explode out of him. He took a large breath, however, and then managed to reply, 'Certainly, sir.' Now was not the time to precipitate his resignation.

Desperate in his general agitation, Tilak half rose, hoping that Dr Prasad had finished.

'Before you go, I would like to ask your opinion about establishing a postgraduate course,' Dr Prasad went on remorselessly. Tilak sat down in his chair again and commended Anasuyabehn to any gods who happened to live in the temple.

He emerged at lunchtime at a loss to know how to communicate with her. He strode across the campus through the broiling heat of the sun. Suddenly his legs faltered and he had to stop in the shade of a tree. He watched the tree ants make a detour round his fingers and continue their endless running up and down the tree trunk, while the trembling in his legs eased. As the faintness passed, he remembered that he had not eaten a proper meal for over a day, and he wondered how to get one without travelling into town; he had only a little rice and lentils in his room.

He remembered John, ever kind and sympathetic.

'Perhaps he'd be kind enough to give me lunch,' he thought, 'and maybe Ranjit could find me a boy as temporary servant.'

A very exhausted Tilak again presented himself at John's door and was fed by a resigned Ranjit and comforted by John, who assumed that his friend's shaken appearance was due, largely, to lack of food and the long session with Dr Prasad about the murdered frog and fish.

Chapter Seventeen

'I thought I might be able to pick up a little Delhi rice,' Anasuyabehn told her aunt that morning, in the hope of justifying a visit to the Marwari Gate bazaar in which the temple lay. They had both been busy, getting ready for the expected arrival of their relations, and Anasuyabehn would, ordinarily, have gone to the nearest bazaar for the day's vegetables. She watched the indecision in her aunt's face. She knew the old woman loved the long delicate grains of Delhi rice, so hard to obtain in Shahpur, even on the black market.

'Well,' the older woman said finally, 'perhaps I could spare the boy for an hour to go with you.'

'I'll be all right alone, respected Aunt,' Anasuyabehn assured her quickly.

'Very well, then. Be a modest, circumspect girl and keep your sari over your head. I hope no Desais see you.'

Anasuyabehn obediently hitched her sari over her head, seized her cotton shopping bag, checked that sufficient money was tied safely in a tucked-in corner of her sari, and fled before Aunt could change her mind.

The bazaar was packed with people. After she had made her purchases, including a seer of Delhi rice from under a stall, she paused apprehensively to scan the crowd for Tilak. A young man on a bicycle eyed her insolently and, as he approached her, began to slow down. She moved hastily closer to the stalls, only to be jostled by a group of millhands going off shift. They touched her obscenely and shouted ribald remarks, as, impeded by the heavy shopping bag, she tried to shrink from them. In a moment, they were past her and clambering into a bus, leaving her nearly weeping with humiliation.

A countrywoman shouted a stream of abuse at them and then called to Anasuyabehn to come closer to her. Anasuyabehn stumbled towards her, wiping her face with her sari and trying not to be sick, while a policeman, rifle on back, leaned against a door jamb and laughed at her.

The woman nodded her head towards the pavement beside her. 'They won't bother you if you don't stray on to the street. Stay here, near us.'

Anasuyabehn nodded and made her way quickly into the temple behind them. She went only as far as the outer cloisters, feeling that Tilak would be sure to find her there.

The building was cool and shadowy. Morning prayers were long since over. The cloisters, with their fifty-two small shrines, were almost deserted. Only at one end a man and a young boy sat together, cotton masks over their mouths, and told their beads. The boy looked up as she entered, but a reproving glance from his companion made him hastily bow his head and continue his prayers.

Anasuyabehn stood leaning against the wall and drank in the peace of the place after the heat and hurly-burly of the bazaar outside. The minutes ticked by and her pounding temples and nausea eased.

Where was Tilak? He should have been there fifteen minutes ago. She went to the top of the entrance steps and looked out over the crowd. No sign of him. She retraced her steps inside and continued to wait.

When her watch told her she had been waiting half an hour, she turned reluctantly and sadly once more to the entrance. Perhaps he had regretted his impetuosity of the previous night and decided that his suit was hopeless.

Head bowed to hide her tears, she did not see, until she nearly trod on him, the monk who had been silently watching her from behind.

Tall, naked except for a tattered cloth covering his genitals, it seemed as if he had no flesh, that the skin was drawn straight over his skeleton. His body was ingrained with dirt and his bald head was covered with sores, where the hair had been painfully plucked out by hand. In one emaciated hand he held a peacock feather and in the other a begging bowl. For a moment, until he drew hastily back from her, her face was within a foot of his.

Her father's guru, his religious teacher, Anasuyabehn realized, with a sense of shock.

As if to pierce her soul, penetrating, bloodshot eyes had looked deep into her own, and made her shiver.

She recoiled from him, feeling as if her mind lay naked to the man and that he had divined her reason for being alone in the temple. She cringed with sudden fear of his supernatural power. Then she bowed low, to touch the horny bare feet.

He knew her. Mehta's daughter, a modern miss with no real respect for her religion. He had warned her father once that he had left her too long unmarried. For his own spiritual good a man must see his children married before he dies. Marry her into an orthodox family, he had counselled. He had heard, however, that he was marrying her, instead, into a monied one.

And now, what was she doing in the temple? She was obviously not there for worship; her clothes were not fresh and she had shopping with her.

He knew that he should not care, that he should turn away from her; but perhaps the child had, of her own accord, sought to return to her religious observances and was not sure how to accomplish this.

Perplexed, he surveyed her ashy face as she rose from her obeisance. She could not go out through the gate until he moved, and he had been so long cut off from any consideration of time, that he was unaware that he had kept her standing there, head bowed, for several minutes.

Anasuyabehn was frozen with fear, as she suffered an intense examination by serene, intelligent eyes, that had spent years looking for the Ultimate Truth, and seemed now to be able to look through her and past her.

She was suddenly acutely aware of her own pettiness compared to men like this. Though she might assure herself that she had discarded her religion, she knew in those scarifying minutes, that it could not be shrugged off like a Kashmir shawl; it was part of the warp and weft of her life, hopelessly woven into her thoughts and actions, and now showing its strength, by making her stand, so frightened, before this uncanny, withdrawn monk.

At last the monk spoke. His voice was soft, so as not to disturb the souls in the air. 'You were looking for me?'

'No.' The answer came in a whisper.

It was an essential part of a monk's creed that he feel no personal interest in anyone. It was laudable, however, and would gain him merit, to hear confession or to instruct in the scriptures. Furthermore, try as he might to conquer it, he was curious to know what had caused her to visit the temple and why she was so obviously terrified.

If he stares at me much longer, thought Anasuyabehn, I shall die at his feet.

The man saw her sway. A bad conscience, he diagnosed.

'You wish to make confession?'

'No.'

'I am here each day. Go home and examine your conscience. You may ask your father to bring you to see me, if you wish, and I will hear you.'

After this pronouncement, he seemed to forget about her, and he turned along the side of the cloister, slowly sweeping the floor in front of him with his peacock feather, so that he would not kill an insect by treading on it. Anasuyabehn tottered out into the blazing sunlight, to the shrieks of the bazaar radios and the vendors' voices.

The bustling crowd around her did little to dispel the mesmeric effect of the monk's frightful godliness. For, to her, godly he undoubtedly was, with a personality purged of all human desire. She felt he did not need to hear her confession to know all that was in her mind.

Hypnotized by the mystic, she forgot to look again in the bazaar for Tilak and the bus was well along the road to home before she remembered him.

Chapter Eighteen

Mahadev Desai's father sat on the worn stone steps of one of the verandas that faced the courtyard of his home. Though the morning sun shone warmly upon him, he was shaking as if with cold. The hands that held the telegram, which his servant had just handed to him, trembled so much that he could hardly reread it, to assure himself that he had understood it.

'Send my brother and my son to me,' he snapped finally, his wizened face looking more than usually owlish as he tightened his lips under his large, hooked nose.

The scared servant flew to obey, while, with quivering fingers, old Desai smoothed the crumpled edges of the telegram.

His second son, his usually blank face full of apprehension, rolled across the courtyard like a billiard ball slowly into a pocket. His uncle followed him, still tucking in his flapping dhoti as he came.

They each read the telegram and, as its full implications sank into their minds, utter consternation made them both burst into speech. Yet the message was such an innocent one. It merely informed them that Mahadev had not arrived on the Delhi Mail and asked on which train he would be travelling.

'The diamonds,' wailed Uncle, his hawklike face blenched.

'The rubies!' exclaimed his nephew, a mass of dithering fat.

'My son,' gasped old Desai. 'My only intelligent son,' and he glared at his second son, who shrank visibly at the insult.

The smell of trouble had by this time brought others to the scene. A knot of servants and hangers-on had gathered at a little distance and were watching the conference speculatively. The daughter-in-law of the wicked tongue could be heard approaching, scolding Mahadev's daughter as she came. The child trotted in front of her, silent and sullen. Automatically, her grandfather hid his fears and called her to him and she thankfully nestled down by him on the step. She stuck her tongue out at her aunt, who mercifully did not see the impudent gesture.

'What's the matter?' the daughter-in-law asked in respectful tones.

'It does not concern you,' replied old Desai coolly. 'I must, however, go out on business.' He turned to his younger son. 'Have the carriage brought out.' His voice sounded as brittle as his frail limbs looked, beneath their thin cotton covering.

The man went obediently, doing his best to crush the rancour he felt at his father's unkind remark. 'It's unjust,' he muttered under his breath. 'I work so hard.'

Old Desai's waspish daughter-in-law hung on to every word, in the hope of obtaining a clue as to what was wrong.

'Daughter,' he addressed her. 'Get out a clean set of khadi and put it in my room. I must change. Your husband will accompany me and will need the same.' He motioned her away impatiently with his walking stick.

The woman's face fell. Her temper flashed out as she called to a servant to get the clothes requested.

'Brother, you must stay here. Several important people are coming in this morning. I'll go to see the Chief of Police immediately.' He sighed deeply, and then exclaimed in apprehension, 'Heaven help us! I hope Mahadev is all right.'

His brother nodded his bald head. 'I was afraid for him when we heard of the robbery,' he said.

'I thought he would be all right,' said the older man. 'He's so quick-witted. I should have sent him by plane – it would have been much safer – though very expensive,' he sighed.

'I've never known dacoits in this district take someone right off a train – usually they rob and murder on the train – or just by – in which case the Railway Police would have found him, and his death would have been reported at the same time as the white woman's.'

'Someone here must have betrayed him, either deliberately or by gossip,' said old Desai suspiciously.

'The dacoits must have been primarily concerned with the registered mail, as usual,' reassured his brother. 'They could, of course, have stumbled on Mahadev by accident.'

Mahadev's father rubbed his chin thoughtfully. 'I doubt if they could have done,' he said at last. 'There was nothing to distinguish him from fifty other Banias who must have been travelling on the train – the boy was himself so sure that he would not be picked out in such an event as this – that is why he carried the stones with him, rather than entrusting them to the registered mail – as you know, some of the stones are particularly good. Our honoured customer, the Maharaja, inherited some excellent ones – and they were a good partial surety for the loan to start his factory. Now he's ready to pay his debt – and we have lost them – and our boy.'

He got up wearily.

'Brother, you had better arm me with some money – and a gift – a good ring, perhaps. Some presents are indicated to speed investigating feet. Arree! Shall I ever see my son again?'

His brother touched his arm comfortingly, and assured him, with more confidence than he felt, that Mahadev was probably safe. The much maligned police were not really so inefficient. There would certainly be a dreadful row about the murder of the English lady and that would galvanize them into action.

The little granddaughter, still as a scared mouse, had all this time been sitting, forgotten, on the step beside them. Her father was a magical person to her, who was often away from home. But when he returned his suitcase was full of presents for her and he had wonderful stories to tell. She opened her mouth suddenly and howled.

Her grandfather and great-uncle jumped guiltily, and, until a servant came to say that the clothing was ready, they kept assuring the little girl that Papa would be all right. She must, however, say nothing about him until Grandpa came home again – and maybe he would bring her a gift from the bazaar when he returned.

'I'll keep her with me,' promised Great-Uncle, and swung her cheerfully up into the air, and carried her off towards the counting house. He stopped suddenly, and turned back to his brother. 'Shall I inform Dean Mehta?' he asked.

'Tell nobody,' replied old Desai. 'Let's first try to find out what's happened.'

Old Desai climbed into the little black carriage, and told his second son to drive fast. No servant went with them. This business had to be kept as quiet as possible, he reflected, if only because he did not wish the Income Tax collector to read in the newspaper anything of their rapidly expanding operations. There was safety in a fair display of poverty. Where riches are splashed about, there come the thieves, the spongers, the hangers-on, the tax collector. Better to hide behind the ancient walls of one's Society, deep in the older part of town. A story of valuable rubies and diamonds lost would alert every robber to the possibility of large quantities of valuables hidden in the floors of the Desai Society, he thought dismally, however poverty-stricken it looked. They would not realize that nowadays money was invested in ships, planes, factories and machinery, instead of being buried as gold.

The traffic was held up by the Red Gate, which was too narrow to allow the vehicles to flow through fast. Old Desai shouted to a toy seller on the pavement, and the man fought his way through the stalled vehicles to the middle of the road. Old Desai solemnly bargained for and then purchased a monkey-on-a-stick.

'Father's reached his dotage,' thought his second son gloomily, as he whipped up the horse again.

Chapter Nineteen

Although the Income Tax authorities might not yet be aware of the extent of Mr Desai's fortune, the police knew of the plainly dressed old man. Doors were immediately opened to him, and it was not long before he was ensconced in a chair in the office of a police chief of gratifying eminence, a small, calm Bengali who had come down from Delhi, armed with instructions to solve the robbery mystery at all costs, before there was a diplomatic row over the death of Mrs Belmont-Smythe.

He sat quietly and listened, while Desai told him of his son's non-arrival at Delhi and his fears for the young man's life. Desai minimized somewhat the value of the jewels he was carrying, but indicated that it was sufficient to tempt a professional thief.

Desai had spoken in Gujerati, his knowledge of English being limited to being able to read it, and his son translated as he went along. There was a pause at the end of the recital during which time the Delhi detective removed his shoes and socks thoughtfully, so that he could sit comfortably cross-legged on his chair. At last he said, 'No body, other than that of the English woman, has yet been found; and these dacoits, as you know, rarely hold anyone for ransom. Perhaps he missed the train.'

These remarks did little to console Desai. 'No. My head book-keeper saw him on to it. Perhaps some of the other passengers saw what happened to him?'

The detective made a wry face and shifted the papers about on his desk.

'We still have in custody a few suspicious characters who were on the train, and we have, of course, the names and addresses of a number of passengers. The majority are untraceable.' His voice rose with decision. 'I'll cause further inquiries to be made, and will have the railway embankments searched again.'

Desai had already decided to obtain the help of his caste brethren in a private search round the scene of the robbery, so he took his departure.

He was conducted to the door, with painstaking respect, by a local inspector, who promised that he would himself again question the railway police who were aboard the train. 'They were overwhelmed by the force of the attack,' he said almost apologetically.

'They always are,' replied Desai dryly, and climbed wearily into his carriage.

As his younger son drove him deeper and deeper into the heart of the city, the old man's spirits sank lower. Why did one scheme and amass money, if it were not for one's sons and their sons? The boy must be dead, dead without leaving a son to tend his funeral pyre, he thought bitterly. The nincompoop beside him had two sons, satanic images of their mother, for whom he felt no affection. It had been Mahadev's sons he had wanted to see before he died himself.

'If he lives, I'll hasten his marriage,' he promised himself.

Hearing his father's mutter, his younger son turned to him. 'Ji?' he queried respectfully.

'Nothing, nothing,' replied Desai testily.

He had told neither Mahadev nor his brother about the opposition of older members of the family to the marriage to Anasuyabehn. The elders had argued that a wealthy girl in the Desai community could be found, a girl strategically placed to increase the power of the caste. Intercaste marriages, they said, dissipated wealth and weakened authority.

Desai had been tempted to agree. When he read the *Financial Times*, however, and when men of other castes planning big enterprises asked his financial help, he felt that to become a power in the new, free India, it was wiser not to emphasize caste.

No one, not even his trusted brother, had ever seen Desai's small private ledger with a swastika drawn, for luck, on its first page. In this, the final results of all his business were entered. He planned that most of what that ledger represented should pass to Mahadev, just as his own father had chosen him to head the business when he had retired. It was, therefore, a good idea that Mahadev have a modern wife, but a wife without bossy caste relations.

The carriage jerked to a stop in front of the plain wooden door behind which lay the Desai Society. Old Desai was helped down from his perch by his son, who handed the horse and carriage over to the care of a servant squatting on the step.

Old Desai went immediately to the counting-house. Partner Uncle was immersed in work, his little grand-niece playing contentedly at his feet with a piece of paper and the office's entire collection of rubber stamps. She received the monkey-on-a-stick with great glee.

'The police,' said old Desai, 'are doing their best, I'm convinced. However, so much is at stake – our reputation for reliability – and poor Mahadev – I'm worried to death about him – that I think we should attempt a search ourselves.'

'I suppose we could,' said Partner Uncle doubtfully.

'Of course, we could,' snapped old Desai. 'We can send for Brother-in-law from Baroda to help organize it, and we have plenty of servants and clerks to help.'

'What about the business?'

'The business can wait,' snorted old Desai, to which unheard of heresy his brother had no reply.

Chapter Twenty

Diana and Dr Ferozeshah's sweeper wearily tidied up the operating room. Dr Ferozeshah, his legs shaking with fatigue, washed his hands and wished he could afford air conditioning. Perhaps next year, he thought. His reverie was broken by Diana's voice.

'. . . and so I promised to go over again today. Would that be convenient to you?'

He turned round, his hands dripping.

Diana was struggling out of her white gown.

'Go where?'

'To that old body in Pandipura. She doesn't seem to be doing very well.'

Dr Ferozeshah surveyed his employee. In spite of her lack of weight, she was plum-coloured with heat and exertion. Too thin, he decided; she needed more rest.

'She'll be all right for a couple of days,' he said, 'and you should rest for a while – we've had a busy morning.'

'I am tired,' admitted Diana, 'but I feel uneasy about her. If you don't want me this afternoon, I could go up on the bus.'

Dr Ferozeshah's perfectly modelled face broke into a mischievous grin. 'All right. Go to see this illustrious patient – and then take the evening off.' He picked up a towel to dry his hands. 'Mirabai can do the evening rounds with me – you've taught her very well.'

A whole evening off was a rare luxury. It sounded as if Ferozeshah was at last satisfied that Mirabai, the new nurse, and a new Sindhi dispenser were competent to undertake some of her work, and she heaved a sigh of relief.

She thanked the doctor, took her handbag from a locked cupboard, and went slowly through the waiting-room for high-caste clients and down the steps to the tree-lined road. She had a room in the house of a widow further down the road, and, as she strolled towards it, she looked back over the previous thirty months. She smiled a little as she remembered how the small private hospital had helped to fight epidemics, patched broken limbs after riots, done operations that in England would have been left to specialists, delivered babies and consoled the bereaved. Though the doctor was making money, much of it was spent on precious pieces of equipment – the X-ray machine, for example, what a help that had been – and the big sterilizer.

When she knocked, her landlady, Mrs Jha, unbolted the front door to let her in. She was a stringy-looking woman, garbed in a plain white sari, her grey hair clipped close to her head to indicate her widowhood. Though she was quite orthodox in her way of life, her grandson, Dr Ferozeshah's lawyer, had persuaded her to take in Diana.

The two women had become good friends and, quite often, Mrs Jha would cook some vegetarian delicacy for the girl and bring it to her. As a caste Hindu, however, she would not eat with her. The line was drawn there.

In return, Diana respected her caste rules and tried not to infringe on her privacy. She never entered her landlady's part of the house lest she defile it. With the aid of a tin bath in her room, she washed herself and her clothes. The sweeper came twice daily through a special sweeper's door into the cupboardlike bathroom, to clean her commode and remove her garbage. Mrs Jha's own servant, for a small tip, drew water from the well in the compound and filled her water-pots on the veranda, both morning and evening. It worked quite well.

Now Mrs Jha was full of news. Mr Lallubhai had sent his peon to ask Diana to attend a meeting at his house the following evening. The man had also brought more news of the train robbery. 'He said,' she commenced in a hissing whisper in case the dacoits might hear, 'that in the bazaar they are saying that this is no ordinary train robbery, and that they must have had local help.' She pursed her lips and glanced over her shoulder, as if expecting to see someone listening to her. 'They think it was not Saurashtrian dacoits who did it – and that makes sense, when you think of it. They wouldn't be foolish enough to kill an English Memsahib.'

She pushed her key ring more securely into the waist of her petticoat, as if to guard it carefully, and looked expectantly at Diana.

Diana, however, knew the value of bazaar rumours, and replied quite cheerfully, 'Except for the murder, the newspaper this morning didn't seem to think there was anything special about it. Just that they were after the registered mail.'

Mrs Jha refused to relinquish one scrap of her morbid excitement, and wagged her head slowly in negative fashion.

'We must be prudent,' she said earnestly. 'When my nephew comes home from work, I shall ask him to clean the gun. And he and his sister can escort you whenever you want to go out.'

Diana restrained the gurgle of laughter which rose in her throat. Mrs Jha's nephew was a huge, flabby, amiable youth and in a crisis, Diana was sure, his only thought would be to find a cupboard big enough to hide in. His shy young sister was hardly necessary to act as chaperon.

She thanked Mrs Jha and retreated to her room.

It was an airy, comfortable room, though, by Western standards, rather bare.

A divan, covered with a homespun bedspread, lay along a whitewashed wall, a few gaily coloured cushions piled upon it. Above this hung a carefully arranged group of family photographs in plain, black frames. There was a small bookcase, crammed with novels, a few travel books, the Bible, a Gita, English translations of the Upanishads and the Light of Truth; on top of it, by a brass vase of wilted wild flowers and grasses, lay some library books, including one of John Bennett's histories. Her few dresses hung on a rail set across a corner of the room, with her shoes in a neat row beneath them. A trunk, its careworn appearance disguised by a frilled cover, held her underwear and a precious tennis racket. On top of the trunk there was a workbasket in which lay balls of wool and knitting needles.

There was little else in the room, except for a small wooden table with its accompanying chair, and a locked cupboard for her modest stores of food, linen, clothing and other oddments.

Diana hurried to her veranda, where she kept her cooking tools and Primus stove. She quickly put together a pan of khicharhi and, while it was cooking, she washed herself and changed into a khaki blouse and skirt, relics of her Mission of Holiness days.

To eat her meal, she sat in a basket chair and looked out over the little courtyard, with its well in one corner and a drooping neem tree in another. Near the well, tiny flowers bloomed between the paving stones, watered by splashes from the water-bucket. A sacred, well-tended tulsi tree flourished in a stone pot in the centre of the courtyard.

Diana never trespassed into the courtyard, and now she thought how nice it would be to do so. 'I'd like a home like this,' she pondered a little wistfully.

'You could have it, if you took a nursing post with a European company here,' she told herself.

'And get caught up in the empty world of club life? Ugh!'

Marriage would also have brought her a home, but she always shrugged when she thought of it. 'I'm past it,' she would say quite philosophically. During her probationer days in Edinburgh she had dated other students, but her shyness made her boring. She had turned to her studies and had become a reliable, cheerful surgical nurse, losing her individuality behind her starched uniform.

It would not have been difficult for her to obtain a well-to-do Indian husband; her ordinary English prettiness was a thing of unusual beauty in Shahpur. She knew, however, that the adjustment to such a life would be too difficult for her.

Her mind wandered. 'What about your new friend, John Bennett?'

Tears stung her eyes. In a moment of honesty, she realized that John had ceased to be only a patient to her and had become a special person, unlike anyone she had met before; a man of integrity, considerable physical strength and high intellect, she reflected wistfully.

She stirred her food around a little, to cool it. Perhaps, she thought rather pitifully, there was good reason for a quiet, older woman like herself to keep away from him, if she wanted to avoid being hurt. Absorbed in his work, he would hardly think about her.

He had an enviable war record and, amongst the University people, he was famous for his kindness – and his celibacy. No hint of gossip ever seemed to touch him, she had observed, not even the assumption, common enough in regard to a man who lived like he did, that he was a homosexual.

She pushed away her half empty dish, and wiped her lips on her handkerchief. 'It doesn't matter, anyway,' she told herself. 'Just because a man is courteous and thoughtful of you, doesn't mean much.'

She pushed back her chair, took a glass and went to a waterjar. She drank a glass of water and also filled a small waterbottle, which she put into her black, nurse's bag.

She picked up her black umbrella and went out to catch the bus.

Chapter Twenty-one

In comfortable solitude, Diana swung along the meandering field path which led from the end of the bus route to Pandipura village. After the smell of the city, the air seemed sweet and heavy with the odour of drying foliage. Even the occasional goat she met stood comatose, the tiny goatherd usually fast asleep in the nearest patch of shade. She became aware, however, of an irritating hubbub further along the path. Loud cackles of laughter and birdlike shrieks smote her ears, increasing rapidly as she approached. When she rounded a bend an unlovely, though familiar, sight met her gaze.

The remains of a dead donkey, by now almost reduced to a skeleton, lay across the path, and though not much was left, four or five vultures still argued and jostled each other over the spoils. One bird had found a particularly succulent morsel and had it clasped in its beak, its bald head and neck bobbing as, with ungainly hops, it tried to find an opportunity to swallow its prize, while the others pushed and shoved around it in an endeavour to rob their companion.

'Blast,' muttered Diana, and drew back hastily.

The vultures ignored her, if they had noticed her at all; they are no animal's prey. They were big birds and Diana teetered uncertainly at the edge of the path, wondering how long it would take them to finish their revolting work and fly away. Finally, she decided to strike into the bush and make a circle round them. She had on heavy shoes and there was little danger from snakes in such heat – most of them would be hibernating. She followed a goat track in and out of the thorny bushes, taking her direction from a distant mango tree which she could see growing further along the path.

Except for an occasional glance at the mango tree, she watched the ground she covered, in case of scorpions. Because of this, she observed a scrap of clean paper clinging to the base of a cactus. Newspaper was not uncommon in the countryside, but any other type of paper was. This was not newspaper. It was linen-backed, with threads still attached to where it had been torn. At one point a light blue line ran across it. Small, unimportant, a piece of rubbish – but out of place.

Her curiosity aroused, Diana stooped to pick it up, and, as she proceeded on her way, she turned it over and over in her hand. Guessing at its origin provided an amusing little puzzle to ease the monotony of her walk.

She reached the mango tree and rejoined the path to the village. The tree gave welcome shade, so she paused to wipe her face free of dust and sweat.

'Namaste, Memsahib,' said a thin, cracked voice behind her.

Diana jumped, and turned towards the voice.

A very old man, who had been sitting in the shade further round the trunk of the tree, was struggling to his feet.

Diana knew him, and sighed with relief. She shoved her handkerchief and the piece of paper into her shirt pocket and picked up her bag and umbrella.

'Namaste,' she greeted the village bone-setter.

He grinned at her, his white-stubbled face dissolving into a mass of wrinkles, and, as she made to continue on her way, he accompanied her. His staff dragged in the sand as he described to her a boy's arm which he had just set. She had once admired an ankle he had set and she had, in consequence, added to his local prestige. He now regarded her as a medical colleague, much to her amusement, though she had to admit that he was surprisingly competent for one who had learned his art only from his father in the traditional way.

'Are you going to Virchand's house?' he inquired, naming the brother-in-law of Diana's patient.

'Yes.'

The bone-setter stumped along for a few yards, and then gave his opinion. 'She'll live, Memsahib. She has been worrying about things which are no concern of hers. Sick people shouldn't worry – it makes them sicker.'

'It does,' agreed Diana.

'The Panchyat will worry about the village – it's *their* job.' His tone was vicious. He would dearly have liked to be a member of the village council himself, but saw no hope of it.

'What's the trouble in the village? I thought there was something wrong when I was there yesterday. Have they been fined for something?'

'Not yet,' replied the bone-setter. He looked up at her from under his grubby white turban, clamped his pinched mouth tightly shut, and refused to say anything more until they reached the village. Still wordless, he saluted her and left her outside Virchand's house.

Her patient was awake and tried to sit up as Diana entered. She made her lie down again, while she took her temperature, which proved to be normal. The deathly look of the previous day had also gone, though she was not very cheerful. The scar of the operation was knitting well.

She sat down on a mat by the bed and advised Virchand's wife how to get the old lady on to her feet again, while the patient herself occasionally put in a word. The young niece brought into the hut a shy mother with a little boy who had a boil, and asked advice. Tea was offered her. Everything was as usual.

Whatever was bothering them must have passed over, Diana decided. She had seen before how a caste group or a family would shut up like clams while they dealt with a domestic scandal or even a murder. Distrusting both police and lower courts, they tried their best not to seek help from anybody in authority.

Diana sighed. They were brave and resourceful, but, because of their poverty, they were open to all kinds of bullying. She hoped, however, that her elderly patient was now safely on her way to recovery and that her brother-in-law would not aggravate her in any way for the next week or two.

The wind was rising, making the sand fly unpleasantly, so she said her farewells. 'If the patient does not seem to be improving, please send a message immediately to Dr Ferozeshah,' she instructed Virchand, sitting in his usual spot on the string bed outside the door.

'Ji, hun,' he agreed, and rose and saluted her.

As soon as she was clear of the village, she stopped to drink the bottle of water she had brought with her. Without water, she would assuredly get sunstroke, and she dared not eat or drink anything in the village for fear of dysentery.

The vultures had departed, leaving the small skeleton to the jackals; a rustle in the undergrowth hinted at their presence. The shadows were lengthening, so she stepped round the skeleton and increased her pace. In the distance she could hear the herdsmen shouting as they rounded up their charges, preparatory to driving them home.

Two red-clad milkmaids, with their big brass vessels of milk, were squatting at the bus terminus. There she hesitated. John Bennett lived not far from the following stop. If she picked up the bus there, she could call in to tell him of the meeting at Lallubhai's house, in case Lallubhai had forgotten to inform him.

She persuaded herself that Lallubhai could indeed be so inefficient, despite his pleasure at John's offer, and walked on. She was followed by the stares and giggles of the milkmaids; her flushed face and short skirts always caused amusement to village women who did not know her.

The compound gate was unbolted, and she pushed it open and went in. John's light was already switched on and she could clearly see, through the open windows, that he already had a visitor.

As she stood uncertainly on the path, shyness overwhelming her, the gate swung slowly shut behind her.

John heard the gate click and turned in his chair to look out of the window. When he saw her, he waved, and a few moments later, he opened the door to her.

He was leaning on his stick, as she entered and stopped just over the threshold. Rather primly, she delivered her message.

'Of course, I'll come,' he assured her. He turned to Tilak, who had risen at Diana's entrance, and introduced him to her.

Tilak put his hands together in salute. What a weird-looking woman – her face was as red as burning charcoal.

She sat down in the basket chair indicated to her, and John sank on to the divan. The divan was low, and he winced; for the thousandth time, he cursed his inability to move properly.

The wince had gone unnoticed by his guests. He turned his attention determinedly to them and they were soon talking quite easily to each other. The story of the dead frog was told once more, and Diana was quick to sympathize. In return, she told them about some of the bigotry she had observed in the Mission of Holiness.

As her shyness receded, her face became more animated and her green eyes twinkled. She accepted a cigarette and smoked it slowly, enjoying the rare luxury of it. John apologized for Ranjit's absence and his own inability to manage the Primus stove to make tea for her. Ranjit had gone, he explained, to find a boy servant he thought would suit Dr Tilak.

The mention of tea brought back her former diffidence. She said hastily that she had not intended to stay, and looked at her watch. 'I think I should catch the next bus,' she said.

Tilak surveyed her gloomily from under lowered brows. He had discussed with John the fine opportunity of the English Fellowship, and had been about to consult him regarding taking Anasuyabehn with him, when they had been interrupted by Diana's knock. Now the moment was gone, taken by this fool of a woman with her maps and her nursing. As he chewed his nails and tried to enter politely into the conversation, the insoluble problem of the passport whirled in his mind.

Diana was picking up her bag and umbrella and John was saying that he should see her on to the bus. But his legs were hurting savagely and his voice did not carry conviction.

Diana sensed his reluctance, though she did not realize the cause. She said stiffly, 'I shall be quite all right alone.'

Tilak had come to the door, too. He felt that John's interest had transferred itself to the woman, and that he would not give his full attention to Tilak's own problems. 'I must go, too,' he said sulkily. 'I have lectures to prepare. Ask Ranjit to let me know about the boy.'

'Certainly,' replied John absently. He looked at Diana a little coldly, feeling that she was, in some way, distancing herself from him. He hesitated, holding the door half open. 'I don't think you should go alone in the dark,' he said to Diana.

Tilak felt he would never escape and he suddenly wanted to get out of the hot little room. 'I'll take Miss Armstrong to the bus,' he offered.

Diana accepted the offer gracefully.

So Tilak found himself escorting an English lady down the sandy lane, past the Dean's bungalow. From the roof, Aunt observed him with astonishment.

At the bus stop, a group of children was playing Horses and Riders. The smaller boys were riding piggyback on the bigger boys, and they pushed and shoved in an effort to unhorse the riders. The fun they were having was infectious, and Diana laughed when one of the riders, with a deft push, caught another one off balance, and, to shouts of acclamation, horse and rider went down into the dust.

The bus arrived in a flurry of sand. Diana hastily thanked Tilak and eased her way into the crowded vehicle.

The little unhorsed rider rolled, puffing and laughing, to Tilak's feet, while, from a nearby house, a shrill voice shouted to the children to come in at once. Three children fled, leaving the fallen one sitting rubbing his back. He looked up at Tilak and grinned beguilingly. Tilak knew him, and his pulses jumped at his good luck.

'You're Mehta Sahib's servant?' he asked.

The boy scrambled to his feet, picked up his black pillbox hat and crammed it back on his head. 'Ji,' he replied respectfully.

'I want you to take a note to Miss Anasuyabehn,' he told the child. 'It is about a special secret with which she will surprise Mehta Sahib, so you mustn't show the note to anybody. Do you understand?'

'Ji.'

Tilak took out his notebook, tore out a page and scribbled a few words on it with his fountain pen. He fished a four-anna piece out of his trouser pocket and handed it, with the note, to the servant.

The boy put the note into his shirt pocket and the coin into the pocket of his ragged pants. He grinned at Tilak and ran happily across the road towards the Dean's house.

Meanwhile, Aunt stumped thoughtfully down the stairs from the roof, where she had enjoyed a short nap. She had just risen from the mat on which she had been lying, when she had observed, over the parapet, Diana and Tilak going to the bus stop.

Still feeling physically and mentally drained after her confrontation with the guru in the temple, Anasuyabehn was seated on the kitchen floor preparing dinner for the visitors. Two chattering female cousins were helping her. The parents were seated on the veranda, sipping lemon water.

The servant had been sent to the house of a neighbour with a full water-pot, the neighbour's tap having ceased to function, and Anasuyabehn said, as her aunt entered, 'I wonder where the boy is? He's been gone quite a long time.'

'Playing with the children down the road,' replied Aunt sourly. 'Saw him just now.' She sat down by a small charcoal fire, which one of the cousins had been tending. She took up a rolling pin and uncovered a pan of dough, which had been put ready for her by Anasuyabehn. The cousin put a pan of oil on to the fire to heat. As the older woman began skilfully to roll out puris on a small pastry board, she said, 'I saw something else, while I was on the roof.' She dropped a puri into the fat and pressed it under with a spatula, while the three girls looked up expectantly. 'That troublesome Dr Tilak was walking down the lane with an English lady – the one who visited Dr Bennett the other day!'

The Dean had put his head round the kitchen door to see how the dinner was coming along. The meal was late, and it troubled him to have to eat after nightfall – no Jain liked to do that. 'Indeed,' he exclaimed. 'You must have been mistaken.'

'My sight isn't that bad,' snapped Aunt. 'Perhaps,' she added cunningly, 'he asked Dr Bennett to introduce him.' That, she surmised, might damn him in Anasuyabehn's eyes. She glanced quickly at her niece, never ceasing the quick rolling of the bread she was making.

The girl sat as if turned to stone, her eyes wide, a lid in her hand poised over a saucepan of vegetables. Suddenly, within her, raged jealousy so raw that she could have spat like a fighting cat.

So that was why he had not come to the temple. Given the chance of an English girl in marriage, he had dumped her like a coolie dumping a bag of sugar.

Aunt smiled contentedly down at her frying puri.

'He would never allow himself to be seen walking with her unless he intended to marry her.' She flicked her sari back from her face and looked up at her brother. 'What do you think?'

The Dean lifted a hand in a dismissive gesture. 'I don't know,' he replied. 'It doesn't matter, anyway.'

Matter? Anasuyabehn nearly screamed aloud at him. It matters terribly, and I don't know how I can bear it.

Chapter Twenty-two

The boy servant slipped silently into the kitchen. No one noticed him, except Aunt, who hissed out of the corner of her mouth, 'And where have you been, Maharaj?'

The sarcasm of the appellation made him cringe. He shrank into a corner, scared by the thought of the money in his pocket.

Consternation grew in him; supposing she found the four-anna piece? Its weight burned against his thigh, its delicious promise of sweets lost in overwhelming fright. If she found the coin, the old owl would shriek and nag at him until she discovered how he came by it; and, dimly, the little boy understood that this would cause not only trouble to himself but, possibly, to his dear Anasuyabehn as well. The fact that the note might be more incriminating than the coin did not occur to him – he regarded it merely as a piece of paper.

In a funk, the child moved to the charcoal bin. As if to make up the fire, he took a piece out and at the same time dropped the coin into the box. It fell with a soft plonk into the slack at the bottom.

At the sound, Aunt turned round. 'Don't make up the fire now,' she snorted.

His fear receded. She had not seen. Obediently, he put back the piece of charcoal and stood waiting for the family to finish their dinner, so that he could have his.

The Dean suggested a walk in the Riverside Gardens. Everyone agreed, and, with a swish of saris, the ladies rose and went to the bathroom to wash their mouths.

Aunt turned to the servant. 'Next time you're sent on a message,' she growled, 'come back at once, do you hear me? At once. Otherwise, I'll take an anna off your wages for every five minutes you're late.'

The boy skulked in a corner and hung his head.

'No dinner, tonight,' added the indefatigable crone. 'Now, clear up the dishes.'

The hungry boy hardly heard her. If they all went for a walk, he would be alone in this terrifyingly big bungalow, where the spirits in the air went *shush-shush* as they flew round the compound; and they rattled at the door bolts and made the curtains flutter at the windows.

As he stared at the discarded brass talis on the floor, they seemed to grow bigger, like staring eyes, too big for a little boy to scour. The littered kitchen floor stretched out before him like the desert of Rajasthan, miles of it to be swept and washed before he might curl up on his mat and lose his misery in sleep. He sat down on the floor and wept loudly.

Anasuyabehn heard the noise and came swiftly back to the kitchen. 'What's up?' she asked her aunt.

'I've told this naughty boy that he can't have any dinner,' replied Aunt.

The sobs redoubled.

Anasuyabehn tried to look stern. 'You're right, of course,' she said, and then paused. 'Perhaps, tonight he could have his dinner, and, if he ever dawdles again, he could go without?'

Aunt got up to follow the others to the bathroom. Over her shoulder, she snapped, 'You spoil him.'

'I'm sure he's very sorry.'

The boy stopped crying, wiped his nose with the back of his hand and nodded vigorously.

'All right, if you wish,' replied Aunt and swept out of the kitchen, all injured dignity. The servant ran to Anasuyabehn and touched her feet.

'Eat quickly,' she told him. 'Wash the talis and clean the floor. You can do the saucepans in the morning.'

'Ji, hun,' he assented, still sniffing, while his eyes made an anxious inventory of the amount of food left in the saucepans. Obsessed by the need to eat, the note lay unremembered in his pocket.

Long ago, in the days of the East India Company, an Englishman had built himself a miniature palace by the river and, round it, had laid out a fine park with a wide promenade along the river bank, the whole surrounded by a high wall. His grandson, an irascible bachelor appalled by the overcrowding of Shahpur, had willed it to the city, to be a park forever, open to all castes and classes to walk and play in.

The people thronged into it, happy to be free of traffic and dust. Admittedly, the grass had worn a bit thin in places, and, at one point, the surrounding wall had broken down, yet it was still a blissful retreat on a hot evening. The palace was now a boys' school, sadly lacking in paint though high in reputation. Like the park, it was open to Untouchables, as long as they could pay their fees.

Beggars were kept outside the gate by an officious chowkidar. They gathered as near to the gate as they could get, however, exhibiting a horrible collection of deformities and lifting distorted hands to the passersby. Like some dreadful opera chorus, they chanted hopefully, 'Ram, Ram, Ram.'

Through this ghastly crew floated like petals on the wind girls and women in pastel coloured saris. They were closely escorted by their white-clad menfolk and were accompanied by a bevy of grave-eyed children. Amongst them, Anasuyabehn walked demurely behind her father and her uncle, a giggling cousin on either side of her, while the two aunts brought up the rear.

Though it was getting late, the park was far from gloomy; each path had its line of electric lights. The evening breeze blew coolly off the river, and the party walked the length of the promenade.

Anasuyabehn found it difficult to maintain her outward composure. Great gusts of fury kept sweeping over her. That Tilak should one day make protestations of love to her, and the next night be seen walking with an English lady was incredible. In this provincial town, nobody would walk alone with an English woman unless he had designs upon her. She forgot that Tilak was from Bombay.

'You're really so dull and depressing about your marriage,' complained one of her cousins. 'I'd give my eyes to be engaged to such a wealthy man – a man who sent me diamonds.' Her voice rose in sharp envy. 'And he looks so handsome in his photo.'

The reminder of Mahadev's generosity struck Anasuyabehn forcibly. She lifted her head proudly and her lips curled in a hard smile. At least her fiancé wanted her badly.

They came to the end of the promenade, and the older ladies sat down to rest for a few minutes on a stone bench, upon which they arranged themselves so that there was no room for anyone else. The two gentlemen walked slowly up and down the path in front of them, while the cousins stood patiently nearby. A lamp illuminated the bench, though it served only to deepen the shadows cast by a huge, drooping tree behind it. Faintly from the burning ghats on the other side of the river came the smell of burning wood, a sad warning of man's mortality.

The cousins grew tired of Anasuyabehn's long silences and ran across the walk to the balustrade, which divided the river shore from the park. Thankful to be alone, Anasuyabehn paced up and down on the grass behind her aunts. Under the shadow of the tree, her green sari made her almost invisible.

A husband and wife, who knew her family, stopped by the bench to pay their respects to the aunts, and Anasuyabehn stepped deeper into the shadow, rather than face another barrage of good-natured jokes about the joys of matrimony. Though very exhausted, she was still simmering with anger.

When she heard the very softest whisper behind her, she was shocked. Stifling a shriek, she turned. 'Go away,' she whispered back to Tilak. 'How dare you come near me? And how did you find me?'

Tilak's black jacket made him invisible against the tree's great trunk, as he breathed, 'Followed you from home. Now, listen. Quickly. Have you a passport?'

Indignation welled up. 'How dare you? How dare you?' she upbraided him.

'I'm sorry, I couldn't get away.'

'No? I imagine you were very pleasantly occupied.'

Puzzled at her attitude, he said irritably, 'Tell me, Rani. Your passport. I have to make plans for us.'

Anasuyabehn peered at him through the gloom. He was so close to her that she could feel his warmth. In the midst of her rage, her physical desire for this handsome man tore through her. One touch from his hand would have diverted the flood of jealousy into channels of self-recrimination and explanation.

'Sister, sister, where are you?' called one of her cousins, running back across the walk.

She whipped round, and, then, forcing herself to advance casually into the light, she called back, 'Here I am.'

Bewildered and frustrated, Tilak slunk into the darkness.

Chapter Twenty-three

Old Desai sat on his wooden divan in his dismal counting house, his portable desk beside him. Sitting near him was his sister's husband, hastily summoned by telegram from Baroda. With him had come his sister's sons, aged fifteen and eighteen respectively.

Leaning against a battered filing cabinet and staring vacantly at the visitors was Mahadev's brother, his face showing none of the sense of panic within him. Mahadev and the Maharajah's jewels were missing and unusual decisions had to be made. He would probably have to go out to help with inquiries amongst dull Hindu clods in the villages, and he was not looking forward to it.

Why didn't his father leave the job to the police?

He knew the answer only too well. His father loved Mahadev above everyone; he would literally leave no stone unturned in order to find him.

The stout, plain man in his round black cap gave a small quivering sigh, and tried not to think of his wife's bitter tirade that morning. She had said she hoped that Mahadev would be found, since there had to be one brain in each generation of the family.

Old Desai turned to the one man in the room to whom he felt close, his Partner Brother, still spry in spite of his years and his sorrows, a man whose sons had died before him. He alone could truly appreciate his dread of losing Mahadev.

Partner Brother's small eyes gleamed behind his heavy, horn-rimmed glasses. 'Well, where shall we start?' he asked.

Baroda Brother took off his pince-nez and polished them, to indicate that he was getting ready for action. Since Mahadev, fleeced by the dacoits, had not arrived at Delhi, he was, in his opinion, lying dead somewhere along the railway track. He kept his belief to himself, however, and suggested briskly, 'We could search either bank of the railway track for some miles on each side of the site of the robbery.'

'The police will have already done that,' said Partner Brother.

The thorough, ponderous mind of Mahadev's own brother had not been idle. 'Father,' he said, with a trace of excitement, 'if there were anything dead within a couple of miles of the railway track, vultures would have come in clouds and would have been clearly visible; the police would have gone immediately to see what was attracting them.'

The other men looked at him in surprise. There was a stunned silence, and then everyone spoke at once.

'He *must* be alive,' said old Desai, his voice trembling.

Baroda Brother-in-law put his pince-nez firmly back on to his nose, and added, 'He must, since his body was not on the train.'

Mahadev's brother gritted his teeth. Even when he showed intelligence, he fumed, nobody really noticed. Even his name was forgotten by most; he was simply Husband or Brother or Son – or, worst of all, Mahadev's Brother – a simpleton in the background of other people's lives, lost in the shadow of a more brilliant brother and bullied by a shrewish wife.

Yet, who supervised all the account books of his father's great concerns? he asked himself. Who checked the incoming interest and made the first moves against those who failed to pay? Who sat up late at night, to comb carefully through each agreement, so that not once had they lost a court case when some outraged landowner took them before a magistrate?

He hoped, in the forefront of his mind, that Mahadev was safe. But, deep inside, he wished savagely that he was lost for good. He chewed again his already closely bitten fingernails.

His father's voice cut through his rumination. 'We'll first inquire of every Desai Society along the route, up to a distance of fifty miles from here. There is no great town to comb, unless he is, say, a hostage, in Shahpur itself – only villages.'

He then began to organize them. 'Dress plainly,' he advised. 'You are moneylenders going about your normal business. On no account mention the jewels. Go by bicycle or by horse carriage.' He tapped his fingers on his little desk, and then went on, 'Take a servant or one of the others with you – if we find the task too great, we'll close the office and use the clerks.' He wagged his finger warningly. 'Be careful to be courteous to the Headman or the Panchyat, when you inquire. And stop at isolated huts – and don't forget the Untouchable quarters.'

All the men nodded agreement.

'Should we inform Dean Mehta now?' asked Partner Brother.

Old Desai considered this question carefully. He would have preferred to keep the matter secret, but the Mehtas might hear a rumour.

A fresh fear struck him. Such rumours might well reach the dacoits. If Mahadev had been left for dead, if he had seen the robbers' faces and they realized that he was still alive, would not they also start to hunt for him?

He winced, as he foresaw a quick knife thrust under Mahadev's well-covered ribs, the moment he showed himself. Impatiently he pushed the unwelcome thought out of his mind, and answered his brother's question. 'I'll go to his office to tell him – so that, for the moment, his family does not have to know.'

He remembered grimly his Baroda Sister's remark, when she had first been asked to act as go-between. She had said, 'The girl is not lucky – she has already lost one fiancé.' He had snubbed her thoroughly as being superstitious and old-fashioned.

The men got up and stretched, and he clapped his hands. When his Chief Clerk came running, he told him to bring in the morning mail, together with his notebook and pencil. While he was doing this, old Desai turned to his younger son and instructed him to stay and mind the business. After he had dealt with his letters, old Desai tottered into the long, dark room which was his general office. His half dozen more junior employees all rose to salute him obsequiously. He made this round of the office daily, pausing to poke into every small detail that caught his eye. Occasionally, he left some young man trembling and ashen-faced, after being upbraided. All his employees were in some way related to him, and it was unlikely that he would ever discharge one of them; but he held the purse-strings tightly in his rheumaticky hands, and it took devoted service and slavelike hours of work to loosen them.

After having left a trail of moral destruction in the office, he returned to his younger son in a more amiable frame of mind. He wanted to compliment him on his deduction that Mahadev was probably alive, and he considered giving him the emerald ring he always wore. He half slipped it off his finger; then his lifetime habit of parsimony re-asserted itself, and he slipped it on again. Words, however, cost nothing, and he left his son considerably cheered up, when he finally climbed into his carriage to drive himself to the University.

From the depths of his dusty cubicle, Dean Mehta's secretary informed him that the Dean was at the Marwari Gate temple and would be a little late that morning. He looked at his watch, and said, 'He should be back in about ten minutes.'

'I'll wait,' Desai decided, and he was shown into the Dean's office.

The secretary returned to his work and Desai could hear him shouting down the telephone. Desai fretted that he should have telephoned before he came. He had a telephone in his office on which he received incoming calls, but he could never bring himself to make a call. Lines could be crossed, he worried, and the contents of very private agreements be overheard by outsiders; skeletons might rattle in family closets; thieves might overhear. The telephone was, indeed, not something to be used lightly. In fact, most telephone calls received by the Desais resulted in one or the other partner driving over to see the caller.

The Dean came in slowly, his ascetic face mirroring clearly his sharp abstinence from food that day and his lack of sleep.

He bade Desai welcome and sent for tea for him. He then sat, amazed, listening to his story. In the back of his mind, he wondered if Mahadev had absconded. Though Desai had not mentioned it, he guessed that Mahadev had been carrying valuables, probably jewellery. A fortune in jewels would be a great temptation to a young man who would know how to dispose of them and who seemed to like living in the West.

They discussed whether to tell Anasuyabehn and decided that she had better know. A rumour would disturb her almost more than knowing the truth of the matter.

The Dean asked what assistance he could give. His brother, he said, had already arrived to help with the wedding and was supervising the delivery of supplies for it.

'If you hear anything that might bear on my son's disappearance, would you let me know?'

'Naturally, I will.'

The Dean forced himself to stand up and see Desai out to his carriage.

As they walked along the corridor, quiet except for the occasional burst of a lecturer's voice as they passed a half-closed door, Desai said that, if Mahadev was all right, he wished to bring forward the date of the wedding. He wanted to send the boy and his new wife to Paris again for a little while.

The Dean foresaw cries of objection from his sisters and his sister-in-law; women were always so fussy about ceremonies – and the astrologer would be full of forebodings, no doubt, at a change of date. He was, however, a little uneasy. Since her first outburst, Anasuyabehn had said no more to him about breaking the betrothal. Aunt had assured him that the girl now seemed quite reconciled to it. Yet, he felt, he would be thankful when it was over; his last family responsibility would have been fulfilled.

As they paused at the top of the front steps, he said, 'The preliminary invitations have been sent out, but I'll hold back the second ones and the special invitation letters, until I hear from you.'

Desai smiled and saluted him. 'A-jo,' he said, and got back into his shabby, little carriage.

Chapter Twenty-four

'Where can a woman cry in peace?' Anasuyabehn asked herself miserably, as she went back home from the park. She felt that if she did not cry soon she would choke. Her last stronghold, her bedroom, was at present invaded by her two cousins. They would not leave until after her marriage – and, after that, she would cease to be a person in her own right and be an appendage of Mahadev's.

Apart from her grief at Tilak's behaviour and her approaching marriage, she was still haunted by memory of the fearsome monk. Her religion, with its ruthless rules for the purification of the jiva, the soul, during each rebirth, had re-asserted itself that morning in a most alarming way.

In betrothing her to Mahadev, her father had broken only a rule of caste, which had crept into the originally classless, casteless Jain belief. Jainism had, at first, been a movement of revolt against caste, she thought, and, to be honest, he was marrying her into a group which epitomized Jain life.

If she ran away with Tilak, she would commit the sin of filial disobedience and would, in addition, marry a man of another religion, a high-caste Hindu. Even to love a man so much was in conflict with the teachings of her religion, she moaned to herself. To become too attached to anything or anybody was a prelude to suffering, and, as tears welled up in her, she knew the teaching had meaning.

'When are the merchants bringing wedding saris to show you?' broke in one of her cousins excitedly. 'I'm longing to see them.'

'Ask Aunt,' replied Anasuyabehn shortly. 'She has it all arranged.'

They turned hopefully to the old lady, to ask about everything to do with the marriage. 'When shall we visit the Desais? Can we go to a potter's yard? We want to mark his wheel with red powder and buy some pots for the marriage booth? And Lord Ganesh must get an offering of rice from us and have his elephant head specially marked, mustn't he, Aunt? Respected Aunt, do tell us?'

Aunt laughed and answered them amiably, while the object of all the preparations trailed slowly behind her and began to regret bitterly her sharpness with Tilak. Perhaps, she argued, he had been held up by his work, so that he could not meet her. And there simply had to be a reasonable explanation of his attendance on Miss Armstrong, if she could only think of one.

The servant had put out string beds on the roof for the gentlemen and on the veranda for the ladies, each bed swathed in a mosquito net.

On arriving home, the Dean immediately excused himself and went to his study to perform his evening devotions, while his more worldly brother betook himself to the roof with a copy of *Gone with the Wind* and a flashlight by which to see to read it. The older ladies retired to one end of the veranda to say their prayers and sink thankfully into their beds. The younger ones sat, crosslegged, on their beds and loosened their long plaits of hair, while they continued to whisper across to Anasuyabehn for some time. She was taciturn in her replies, however, and eventually feeling a little deflated they curled up and slept.

Anasuyabehn could not rest. For greater comfort, she took off her blouse and wrapped her sari loosely round herself. Her throat ached with suppressed tears.

Finally, she slipped out of bed and went into the house. There was no light under the study door, so she assumed her father had gone up to bed on the roof. She made her way to her own room and switched on the light. The heat of the house was almost intolerable, but the need to cry was urgent. She paced up and down restlessly; the tears, so long repressed, would not come.

Undeniably, Tilak still had the intention of marrying her; otherwise, he would not have bothered to follow her to ask about the passport. She understood the importance of the question; a large deposit was needed in order to obtain one, and government procedure was extremely slow.

Well, she had a passport, obtained when she had accompanied her father to a conference in Sri Lanka. The problem was how to get this information to Tilak and how to ask his forgiveness for her rudeness.

Her cotton sari was soaked with perspiration. She went to the window, opened it and leaned her head against the iron bars. There was not a breath of wind. She stared aimlessly out at the rural scene lit by a moon partially shrouded in dust. She hoped that houses would never be built behind her father's bungalow.

Then she remembered that, unless Tilak moved quickly, she would soon leave this pleasant home for the cramped and ugly Desai Society, behind high walls in the inner city. She had not yet seen it, but she could well visualize its crumbling walls and worn steps, its wavery, tiled roofs, its lack of fresh air. Aunt had told her that not many people lived in its multitude of rooms, that the business took up a number of them. She thought of Mahadev's little girl wandering, solitary, through them. What was she like, after being pushed about by a spiteful aunt? Anasuyabehn felt suddenly cold at the thought of having to establish her seniority over her future sister-in-law – her aunt had warned her about this. And then there was the lonely, sad uncle whose wife and children were already dead. What was he like?

'I can't face it,' she cried softly. 'Tilak Sahib, how can I get a note to you?'

Her question was answered as if she had rubbed a magic lamp. From outside the window came an urgent whisper, 'Put the light out.'

Mouth half-open in surprise, she stood motionless, and then began to giggle almost hysterically.

'The light, Bahin.'

Still giggling, she went obediently and switched the light out.

'Come to the window,' pleaded Tilak.

She stood with her hand on the switch, trying to calm herself. She succeeded only in bursting into tears.

'Come, Rani.'

She ran to him, tears pouring down her face. Putting her arms through the bars, she clasped them round Tilak. A very delighted Tilak slipped his arms through the maddening bars to hold her as best he could. The bars bit into their flesh.

'My love, my dear love,' he murmured. Endearments and passionate kisses passed between them, and the passport was momentarily forgotten.

Suddenly, from the roof, Anasuyabehn's uncle shouted, 'Who's there?' Keener of hearing than his elder brother, he leaned over the parapet and swung his torch wildly about, the darting beam moving too fast to pick out any single detail.

Without a further word, Tilak slid away from the windowsill. Like a squirrel, he streaked along the backs of the bungalows, then cut across the field path into common land, where he lay panting in the dry grass, until the lights went out again in the Mehta home. Then he jogged back to his room, cursing under his breath.

Chapter Twenty-five

The following day, Dean Mehta asked his brother to come into his study. 'I must tell you something,' he said.

His brother had just washed his mouth out after lunch, and a few drops of water still clung to his chin. As he followed his brother into the stifling room, he dabbed his dripping face on his sleeve.

Contrary to the best advice of his guru, the Dean had an electric fan. Though he could not bring himself to stop using it altogether, he turned it off during his fast days.

'A fan,' the guru had said, 'injures the souls in the air. Yours, being electric, can also kill insects.'

Today, the fan was back in its cardboard box, and the windows were shut to keep out the onslaught of the afternoon sun. The heavy Western desk and chairs, the crowded bookcases, added to the oppressiveness of the atmosphere. Because of the extra people in the house, the boy servant had not had time to attend to the chattyas, the heavy copra mats which covered the outside of the windows and usually dripped comfortingly with water to cool the room. There was nothing to mitigate the sweltering weather.

The Dean's brother wondered how he was going to endure the house for a whole month. He deposited himself on one of the stuffed chairs, which immediately caused him to perspire even more.

The Dean told him briefly of Mahadev's disappearance. He did not mention his own suspicions that Mahadev might have absconded. He ended by saying, 'I shall, of course, tell Anasuyabehn. She has a right to know.'

'Anasuyabehn isn't very lucky, is she?' his brother responded glumly. 'If Mahadev turns up, we'd better hold the marriage as soon as possible, before anything else happens.' And then I can go home to an air-conditioned house, he added to himself.

'It's odd that you should say that. Desai said the same thing this morning. They have some business in France they want to send Mahadev to attend to; they want his wife to go with him.'

The younger Mehta scratched miserably at the sweat rash on his stomach. 'Certainly we can manage it, if Sister is agreeable.' He examined the backs of his hands thoughtfully; the skin was already dry and cracking from Shahpur's desert climate. 'Anasuyabehn was not very keen on this match, was she?'

'Not at first,' replied the Dean. 'It came as a surprise to her. Her aunt assures me that she's quite happy about it, now she knows more about the family.'

'It was a pity we could not find her a scholarly man.'

'Well, those we considered were either without prospects – and I wanted her to do better than our poor sister – or they were personally unprepossessing. And young Desai is really keen on her. He sent her a superb diamond, you know.' He sighed, and then added a little defiantly, 'He's not ignorant either. He's a matriculate and has travelled a lot.'

The younger Mehta nodded. Then he suggested, 'Perhaps she should be a little more tightly chaperoned until her marriage – to avoid any hint of scandal.'

'Scandal?' The Dean looked shocked.

'Well, you know what people are,' his brother said defensively. 'She has a lot of freedom.'

'Well,' responded the Dean. 'We'll tell her aunts that she is not to go out of the house alone.'

Relieved that he had persuaded the Dean to have Anasuyabehn chaperoned, without having to mention to him vague suspicions aroused the previous night, he offered to send the girl in to see her father.

He found the ladies on the veranda. Each had a piece of needlework in her lap, but they, too, were wilting from the heat, and the needles were not being plied. When he came over to them, Anasuyabehn got up from the floor and her uncle could not help but observe the change in her from yesterday. The silence and the pinched look had gone from her. She was radiant, and when she spoke it was with the excitement of one in a fever.

He told her to go to her father and he watched her, as she vanished into the bungalow. He felt that she certainly had the strength of character to carry on an intrigue with a considerable amount of duplicity. Had he heard a man's voice last night or had he imagined it? he asked himself. Had she been saying her prayers, as she said she had? One did not pray in the dark, and, as he came down the stairs from the roof, he had distinctly heard a light being switched on. Her window had been shut, when his wife had gone into her room – he had asked particularly. Miss Anasuyabehn was up to something, he was sure, but he could not accuse her without proof.

He was worried about a scandal for another reason. Soon his daughters would face the same shortage of marriageable men as Anasuyabehn had. He did not want the problem made worse by a scandal in the family. Some castes were short of women and a girl could take her choice of eager young men, but amongst the Mehtas, at the moment, there seemed to be a real dearth of males. He must tell his wife to watch their girls, he decided.

Further down the veranda, Aunt was watching *him* out of the corner of her eye, wondering why the Dean had sent for his daughter. She, too, was giving thought to possible husbands for her nieces, and was going over in her mind all the young men who might be eligible. Unlike their father, she had taken into account that they were nearly a decade younger than Anasuyabehn – a different generation. 'Ah,' she exclaimed, satisfied, as she managed to thread her needle and at the same time recollect a possible sixteen-year-old boy.

Chapter Twenty-six

'This man you've sent me to work for, this Tilak Sahib, is very strange,' remarked Tilak's new servant to his uncle, Ranjit.

'He's no stranger than most modern people. Be thankful for a job. Now you can eat well – and, with care, you can make a little money,' Ranjit scolded.

They were seated on John's back veranda, sharing what was left over of John's breakfast porridge. Having dispatched Tilak to his lectures, the nephew was on his way to the vegetable bazaar and had stopped for a minute or two to report to his uncle.

When he saw that Ranjit was cross with him, the boy immediately became obsequious. 'I'm grateful for the job, Uncle.'

'It isn't Tilak Sahib's fault that he has to cut up fish for a living,' Ranjit remarked. 'It's his father's fault for training him so.'

'Is he a fishmonger?' the boy asked, horror creeping into his voice. 'I thought you said he was a professor.'

'He is, he is,' replied Ranjit testily, as he collected up their dishes. 'He studies the insides of fish and frogs.'

The nephew's distaste, as he digested this information, was apparent on his ratlike face. Then he said uneasily, 'He went for a walk in the middle of the night – so late that the moon was beginning to set. What man in his senses would do that?'

Ranjit had the answer immediately. 'Perhaps he went to look at his experiment in the University.'

'What's an experiment?'

'I don't know,' said Ranjit truthfully, 'but I have heard from other University servants that, sometimes, professors go at night to check their experiments.'

'Oh,' said his nephew, and was satisfied.

Tilak was, however, news. Ranjit mentioned the late walk to another servant, joking that he might be hunting for another frog. This servant told the joke to someone else, and in due course it reached Miss Prasad's woman servant, who was one of Aunt's main sources of gossip, and Aunt learned that mad Dr Tilak went hunting frogs all through the night. She filed the information, with a lot of other more juicy titbits, for further use.

In the late afternoon, Ranjit went to town and ordered a tonga to come out to the house that evening, to take John to the home of Mr Lallubhai, one of the district's wealthier millowners.

Though Lallubhai was very rich, he was also a very conscientious man. His mills might hum with machinery forbidden by the Jain religion and turn out more cloth than any other works in India, but he combined in himself much that was good in a Jain gentleman. He provided housing for his workers which was the envy of other Shahpur citizens packed together in shocking slums. A small hospital, properly staffed, took care of the health of his workers, and a school for children up to the age of ten had recently been opened in his compounds. When building his house, he had installed outside his gates an extra water tap. This tap was considered miraculous because, no matter what the time of day, water ran out of it – and it ran fast, unlike the miserable trickle of the municipal supply. The tap was for public use, for all castes, and it was used with gratitude by Jain, Hindu and Muslim.

As John paid the tongawallah, and the chowkidar opened the gates for him, he watched the red-clad or white-clad women filling their water-pots. Amongst them stood Diana wiping her hands with her handkerchief. She smiled when she saw him, and the women all paused in their task, while they watched the couple.

She held out her hand to him, her discomposure at the end of their last meeting forgotten. 'My hands felt filthy from travelling on the bus, so I was washing them,' she explained.

John nodded, continuing to hold her hand and smile at her; she had four blue bracelets on her wrist, he noticed, and a hell of a lot of freckles.

A burst of giggles from the women, as they hoisted their water-pots on to their heads, made him drop her hand hastily. 'We should go in,' he said.

They turned and went through the heavy gates covered with beaten silver, and approached the huge, marble-trimmed bungalow. One broad picture window was lit up and they could see, on the inner wall of the room, a large copy of the famous painting of Gandhi and Nehru sitting together, a picture which graced many Indian homes. John grinned. The austerity of the great leader, clad only in his loin-cloth, seemed a bizarre comment on the ostentation of the house.

John's stick clicked across the terrazzo terrace. He could not think of anything to say to Diana and felt awkward in consequence. He thought she looked charming and he wondered that she had not been approached by someone like Lallubhai to become either his mistress or his wife. Diana could have told him, had he asked, that she had become quite adept at turning down such offers.

He found himself indulging in thoughts suspiciously close to jealousy, when Lallubhai seated her on a settee next to him. Lallubhai's wife also noticed the seating arrangements. She was an extraordinarily beautiful Madrasi woman, her red sari draped round her shoulders to make a frame for a face marred only by an expression of cynical boredom. John bowed to her and sat down himself. She may be beautiful, he brooded sourly, as he accepted glasses of water and fruit juice from a bearer, but in this provincial backwater, Diana, with her red hair, is unique.

Lallubhai cracked a joke with Diana and made her laugh. Then he called the meeting to order. He might enjoy dallying with a pretty woman, but he was, first and foremost, a businessman with little time at his disposal.

Within half an hour, John found himself with enough mapmaking to last him through six months of spare time. A garrulous assistant from the City Engineer's Department, already overwhelmed at being amongst such wealthy people, was appointed to help John.

John was amused by the expressions on the faces of the remainder of the Committee, as Lallubhai apportioned to each of them a slum district to be visited, censused, as far as possible, and recommendations made regarding it. Since many of the slums were as horrifying as those of London in the eighteenth century, John was not altogether surprised at their sudden lack of enthusiasm. The police hardly ever visited such places and they were avoided by the health authorities, except at times of epidemics. The whole Committee quailed visibly and began to make excuses.

At last, a Christian missionary spoke up. He was a ghostlike, malaria-drained man from the American Middle West, white-haired, withdrawn. Though his voice was querulous, his white hairs demanded respectful attention.

'Gandhiji said that we *must* help ourselves,' he told them gently. 'If we can clean up and improve the city, we shall be acting on his behest. A healthier city benefits all of us – we shall have less to fear from disease, for one thing.' He paused, and put his hand on the back of John's chair for support.

John remembered when he had first come out to Shahpur, a brash, vulgar man with a text always on his lips. He had not had much success with his mission, but Shahpur had moulded him into a very fine person. Now, he put courage back into the Committee. He shamed them with Jain and Christian texts and his own eighteen years of work in the city. As they rose, they promised, resignedly, to do as Lallubhai had asked them.

The old missionary sank down into his chair again, and John shifted himself round so that he could shake his hand. At the same time, he became aware of Lallubhai's rumbling bass voice, accompanied by Diana's protesting contralto.

'Miss Armstrong, you cannot go home alone at this time of night, even in a tonga. I won't hear of it. I have ordered a car for you; it will be at the front door in a few minutes. Unfortunately, I cannot accompany you . . .' He looked round, and at the same moment John turned back from the missionary. 'Ah, my dear Dr Bennett, I wonder if you would take care of Miss Armstrong. My chauffeur will drive you both to your respective homes.'

Diana's green eyes twinkled momentarily, though she resented John's obvious alarm.

'Why – why – of course.' John leaned heavily on his stick, as he got up from his chair. 'Delighted.'

Snugly ensconced in the back of Lallubhai's air-conditioned Cadillac, the uniformed back of the chauffeur comfortably anonymous in the darkness, Diana sat quietly by John, her hands folded in her lap. Nothing indicated the dejection within her. He had not really wanted to escort her – and why should he? She felt, suddenly, despairingly lonely.

'Do you think this survey will ever be carried out?' John asked her. Her sweet and heavy perfume was from Lucknow, he guessed.

'Yes, it will,' she replied. 'Lallubhai will see to that. He is so powerful – and he has a most vindictive tongue at times.'

So she didn't like Lallubhai all that much. In case the chauffeur understood English, he quickly changed the subject.

He said cautiously, 'I wonder if you would like to walk for a little while in the Riverside Gardens?'

She sparkled immediately and said she would.

John redirected the chauffeur, much to the man's disappointment. He had been wondering what an Englishman did when he was left alone with a gorgeous woman, and now he would probably never know. He clicked his tongue irritably and swung the car around.

A Cadillac stopping by the park gates caused a rush of beggars, each with his cry of woe. John had a busy moment or two while, with his stick, he kept them away from Diana. With good humour, he spoke to them in Gujerati, the homely language learned as a child from his beloved Ayah.

'Hey, Brothers,' he cried. 'Leave me enough so that I, too, may eat.'

They grinned at him, and whined, 'In the name of God, Sahib, you do not know the pain of an empty stomach.'

'I do know,' he said, and pushed pennies into sore-covered hands. The memory of his hunger in prison made him generous. 'Now, chelo,' he ordered them, and the chowkidar reinforced his order to them to go, by threatening them with his lathi.

Though she was not afraid, Diana kept close to him. So often, she had to face such people alone. Though their diseases, their starvation, their filth grieved her, one could get overwhelmed by sheer numbers.

They strolled into the nearly deserted park and John's stick thumped heavily on the asphalt path.

A man who had been leaning on the balustrade, his head buried in his hands, looked up suddenly. They were upon him before they realized he was there.

The light of a lamp fell full on Tilak's face, a face ravaged by weeping and lack of sleep, so filled with despair that it was hard to recognize the usually fretful, dogmatic man.

'Are you ill, old man?' John asked in concern, while Diana diplomatically stepped back a little.

'No, Bennett Sahib.' Tilak straightened up and made a great effort to appear calm. He rubbed his hands over his face. 'I may have a touch of fever, that's all. I thought it might be cooler down here. The servant you sent is very good – cooks quite well – and it hasn't dawned on him yet that the tradespeople pass our room by.' He rattled on, 'Ah, Miss Armstrong – it's pleasant down here, isn't it?'

Diana smiled shy acquiescence. Her nurse's eyes ran over the careworn face. Yes, probably fever – though, to her, he seemed terribly distressed mentally. Pity overcame her disappointment at not having John to herself.

John prepared to say goodbye and walk on with Diana, but Tilak was reluctant to let them go; it did not occur to him that there were times when John could do without him. When they moved, he moved with them, talking about odds and ends of campus news.

At first Diana left John to answer him. The serenity of the night enfolded her, a golden moon in its first quarter, a cloud of stars, the perfume of flowers ground to dust in the scorching daytime heat. Then, feeling that perhaps she should help John out, she interrupted the men to say brightly, 'Isn't the sky clear! No wonder poets praise the night.'

Tilak pounced on her remark and said, 'Poets create romantic illusions, Miss Armstrong. Romance has no place in India.'

His sharp response was unexpected, and she replied a little nervously, 'Come now, Dr Tilak. Indians are just as romantic as Westerners, and the winds of change have made them more able to express it, nowadays.'

'There *are* some of us who try to assist the wind, Miss Armstrong,' he admitted. He shivered, though there was no breeze to chill him.

John had listened uneasily to the exchange, and now he said, 'You're shivering. Perhaps you've a touch of malaria. You should get into bed soon.'

Tilak shrugged, as if to indicate that it did not matter if he had.

They returned to the gate. John gave up hope of having Diana to himself that evening; it would have to await another opportunity. 'Let's take a tonga between us,' he suggested. 'We can take Diana home first.' Tilak agreed absently and left John to bargain with the tongawallahs. A bargain was struck with a Muslim as thin and brown as an old pipe cleaner, and they climbed into the awkward little carriage.

In the enforced proximity, knees touching, bodies swaying together, the two Europeans could feel Tilak continuing to shake. They both expressed their concern.

Tilak shook his head. 'It's – how do you say in English – a goose walking over my grave. I'll feel better later on. Don't worry.'

As they passed under a street lamp, however, Diana saw that his eyes were fever-bright. He's terribly overwrought, she thought anxiously. She ventured to advise him, 'As a nurse, I prescribe three aspirins and bed.'

He agreed to do as she had said. How could he explain to her, he thought, that the shivering was caused by a fearful apprehension? A primitive scenting of danger to himself.

He was overwhelmed by worry that he would not be able to whisk

Anasuyabehn safely away, before she was married to Mahadev, and that it was almost impossible to communicate with her. His nerves were screwed to breaking point and he did not know which way to turn.

At Mrs Jha's house, John got down to see Diana safely to her door. He waited patiently while Mrs Jha could be heard fiddling with the great brass bolts on the other side. He looked down at Diana. She smiled at him, and very gently he bent down and kissed her on the cheek. At that moment Mrs Jha was checking on them through her peephole. She was greatly shocked. Her thin lips were even thinner, as she let her lodger in.

Diana herself was agreeably surprised and gave him another smile, as he said goodbye.

He climbed back into the carriage and said to Tilak, 'We can go first to your hostel and the tongawallah can drop me on his way back to town.'

Tilak had been wrapped in his own thoughts, but he said that he would prefer to get down at John's bungalow and walk over to the hostel.

'But you've got fever,' protested John.

'It's a fever of the mind,' Tilak snapped, his voice full of wretchedness.

'All right,' agreed John, and at his bungalow they had an amiable argument as to who should pay the tongawallah. John won, on the grounds that he would have taken a tonga, anyway. He was worried enough about his friend to offer him a drink before he went to the hostel, and this was accepted by Tilak with evident relief.

Tilak sipped cautiously at his whisky and water. It did not taste quite as foul as he expected; he would rather have died than admit that he had never tasted whisky before. Shahpur was a prohibition area, and John obtained a small ration of whisky each month, on the grounds that he had drunk it all his life and was, therefore, an addict. He was much teased about it.

Troubled by the ravages wrought on his friend in a few distressing days, he watched Tilak thoughtfully, as he sipped his own drink.

The unaccustomed alcohol loosened Tilak's tongue. He spoke first of the English Fellowship and then, more slowly, about his desire to take Anasuyabehn with him as his wife.

When he heard this, John sat up in his chair, pain in his legs forgotten.

'Look here,' he said. 'The only way in which you can marry Anasuyabehn is by formally asking her father, or getting your uncle to ask for you.'

'If she has a passport, she could be married to me in a civil ceremony in Bombay and we could go straight on to the ship. The problem is that the Fellowship does not commence until October, and she is scheduled to marry this Desai fellow next month.'

'That would, anyway, be tantamount to an abduction in the eyes of the law, here. Dr Mehta is my old and trusted friend; I could never be party to the abduction of his daughter.'

'I'm not asking you to be.'

'Well, there's another point. I wouldn't like you to face a charge like that in a local court. Apart from its being a very serious charge, you're a Maratha – and they'd have your blood.'

Tilak made a face. 'Gujeratis are not very fond of us, are they? We are also not very fond of them.' He sighed heavily. 'You know perfectly well that the Dean wouldn't even give me a hearing. Every time I meet him in the corridor I can see him trying not to throw up again – and some of his Arts colleagues are positively insulting.'

John sat taut and attentive. Unless he was stopped quickly, Tilak might ruin himself, and end up being thrown out of the world of scholars – and out of his family, as well. He suggested gently, 'Look, Tilak. You've got this Fellowship. Take it. Go and work under Diamond – it's a chance in a thousand. Forget about Anasuyabehn. Mahadev is a decent man in his way, and her father, I believe, knows it.' He paused for breath, and then added persuasively, 'There are other women in the world, Tilak, women educated to your level. You'll find someone else in time.'

While John had been speaking, Tilak had left his chair and, with his hands clenched in his pockets, had been walking slowly up and down the room. Now, he went to the door and flung it violently open. He glared out at the inky shadows in the compound.

He was furious; he dared not speak. One word would have loosed an avalanche of anger on to John – and in his heart he knew that John was the only true friend he had in Shahpur.

He ran down the steps into the darkness. The compound gate slammed after him.

Chapter Twenty-seven

Mrs Jha shut the door on John, replaced the padlock, and then turned to Diana. Beneath hooded lids, her black eyes were full of suspicion, and her lips were tight with disapproval; it was not seemly for a young woman to be seen home by a man. When previously Diana had been to meetings at Lallubhai's house, she had always been driven home with a number of guests, both ladies and gentlemen, in the car. Once she had arrived home having been driven in solitary grandeur by Lallubhai's chauffeur, which was bad enough; but after all a chauffeur was hardly a man at all. Now Mrs Jha awaited an explanation, while Diana stood in the hall in a half dream.

Mrs Jha rattled her keys, and Diana came out of her reverie. If she did not wish to lose her room, some explanation of John's presence was necessary.

'Mr Lallubhai asked Dr Bennett to bring me home,' she said. 'He's a very learned man – some people say he is a sage – who lives near the University. He writes history books about the Gujerati people.'

Mrs Jha's imagination was captured.

'Books about us?' she exclaimed.

'Yes,' replied Diana, with suitable gravity. 'He's made the Gujerat famous in America and England, as a place of learned and pious people.'

'Ramji! Fancy, books about us. And he is a sage, you say?'

Diana smiled.

'Well, not quite,' she said, 'but he lives a bit like a monk.'

Mrs Jha's face fell. Although she had disapproved of Diana's being accompanied home by a strange man, she was disappointed at being robbed of a secondary interest in a romance. A sage, indeed!

She moved down the passage, hitching her sari as she went, while Diana turned towards her room. Sages in ancient days were known to fall from grace, the old lady ruminated hopefully, and this one had certainly kissed the girl, which was quite shocking.

Diana took off her dress and wandered about her room in her cotton petticoat. With a mind hopelessly overstimulated, she abandoned all thoughts of going to bed for some time and decided that, in spite of the noise it would make, she would do her washing.

She got out the wooden paddle with which to beat the wet clothes on the veranda floor, a bucket of water made warm by the sun, a bar of common soap and the cardboard box of dirty clothes. Methodically, she sorted the clothes, taking each garment carefully out with her fingertips and shaking it well away from her, in case a scorpion or a snake should have taken up residence. Then she went through her skirt and blouse pockets to remove dirty handkerchiefs.

And there it was.

Fluttering silently to the floor from a handkerchief, a minute piece of paper with a blue line across its creamy whiteness. Diana watched it fall, her brows knitted in perplexity.

'Now where did that come from?' she muttered, and bent down to pick the scrap up.

The movement reminded her. Of course, she had picked it up on the way to Pandipura. She smiled at the thought of how she had amused herself by wondering how it came to be at the foot of a cactus in the bush.

Then the smile died, her eyes widened. She knew what it was.

The dead donkey! Her patient's fear! The missing noise in the village! It all fell into place.

Her first thought was to run to the police. But, no. These were not like British policemen – she might find herself in a dreadful mess with them. Then go to ask John's advice? That was hardly practical at eleven at night.

Her heart pounded and she ran her fingers feverishly through her red hair, as she sought for the best way of dealing with the unnerving revelation.

'Perhaps I should do nothing at all,' she dithered uncertainly. Then she remembered the Englishwoman lying dead in her First Class carriage in the robbed train, and indignation rose in her.

'It might have been me,' she thought.

Absent-mindedly, she picked up a garment, damped it and began to scrub soap into it. She rubbed and scrubbed and beat the washing in a spreading sea of soapsuds on the veranda floor. Then, as she rinsed her clothes in a bucket of fresh water, she decided that Dr Ferozeshah would be the best person to consult. He was intimately bound up in the life of the city and would understand all the factors involved.

'I'll ask him as soon as I go on duty,' she decided, and shook out a towel so forcefully that it made a sound like the crack of a bullet.

Chapter Twenty-eight

Unwilling to take a tonga, which would draw too much attention to them, and having long since exhausted the limited bus service, the uncles of Mahadev trudged from village to village. Where there were Desai Societies in a settlement, they commenced their inquiries at them. Failing that, they went to a member of the Panchyat, the Village Council. They did not neglect the miserable corners in which lived the Untouchables; the weavers, the tanners, the lavatory cleaners. Though they tried to make their inquiries casual, the news flew from mouth to mouth and, at times, a train of curious children and officious, advice-giving elders trailed along with them.

Occasionally, their queries about a Bania they were to meet and had somehow missed, as they put it, caused an electrifying attention, and they discovered that police, on bicycles, had already been through some of the villages seeking clues to the train robbery and a missing man.

After he heard this, Partner Uncle hired bicycles from a small shop. He and his servant wobbled along sandy lanes, cursing the heat and the dust and the smells, but progressing at least a little faster than they had done previously.

Partner Uncle was not a young man and, by late afternoon, he was trembling so much from exhaustion that he could no longer balance on his bicycle. When they reached a small well, he bade his servant dismount.

A young Hindu shepherd was drawing water for his sheep. The flock baaed and swirled around him, as he filled a trough for them from the waterskin. He paused, and politely offered water to the weary travellers. They thankfully squatted down, and he poured water from the skin into their hands. Trickles of the cool liquid ran down to their elbows and splashed pleasantly on to their sandalled feet.

With a grunt of relief, Partner Uncle wiped his dripping chin on his sleeve and sat down, cross-legged, under a nearby tree which gave a straggling bit of shade. His servant sat with him.

Both shepherd and sheep eyed them doubtfully. Then the shepherd settled his plum-coloured turban more firmly on his head and returned to watering his flock. As he guided the rope quickly over the well wheel, he shouted above the noise of the sheep, 'Have you come far, Brother?'

'We have,' replied Partner Uncle. Then he asked, 'The railway must run quite near here?'

'Yes,' agreed the young man and gestured towards the horizon. 'You can see the telephone poles that run along the top of the cutting.'

Uncle scrambled up to have a look.

'That's where the train robbery took place,' went on the shepherd.

'Were you here when it happened?' asked Partner Uncle, with sudden interest.

'No, sir.' He bent over the trough to empty the skin, still looking at the Banias out of the corner of his almond-shaped eyes. 'I took the sheep home, because I felt a dust storm was coming. It was time for supper, anyway.'

'Yes?' encouraged Partner Uncle, sensing that there was more to come. A blankness crept across the shepherd's handsome face, however, and he silently let down the waterskin into the well again. The wheel squeaked mockingly.

Frustrated, Partner Uncle tried again. 'Have you seen another Bania going this way? We were to meet him at the village back there, and we have somehow missed him.'

This innocent question caused the shepherd to blench. His hand shook so much that the rope nearly came off the wheel.

Used to the evasions of bad payers, Partner Uncle suddenly roared at him, 'You *have* seen him. Has he been hurt – or robbed?'

The boy cringed. 'No, sir. No.' His eyes were wide with stark fright. 'No – no one's passed this way today – except for the milkmaids going to and from town – and the vegetable sellers very early this morning.'

The sheep scattered uneasily at the sharp voices. Uncle's voice came like a trumpet. 'Perhaps not today – but a day or two back. He did, didn't he?'

'Sir, I don't know your friend,' came the fearful reply. 'I've no remembrance of a stranger doing business in our village.'

Uncle's voice dropped, and he wheedled, 'Come, lad, I mean no harm – but I do need information about such a man. I'm sure no traveller would be assaulted in your village. You can, therefore, safely tell me what it is that you have seen.' He palmed a couple of rupees and let them show out of the corner of his hand.

Grey-faced, but with his eyes on the money, the boy began to babble. 'Sir, we stole nothing. We took good care of the stranger – yet, it's best when dacoits are about to say nothing.'

'Quite, quite,' agreed Uncle, trying to be patient. He made himself smile as he looked down at his plain, respectable white shirt and homespun dhoti. 'It's obvious, at least, that I'm not a dacoit – only a businessman from Shahpur. You can speak safely to me. I'll tell no one else.'

'True, Bhai,' replied the shepherd, trying to stop quivering.

'Well, what happened?'

The shepherd gulped. 'Sir, it was like this. My eldest brother was returning from market in our ox-cart – on the day of the storm. He knew a storm was coming, too, so he took the new road along by the railway – it's easier for a cart to travel on, though it takes a little longer.'

'This was on Monday afternoon?'

The boy counted on his fingers. 'Ji, hun,' he agreed. 'It was already dark by the time he reached the cutting and the storm was howling round him. Being alone, he was afraid and he stopped to light the lantern for the cart. In the darkness and the wind, he couldn't find his matches, and then he heard horses nickering and thought they must be tied to trees nearby. Now, horses are not much used here, sir. And my brother wondered who would stop in such a lonely place in a storm – they would surely press on to seek shelter in our village. My brother became too afraid to advance up the road, so, as quietly as he could, he drew the ox-cart off the road and tethered it, hoping that the cacti would mask his presence.'

Partner Uncle could well visualize the nervous, superstitious peasant caught in the storm and fearing devils, robbers, angry gods.

'Yes, yes,' he said impatiently.

'My brother crept away from the cart and lay in a hollow. He saw flashlights flick on and off, but the dust was so thick and the night so dark, he couldn't see who was holding them. Then, through the earth, he heard the vibrations of the Delhi Mail approaching. There was a big explosion – and rifle fire – and the train stopped, instead of roaring onwards.'

The shepherd had now forgotten his fear and was absorbed by his story, embroidering in the details. 'He thought for a moment that the war with Pakistan had started – because we're only forty miles from the border, sir. Anyway, there were shrieks and cries – a woman screaming, and a rush of people, first down the cutting and then up again. Along the road and then across country the horses clattered, like devils sucked up into the sky.

'My brother lay perfectly still, quite safe, thanks to the storm – and, after a while, he heard the railwaymen shouting to each other, and the train started up.'

'The Bania?'

'I'm coming to that, sir. Did you say two rupees, sir?'

'Four, if you can tell me where he is now.'

'I don't know exactly where he is, sir.'

'Well, what *do* you know? Why are you telling me this long tale, which I can read in any newspaper, if you don't know?'

'Peace, Brother,' the shepherd's voice began to shake again. 'How will you understand if I don't tell you from beginning to end?'

Anger being a mortal sin, Partner Uncle did his best to swallow his. 'Well, what happened then?'

'My brother lay a long time in his hiding place. When nothing more happened, he crept back to the ox, listening intently. He got the cart back on to the road again and wrapped his turban round his face, because the sand was still blowing. He led the ox, for he still feared to show a lantern light, and continued slowly down the road. He had not gone very far, sir, when he heard a loud groan, right at his feet. Now, what would you have done, sir?'

With eyes closed, Partner Uncle stood up and stretched himself. 'I'd have fled,' he said sarcastically and then swore under his breath, mentally promising forty-eight minutes of penance to wash out the oath.

'Not my brother,' boasted the shepherd with pride. 'He looked about him, and, by the side of the road, saw a vague white bundle – like a fallen ghost.' He paused for effect. 'It moved a little. He advanced carefully, fearing it might be a wounded dacoit. It was a big, stout man weeping with pain – a townsman, he guessed.' The shepherd spread out his hands in a gesture of helplessness. 'My brother didn't know what to do. He went to the cart to get the lantern, however, and succeeded in lighting it.

'The man was a sorry sight, his face all covered with blood.'

Partner Uncle exclaimed in alarm.

The shepherd nodded, and went on, 'My brother wiped the blood from his nose and eyes. He tried to lift him up to put him on the cart and bring him home, but the man was too heavy for him and cried out in pain.'

Partner Uncle was, by this time, striding up and down in great apprehension. He stopped in front of the shepherd. 'Well, what next?'

'Brother took the blanket from round his own shoulders and covered the man with it – a good blanket, sir, now ruined by blood. He whispered to the man to try to keep quiet and he would bring help. He then tethered the ox again – because oxen are slow, sir – and ran home in the teeth of the storm.

'Five of us went out in that terrible storm, sir, and found the man and put him in the cart and brought him to my father's house. My mother washed away the blood and found he had two wounds, one on the top of his head and one in his shoulder. He was unconscious but mother said no bones had been broken. She bound him up – and all night we sat and wondered what to do. Ours is a very small village, sir, since the cholera killed so many, and my father is the eldest elder. The responsibility was his.' The shepherd paused for breath, and then asked, 'He must have been a passenger on the train? Would he be your friend?'

'I believe so,' replied Partner Uncle, and then, as the shepherd showed no sign of continuing the story, he queried, 'Well?'

The shepherd evaded Partner Uncle's anxious glare. 'Sir, the sun is going down. I must take the sheep home.'

Partner Uncle swelled with sudden rage; the veins on his forehead stood out. He swept his arms above his head and shook his fists, like an avenging god. 'What is this?' he shouted. 'What happened to my nephew?'

The countryman cringed, and responded uncertainly, 'Your nephew? Sir, you *must* speak to – to father.'

Partner Uncle screamed again in rage, his voice echoing round the empty countryside. Pointing a finger at the unfortunate shepherd, he advanced threateningly towards him, only to be brought up short by milling sheep. The boy stammered, 'Come home with me, sir. Father will explain to you.'

The frightened sheep eddied between them. Afraid that his furious master would have a fit, the servant caught him by the arm, and implored, 'Master, keep calm.'

Partner Uncle shook off the restraining hand, but he did thereafter try to control himself. 'Very well,' he snarled. He picked up the hired bicycle and motioned to the servant to pick up his. The sheep were called and herded to the path. In the blinding dust raised by ninety-six little feet, Partner Uncle followed the flock and its shepherd.

Partner Uncle found little solace in being half-choked by dust, but his anger cooled and his quick brain went to work. It did not take him long to realize why the boy had stopped his tale where he had. After cleansing the wounds, the old father would naturally look to see if his unexpected guest had been robbed, by checking his money belt; and if it was indeed Mahadev and his money belt was still round his waist, the old man would have been faced with the terrible temptation of a fantastic fortune having arrived in his poverty-stricken hut. How easy to add to Mahadev's wounds, take him back to the cutting during the night and bury the money belt under the floor until such time as it seemed safe to remove himself, his family and the fortune to another part of India.

During the twenty minutes' uncomfortable walk, Partner Uncle felt it would be a miracle if Mahadev and the jewels were both safe.

Infinitely thin and wrinkled, Jivraj lay on his string bed. He struggled up to speak to Partner Uncle, however, and bade him sit beside him while he heard his business. Then with many a sly look over his shoulder, he confirmed his son's story of the robbery, and sent for his elder son, his nephews and his brothers, who all corroborated it. Though dreadfully afraid, not one of them said a word of how the robbers themselves had pounced on the village, uttering terrible threats and sweeping away all their donkeys with a promise of their safe return in a few days' time. In a matter of minutes in the dark night they had come and gone, leaving dismay and near panic behind them. And then, before the night was done, Jivraj had been faced with the problem of the wealthy, wounded stranger.

Now he must cope with this hard-faced Bania, just when it appeared that the train robbery was all but forgotten and all that remained was for the donkeys to be returned; he had no doubt that they would arrive home safely since their loss would cause comment all over the district, and the robbers would not wish to leave any indication of how they got out of the province.

'But where *is* my nephew?' demanded the frantic Uncle.

'Ah, Sahib, has no word come to you from the police?'

'No!'

Jivraj looked bewildered.

'But the doctor promised to find out who he was and inform the police, so that word might go out to his family.'

'Doctor?'

'Yes, Sahib. The morning after the robbery the stranger had high fever, and we feared he might die.' He looked helplessly at Partner Uncle, 'And then how would I explain away to the police a corpse with wounds?'

Another man pushed his way forward. 'I remembered that I had heard the white doctor was visiting a few villages away, so my son went for him.'

Partner Uncle took a large breath and relaxed a little. 'Did he come?' he asked.

'Oh, yes. He came with his big lorry. He said the Bania was very sick and had a bullet in his shoulder. He also needed medicine which the doctor didn't have with him. He asked what had happened, and we told him. Then he brought a cot from his lorry and we put the Bania on it and lifted him in. The doctor Sahib said he would take him to his hospital and inform the Shahpur police. We were deeply afraid of being implicated in the train robbery.' He stopped and looked uneasily round the group of anxious men who had gathered. 'The doctor said he would explain to the police for us – that he knew us to be honest men. He comes to the village occasionally.'

Partner Uncle stood up. 'Where's the hospital?'

The villagers looked at each other. Then one said, 'It's to the north – on the other side of Shahpur – ten or fifteen miles from here.'

'That side of Shahpur is desert. There couldn't be a hospital there.'

'That's where it is.'

A younger man bent down and whispered in Jivraj's ear, and Jivraj said to Partner Uncle, 'It's a God hospital – a Christ one.'

'Ah, a mission?'

Dusk was falling, and a woman of Jivraj's family came out of the hut with a lighted charcoal fire held in a pair of tongs. She put it down, put a covered bowl by it and began to slap rolls of dough between her hands to flatten them into rotis, preparatory to cooking them.

Jivraj looked at the exhausted old moneylender and was touched by the sadness in his face. 'Sir, if you can eat our food, one of my sons will serve you under the tree over there.'

Moneylenders are not popular in villages and Partner Uncle was surprised by the offer. He was glad to accept, however, and then he added, 'It's too late to find the hospital tonight. I'll return to Shahpur and set out again early in the morning.'

To his surprise, Jivraj said, 'To return to Shahpur from here is very simple. When they made the new road, they built a station for us at the nearby railway. In about an hour's time, a local train will come down the line. It's about a mile to the station.' He bridled with pride in the new facility.

So Partner Uncle found himself eating good millet bread and sag with a little yoghurt, under a tree in a strange village, and ruminating on the unexpected courtesy and kindness of country folk. Deep inside he felt a trifle ashamed of the many times he had, in years past, pounded money out of just such people.

'Ah, well, they owed it,' he thought, as he scraped the last bit of sag off the palm leaf on which it had been served.

'Not at 144 per cent interest,' said his conscience.

The young man who served him was the shepherd he had met at the well, and he put the promised four rupees into his hand; the boy took them without protest, as his due. An older man then brought a lantern and led them, as they pushed their bicycles, over an almost invisible track down to the small railway station.

There are no words of thanks in the Gujerati language and Partner Uncle did not offer to pay for his meal, but the villagers knew and Uncle knew that a bond of hospitality had been forged between them. One day, when the opportunity arose, it would in some way be repaid.

Less than two hours later, Partner Uncle was reporting to old Desai, who himself had had a fruitless day.

'I know of the hospital,' said old Desai. 'It is called the Mission of Holiness. Once I met that doctor.' He picked his toes thoughtfully. 'I formed the opinion that he was not altogether trustworthy – you know how one senses it?'

Partner Uncle sighed, and nodded.

'Tomorrow, Baroda Brother and I will go to the hospital and inquire. You must rest.'

Partner Uncle agreed. It did not occur to either of them that the Mission of Holiness might be on the telephone – nor was it.

Chapter Twenty-nine

Tilak never remembered clearly how he got through the night and the following morning, after leaving John so precipitously. A veil seemed to be cast over his conscious mind and he was guided merely by habit.

Realizing that the Sahib was in some way ill, his servant made up his bed and suggested that he sleep. He helped Tilak off with his clothes and held back the mosquito net while his master silently clambered into bed. After a while, he slept.

Soon after daybreak, the servant brought him hot water for shaving and then a brass tray of breakfast. After he had laid out clean clothes, he sat down in a corner and wondered apprehensively what Uncle Ranjit would say if he ran away.

Tilak shaved mechanically, turning over his lecture notes as he did so. A plop of shaving soap fell on them and he wiped it carefully away with the towel. He continued to read while he ate wheaten porridge and drank some milk. Then he put the notes into his briefcase, dressed, gave the servant money for the day's food, and walked down to the University.

Though the sun was already well up, he shivered occasionally as though he were cold. It was not chill, however, but rather an inner perception that he faced a long, hard road to travel. He felt helpless, unable to accept the bitter facts regarding Anasuyabehn, which John had pointed out the previous evening.

When he arrived at the Arts and Science Building, some of his students were hanging about outside it. They looked sullen and turned away from him, but he was too absorbed in his own problems to notice them. Inside, other students were hurrying to lecture rooms. They stared at him as he strode unseeingly to his own lecture room. He opened the door and walked in.

The room was empty.

Surprised, he looked at his watch. He was punctual. He put down his briefcase and took a few uncertain steps towards the window. Then he wheeled around and went out to the corridor again.

While the last students scurried through doors, like rabbits down their burrows, the Vice-Chancellor's secretary hurried up to him.

Tilak asked, 'Do you happen to know if they changed the room for my lecture? Is the Dean in yet?'

The secretary blinked excitedly from behind thick spectacles. 'The room? I don't know. The Dean has just gone over to the English Department. Dr Prasad, however, wishes to see you now.'

'I can't possibly see him now. I have a lecture – only all my students seem to be late or are in the wrong room.'

The secretary replied portentously, 'They are not late, Sahib.'

'What do you mean?' A fuming irritation at the fool standing before him began to invade him. 'Well?' he snapped.

'They're on strike, Sahib.'

'Strike?'

'Yes, Sahib. That's why Dr Prasad wants to see you.'

Seated in front of the Vice-Chancellor, Tilak looked at him amazed. He had not heard Dr Prasad's opening words, except that he realized that his tone was sympathetic. Now Dr Prasad was saying, 'This is a situation which I had not foreseen. It will be the work of three or four hotheads. I have sent for Dean Mehta – he will know who are likely to be the miscreants, and I can assure you that disciplinary action will be taken.'

He waited for Tilak to say something, but Tilak was so taken aback that he was beyond words. All this because of a little dissecting? It was absurd. Yet, in his heart, he knew it was not absurd. He had struck at the roots of Jain belief.

'Would you like to take some leave while we deal with this?' asked Dr Prasad.

'Of course not,' Tilak assured him. Anger began to take the place of surprise and he felt like throwing something at the dolts who could not see that India, whether its inhabitants liked it or not, was a part of the twentieth century.

'I suggest leave, my dear Dr Tilak, because Dr Bennett mentioned to me, when I saw him recently, that you had had a brick thrown at you. It disturbed him because it happened on campus – and students are apt to be a little unstable.'

'Are you afraid of violence of some sort?'

Dr Prasad hesitated, and then said, 'I shall try to avoid it, of course.'

'Well, I'm not afraid of it – my mother and sister have gone back to Bombay, so I don't have to worry about them.' He laughed sardonically, and commented, 'It would be ironical if our Jain friends took to violence to defend non-violence!'

'It would, indeed,' agreed Dr Prasad sadly. 'But I hope it won't come to that. Meantime, I really think it best if you went on leave for two or three weeks.'

An hour later, the University's Head Peon was dispatched to town to make a reservation on the Bombay Express for that afternoon. Tilak's servant went scuttling down to the river, to rescue his master's shirts from the boiling vats of the washerman, and Tilak himself tried to deal with the chaos in his room.

Sheets, mosquito net, blankets, bedding roll, were spread all over the floor, as a result of his flustered servant's efforts at packing. Clucking with irritation, Tilak made up his own bedding roll and packed a trunk with his books and papers. As he worked, he considered how to let Anasuyabehn know of his impending absence. Dr Prasad had turned down the idea that he remain in the city, but not teach. 'It's better to be right out of it,' he had insisted. He felt physically weak and the sweat rolled down him, as he struggled with leather straps and recalcitrant buckles.

He began to weep helplessly and sat down suddenly on the bedding roll. Would it be better simply to walk out of Anasuyabehn's life? Go away to Bombay and never come back?

He gave a shuddering sigh. He couldn't do it; he must at least let her know what had happened. After a little consideration, he decided to ask John to deliver a note to her.

He scribbled a quick explanatory note to her, saying he hoped to return in two weeks, and enclosed it, unsealed, in another note to John. His servant could take it over to him.

Anasuyabehn, too, had spent a bad morning, wondering how to inform Tilak that Mahadev was missing, that there was a chance he had been killed, but that, if he were found, her wedding would take place sooner than expected.

She did not want to wish a man dead. This unexpected happening, however, made her hope that he would be missing long enough for the marriage to be deferred.

In the late afternoon, while the aunts and her cousins slept and Dean Mehta went back to the University, she sent the boy servant to the students' hostel, with a cryptic note giving some indication of her predicament.

'Go first with this,' she instructed him, as she handed him the chit, 'and, on the way back, buy some fresh pan leaves from the pan seller up the road. Give the note only to Dr Tilak. Nobody else. Do you understand?'

The little boy grinned slyly and slipped quietly out of the sweeper's door and up the field path. At the hostel, he found himself facing a padlocked door.

The wife of a student, baby on hip, was standing at the door of the next room, and she asked him what he wanted. He told her that he had brought a letter from Dean Mehta's daughter to Tilak Sahib.

'From Dean Mehta,' she corrected.

'No. Bahin wrote it herself.'

The woman looked thunderstruck. Then she said cunningly, 'Leave it with me, little Brother. I'll give it to him when he comes in.'

He held it behind his back and took a step or two away from her. 'No. It's for Tilak Sahib only. When will he be back?'

In a fury of curiosity, the woman answered him, 'He went away with all his luggage this afternoon. Perhaps he won't come back.' She started to advance towards him. The child turned, and ran helter-skelter down the stairs.

The middle-aged mother of another student opened her door further down the passage. 'What was that?' she asked the woman with the baby.

The woman told her, and so the story was sent on its way. Two days and several dozen gossips later, it was said on the campus that Dean Mehta's daughter was pregnant by Dr Tilak, who had fled to escape the consequences.

Chapter Thirty

While Dr Ferozeshah was preparing to receive the morning rush of outpatients, Diana showed him the piece of paper she had found and told him of her deductions.

'Keep out of it,' Ferozeshah advised promptly.

'But the police might be able to trace the dacoits if they knew about this,' protested Diana. She was dressed in her white, nurse's uniform and was getting together the doctor's stethoscope, his thermometer, cotton wool and bottle of disinfectant and putting them ready on his desk.

In response to her protest, Ferozeshah said firmly, 'Never go near the police unless you have to.'

'I haven't done anything wrong!'

'Neither of us has. But once they are here, they'll hang around and expect to be fed – and if we really want anything done, they'll expect suitable baksheesh.' He finished buttoning up his white coat.

'Oh,' said Diana, immediately deflated.

'Cheer up. I'm sure you're right. But, at best, that piece of registered envelope you found is a clue; it's not concrete evidence against the dacoits. And, you know, the villagers will be punished – and the dacoits would still get away with it.'

That evening, after an early dinner, Diana went on the bus to see John and ask his opinion. Ranjit admitted her and managed a polite smile, a smile that faded immediately he returned to his back veranda; it was replaced by a look of great anxiety.

John agreed with Ferozeshah. 'I've heard that they have sent a good man down from Delhi to investigate, because of the murder of that Englishwoman. Let *him* get on with it.'

Diana sighed. 'I suppose you're right – I felt so clever working it all out. But how will those poor people in Pandipura cope?'

'I bet the donkeys are back in the village by now. The villagers haven't suffered much and they'll all be as quiet as mice – they don't want the dacoits to burn the place flat next time they come this way.'

'That's awful! It's bullying!'

'We live in an awful world,' responded John almost flippantly.

His acceptance of human wickedness surprised her. It savoured of a Hindu outlook.

He continued. 'They probably had a plan to get the proceeds of the robbery out of the province and, because of the storm, it went wrong, so they pounced on the nearest village – they needed transport that fitted into the landscape and could carry, say, builder's sand, with the loot buried in it. Donkeys would be perfect. Horses stick out like sore toes, here.'

'Why use horses at all?'

'Speed – to get away from the scene, in the first instance. They probably had a string of camels waiting, and missed them in the dark and the dust.'

'My patient was so frightened and worried that she nearly died.'

'That's too bad. Is she all right now?'

'Yes. She'll be OK.'

'Good. I say, can you stay to dinner?' he asked shyly.

Diana looked up at him and smiled. 'I'd love to,' she said, and hoped she could eat a second meal.

John took up his stick and went to consult Ranjit. The bearer agreed morosely that he could provide enough food. John turned to go back into his room.

'Sahib . . .'

'Yes?'

Ranjit, seated on the floor in front of his precious Primus stove, looked up. He looked as sour as a piece of dried tamarind. 'Nothing, Sahib,' and he leaned forward to pick up his paring knife.

Really, John thought, Ranjit was a queer old stick sometimes.

As he re-entered, John asked Diana, 'Do you happen to know Anasuyabehn Mehta?'

'No. Who is she?'

'Dean Mehta's daughter. Lives a few doors down. I just wondered.' He did not like to say that in his cash box lay the love letter for her, left by Tilak's servant earlier that day, which he wanted delivered to her. He had read it. It said simply that Tilak had to return to Bombay and was consulting his uncle. It would mean the world to Anasuyabehn, and, even if Dean Mehta saw it, there was nothing dishonourable in it.

Diana watched him cross the room, leaning on his stick. 'I don't think that you need to use that stick all the time,' she said abruptly.

Startled out of his thoughts of Anasuyabehn, John glanced down at the offending stick.

'Do you have any pain now?'

'Not often, unless I've hit myself on something.'

'I don't think Ferozeshah has examined you for a long time. He's been rushed off his feet.'

'Oh, I only ask him for a sedative. In England, they told me not much more could be done.'

She gazed at John standing uncertainly before her, his face slowly reddening with embarrassment.

'Forgive me,' she said gently, 'for being so personal – but I saw a fair amount of similar injury during the war and how it was treated. I believe you could learn to walk without a stick – and quite straight. It would mean that the rest of your body wouldn't ache so much from being out of position. I imagine it does ache?'

He nodded, and she got up and went to stand in front of him. 'Would you like to try?' she asked. 'I'll help you.'

She was not a tall person and seemed very diminutive to him. Her eyes crinkled up with humour, and she said, as if she had read his thoughts, 'I'm quite strong.'

'I wouldn't mind having a bash at it.'

'OK. I need first to see exactly how you put your feet down. Put your hands on my shoulders and I'll walk backwards, while I watch your feet.'

He laid his stick on the divan and shyly put his hands on her shoulders. It was so long since he had touched a woman that, at first, his thoughts were not about learning to walk. He stumbled, only to be steadied by a surprisingly strong arm round his waist.

Diana held him for a moment; then quickly let her arm drop, afraid that her instinctive movement might be misconstrued. John was thinking, 'She's too bloody innocent for words.'

'Let's try again,' she said in her bright, professional voice, and he glumly gave his attention to what she was saying.

He held on to her and advanced as she retreated.

Ranjit peeped through the half-open door and was horrified to see such abandoned behaviour. He went back to his cooking pots wagging his head in a hopeless fashion.

It was even worse when he went in to announce dinner. The copper and the dark heads were bent close together over the desk, while the Memsahib drew indecent pictures of men doing peculiar actions with their legs.

Ranjit hardly slept that night.

Chapter Thirty-one

On a littered desk, lay Mahadev's money belt like a pallid, dead snake. Seated before it was a man leaning his head on his clenched fists. He had not moved for twenty minutes.

An increasing ruckus outside the window reminded him that patients were gathering there for morning surgery. He lifted his bald head wearily and rubbed his eyes with his knuckles, to look around his cluttered little office, where the few pieces of furniture were all piled high with dusty records. The corners of the room were festooned with cobwebs, and the uncurtained windows were opaque with dust, a myriad of smears and finger-marks. One window was open and, through it, he could see the dreary, flat, semi-desert landscape shimmering in remorseless heat.

The chatter outside the window increased; the Mission of Holiness was a very busy place, and the missionary himself felt tired to death.

He opened one fist.

On his soft, white palm glittered a beautifully cut ruby, its perfection undimmed by the gloom of the office.

It must be worth thousands, he thought, and glanced at the money belt in front of him. There must be a fortune in that!

The money belt was a plain strip of grubby white cotton, which had been folded and stitched down one side. Along the whole length of the belt, at about one and a half inch distance from each other, lines of stitching divided the belt into small compartments. Judging by the feel of it, each compartment held a stone at least as big as the ruby.

''Strewth, I wonder what it's all worth?' he muttered. 'I bet it'd buy a hundred new hospital beds, the salary of another doctor, two nurses and an operating room – and a stack of penicillin ceiling high. And bibles – dozens of them in Gujerati.'

He again looked at the ruby and smiled grimly.

'I could sell a gem like that in the jewellery market of Bombay or Delhi as easily as falling off a log – and who would know? I can simply say that he had no belt on him when he arrived here.'

As he ruminated, the waiting patients outside were being marshalled into a queue by a middle-aged Indian. The missionary had found him in a ditch, the sole survivor of a family of refugees from Pakistan who had died of starvation.

The whole queue would be suffering from malnutrition, thought the missionary despondently, apart from their heat boils, their venereal diseases, their tuberculosis and heaven only knew what else.

There was a knock on the door, and he hastily swept the belt into his desk drawer, and stood up.

It was only the woman sweeper coming to do the floor, and he walked up and down one side of the room while she swept the other side. The ruby was still clutched in his hand. What was he to do? And who was this man, anyway?

In the waist of his homespun dhoti had been knotted a return Interclass train ticket to Delhi. A small purse, pinned in the same place by a large safety-pin, had yielded twenty-three rupees and some change. His linen had, at one time or other, been marked with a D in Western script. Having found the money belt, the missionary could well understand why his patient had made such a frantic effort to escape from the train.

The sweeper opened the door to the passage and swept through it the dust she had collected. She began to sweep her way slowly and ineffectually towards the front door.

From beyond the door she faced, came the sound of loud, authoritative voices. A rifle butt was banged on the woodwork.

With lightning speed, the missionary shut the door of his office, snatched the money belt out of the drawer and bundled it and the ruby into the wall safe.

The sweeper opened the door and came flying into the room, at the same time trying to touch the feet of the police officers accompanying her. After them came the Mission's head nurse, protesting in Gujerati that the Doctor Sahib was very busy. It seemed suddenly that the room was filled with armed men, though, in fact, there were two police constables with rifles and one officer with a pistol in his holster.

Calmly and benignly, the missionary rose from his desk chair, one hand raised as if to bless. On the desk lay his bible, open as if he had been studying. 'Good morning, gentlemen. What can I do for you?'

The belligerent attitude of the police gave way to faint respect. The small man with the pistol stepped forward and answered him in good English. He said that they were looking for a missing Bania and that they had heard that he had recently had a Bania as patient. Before he could be answered, he turned to the constables and told them to wait outside.

The missionary answered calmly, 'Please sit down,' and motioned his unwelcome visitor to a chair. With his eyes on the doctor, he sat down with a rattle of accoutrement.

On his part, the missionary weighed up his visitor. A Bengali by the accent, supremely shrewd, a very senior police officer judging by the good cut of his khaki uniform. From a corner, the head nurse watched them both, and tried to stop his teeth chattering.

'We do have a man here, who by his dress appears to be a Gujerati Bania,' agreed the missionary.

'I believe he arrived here under unusual circumstances and that he had a bullet in him.'

'Yes. He has had high fever for three days, so we have no idea who he is. Had his temperature not gone down during the night, you would have heard from us today. He is now under sedation. He is obviously exhausted and needs to sleep.'

'I'd like to see him,' said the officer, still watching the missionary.

'He won't wake for at least two more hours. You could try waking him now, of course, but I doubt whether you would get any coherent response from him.'

'You should know that in circumstances such as these, the police should be informed immediately.'

'Ah, yes, of course, quite,' the missionary was at his vaguest, with a gentle smile. 'We have no telephone – and we are so busy – you have seen the queue outside. I could not spare anyone to go to town. I knew he would recover. It was not a question of murder.'

'It's a question of attempted murder,' replied the Bengali tartly. 'I'll leave a constable to sit by his bed, and I'll return in about two hours; I've other business in the neighbourhood.' He stood up, ready to leave. 'Exactly how did this man come to you?' He had already heard the story from the Mission's lorry driver, who had been roughly questioned a few minutes before, but he wanted to hear the American's version.

Now, he found that it tallied quite well with what he already knew.

'The Pandipura villagers saved his life, of that there is no doubt,' the missionary told him. 'They are to be commended.'

'It would seem so,' grunted the officer.

After the officer had gone, the American took out the money belt and carefully eased the ruby back into it. Then he went to see his patient.

Mahadev was sleeping quite relaxedly and his colour was good. By the bed sat a police constable, his rifle across his hairy knees. He was already dozing.

'Are you ready, Doctor Sahib?' his nurse inquired. 'There's a long queue.' He had his hand on the door latch of the dispensary.

The American sighed and said he was ready. How much penicillin would a ruby buy, he wondered?

Chapter Thirty-two

That morning, old Desai was so anxious that, for the first time in his life, he missed reading his morning mail. After drinking a glass of milk, he set out at daybreak for the Mission of Holiness. A servant drove the carriage, and Desai snarled at him unceasingly to hurry.

The old man had a brass box of lunch on his knee and a full water-jar on the seat beside him. Next to the water-jar, sat Baroda Brother. He was placidly polishing his spectacles on his shirt end; the morning was relatively cool, and he was enjoying the drive through the half-awakened city. By the driver sat his son, thrilled at the adventure.

The narrow city streets gave way to wide gravel boulevards, lined with trees shading the graceful houses and bungalows of the city's well-to-do millowners. These petered out to become a rough track; and the last mile was little more than lorry wheelmarks in the sand, through which the horse could hardly drag the carriage. Finally, the passengers got down and walked along beside the vehicle and made better progress.

Meanwhile, Mahadev lay in his hospital bed, under a mosquito net, and listened. His head ached so intolerably that he could not bear to open his eyes. When he tried to shift himself slightly, the pain in his back made his senses reel. One of his arms seemed to be tied to his chest. A short distance from him a number of voices made a steady hum – he wondered if it were the dacoits and lay very still, so as not to betray his presence.

Then he realized that he was in a bed of sorts, and made himself open his eyes for a second. He caught a glimpse of an old-fashioned English screen making a wall around him. Above the wall, he could see a shelf with glass containers sitting on it; over them a squirrel scampered.

He tried to think.

That was it! The trip to Delhi, to return the Maharaja's jewels. He had borrowed against them to set up a radio factory and now he wished to pay his debt.

The jewels!

With his unconfined hand, Mahadev felt round his waist. The belt was gone.

The shock was so alarming that he tried to sit up, only to fall back as rivets of pain went through him.

'Doctor Sahib,' called a voice beside him, and he forced himself to open his eyes again.

He did not know what he had expected, but the sight of a constable gaping down at him was a further shock. Apprehension about the loss of the stones gave way to fear for his personal safety. What had he done that he should be under arrest? In a split second, Mahadev saw himself flung into a filthy prison or, at best, reduced to utter poverty, a lender of single rupees.

In response to the call, a man came round the screen. An Englishman! The sense of lunatic nightmare increased.

'Ah, I see we are better,' the missionary said, his professional smile covering his own despair. 'I'm probably damned if I steal that belt,' his thoughts ran, 'and, if I don't, I'm condemned to this unmerciful round of watching patients suffer for the lack of simple drugs. Why, O Lord, why?'

He took the patient's wrist in pudgy, capable fingers, and added to himself, 'And if this guy pays his bill, I'll be lucky.'

'How's the head?'

Mahadev ignored the question. 'Where am I?' he asked.

'You're in the Mission of Holiness Hospital. I brought you in from Pandipura, near Ambawadi.'

'How badly am I hurt?'

'Bullet lodged in your shoulder – I've got it out, and a neat furrow across your skull where another one hit you – that was a near thing.' He turned and asked the constable to help him prop up Mahadev, while he looked at the head wound. The constable, who had never been in a hospital before, was fascinated, and did what the doctor ordered very carefully. Mahadev cried out with pain, however.

The doctor was undoing the bandages round his head. 'You'll be OK,' he assured the shattered moneylender, who was certain nothing would ever be OK again. The conversation was in Gujerati and the police constable watched and listened attentively. 'What happened? Do you know?' the doctor asked.

'The dacoits must've been short of men, because none of them caught hold of my carriage door, so I opened it and slipped down on to the track and ran for the embankment. A huge dust storm was raging – confusion – horses – screams. I started to climb further up the embankment where there were trees and bushes. They must have seen the movement.' He sighed and winced. 'When I came round, the train had gone.' He stopped; the effort of talking was too great. The missionary removed the dressing, and when the pain of it subsided, he went on, 'I remember trying to crawl to the new main road – and a woman washing me.'

The constable spoke. 'It's better to stay in the train in a raid by dacoits. If you hand everything over quickly, you're usually all right. Not so with Muslims, of course.'

Mahadev looked at him sourly and nearly shrieked when the missionary muttered, 'Ah, healing nicely,' and clapped a new dressing on to his head. When he had replaced the bandages, he said, 'Well, sir, you've had a lucky escape. Later on today, you could try moving around a little. But, first, I want to look at your shoulder. And I want to know who you are, so that I can inform your family.'

Sulkily, Mahadev told him. He wanted to ask where his money belt was, but was frustrated by the presence of the constable. Never tell the police anything, had been drilled into him from childhood. Of course, he thought miserably, the police themselves might have the belt, in which case he would leave to his father the delicate negotiations to get it back.

'What day is it?' he asked, and was thoroughly perturbed to hear that it was Friday morning. The raid had taken place on Monday evening.

As the doctor worked, he chatted, partly to cover his own worries and partly to reassure his patient. 'A police bigwig will be here in about half an hour, to question you,' he informed his patient.

'A *Delhi* police chief,' interjected the constable reverently. He had parked his rifle against the bed, so that he could see better what the doctor was doing.

Mahadev closed his eyes and tried not to feel too bitter. A Jain gentleman was forgiving, patient under affliction. He did not feel like that – only cross and petulant and dreadfully weak.

He realized that the glass bottles ranged around the wall contained pickled specimens of foetuses, and his empty stomach began to heave. Fortunately, a woman in a white sari brought him some water to drink and distracted his attention. She was followed rapidly by the tramp of boots across the floor, heralding the return of the tiny police chief.

A little later, a triumphant and much relieved old Desai was shown into the dispensary. He stumped across the room, muttering that private initiative had been better than the perfidious police force. Had he not found his son himself?

He was much chagrined when, rounding the screen, he saw a very yellow and shrunken Mahadev lying on a bed and an obviously frustrated and fuming police chief sitting cross-legged on the chair beside him; Mahadev was not going to be much use as a witness.

The police chief looked up, as the old man entered, followed by his brother-in-law and nephew. He understood something of what was passing through old Desai's mind. The police had, in finding Mahadev first, scored over him. He immediately felt better and rose politely to salute him. 'Here is your son, sir. You may take him home as soon as you wish.'

Driving back from the Mission of Holiness in the early afternoon, old Desai was very quiet. It had been agreed that Mahadev should remain in the hospital for two more days. Baroda Brother-in-law asked him, 'Are you worrying about Mahadev?'

'No, the boy is obviously recovering. That English doctor knows what he is doing.' Old Desai could never remember that Americans were not English.

'It's what he was carrying?'

'Yes. We couldn't ask him with the police all round him.'

'Where do you think it is?'

'It's not with Mahadev. He touched his waist and made a tiny gesture to indicate that.'

'It'll be a frightful loss.'

'We shall have to pay. It's our reputation which is at stake. We've never failed to return securities lodged with us.'

'Do you think the train robbers took it?' asked Baroda Brother, thankful he did not have any share in Desai's business.

Desai replied slowly, 'I suspect that the English doctor has it.'

'What? He would've told us.'

'Not all English people are so honest.'

'It couldn't be. Anybody could've taken it when he was unconscious.'

Old Desai did not agree. He had not built up his enormous business without acquiring a profound knowledge of human nature. Like the Bengali detective, he sensed that the Mission doctor was hiding something. The man was disturbed in some way, and such a fortune would tempt the holiest of men.

'Have you told the Maharaja anything yet?'

'I sent a telegram saying that our representative would be with him in a few days' time.' He chewed his lower lip. 'I don't know yet *what* we send him, however.'

Their gate was opened by the chowkidar, who had been watching for them, and the whole family and staff swooped upon them.

Old Desai creaked slowly down from the carriage. He picked up his silent, wide-eyed, little granddaughter. 'Papa is coming home in two days' time,' he announced to her, 'and I think Aunt should get the tailor to stitch you a new dress for the occasion.'

The child smiled and relaxed, her head on his shoulder. Dear Grandpapa.

Chapter Thirty-three

'I wish your father would make up his mind when the marriage is to take place. Everything is upset. The astrologer says he can't find a better day than was originally arranged. Now it's got to be changed, and the wedding invitations have the wrong date on them,' Aunt grumbled to Anasuyabehn.

Anasuyabehn hardly heard her. The boy servant had just returned from his visit to the hostel. She could see him through the window, cowering in a corner of the compound, apparently afraid to enter the house.

'Your father said that it was your future father-in-law who wanted the date brought forward,' chimed in the visiting aunt.

'I should imagine that the tailors will need at least another three weeks to finish the stitching,' interpolated the eldest cousin. She was stroking, with avaricious fingers, a gift of three silk saris still sitting amid its wrappings on the floor.

Aunt pursued the subject of the change of date. 'I don't quite know what the fuss is about,' she admitted. 'Mahadev has not yet returned from Delhi.' She wondered if there were any truth in the rumour she had heard that he had disappeared, but felt it wise to keep that to herself. She turned again to Anasuyabehn. 'Immediately after your marriage you are to go to a place called Paris in England – very strange to me – in my day, you would have remained at your father-in-law's house.'

'Ji, hun,' agreed Anasuyabehn. She went to the window. 'Bhai,' she called to the servant. 'Hurry up, now. Light the stove on the veranda for me, and put some water on for the lentils. I'll be out in a minute.'

'Let me help,' offered a younger cousin, who had taken a great liking to Anasuyabehn.

'No, no. The boy will do most of the work – I must just guide him.' She made an effort to smile at the golden-faced girl, and, after a little while, made her escape to the side veranda, where she could already hear the fire crackling in its little stove.

'Gone away?' she exclaimed to the boy, as he handed back her note.

'Yes.'

'Who told you?'

'A lady next door.'

'Did she see the letter?'

'No, Bahin.'

'Good boy.' Her whole body trembled with fear and, again, before her eyes danced the calm face of the monk, the all-seeing eyes ripping her secrets from her. Bad actions brought bad results. Had Tilak fled because she was already affianced? How cruel could men be? He had promised – and he had failed her.

She held on to an old water-pot stand for support, as the veranda whirled around her. She felt trapped, like a ground squirrel cornered by dogs. Until Tilak came striding into it, her life had seemed useless and empty. Now, he was gone like fluff on the wind, without a word to her. Spasms of pain shot through her and perspiration poured down her face.

Her cousin wandered through the door from the kitchen. 'Bahin!' she cried in alarm and ran to her. She put her arms round the swaying girl, while the servant squatting by the fire watched nervously.

'I'm all right,' murmured Anasuyabehn through clenched teeth, '. . . heat made me faint.'

'I'll get mother,' said the girl.

'No,' cried Anasuyabehn sharply. 'I'll sit down – it's only heat.'

Her cousin lowered her carefully to the floor and she leaned her head against the cool stone of the water-pot stand. Her cousin took the water-ladle from its hook and filled a brass jar with water. She then dipped her sari end into it and, kneeling down by her, she dabbed Anasuyabehn's face with it.

The cold water revived her and she surreptitiously slipped her note to Tilak into her waistband, under cover of her sari. Then she very gratefully put her arms round her cousin and leaned her head on her shoulder. Her cousin, mystified but sympathetic, held the trembling bride-to-be, and instructed the servant to get on with his work.

'Let me ask mother to come,' she begged Anasuyabehn, after a few minutes.

'Don't worry. I stayed too long in the sun this morning, talking to Savitri.' Her courage came slowly back to her and she again was able to put on her armour of patient amiability, so that her cousin was finally convinced that, indeed, nothing much was wrong.

Chapter Thirty-four

A week later, Mahadev Desai, accompanied by several members of his family, came to the Dean's home for a little ceremony. Some fruit and a green stick were solemnly buried in a hole which was to hold one of the supporting poles of the wedding tent. The story of his adventures had preceded him and, with his arm in a sling, he was looked upon as something of a hero. He was unusually pale and moved about very carefully. He was allowed to see his bride-to-be at the ceremony, but did not get much chance to speak to her. After the visitors had had tea and departed, three carpenters took over the compound and proceeded to dig holes all over it for the remainder of the supporting poles.

Their activities impeded the delivery of sacks of grain, sugar and pulses and tins of vegetable oil, all of which the Dean had had to buy on the black market, because some were rationed and some were in very short supply. He and Aunt, therefore, went to the big storeroom to see the stuff weighed. They already had a house full of guests and, closer to the wedding day, would have to feed many more, including the Desai contingent. To accommodate everybody, a house down the road had been rented.

There was a lot of gossip amongst his current guests on the pros and cons of the marriage; such things were always picked over and examined in detail in families. But it was public gossip which was worrying Aunt, as she scolded the coolies for being clumsy.

That morning, the Vice-Chancellor's ayah had dropped in to pay her respects. The ayah always knew a lot about the doings on campus, so Aunt had edged her away from the visitors and back to the compound gate, while they talked. The ayah was simply breathless to confirm with her that what she had just heard was not true and that the wedding was, indeed, going forward. She felt it her duty to inform Aunt that there was a rumour that Anasuyabehn was expecting by Dr Tilak and that he would be forced to marry her. Aunt had been shocked to her very sandals, had scolded her and sent her packing with instructions to deny such a calumny everywhere.

Anasuyabehn was not with child, that, at least, Aunt was sure of. Only last week she had kept the three days of retirement from cooking and other household tasks, which she had kept ever since she was fourteen. And Aunt had herself dispatched the bloody clouts to the Untouchable washerman. As for her virginity, that was another matter. And Aunt was very apprehensive about this.

Anasuyabehn had done obediently everything she was required to do in connection with the marriage. The whole family had, on Mahadev's return, been to dinner at his house and the girl had sat quietly with the women who would be her in-laws. Mahadev's little daughter had been brought to her during the meal, and she had persuaded the child to sit with her and had fed her with food from her own tali. According to the Dean, this had pleased old Desai greatly when he heard about it. Mahadev had put in a limited appearance because he was still quite weak, but he had smiled on his bride when she arrived. But would he, quaked Aunt, smile if he had been cheated?

She picked up a paper which was being blown about in the draught, her mind elsewhere. She could not read, so she handed it to the Dean. 'Is this a receipt we should keep?' she inquired.

The Dean, who was tired, unfolded it impatiently and glanced down at it. His expression changed and he closed his hand over it quickly. 'Come into the study,' he commanded Aunt. Puzzled, she followed him. 'What's up?' she asked.

The Dean closed the door after them. 'Where did you find this?'

Aunt shrugged. 'It was on the floor. What is it?'

'Beloved,' read the Dean, a break in his voice. 'Meet me at the far end of Riverside Park tonight. I will wait from 9 till 11.'

Aunt felt sick. On top of what she had heard that morning, this was too much to bear. What could she say? The hope of being regarded as the family's finest matchmaker suddenly vanished, with all the delights that such a reputation would bring. Instead, she heard the sniggers of the womenfolk and the dirty jokes of the young men. Somehow the Desai marriage had to be saved.

'Is it signed?' she asked, to give herself time to think.

'No. I know the handwriting, though. It's quite distinctive.'

'Whose is it?'

The Dean looked very grim. 'It's Professor Tilak's. He and Anasuyabehn – I would never have dreamed of it!'

I might have done, thought Aunt, if I'd thought about it. With an effort, she asked, 'Is it addressed to her?'

'No.'

'Then it may belong to one of her cousins.'

The Dean disagreed. 'I doubt if they've even met him.'

Suddenly he pounded his desk with his fist. 'The stupid girl!' he shouted. 'Bring her to me *quietly* – before that mob outside realizes that anything is wrong.'

Aunt hurried to Anasuyabehn's room. Before opening the door, she slowed to her usual shuffle. Anasuyabehn was seated cross-legged on her bed with three cousins and Savitri. Curled up together, they were chattering amiably. Anasuyabehn was listening, her deepset eyes ringed with black, her mouth drooping.

How ill she looks, thought Aunt. Not at all like a girl about to be a bride. And all Aunt's misgivings returned.

As she approached the girls, she forced herself to smile. 'Your father wants you in his study, niece. Run along, now.'

Anasuyabehn slipped off the bed and hastily smoothed her hair and hitched up her sari. Since the safe return of Mahadev, she had steeled herself to face the fact that Tilak had deserted her and that she must marry the big, widowed moneylender.

The pain of Tilak's leaving her was almost more than she could bear. It ate into her like an acid, an unbelievable anguish. She felt removed from events around her; everything seemed distant and unreal. The slightly smutty jokes her cousins had been making seemed sickening to her; she could not laugh.

The only person who impinged upon her understanding was Mahadev himself. His first task upon his return had been to call upon her, despite the agony of being jolted along in his carriage. They had faced each other, not knowing what to say in front of their relations, she resentful, he longing. Through her misery, she had realized that within him lay a powerful personality; he was not to be trifled with.

When she had been to dinner at the Desai Society, he had found a moment in the bustle of departure to hold her hand. She had looked up in astonishment at the firm, warm touch, her first physical contact with him. He had laughed down at her and she had caught a glimpse of a man instead of a moneylender. She had been afraid.

As she entered her father's study, closely followed by Aunt, she inquired politely, 'Ji?'

She was shocked, when he shouted at her, 'What's the meaning of this?' and thrust a sheet of paper at her.

Bewildered, she took it from him. It was worn at the corners and must have been lying about for days. She bent her head and read it.

Her first reaction was one of overwhelming joy. So he had tried to communicate with her. A singing happiness made her giddy for a moment. She kept her eyes on the missive. The paper was much handled. When had it been written? Of course! He had been in the Riverside Gardens with her. The joy faded, but she held on to the paper tightly – it was part of him.

'Well,' snapped her father.

The desire to protect Tilak was instantaneous, and with elaborate care she lifted her eyes to her father. She made her eyes twinkle and her lips curve in a smile. 'We seem to have stumbled on somebody's little romance – where did it come from?'

Aunt was watching her intently. She's clever, she thought, but not quite clever enough. That letter is hers, all right.

She continued to stare out of the corner in which she squatted, as the Dean, his burst of temper unexpectedly checked, asked, 'Well, isn't it yours?'

'I've never seen it before,' replied Anasuyabehn quite truthfully. 'It's very old. I wonder where it came from – it isn't even signed.'

'Oh, I know who wrote it – the writing is unmistakable.'

'Who?' asked Anasuyabehn, ignoring her father's angry frustration.

'That doesn't concern you, daughter, since you say it is not a letter to you. If it's not yours . . .' He glared at her. 'Then the wind must have blown it in.'

'We've had a great many visitors, including the Desai family,' Anasuyabehn pointed out. 'Any of the younger women could have dropped it.'

The Dean was stopped in his tracks. 'Of course,' he muttered. 'Of course.' He sat down in his chair and tapped his fingers on the desk, while Anasuyabehn waited politely. 'I'm glad that you have not done anything despicable.'

'What she says is very likely,' Aunt interjected, and Anasuyabehn was grateful for the unexpected support.

The distant buzz of talk from relations on the veranda suddenly ceased, as if it had been switched off. Aunt looked towards the door of the room, as if she would love to go to investigate.

Outside, an English voice asked for Dean Mehta.

'Dr Bennett!' exclaimed the Dean. Then he sighed. 'This note is not yours?'

'No, father.' Anasuyabehn hated to lie to her father, but could not find any other safe answer. She turned to go.

There was a knock on the study door. The servant showed John in.

He was carrying a parcel and stood diffidently blocking the doorway, not realizing Anasuyabehn's frantic need to escape.

'I've . . . er . . . um,' he began, and looked down at Anasuyabehn. God, how ill the girl looked and almost as if she were going to cry. 'I've brought a little something for Anasuyabehn, if she may accept it. I – er brought it myself, because I was afraid any other carrier might drop it.'

He did not add that he had in his pocket a letter which had far more import to her. Tilak was a damned pest to leave him such a job. He had racked his brains for days to find a way to get the letter to Anasuyabehn, but no opportunity had presented itself. If he had posted it, he knew that the Dean would automatically open it and read it himself, before giving it to his daughter.

Now, on his desk at home, lay his invitation to her wedding reception. And he did not know what else to do, other than buy her a present and watch her marry a man she did not want to marry. Poor kid. She would get over it, he supposed; Mahadev was no fool and presumably knew a bit about managing a woman. He hoped that when Tilak heard the news of the wedding being hastened, he would not blow out his brains.

Caught between loyalty to his old mentor, the Dean, and affection for Tilak, he now stood in the middle of the Dean's study, a box of fine English china in his arms, sensing that he had stumbled in on some kind of domestic crisis.

Dean Mehta was the first to regain his equilibrium. 'Come in, come in. You shouldn't put yourself out on our behalf.' He watched, with growing astonishment, as John walked slowly, but quite straightly, to his desk to put the parcel down. 'You're not using your stick,' he exclaimed.

John grinned with satisfaction. 'Trying to manage without it. I left it parked on the veranda.'

'Well, well. That's excellent. Anasuyabehn, bring a chair for Dr Bennett.'

Anasuyabehn pushed a chair up behind him, and John sat down rather suddenly.

He smiled up at the careworn girl. 'I've brought you an English tea service,' he told her. 'I know the family will shower you with all kinds of beautiful things, but I thought you might enjoy some china – something different.'

Anasuyabehn shyly thanked him.

'May I wish you much happiness,' he said gently.

As if in unbearable pain, her creamy eyelids half-closed, while she nodded a polite acquiescence. John cursed himself for being a clumsy clod; yet he knew that he could not tell her father. Either she or Tilak must speak up.

Anasuyabehn had turned back to her father, 'May I be excused, father? Savitri is waiting for me.'

Her father, his hands clasped on his desk, nodded absently. She said thank you in English to John and went quietly out of the room. Aunt slid after her, making a polite namaste towards John as she passed him. He jumped, not having noticed her presence.

Savitri! Why hadn't he thought of her before? A thoroughly modern woman, who drove her own car and was liable to shock everybody by talking about trial marriages. He was certain she was tolerated in the Dean's house only because her father was a Professor Emeritus. She and Anasuyabehn were great friends – and she was smart.

Whether Anasuyabehn was actually married to Mahadev or whether she was not, she was, John argued, entitled to receive any correspondence addressed to her. Thin, bespectacled Savitri would enjoy being the messenger. Who knows? he reflected. Tilak just might be able to turn the tables, in an honourable and decent way.

And in Bombay, Tilak pleaded for Anasuyabehn before a sardonically amused uncle and a bewildered, affectionate mother. 'You could telephone the Dean at the University,' he begged.

Chapter Thirty-five

The Desai business was too large to be totally neglected during the week before the wedding. Old Desai, Partner Uncle and Mahadev, therefore, stayed in the Desai Society, while the rest of the family moved over to the house rented by Dr Mehta for his guests.

Mahadev had had a trying time commuting between the Society and the Mehtas' home, to attend the various ceremonies preceding the actual wedding day. Though his head ached abominably and his left arm was still in a sling to protect the shoulder while it healed, his paternal aunt had insisted, at one of the ceremonies, that he must have the traditional iron ring tied into his hair. It seemed that every time he lay down, he lay on the ring. He wished passionately that the Mission doctor had shaved his head completely, when preparing to stitch up his wound; instead the doctor had considered that he might be a Hindu and had, therefore, kindly left one longish tuft, to which the ring had been appended.

His father and his Partner Uncle had spent weary hours with him discussing the expansion of the French business. They were all agreed that, in these uncertain times, they should have some money invested outside India.

In one of the earlier marriage ceremonies, he had sat in the flapping marriage tent, with a silent, veiled Anasuyabehn beside him, and had hardly glanced at Ganesh, the benign elephant-headed god, remover of hindrances, who was being worshipped. His mind had been filled with the legal difficulties of the French investment, so much so that he had jumped when a lucky woman, taking four pieces of wood and dipping them in oil, had touched his forehead with them. Then the ring had been tied into his hair.

Ceremonial gifts of rupees had been given to him and to Anasuyabehn. Other money gifts had also been presented by relatives, to be kept until after the ceremony, when they would be divided between his and Anasuyabehn's paternal aunts.

A company of elderly Jains had been specially invited for the later ceremonies; they would inspect the quality and the quantity of the wedding gifts.

Mahadev sighed frequently. Though the marriage festivities would be briefer than those for his first marriage, they were time consuming. It was well that he had been able to get plane reservations for Paris for the second day after the vows had been completed.

Gradually, however, as the day of the actual wedding came closer and his health improved, his mind turned towards his bride and he began to think of the pleasures of again having a wife. He dearly wished to please her and to see her eventually installed in a modern house of her own, where his little daughter might thrive better and have brothers and sisters. He never doubted that Anasuyabehn would care for the child, and in this he was correct.

One morning, he had to compose convincing arguments to persuade the Government of India to allow an overseas investment, and when he finally put down his pen, it was with a feeling of relief that he had done it skilfully. He sat in his dreary office, feeling wells of hopeful anticipation rise in him. He collected up his papers and at the same time began to sing a morning raga. The clerks in the counting house lifted their heads in amazement, as the strains of this devotional hymn came rolling out of the private office.

With a fine disregard for his comfort, Mahadev's brother had been ordered to oversee the wedding party at Dean Mehta's rented house and to travel back and forth daily to supervise the counting house. Now, while Mahadev carolled away in his room, in another little office his younger brother was inquiring of his father, 'What are we going to do about the Maharaja's jewels? I sent a telegram saying we would send another messenger. But what are we to do now?' His plump face creased with anxiety.

His father leaned back on the sausage-shaped pillows of his divan. 'Humph. Didn't Partner Uncle tell you? We shall indeed dispatch another messenger. You're going to go – and take the stones with you.'

He watched in quiet amusement, as his son's weak mouth opened in surprise. There was also a gleam of fear in the younger man's eyes – he knew he was no hero, and he dreaded violence of any kind.

'You'll go by plane – in spite of the cost,' his father assured him.

'But we haven't got the jewels?'

'Oh, yes, we have,' the old man chuckled. 'I put them in the strongroom myself.'

Relief replaced anxiety. 'But . . . but . . .'

Old Desai wagged his finger at his son. 'Your brother's sagacity is something to emulate.'

The younger man appeared to shrink into himself. The small button eyes almost vanished amid the folds of fat. The chin sank down to the chest and the chubby fingers were clenched. So the almighty Mahadev had done something wonderful again.

'What did he do?' he inquired dully.

Old Desai clasped his hands over his stomach. 'Well, it was interesting. Your uncle and I were sitting by the bed at the Mission, wondering how to broach the subject of the missing money belt in front of a constable, who was still there. We didn't want to accuse anyone of taking it, and find we had a libel suit on our hands. Anyway, when Mahadev was dressed and ready to be discharged from the hospital, he sat on the edge of the bed, to rest himself before making the further effort of going to the carriage.' Desai ran his tongue round his few remaining teeth, while he looked at his dejected younger son.

'Well?'

'He was quite clever. When the Mission doctor entered the room, he looked at him and said, "I'm ready to put on my money belt now. Will you kindly fetch it for me?"'

The younger brother was intrigued. 'What happened?'

'The doctor replied, "Certainly." And then he went to get it.'

'How extraordinary!'

'Yes, it was. If he had not intended to keep it – if he could – the Mission doctor would surely have mentioned to Mahadev that his valuables were being kept in safety. With his simple request, Mahadev gave the impression that he remembered the belt being removed from him by the doctor.'

The brother sighed, and old Desai glanced again at him. In comparison with Mahadev, the boy was dull. He was, however, extremely useful; he dealt with all the irritating details of the business. Old Desai thought suddenly of the Maharaja and his brand new radio factory. The Maharaja might be willing to pay an experienced accountant very well, to come to him. And all over India new enterprises were springing up which needed more than an abacus-rattling clerk to keep their accounts; his younger son might easily plunge into a new life, away from his family.

Old Desai did not like these ideas; the boy was flesh of his flesh; he did not want to lose him.

He picked up a memo pad from the portable desk beside him on the divan, and unscrewed his fountain pen. As he addressed his son, he wrote down each point. 'Now that you have reached years of discretion,' he said, as if he had been patiently waiting for his younger offspring to grow up, 'I shall put more responsibilities on your shoulders. I can no longer travel, as I used to, and your uncle is also feeling the strain. This Delhi trip will be the first of many for you, for Mahadev has, in addition to his other responsibilities, to watch the Paris and Bombay businesses.'

He could almost feel the relief shooting through his son's veins. Just to get away from his wife, thought the old man grimly, would probably cheer him up. And to travel on a plane was definitely prestigious. Though it pained him to say it, he added, 'And you will need to draw more money in future.'

The plump figure ceased to slump. It expanded to its full girth. Dignity descended upon him like a new garment slipped over his head. As a trusted representative of the family, always bustling off to new places, he would at last be able to patronize his wife.

As expected, the Desais had not yet paid their hospital bill. The medical missionary, however, knelt by his bed and thanked the Lord for removing the temptation of the money belt. The muttered prayers ceased for a minute or two, while the sorely tried worshipper rested his head on his string bed. Then, in an almost businesslike voice, he again addressed his God, 'And now, Lord, about some funds. The need of your children is terrible. Must they suffer so?'

Perhaps God heard, for about that time some ladies in California met together and, for the sake of something to do to fill their spare time, decided to have a fund-raising drive to extend the Mission of Holiness near Shahpur in India.

Chapter Thirty-six

Though Savitri and her parents, being Hindus, had not been asked to Anasuyabehn's wedding, they were, like John Bennett, invited to a reception to be held after it. Because she was a close friend, however, Savitri came and went freely in the house. Her thin scornful voice mocked the ancient ceremonies, until Anasuyabehn asked her wearily to cease.

Though Savitri's eyes were myopic, they missed little. She had guessed from Anasuyabehn's lack of enthusiasm that her friend was not very keen on the marriage. She had suggested that if Anasuyabehn was not happy she should refuse the offer. Anasuyabehn had said dryly that she had not been given much opportunity to do so; everything had been fixed before she was consulted. When Savitri mentioned this to her own parents, they had ordered her to hold her tongue; Dean Mehta knew what he was doing. Rather cowed by her parents' joint outrage at her attempted intervention, she had obeyed.

Her spirits crushed by Tilak's apparent desertion, Anasuyabehn wanted to curl up in some secret lair and never come out again. But she was being carried along by events and had no one to trust, except her father. She clung to the idea that the reward of filial obedience was a well-ordered and contented life. Clutching at this frail hope, she complied with all her aunt's requests. In any case, what use was there in fighting when there was no one for whom to fight?

She had spent one night seething with rage and frustration, asking herself madly why Tilak should so suddenly vanish. Involved in the preparations for the marriage within the two families, she had not heard the rumours as to the cause of his quick departure. It had naturally not occurred to her father or the Vice-Chancellor to tell her the exact reasons.

The white light of morning had brought a dawn of commonsense. Tilak was an honourable man. Perhaps he had left her because she was already affianced and, anyway, of another religion and caste. The furious temper was curbed, the burning desire held down. She bowed her head and told herself, without much hope, that true happiness was to be found in a loyal partnership with a man chosen by one's parents.

On her wedding morning, she submitted quietly to the ministrations of her cousins and aunts. They bathed her, washed and oiled her hair and plaited it with flowers. With great care, her eldest cousin knelt before her and painted her face with delicate flower designs. Another one stained the palms of her hands and the soles of her feet a soft orange. Finally, they wrapped her in a fine red silk sari embroidered with gold thread.

Before they pulled the sari end down over her face, they brought her a mirror, so that she could admire herself. She looked into its shiny depths and saw a stranger, a very glamorous one. She looked at the image expressionlessly; then she thought of Tilak seeing her when the veil would be lifted, and her lips curved in a gentle smile. The smile faded. Bitter tears welled up and coursed unrestrainedly down her cheeks, to spoil the paint and to trickle over the large, glittering nose-ring and fall like small diamonds into her lap.

The cousins laughed and mopped up the tears. They touched up the painted flowers and agreed that everybody cried when they had to leave their home.

'When you've got a little son in your arms, you'll be truly happy,' Aunt assured her.

Dressed in their best, the families were waiting in the compound. She had, therefore, to compose herself and join them in worship, her face mercifully veiled.

Fourteen young girls were merrily feasted. Armed with gifts of wheat, dates and coconuts, they then streamed down the lane, where a potter awaited them. He cheerfully supplied them with four water-pots.

The fun of a wedding overflowed the compound and spread around the neighbourhood. Little groups of servants, sweepers and village people on their way to town stood in the lane, to glimpse what they could of the fine clothes and jewellery. At the side of the house, the caterers built up their great charcoal fires again and again, and sweated and shouted and turned out innumerable sweetmeats and savouries.

In the storeroom, the Dean's younger brother, with a couple of nephews to assist him, doled out sugar, nuts, flour, spices, oil and vegetables, with a sure hand, seeing that nothing was wasted or stolen, and that yoghurt and water were kept cool and not spilled.

A small band of musicians drummed and squeaked in a corner, their well-practised efforts often lost under the babble of dozens of voices.

The Brahmin, who would officiate at the actual marriage rites after sunset, was fed and fussed over, his shaven head and gnarled hands gesturing a polite 'No', as his palm leaf plate was heaped higher and higher.

The Dean wished that his daughter's wedding should be a joyous occasion. He sailed amongst his guests, greeting them jovially, giving no hint of his inward worry about Anasuyabehn, with whom he had spent an uncomfortable half-hour the evening before. In response to his forecasts of a happy family life, she had responded sadly with a simple, 'Yes, father.' He hoped sincerely that Mahadev knew enough to make her happy.

Meanwhile, in the rented house, a slightly abashed Mahadev was submitting to other ceremonies. Still clucking about the mess his shorn head was in, his paternal aunt replaced the iron ring attached to his topknot with a silver one. With suggestive jokes, the barber washed and powdered one of his toes. A group of giggling young women swooped on him and fed him with sweets.

His friends then helped him mount a decorated horse. His shoulder objected strongly to the exercise, and he winced. As they rode to the temple to worship, they chaffed him that he was lucky the dacoits had left him able to consummate the marriage.

In a splendid procession of cars, horses and pedestrians, he was taken from the temple to Anasuyabehn's home. His heart beat furiously under his silk shirt, and he hoped the girl would like the jewellery he had bought her.

The sun was going down, as they went through the streets. Women and children lolled on the little verandas above the shop fronts, as they waited for the evening breeze to come rippling down the ovenlike, smelly streets. On the pavements, their menfolk squatted idly, smoking and gossiping after their evening meal.

The flickering lights of the procession brought everyone to their feet. At one corner, a beggar in the crowd stood and cursed. He shook his fist at the bridegroom. The bystanders laughed at him; they knew him well. He was harmlessly crazy. They knew he hated the Desais because they had foreclosed on his little shoe shop and forced him into beggary; but, then, none of them liked moneylenders.

As gold and silver trimmed saris, gold bracelets and jewelled necklaces glimmered in the beams of the car headlights, the watchers admired unrestrainedly. They sniffed appreciatively, as waves of flower perfume passed over them from the multitude of garlands carried in the procession. The men admired the horses and the shining cars. Except for that of the beggar, there was no animosity at the display of wealth; they enjoyed the spectacle and never thought of it in relation to their own pressing needs. The Desais, however, were not very trusting. The walking ladies were confined within heavy ropes carried on either side of the procession by their servants and younger male members of the family. Nobody was given the chance to snatch at so much as an earring.

In the centre of it, Mahadev, his pain soothed by aspirin, his spirits high, enjoyed the pomp of his wedding day. Unhaunted by thoughts of his first wife, for whom he had gone through the same performance, it was as if he went to his first marriage. This time, he told himself, he was marrying for love, and he knew a great content from the thought of it.

The compound had seemed quite full before the advent of the Desai party. Now it was jammed. Space was somehow made, however, for the bridegroom to make his way to the bungalow, where a crushed Anasuyabehn sat dully behind a curtain.

As required, she spat betel juice at him, while her maternal aunt, in lieu of her dead mother, marked him with auspicious marks and threw little balls of rice and ashes over him. The aunt then waved a vessel of water over his head, managing not to splash his magnificent, flower-bedecked, silk turban.

From behind the thin curtain and her shrouding red sari, Anasuyabehn watched him out of the corner of her eye. He looked very fine in his bridegroom's clothes, and there was nothing about him to which she could truthfully object, except that he was not Tilak.

Escorted by their relations, the couple were now taken through the stifling March heat, to the marriage tent. There, a committee of leading Jains awaited them in festive mood. Mahadev's friends brought forward his gifts to the bride and laid them before these gentlemen, who rapidly totted up their value, were greatly impressed by it and announced that the gifts were most generous. The gifts were then handed over to the bride's friends.

Mahadev and Anasuyabehn were seated side by side and shook hands with each other. Under the stare of so many witnesses, Mahadev did not dare give Anasuyabehn's hand a hearty squeeze; he had to content himself with a light shake. The end of her sari was then tied to his scarf.

One of his friends brought him a box, which he handed to Anasuyabehn. When she opened it, her aunts leaned forward eagerly to view its contents. Rings and bracelets of solid gold made them gasp enviously.

With his face aglow, Dean Mehta brought his offering for his beloved daughter. Iridescent saris, blouse lengths and petticoat lengths to match, a finely-wrought gold necklace, more gold bracelets. Anasuyabehn had never owned so much in all her life. Father has spent too much, she fretted, and wondered if he would have enough money to retire on; then she remembered that he would need no money. As a monk he would need nothing, not even her. She would have no one to turn to – except her husband. She sighed a little sobbing sigh. Hearing her, Mahadev turned quickly towards her but could see nothing but the vague glimmer of her face behind the silk.

In the half-light of the oil lamps, old Desai seemed to float towards his son. Aided by an ancient cousin, he washed one of his son's hands; Anasuyabehn's maternal aunt did the same for her. She then placed Anasuyabehn's hand in that of the groom. Mahadev cheerfully held on firmly and, despite her depression, Anasuyabehn was forced to take cognisance of the fact that the man sitting by her was real, with needs to which she must give attention. She began to tremble and Mahadev, feeling it, massaged her palm gently with his fingers. He tugged her to her feet and they solemnly circumvented the flickering fire before which they had been sitting. Four times, left to right, they paced together, while lucky women pressed forward to receive sopari nuts from Mahadev; thus must husband and wife walk together equally, like oxen, pulling the wagon of life.

Sweets cooked by a Brahmin were offered to the couple and were formally refused.

They walked together into the house, where worship was offered to Anasuyabehn's gotrija, her kinsmen of lineal and collateral descent from a common ancestor.

The couple were, next, to go in procession to the rented house for a similar ceremony in honour of the bridegroom's ancestry. The day had been a long one and, before setting out, Anasuyabehn whispered rather frantically to her maternal aunt, and was given permission to go to the bathroom, escorted by her favourite young cousin.

The sweeper's door into the bathroom had been left open for ventilation and, when she went to close it, she saw to her astonishment Savitri standing hesitantly on the field path.

'Hey, Bahin,' cried Savitri, stumbling towards her along the rough path.

'Hurry up,' whispered her cousin, from the other side of the door which led into the house.

'Anasuyabehn,' panted Savitri, keeping her voice low. 'I've been trying for two days to get you alone – and now I don't know what to do – it's the letter.'

'What letter?' Anasuyabehn pushed her veil back from her eyes, so as to see her friend's troubled face more clearly.

'From you know whom – John Bennett gave it to me – he couldn't deliver it himself – though he said he called on you.'

Anasuyabehn remembered John bringing the box of china himself. By all the gods who ever reigned, he had had a letter to deliver! The trembling which had begun in the compound became a helpless shake.

'Give it me.'

'Come on,' urged her cousin and opened the other door.

Savitri ignored the young girl and took the letter from under her sari.

It smelled faintly of her perfume and Dr Bennett's tobacco, and the envelope was quite dirty.

Ignoring her watching cousin, Anasuyabehn tore open the envelope, her fingers clumsy. The cousin pressed forward, but a glare from behind Savitri's heavy spectacles made her shrink back.

And so the screw was turned once more.

The gentle, courteous words and promises, so quickly penned, seemed to hit her under the heart. The pain was so intense that she cried out, before she fell fainting into Savitri's skinny arms.

The shocked little cousin rushed forward and together they half dragged, half lifted, Anasuyabehn into the passage. The younger girl opened her mouth to call her mother, but Savitri was made of sterner stuff, and whispered, 'Shut up. Wet your hankie under the lavatory tap – quick.'

The cousin obeyed.

The touch of the water on Anasuyabehn's face failed to bring her round. Her aunts could be heard calling to her to hurry. There was a shuffle of footsteps on the veranda. Savitri rose, and ran towards the footsteps, while the frightened cousin pillowed Anasuyabehn's head in her lap.

A bevy of ladies hurried into the passage, calling, 'Hurry up!' In the background, Mahadev inquired if anything was wrong.

Savitri composed herself and said quietly to the first lady, 'Anasuyabehn has fainted. It must have been the heat and the excitement.'

The little cousin discreetly slipped the note from under Anasuyabehn's trailing veil and stuffed it down her blouse. She had no idea what the letter was about, except that it must be most important to Anasuyabehn. With thumping heart, she gave way to Aunt and wrapped her sari loosely round herself, to hide the telltale bulge.

Between them, the ladies got Anasuyabehn on to her bed and crowded round her, chattering anxiously, while word spread in the compound that the bride had been taken ill. 'A bad omen,' muttered one old lady to another.

Dean Mehta, old Desai and Mahadev pushed their way into the crowded room. To give the patient air, the Dean ordered that the room be cleared, except for the three gentlemen, Aunt and Mahadev's aunt. This was done, though the little cousin continued to stand, unremarked, by the head of the bed. Savitri had considered it prudent to sidle quietly out of the house through the sweeper's door.

A lota of water was brought by the boy servant and Aunt sponged her face. After a few minutes, the eyelids fluttered under their smudged paint – and closed again, as she realized her predicament. She was now legally married to Mahadev – and, far away in Bombay, Tilak was trying to start negotiations to marry her; he had not deserted her, he had not run away. He loved her and she loved him. Waves of grief broke over her, as if someone had died, and she sobbed helplessly before her astonished relatives.

How many times do we die in our lives, she wondered, our spirits crushed and broken? And yet the body lives on.

The marriage garland round his neck withering in the heat, Mahadev could bear the sobs no longer. Regardless of convention, he pushed Aunt away. Kneeling by her bedside, he took her hand and himself massaged it gently to get the circulation going. At first Anasuyabehn neither knew nor cared whose hand held hers, whose fingers carefully rubbed her wrists. It was, nevertheless, comforting, as if someone, at least, realized her suffering. Eventually, the weeping ceased. She lay with eyes closed, while Aunt leaned over and gently wiped the wet cheeks.

Her eyelids felt heavy, too heavy to open, but Mahadev waited patiently, and, finally, she did open them, to come face to face with the anxiety and fear clearly mirrored in his usually cold, intelligent eyes. Dimly she knew that, of all the people gathered round her, Mahadev cared the most – and Mahadev was innocent – he had not done anything that contributed to her predicament; she had received nothing but kindnesses from him. 'I'm sorry,' she said, and closed her eyes again.

Old Desai and Dr Mehta were relieved to see her come round, and began in hurried whispers to debate what they should do. Aunt interposed to say that the wedding must go on, as soon as Anasuyabehn was a little recovered; it would be too unlucky otherwise.

Anasuyabehn felt so tired that all she wanted was to be left alone. But Mahadev was there, still rubbing her hands. With a great effort, she swallowed her tears, opened her eyes again, and said that, if she could have a very hot, strong cup of tea, she thought she could go on – the time taken to prepare it, she argued, would give her a few minutes of rest.

Mahadev laughed out loud with relief. He whispered that she could have the whole of Gujerat if she wanted it. She made her lips smile.

The tea was made, the guests reassured, and, by the light of the moon, they set out in procession for the house rented by Dean Mehta. Laden with sweets, dates, money and the kernels of four coconuts, the Mehtas returned home exhausted, to go to bed for the remainder of the night.

The following evening, shaken but composed, Anasuyabehn sat quietly amongst her cousins, while the committee of eminent Jains inspected further gifts from her family. Then alms were distributed to an eager crowd of beggars and saddhus waiting at the compound gate.

Normally, the guests would have been feasted for several more days, but Mahadev had to go to Paris, so, to the sound of steady drum beats, Anasuyabehn dipped her hand in red powder and marked the house walls with the imprint of her palm. In the marriage tent, she impressed an auspicious mark on Mahadev's brother's forehead, making the gesture very respectful and leaving him beaming contentedly. Someone handed her yet another sari, and she wondered vaguely how many dozen she now owned. A coconut was put into her hand and, with Mahadev smiling down at her, she stepped into his carriage. Another coconut was put under the wheels of the carriage and the vehicle jolted over it to break it. The pieces were then offered to her, with four sweetmeats and two brass vessels.

The driver whipped up the horse. Cars and carriages slid out before and behind them. In procession, they made their way into the old part of the town to the Desai Society.

'This is it,' she thought numbly. 'In that old house they will have prepared a bed covered with rose petals and I will sit on it and Mahadev Desai and I will be alone for the first time.' She knew what to expect and she felt dull and lifeless. She could feel the warmth of her husband's thigh against hers, and she turned towards him instinctively. 'Don't be afraid,' he told her gently. 'Everything will be all right.'

At home, the Dean looked at the imprint of his daughter's hand and prayed for her. Then he went to say farewell to most of the guests, pressing some to stay a few days more. He did not yet want to be alone.

In the hopelessly untidy kitchen, deserted for the moment, Anasuyabehn's faithful little cousin surreptitiously read Tilak's letter. Through the crumpled paper, she saw Anasuyabehn's face, so colourless, so dead, her lips hardly moving as she forced herself to say, 'Burn it.' To the young girl it was as if something in the new bride had burned with a mighty flame and was now cold ashes, and the youngster trembled with fear of love not yet experienced.

She struck a match, lit the letter and held it in her hand until it was reduced to a tiny corner of paper attached to curling, black embers. Then she dropped it into the ash-choked charcoal brazier.

Chapter Thirty-seven

On the morning after Anasuyabehn's departure, Aunt stood on the veranda and surveyed the appalling muddle. Pieces of tissue paper, palm leaves, withered flowers and garlands, two pieces of cloth flapping loose from the marriage tent, a pair of chuppells abandoned on the steps; behind her, in the kitchen, a mass of teacups and glasses to be washed, and unsorted laundry to be dealt with, seven house guests still to be fed, and a reception for some thirty people to be arranged for that evening. The last item, thank goodness, would be dealt with by the caterers and her younger brother; she could already hear him talking to two of the cooks; and Dean Mehta, she supposed rather sourly, was probably at his devotions. Lucky for some people that they had so much time for prayer and meditation; she herself had to be content with hastily repeated mantras as she made the morning fire.

The postman, his khaki uniform already black with sweat, picked his way through the debris and handed her the morning's letters.

Although she could not read, she recognized amongst them the handwriting of a great-uncle who had been invited to the wedding. What a mercy that old windbag was too old to travel, a walking gossip column, who would have smelled out the rumour about Anasuyabehn and would have retailed it on every veranda between Shahpur and Calcutta. She sighed, when she thought about this, and hoped that Anasuyabehn's first child would not arrive before ten months – in fact, twelve months would be better.

When she knocked at the study door and opened it, the Dean still had his rosary in his hand. She put the letters on his desk and retreated to the kitchen.

After he had put his rosary into its box, the Dean mechanically opened his letters. It was with considerable shock that he read Tilak's uncle's preliminary inquiry regarding a match between his nephew and Anasuyabehn.

It seemed to him, at first, that he must have misread, and he perused again the careful description of Tilak's assets, both physical and monetary. But there was no doubt that it was an offer for his daughter.

Here was proof that the girl had lied to him. His little daughter had lied. He was engulfed in wretchedness. What had she been doing?

As he stared at the letter, his fear and disappointment at his daughter gave way to anger against the hapless Tilak. He tore the letter up and flung it into his wastepaper basket.

If he heard so much as a breath of scandal about Tilak and his daughter, the man should go. If it were the last thing he did as Dean, Tilak should be made to rue the day he ever tampered with Anasuyabehn.

The letter from Bombay crossed with one from John to Tilak, in which he told of entrusting Tilak's letter to Savitri for delivery. He wrote also of the haste with which the marriage was being solemnized, and that he hoped that Tilak would find someone else and be happy with her.

When the servant brought John's letter to Tilak, he was sitting by his mother's couch while she had her morning tea. As he read the missive, a fearful numbness crept over him, and his mind refused to accept the news it contained. He continued to sit, the letter in his hand resting on his knee, while the numbness gave way to a ghastly emptiness.

It seemed to him that he had been stripped of his clothing and walked by himself through a vast empty space, a cold wind beating upon his bare flesh. It seemed that he walked for a long time, ignoring the wind, refusing to be afraid, and gradually his senses returned.

When he opened his eyes, he did it carefully and slowly, as if letting in the light would also let in something horrible; but it was only his mother's troubled eyes which met his.

She had put down her cup in her saucer, and she asked, 'What's the matter?'

Tilak was unable to speak. He handed the letter to her and she read it, her English being quite adequate to the task.

'Your friend in Shahpur – the Englishman?'

'Yes.' With that single word, all the emotion which he had tried to control since he left Shahpur suddenly erupted. He fell to his knees by the couch and buried his head in the Kashmir shawl draped over it. He hammered the couch with clenched fists. 'Why couldn't Uncle get through on the telephone?' he almost screamed.

His mother put down her cup and saucer with a clatter, and leaned forward to put her arms round her wilful, dreadfully hurt son. 'The lines to Shahpur were simply choked by calls, my dear child. Uncle couldn't help that – it'll be years before we get a proper service.'

Chapter Thirty-eight

Because both Tilak's uncle and his mother feared a nervous breakdown, they did their best to dissuade Tilak from returning to Shahpur.

'There's nothing you can do, my son.'

'I know that, mother. But I want to see the Vice-Chancellor and find out how things are in the University, and I would like to hear from John Bennett exactly what happened.'

Though he was obviously distraught, he was, they felt, trying to be rational, so they reluctantly agreed to the journey. The following morning, he and his servant arrived at Shahpur station. In the vast Victorian waiting-room there, he took a shower and changed his clothes. He was calm enough to eat a little breakfast in the empty first-class dining-room, while his servant ate in less sumptuous surroundings at a platform stall.

He had an overwhelming desire to see Anasuyabehn once again, just to look upon her face. He told himself sardonically that one is permitted to look on the face of one's dead. He did not wish to call on her; apart from it being too modern an idea for the Desais to accept, it would awaken again in her the despair she must have felt at having to go through with her marriage. But just to see her passing by was a gnawing need.

The servant came into the dining-room to inquire what he should do next, and Tilak instructed him to take his luggage to his rooms in the students' hostel.

The servant looked scared, and whispered that perhaps the Sahib should not show himself there for the present. Wouldn't a hotel be safer?

Tilak told him roughly not to be a fool. The students were not going to hurt him. 'For myself, I may stay a night or two with Bennett Sahib. I have to see him.'

Satisfied, the servant went away to find a porter.

After giving up his ticket, Tilak went through the barrier. He hesitated on the steps outside, and a motorcycle rickshaw drew up quickly by him. 'Sahib?' the man queried hopefully, revving his engine.

'Do you know the Desai Society – the one in the city centre?'

'Ji, hun. Everybody knows it.'

'Right. Put me down fifty yards before you get to it.'

They drove through narrow alleyways thronged with people, then into an area where the alleys were little more than passages lined with the high boundary walls of various Societies. They came at last to a square which held the goldsmiths' bazaar, and there the rickshaw wallah stopped.

He pointed to an archway on the other side of the square. 'Through there, Sahib, is a vegetable bazaar. Opposite it, is the Desai Society's gate.'

Tilak paid the man without comment. He had a shrewd suspicion that he had been taken on a tour of the old city and that probably there was a much shorter route from the station, but he could not be bothered to bargain; his mind was on Anasuyabehn.

Uncertain what to do, he walked through the archway and found the compound gate without difficulty. A few women and children were standing near the gate, sweepers or the very poor, and one or two professional beggars squatted with their backs against the Desais' wall, their begging bowls in front of them. Tilak hastily crossed the tiny square and pretended to look through the vegetable bazaar.

'What are the people waiting for?' he asked a stallholder.

The stallholder told him of the great marriage just performed. Today, the rumour was that the bridegroom was going to take his bride on an aeroplane. He thought that the women were waiting, in case, at the time of departure, the Desais felt like giving a little more in charity.

As he was talking, a taxi came from the further side of the little square and drew up at the gate.

The compound gate was opened by a chowkidar, who immediately kicked one of the beggars to make him move out of the way. The grumbling beggar moved about six inches and then was forced to his feet by the rush of onlookers who closed in on the entrance. Tilak himself was propelled, not unwillingly, towards the gate by a couple of eager youths and three giggling country girls, and was soon hemmed in by a small crowd.

A servant put two suitcases into the taxi. Then a very old man in horn-rimmed spectacles was assisted in, while the crowd murmured in nervous awe; everyone knew of old Desai.

Surely, the bride would come now. The women pushed forward and Tilak, to his consternation, found himself to the front of the crowd with the beggar who had been so ignominiously kicked, and rows of women pushing behind.

A murmur of women's voices came from within the Society. Anasuya-behn, her face half obscured by her flowered silk sari, stepped on to the street, followed closely by a man in white khadi, who, Tilak presumed, was her husband. They were followed by several ladies and gentlemen who stood around the gateway. Anasuyabehn turned her head, as if to say goodbye to one of the ladies – and then she saw him.

For a moment she stood transfixed, the words of farewell unspoken. She lifted her sari further over her face to shield herself from the gaze of the jostling relations.

Oblivious of the reason for her momentary pause, Mahadev put his arm gently round her back to move her towards the taxi, and in the self-same second the beggar, knife in hand, lunged forward as if to stab her.

Tilak saw the knife flash as it was drawn and he leaped between them, taking the knife in his own back, as he and Anasuyabehn crashed to the ground.

She screamed as she fell and, in the rush of people towards her, the beggar turned and ran for his life.

A shocked Mahadev beheld a man with a knife in his back lying over his new bride. The crowd began to move hastily away, while the chowkidar lifted Tilak up slightly so that Mahadev could get at his wife. He pulled her free and lifted her to her feet. She was dust-covered and bruised, but was able to stand on her feet, one hand to her mouth, as Partner Uncle bent and very carefully withdrew the knife. He tore a light cotton shawl from round his neck and pressed it on the wound, while he shouted for someone to bring a string bed to carry the man into the compound.

From his more elevated position in the old-fashioned taxi, old Desai had watched with horror. Now he scrambled out and went to Mahadev. 'Is she hurt?' he asked anxiously.

Mahadev was gently wiping his wife's bruised cheek. 'No bones broken,' he said. 'The man seems to have taken most of the fall, somehow.'

Old Desai whipped round to look at his Partner Brother kneeling by Tilak. Partner Brother looked up and said, 'He's dead.'

Anasuyabehn turned her face into her husband's shoulder, while a Desai aunt tried to persuade her back into the compound. Mahadev, his face deadly pale, held the shuddering young woman. 'Wait a minute,' he urged the aunt.

Old Desai turned back to his son. 'Take your wife and go to the airport. Catch the plane. This is a police matter, and they'll keep you here for weeks as a material witness. Your wife can tend her bruises and change her sari in the airport.'

Mahadev stared at him, overwhelmed for the moment by the sight of murder.

'Go, boy, go,' his father urged. 'That knife was meant for *you*. Your wife nearly died instead of you, because just at the very second he struck, she moved in front of you. Seated in the taxi, I saw exactly what happened, and I fear there may be other dacoits nearby who will make a second attempt.' He paused for breath, an old man fearing the loss of his eldest son. He caught at Mahadev's sleeve. 'Wake up, boy, and get into the taxi, quickly.'

Mahadev forced himself to speak firmly, as he wrapped Anasuyabehn's sari end round her bruised arm. She was not weeping, only breathing heavily, her face almost colourless. He half-lifted her into the taxi and, when he followed her, she clung to him, burying her face in his shoulder. During the nights he had spent with her, he had been very gentle, making sure that she was pleasured. Last night, he thought with a sudden glow, she had turned willingly to him and had responded to his overtures.

Despite the shocked looks of two older ladies, who had scrambled into the taxi after him, he continued to hold her and to whisper to her not to be afraid; he would protect her.

Thankful to get away, the taxi driver hooted to persuade the stallholders, who had replaced the original crowd, to get out of his way while he turned in the small space.

At a point where the narrow street he was travelling debouched into a main thoroughfare, he was stopped by an armed policeman. The constable flung open all the doors, took a good look at the passengers, made sure no one was hiding under the seats, and then motioned them onwards.

Through his mirror, the driver saw a police jeep ease its way into the rabbit warren he had just left.

Chapter Thirty-nine

Immediately the police jeep was noticed coming down the lane, the stallholders shot back to their vegetables and began assiduously to rearrange them; the open-mouthed women pulled their plain white saris over their heads and became anonymous bundles hurrying through the far archway, following their menfolk. After them ran a bunch of little urchins afraid of being left behind.

The old American army jeep slid to a stop on its smooth tyres, and the Bengali police chief leaped out. A constable dropped off the back of the vehicle and hammered on the door with his rifle butt. The iron bar across the inner side squeaked as it was turned, and the nervous chowkidar let in both the police chief and three constables.

Despite the melting away of possible witnesses, which he had observed as he came into the small bazaar, the Bengali was hopeful that he might now get a lead on the dacoits. In the back of his mind, he had rather expected that an attack might be made on Mahadev. The passengers in the held-up train would have seen only a vague collection of men with their faces covered; Mahadev had left his carriage and might easily have seen how they moved the loot.

Old Desai was amazed to see the police arrive so fast. He was in the process of going through Tilak's pocket book, so that he could identify him when he himself telephoned the police.

'I telephoned them as soon as I saw what had happened,' his younger son told him.

The Bengali, as he approached and heard his remark, smiled with approbation on the stout accountant. 'Very wise,' he told him. 'There are not many entrances to this area, and I sent men on bicycles to block them immediately.' He shrugged, as he approached Tilak's body, lying on a narrow bed in the shade of a loggia. 'Of course, if the man climbed a wall and went through one of the Societies, we might not be lucky.'

Chairs and glasses of water were brought and, while his men lounged on the other side of the compound, the Bengali got down to detail. The contents of Tilak's wallet had hardly yielded the letters about the Fellowship, which gave his name and Bombay address, before old Desai's office telephone rang. A nervous clerk came to say that the police chief was wanted on the line.

The Bengali listened intently and said, 'Charge him.' He slammed the receiver down and came crossly back to the waiting Desais. While they waited, he sat down and lit a cigarette. At last, he addressed old Desai.

'We've got the man. He ran into the arms of one of our men on his usual beat, struck the constable and was arrested for assaulting a police officer. He fits your description.'

Everybody present sighed with relief. The Bengali continued to stare at the body. Then he added, 'He's not a dacoit. He's known to the beat constable. He was a shoe merchant on whom you foreclosed, and he's been known to utter threats against you.'

'I didn't recognize him,' said old Desai.

'There's a lot of difference between a well-to-do merchant and a mad, starving beggar,' replied the Bengali and swung off his chair and on to his feet.

The group of men in front of him stiffened visibly, as they realized his contempt for them, in spite of their wealth.

The detective called his men over, and told them to bring a stretcher and remove the body.

He had seen a lot of death, had this small Bengali; yet it angered him that a man clever enough to obtain an English scholarship had died instead of one of these accursed moneylenders. His small, snakelike eyes regarded Desai. 'You were fortunate that such a brave man was near. Otherwise, you would undoubtedly have lost your son.'

'Yes,' said Desai, who by this time was feeling that he had had as much as he could endure, 'I am grateful to him – very grateful.'

Remorselessly, the Bengali then went on to upbraid him for allowing a material witness like Mahadev to depart from the country.

Old Desai was nearly sulky when he replied, 'I was afraid there might be other dacoits in the crowd; they might have struck again. How was I to know he was only a debtor of ours?'

After warning old Desai to hold himself in readiness to attend the inquest and the subsequent trial, the detective followed his men swiftly out of the compound, and left the demoralized Desais to their own consciences.

As the stretcher-bearers lifted the stretcher to put it into a small van which had drawn up behind the jeep, the Bengali stopped them. He lifted the cloth laid over Tilak's face and looked down at the beautiful, calm features. He was remembering a remark of one of the older ladies, when he asked if anyone knew the victim. She had said, 'Our new daughter seemed to know him – she turned to look at him, before he was struck down.'

As he let the cloth drop, he muttered, 'I wonder why you were in this unlikely part of town this morning? Was there a connection between you and the new bride?'

The puzzled bearers pushed the stretcher into the vehicle and slammed and locked the doors.

The Bengali returned to his jeep and climbed in beside the driver. He wondered if he had stumbled on a love affair as well as a murder, and, with all a Bengali's understanding of the passions of human nature, he decided it was unnecessary to intercept the younger Desais at the airport; he could get a conviction without them. In his own mind he was certain that the victim had given his life for the sake of the girl – old Desai's exact description of the movements of his son and his wife and the beggar at the moment of the tragedy made that fairly clear.

As his driver took him slowly through the ancient streets, he thought about Mahadev Desai and his new wife, and then about the fine scholar whose life had been so summarily ended. There was a story there, he was sure of it.

He threw his cigarette end out of the window and it was immediately pounced upon by a beggar. Who am I to muddy the water further, he asked himself angrily. Tilak Sahib, rest in peace; I'm going to hang the bastard that killed you; but it's one of those cursed moneylenders who should be at the end of the rope – they drove him mad.

Chapter Forty

The news of Tilak's murder came too late for that day's newspapers, and the Bengali police chief, taking his address from the letters found on him, informed only his family in Bombay. Neither John nor the barber who had come to cut his hair that afternoon, were, therefore, aware of it. John, however, was not in the best of tempers; he felt indescribably petulant and he had been unable to concentrate on his writings. The arrival of the barber had been a relief, and he limped out on to the veranda and sat down in his basket chair.

The barber wrapped a clean towel round his neck.

'Have you got my comb and shaving brush?' asked John. 'I prefer them to yours.' And he looked with distaste at the grubby shopping bag of barbering necessities lying on the veranda floor.

The barber looked pained and his beautifully waxed moustache twitched with irritation, but he answered, with a slight bow, 'Of course, Sahib. Ranjit has brought everything, including hot water in your own lota.' He pointed to the little brass vessel sitting on the veranda rail.

'Good,' grunted John. 'Very well.'

The barber began to comb. Since all Englishmen have an unnatural interest in the weather, he talked about the weather. Diplomat, gossip, messenger, the barber studied all his customers, and, as he went from house to house and village to village, he retailed the news, views and scandal of the district, slanted according to the views he supposed his customer of the moment held.

'Getting a little thin just here,' he announced, planting an accusing finger on a non-existent bald patch amid the thick thatch on John's head. He put down his comb and rummaged in his shopping bag.

'To avoid losing one's hair it's important to oil it daily. Now I have here a new oil which many of my customers are finding most efficacious . . .' and he waved a bottle in front of John's nose.

John blinked as the bottle sailed dangerously near, but managed to read *Asoka Medicinal Hair Tonic* on a flowerdecked label.

'What does it smell like?' he asked doubtfully.

The barber whipped out the cork and a tremendous perfume immediately enveloped them both.

'I'd rather be bald,' said John decisively.

The barber bit his lower lip and looked hurt, then he surveyed John's head from the front, cocking his own head first on one side and then on the other. 'Well, of course, it doesn't show in front,' he said at last, 'but it won't be long.'

'I couldn't stand it,' said John, all his sales resistance hastily marshalled. 'Perfumes – er – perfumes make me sneeze,' and he sneezed to demonstrate the fact.

The barber leaped out of range of any droplets, and said with a regretful sigh, 'Pure mustard oil might help, though I think it's really too far gone for that.'

Frown lines on John's forehead warned him that his customer was getting irate.

'Well, well, never mind,' he said. 'I expect you would like a shave, as usual, Sahib.'

'Yes,' John replied.

'Ears cleaned? They need it – you've got hairs growing in them.'

'Very well,' his customer agreed resignedly.

'Nice wedding Mehta Sahib had for his daughter,' said the barber as his scissors clipped merrily.

'I expect so,' said John. 'I didn't go to the wedding – only to the reception for friends the next day.'

'Oh, it was very fine indeed, though the number of guests was limited by the size of the compound. She has married a very fine gentleman – his toenails were clean and well clipped,' he added as a professional detail.

'Did you get the toe powdering job?'

'Yes, indeed. I did his brother, too, when he was married.'

'Decent tip?'

'Fair, fair.' The barber did a rapid run round John's left ear with the scissors. 'Of course, they're moneylenders – but so rich, Sahib, it is unbelievable. You should have seen the gifts.'

'I can imagine them.' John ducked as the scissors shot across his forehead.

'Keep still, please, Sahib.'

The barber stepped back in order to view his handiwork, and then said coyly to John, 'I hear you're considering marriage, too, Sahib.'

'What?' shouted John, sitting up in his chair so suddenly that he nearly lost an eye to the advancing scissors.

The barber jumped backwards, scissors held engarde, his professional aplomb severely shaken. 'I – I – er just heard a little word about it,' he said, eyeing John nervously.

John laughed at him and relaxed again into his basket chair.

'Wherever did you hear it?'

The barber took up his comb and combed furiously, while he considered his reply. He bent his head to look at the hairline he had trimmed. 'I think that'll do,' he muttered, and whipped a hand mirror out of his shopping bag.

John glanced at himself in the tiny mirror. 'OK,' he said. 'No oil. Where did you hear it and who is to be the bride?'

'Aren't you going to be married, Sahib? I must say I thought it unlikely, in spite of other rumours to the contrary.'

He looked down at John's spare body and the hurt legs.

John was irritated by the look. 'Well? I want to know who I'm to marry – Miss Prasad?'

The barber ventured a snigger at the mention of this prim, dedicated female. 'No, no, Sahib. The English lady with the copper-coloured hair, Sahib. She's often in the villages, working with Dr Ferozeshah. I don't know her name.'

'Oh, Miss Armstrong. Well, she's a friend of mine. I wonder why anyone should think I'm about to marry her, though.'

'It was your inquiry about the house which Dean Mehta rented temporarily for his daughter's marriage. It's to let again. A good house, Sahib, with its own well.'

Despite being smothered in shaving soap, John sat bolt upright in his chair.

'Look here,' he almost shouted, 'I haven't made any inquiries about that house.'

The barber tut-tutted and wiped soapsuds off John's eyebrows.

'The landlord himself told me, Sahib; I came straight from him to you. He said you had asked about repairs and rent, so naturally he assumed you were about to marry – the lady comes to see you regularly.' The barber waved his razor in the air rather hopelessly. 'It seemed quite natural, Sahib.'

John sniffed. 'I've made no inquiries and I don't intend to get married just to please my neighbours. The man must be out of his mind.'

'Just bend your head a little to the left, please, Sahib. That's better.'

The fearsome razor swept gracefully round his neck. 'Your skin is not what it might be, Sahib. The sun is very hard on white skins. Now, I have here . . .'

'No,' snapped John resolutely. 'My old red hide is doing quite well, thank you. Married, indeed.'

'Well, Ranjit said it would be quite soon.'

'He did, did he? Hmm. I suppose it was he who actually saw the landlord?'

'Of course, Sahib.' The barber was by now completely bewildered, and silently tackled the cleaning of John's ears, while John sat and fumed.

The mirror was again produced and John looked at himself.

For the first time for years he really considered what he looked like. Heavens, his face was seamed and weatherbeaten, and was that really grey hair at his temples? Surely, at thirty-four he should not be grey?

The crushed barber saw his client's fingers stray up over the offending skin and hair and hastened to pay a compliment.

He smiled ingratiatingly and said, 'Most distinguished-looking, Sahib.'

'Humph,' said John, nonetheless slightly comforted. 'How much?'

The barber was paid, packed his shopping bag and retreated down the path to the compound gate, promising to come again in two weeks' time.

'Ranjit!' roared John, and, at the tone of voice, Ranjit appeared with the speed of a rabbit, hastily wiping his wet hands on his sweat cloth.

'Just what have you been doing? That lunatic of a barber said you were inquiring about the house for rent down the road.'

Ranjit swallowed, considered what he should say and only succeeded in looking very guilty.

'Well, Sahib, it . . . er.'

'The wretch suggested I was going to be married . . . now I'll be bothered by everybody asking me if I am, blast it, and every tradesman in the district will try to sell me things. What on earth have you been doing?'

'I happened to meet the landlord, Sahib, and I asked him – er, out of general interest, Sahib. You will remember that we were talking about the need for you to have a better house a little while ago?'

John took a large breath and reminded himself that Ranjit was his most devoted friend.

'And getting married?'

This question in Ranjit's opinion demanded a straight answer. It was obvious that his young master – John was permanently about eighteen in Ranjit's mind – did not know what he was doing. Otherwise he would not ask such a silly question.

'Sahib, even in England, if you favour a young woman with your interest and she eats with you and you sit close to her, doesn't that mean that you'll marry her?'

Despite his indignation, John's eyes began to twinkle. 'It depends on your intentions.'

'A man such as yourself could not possibly have any intentions, except marriage,' declared Ranjit stalwartly, but wondering suddenly if Englishmen were, perhaps, a little like Indians in some respects.

John's temper had cooled. He took out his pipe and lit it, putting the dead match carefully back into the box, before he answered.

'I've no intentions at all, Ranjit. You know that my legs are a mess. They don't work very well and they are scarred. I'm also no longer young. I wouldn't like to ask a woman to marry such an old crock.'

Seeing that the storm had passed, Ranjit ventured to sit down on the top step. He rubbed the grey stubble on his chin, as he considered John's last remark. He loved his master, as if he were his own son, and enjoyed serving a bachelor, but lately the Sahib had been fretful without reason. He had seen him watch the little Memsahib go down the path to the gate, and then turn back to his desk, to sit silently staring at the papers before him, unable to work.

It was the law of all Hindu families that parents should marry off their children. Men and women should enjoy their spouses and only in age turn to asceticism. The Sahib had never known the joys of marriage and this was not normal.

Few servants liked to serve a married couple – wives had a habit of poking their noses into every domestic detail – but Ranjit was prepared to do this, if it made his master content. He, therefore, cleared his throat, blew his nose, and went into battle.

'Women, Sahib,' he began, 'are peculiar creatures. When they care for us, it is frequently because of our deficiencies and stupidities.'

John blew a cloud of smoke, and laughed.

Ranjit looked indignant. 'You laugh, Sahib, because you have no experience. The little Memsahib . . .'

The laugh died in John's throat. 'Well, what about her?' he asked quite sharply.

Determinedly, Ranjit plunged on. 'The little Memsahib doesn't see that you are a little older than some. She does not *see* your sick legs, though she will help you to cure them. She sees only you, Sahib.'

John looked silently out over the shabby compound. Ranjit had the eyes of a vulture, missing nothing.

At last he said, 'Have you asked the lady for me, Ranjit?'

'There is no need, Sahib. It is in every look she gives you.'

'Do you like her, Ranjit?'

'Yes, Sahib.' He searched for words, pulling nervously at his little pigtail at the back of his head as if to stimulate the brains within. 'More than other English ladies I have served.'

'Ah, well, Ranjit. Cats can look at kings, and I suppose I can look at a pretty woman sometimes. Now I am going to think about this map I am to draw for Shri Lallubhai. Go away and make me some dinner.'

'Ji, hun,' assented Ranjit, heaving himself to his feet and wondering if he had done any good at all with his attempt at matchmaking.

Dusk came while John was still working on the map. Lacking a large table, he had pinned big sheets of paper to the walls of his room. Propped up by the end of his table, he stood in front of these, pencil in one hand and ruler in the other, while he roughed in the districts that he knew. He hoped that his assistant from the City Engineer's Department would be able to add more details to his work.

He had turned to pick up a fresh pencil and to switch on another light, when he thought he heard the compound gate click. He paused, took up his stick and went towards his open front door.

It was much darker than he had realized, the stars already lay like brilliants on indigo velvet and the world was quiet with after-dinner hush.

She saw him before he saw her, his spare figure silhouetted against the light of the lamp, and she came towards him like a drifting ghost.

'Diana,' he exclaimed.

The sound of her first name made her pause, then she came swiftly up the steps, her arms full of rolls of paper, her face aglow.

He took the rolls from her and tossed them on to his couch, then took her arm and drew her into the softly lit room. He did not let go of her arm, but stood looking down at her.

'This is a pleasure,' he said.

'Ranjit said in the bazaar this morning that you wanted to show me the map, so I came as soon as I could and brought that stuff from the City Engineer.' She pointed to the pile of papers, and then realized that he was still holding her bare arm. She faltered, and looked up at him a little beseechingly.

'Ranjit is apt to be a trifle premature,' he said rather grimly, and continued to hold her arm and look at her, until her pulses quickened and she dropped her own gaze, lest he realize how disconcerted she was.

'Come and sit down,' he said, and led her to the couch. He moved the blueprints and sat down beside her. He had never done this before, and she looked at him out of the corner of her eye. He caught the look and she smiled at him. The tight, withdrawn expression on his face faded, but he continued to look at her as if he had never really seen her before. He knew suddenly that he wanted her like he had never wanted anything for years. Not only did he desperately want her in his bed, but he wanted her to be opposite him at breakfast, to listen to his hopes and fears – and even to his very bad jokes. He slowly let go of her arm. Dare he ask her?

His eyes moved over the short, red-gold hair to the little, freckled triangle of skin under her throat, burned red by the sun, and he realized that she had on a different dress, the neckline of which plunged and curved delicately over full, white breasts. It was a dress meant for dinner dates and moonlit evenings, not for hard work on maps. He chuckled, and grinned at her engagingly.

'Could you stay to dinner once more?' he asked hopefully. 'I don't have enough company these days.'

To his further amusement, she blushed furiously, scarlet running up to her hairline. She fingered her glass bangles nervously, before she answered.

'Ranjit said you would expect me to stay to dinner whenever I came. He said you always asked people because you didn't like eating by yourself.' She said it teasingly, as if to belie the telltale blush.

It will be a marvel if he hasn't asked her to stay to breakfast as well, he thought, but he answered without hesitation, 'Ranjit is quite right.'

'Then I shall be delighted to stay.'

John stood up and went to the window.

A well burnished moon was rising. The University gardens would be a pretty haven tonight, he thought, and he turned back into the room, his mind made up.

'Ranjit,' he roared. 'Make dinner for two. Armstrong Memsahib has come.'

Ranjit came through the door from the back veranda. He had shaved and had on a clean shirt. He grinned toothlessly, as he announced, 'Dinner is ready now, Sahib, and there is plenty for two.'

'Ranjit, you are a genius.'

And Ranjit viewed the rather self-conscious couple and replied contentedly, 'Yes, Sahib.'